PRAISE FOR THE NOVELS OF RONI LOREN

"Hot and romantic, with an edge of suspense."
—Shayla Black, N

"Unique and emotional."

"A mix of blistering (and kinky) se_____ angst, and
dangerous suspense."
—Romance Novel News

"A must-read!"
—Nocturne Reads

"[A] steamy, sexy, yet emotionally gripping story."
—Julie Cross, author of the Tempest novels

"I dare you to even attempt to put it down."
—Cassandra Carr, author of *Burning Love*

"An angsty backstory made beautiful by a hero who doesn't know
how perfect he is. Don't miss this Ranch treat!"
—Carly Phillips, *New York Times* bestselling author

"Steamy, occasionally shocking, and relentlessly intense, this book
isn't for the faint of heart."
—*RT Book Reviews*

"Loren does an incredible job portraying the BDSM lifestyle in a
sexy and romantic way . . . Loren should definitely be put on the
must-read list."
—The Book Pushers

"Like a roller-coaster ride . . . When you hit the last page, you say,
let's ride it again."
—Guilty Pleasures Book Reviews

"Roni Loren's books are masterful, story-driven, sensual, and very
erotic . . . Definitely one of my have-to-get-as-soon-as-possible
series!"
—Under the Covers Book Blog

CALL ON ME

RONI LOREN

BERKLEY BOOKS, NEW YORK

BERKLEY

An imprint of Penguin Random House LLC
375 Hudson Street, New York, New York 10014

This book is an original publication of Penguin Random House LLC.

Library of Congress Cataloging-in-Publication Data

Loren, Roni.
Call on me / Roni Loren. — Berkley Trade paperback edition.
pages ; cm
ISBN 978-0-425-27839-0
I. Title.
PS3612.O764C35 2015
813'.6   dc23
2015005703

PUBLISHING HISTORY
Berkley trade paperback edition / July 2015

PRINTED IN THE UNITED STATES OF AMERICA

10 9 8 7 6 5 4 3 2 1

Cover art: Flounces © Irina Fedotova / Shutterstock.
Cover design by Diana Kolsky.

Penguin
Random
House

To all those readers who demanded
that Pike get his own story, this is for you.

ACKNOWLEDGMENTS

To Donnie, for always being my biggest cheering section. I know living with a writer can be . . . interesting. Thanks for always being up for the challenge. Love you.

To my son, for keeping me on my toes and making sure I never take life too seriously.

To my parents, for being so damn cool and supportive (and for watching kidlet when I go to conferences or need a vacation). And to all of my family, for being so encouraging.

To my agent, Sara Megibow, for your unflagging support and fangirling.

To my editor, Kate Seaver, for your insight and belief in my books.

To Julie Cross, Jamie Wesley, Dawn Alexander, and Genevieve Wilson, my fellow writers in the trenches. Thanks for being the girls I gossip with, vent to, and cheer with at the virtual watercooler.

To Taylor Lunsford, for always being willing to give me a last-minute read when writer insecurity is cropping up.

And finally, to my readers, you are the ones who keep me at this keyboard every day, striving to write the best book I can. Thank you for spending time with my characters and books. I am forever grateful.

ONE

"Are you touching yourself?" The voice in Oakley's ear sounded labored and overeager—like a Saint Bernard attempting phone sex. He was probably drooling, too. Lovely.

"Yes, you make me so hot . . ."—she quickly checked the sticky note she'd put on the kitchen island—"Stefan."

Stefan. Literature professor. Single. Six foot five.

That's the info he'd given her. Which probably meant: *Steve, unemployed, married, and five-six on a good day.*

He groaned. "You're so sexy."

Sexy? *Two points off for lack of originality, Mr. Lit Prof.* Though, even the suave guys tended to forget their vocabulary when they got to this point in the conversation. Oakley covered the mouthpiece on her headset and turned off the timer on the oven. If nothing else, she was impressed the guy had lasted through the full baking time.

"Thanks, sugar," she said, letting her tone drop into a lower register.

"God, your voice is so fucking hot."

That she heard a lot. A record company exec had once deemed her voice "smoky, X-rated perfection" when he'd heard her demo. At the time, she hadn't considered how inappropriate it had been for a grown man to tell a fifteen-year-old kid that. But her raspy voice had gotten her the gig then, and it had gotten her this one now. Though, admittedly, the bar wasn't set quite as high for this current one.

"I'm gonna give it to you so hard, Sasha," Stefan ground out. "I can feel your hot mouth closing around me."

Oakley donned oven mitts and leaned down to pull out the tray of brownies. The smell of chocolate and the heat of the oven hit her with full force. She inhaled deeply. "Mmm, that's *so* good. I could just lick up every last bit."

"Yeah," he panted, the sound of his slick, pumping fist obscenely clear through the receiver. "That's right. Show me how much you want it."

There you go, Steve, you go on and get your money's worth. Oakley set the tray of brownies on a trivet and tugged off the mitts. Her stomach rumbled. She'd stayed up late enough that her body was looking for dinner number two. But these weren't for her.

She glanced toward the darkened hallway and the stairs beyond. Well, maybe one little corner piece wouldn't be missed. She cut a small square and dipped her fingers in to grab it. But as she lifted the brownie, her knuckles grazed the searing hot pan.

"Ah, shit!" she hissed, jerking her hand back.

"Oh, yeah, let me hear it," Stefan said on a moan. "Come with me, baby."

Oakley shook out her hand, sucking air through her teeth, and tried to keep the pain out of her voice. Her phone companion thought she was mid-orgasm. She threw in an *oh, oh, oh* and ran to the sink to plunge her fist into the dishwater she'd drawn to soak the mixing bowl.

Stefan made choked sounds as he reached his own release. In another world, maybe it could've been an erotic moment. She'd talked a guy into an orgasm. He was calling her name. But the name was fake and so was the talk. And though she held nothing against the guys who called—after all, they helped her pay the bills—her libido had long ago crawled into a dark corner to die a quick, peaceful death. Even if she imagined the guy on the other end of the line looked like Johnny Depp or Justin Timberlake or something, she couldn't drum up one ounce of interest.

Stefan panted heavy, wet breaths right against her ear, resuming his resemblance to a Saint Bernard. Maybe she should offer him a "good boy" or a Milk-Bone.

"That was amazing," she said, using her husky, after-sex voice as she soaked her hand in the water. "Thank you, Stefan."

Panting. Panting. That was the only response.

Then a tight, high sound—whistling.

No. *Wheezing.*

Uh-oh. "Stefan? Are you okay?"

Those squeaking breaths continued for a few seconds then: "Yes . . . I'm . . . fine."

He didn't sound fine. "Stefan, if you're having an asthma attack or chest pains or something, you need to call for help."

"Can't . . ." He gave a ragged cough. "My wife . . . can't know . . . I'm down here this late. She'll know I'm up . . ."

He coughed again.

Jesus Christ. Oakley shook the water off her hand. "What's she going to think when she finds you dead in the basement? Hang up the phone and dial 911."

"I—"

"Stu?" a sharp voice said in the background. "What are you doing down here? *Stu?*"

"Oh, shit," Stefan/Stu said between wheezes.

The dial tone buzzed in Oakley's ear a second later.

She pulled off the wireless headset and sagged against the fridge, exhaling a long breath. Okay. It would be all right. Stu's wife might kill him when she found him with the phone to his ear and his underwear around his ankles, but at least the guy wouldn't die of a heart attack on Oakley's watch.

She could handle a lot of stuff—callers threw all kinds of bizarre shit at her—but she couldn't be responsible for helping kill one. It was bad enough that she'd just contributed to strife in another marriage.

Gold star for her.

It shouldn't bother her. The guys who called were grown men making a conscious decision to seek out paid phone sex. She was simply the tool of choice. Another night, they may download porn and watch a dirty movie instead. If she'd learned anything during her years of doing this job, it was that it wasn't personal. She had a job to do. The callers needed a faceless someone to fill in for their fantasy that night. The relationship was purely transactional. And hell, she'd been used for free by enough people in her past. Now she was at least paid for it and not getting emotionally annihilated in the process. But still, sometimes she felt like the drug dealer, giving addicts easy access to their vice.

She rolled her shoulders, trying to shrug off the stress of the call, and dug a tube of antibiotic ointment out of the junk drawer to slather on her burned knuckles. It was past two and she really needed to get to bed, but there was no way she'd be able to sleep after that burst of adrenaline from the call.

Plus, she'd never gotten her dessert. And right now, she could use a big honking piece of chocolate.

She went back to the brownies. They'd cooled enough by now, so she cut herself a bigger square than the original corner she'd planned and took a bite. She closed her eyes. *Yeah, that's the stuff.*

After pouring a big glass of milk, she brought that and the rest of the brownie to the table. She glanced at the walkie-talkie she'd placed on the table, the soft white noise relaxing her, and leaned back in the chair to enjoy the solitude. She was used to pulling the night shift by now, but usually she fell into bed after the last call, grasping for any shreds of sleep she could get before the alarm went off to start her real job. But it was nice to sit for a moment and simply be.

She polished off the last bit of brownie and milk and brought her glass to the sink. The exhaustion was settling in full force now. She braced her hands on the edge of the counter and eyed the soaking dishes. Her mother had always had the rule to never go to bed with a dirty sink—as if a bright, gleaming, empty sink was some sign of how together the household was. Maybe it was.

Oakley turned away from the dishes. They'd have to wait until tomorrow. She didn't have it in her.

She put foil over the rest of the brownies and grabbed the walkie-talkie and her headset. She should be able to get at least four hours of sleep. But right as she flipped off the light, the walkie-talkie beeped.

"Mom?"

Oakley halted, startled by the sudden break in the quiet. She pressed the button on the side of the device. "Yeah, baby?"

"What's that smell?" Reagan asked, her voice groggy from sleep.

Oakley shook her head and smiled. She should've known the bionic nose would pick up that scent even in her sleep. "It's just the brownies for your bake sale tomorrow."

"It's not my bake sale. It's the school's," Reagan corrected.

"That's what I meant."

"But that's not what you said."

Oakley leaned against the wall in the hallway. This was an argument she'd never win. Reagan was into exactness. When Oakley told people Rae was eleven, Rae would jump in and specify how many months past eleven she was. "I'm sorry I said it wrong the first time. Now go back to sleep, sweethcart. I don't want you to be tired in the morning."

"Did you put nuts or caramel in them?"

"Of course not. I know you're a brownie purist."

"Okay. Good," Reagan said, and Oakley could almost hear her daughter nodding. "Thanks, Mom. Love you."

Oakley pressed the walkie-talkie to her chest for a moment, warmth filling her. "Love you, too, Rae. Good night."

Oakley headed to her bedroom, listening to the footfalls upstairs and the flush of the toilet as Reagan made a quick trip to the bathroom. She must've really had to go because Rae hated getting out of bed in the middle of the night. And she outright refused to come downstairs after dark—a phobia she'd developed years ago and hadn't been able to shake yet.

Hence the walkie-talkies. Oakley had gotten tired of Reagan yelling from afar anytime she needed something at night. And leaving every light blazing through the house all evening wasn't an option either. The electric bill was already high enough.

Bills. No, she wouldn't think about that now. Even though she could see the stack staring at her from her desk. The gas bill. Rent. The quarterly installment for Reagan's private school and therapies.

She couldn't face that tonight. Plus, she knew the due dates by heart so she could hold on to her money until the very last minute without being late.

She closed her bedroom door and walked over to her computer to wake the screen. Her sign-in page for the service she used to get her calls was still up. It showed how many minutes she'd logged tonight. Not bad. But she was six minutes shy of hitting the bonus level where she got an extra fifty bucks for the night. Stu's health scare had cost her more than stress.

She sighed and sagged into her desk chair. Fifty extra dollars could pay for that pair of lime green Chuck Taylors Reagan wanted for her birthday.

Oakley yawned and checked the box that indicated she was available to take a call. Her cell phone rang within seconds and she slipped on the headset again. "Hello, this is Sasha. Ready for a fantasy night?"

"So ready," said the deep-voiced caller. There was male tittering in the background.

Great. A frat-boy call.

"What are you wearing, Sasha?"

Oakley looked down at her oversized T-shirt and yoga pants. "A sheer robe with nothing underneath."

"Aw, yeah," the dude said. "How big are your tits?"

Oakley put her head to her desk. Six minutes. She only needed to keep them on the phone for six more minutes.

Six.

Five.

Four.

Three.

They hung up at two, laughing in the background as the phone went dead, their Truth or Dare game complete.

And she was short.

She lifted her head and checked the Available box again.

"Hello, this is Sasha . . ."

TWO

The chick in his living room was taking a selfie next to his gold record. Pike leaned back, watching her through his half-open bedroom door. "Fantastic."

"What's fantastic?" his friend Gibson asked on the other end of the line. "Did you even hear what I said?"

"No, I didn't. And what's fantastic is that I have a seriously hot B-list actress in my living room, who was all kinds of cool after the show tonight but is now snapping duckface selfies in front of my shit."

Gibson snorted a laugh. "At least she's not using you just for your body."

"That I'd be okay with. But this . . ."

"Hey, if there's no selfie for proof, the event never happened. At least that's what my niece tells me. It's like a tree falling in the woods."

Pike sighed. "Observation: Duckface is a friend to no one."

The longer Pike watched, the more he regretted his decision to bring this woman home with him. He'd been buzzing off the energy of the performance tonight and had wanted to keep that feeling going. Darkfall had kicked ass on stage and had impressed the promoters who were putting together some of this summer's biggest tours. If Darkfall landed a sweet opening spot with some big-time band, they'd have a chance to recapture some of the traction they'd lost when their lead singer had taken extended time off between albums to get surgery on his vocal cords. In some ways, tonight felt like a rebirth of the band, and he wanted to celebrate.

And usually the only thing more exciting than pounding the drums, making thousands of fans scream, was making just one scream. But as he watched his date take another photo of herself, he was losing his enthusiasm for his plan.

Maybe a chill night at home with the dog would've been a better idea.

Monty barked from somewhere in the living room, protesting the fact that Pike hadn't given him his requisite belly rub and dog biscuit when he'd come home. He'd been too busy pouring a drink for his guest.

"What's her name?" Gib asked.

Pike scrubbed a hand through his damp hair. "Why does that matter?"

"Come on, tell me that you're not that big of a dick and you remember her name."

Pike grimaced at Gib's tone. This is what he got for hanging out with businessman types instead of fellow musicians. The suits had a different code of conduct. With the guys in his band, remembering names was only expected *after* you slept with someone. Luckily, Pike's memory was good. "Lark Evans."

"All right. Hold on a sec." The clicking of a keyboard sounded on the other end.

"Gib, look, can we talk about whatever you were calling for tomorrow? I'm ignoring my company." He walked away from the door and dropped the towel from around his waist to pull on a fresh pair of well-worn jeans. "I told her I'd only be in the shower for a minute."

"Ha! I knew it," Gibson said, triumph in his voice.

"What?"

"Your girl's on Instagram. And guess what pics are making their way around the world as we speak?"

Pike sighed.

"Damn, she is hot, though," Gibson said. "Duck lips notwithstanding."

"Which is why—"

"Ah, shit. You're gonna love this. Wait for it . . . Caption to the pic: *Hanging out with Spike, the drummer from Darkfall!* Hashtag: *hawt.*"

"Hold up. *Spike?*"

Gibson burst into laughter. "Spike! Man, she doesn't even know *your* name. How very rock star of her."

Pike looked to the ceiling, letting that sink in. Karma was a fucking bitch. "You are totally ruining my hard-on here."

"Now don't kid. I know my deep, brooding voice makes you hot," Gib said. "Want me to talk dirty to you, Spikey?"

Pike grinned. "So it's finally happened. You're going gay for me. I'm flattered. Of course, it was inevitable. I mean, have you seen me? But I hate to break your heart, Gib, I only play for one team."

He sniffed. "If I were gay, I'd have way higher standards than you. That record would need to be platinum."

"Aw, love you, too. I'm even making my duckface for you." He made a loud kiss sound. "Now I'm letting you go because, unlike you, I'm about to get laid, son."

"Fine. But call me back in the morning. I have a charity thing I need to run by you."

Pike tucked the phone between his shoulder and ear and pulled his bedside drawer open to check the condom supply. "The Dine and Donate event? I told you the band's in again this year, if you need us."

"No, this is for something different. More of a favor than anything else."

"Sounds ominous. But yeah, call you tomorrow."

"Cool. Now go rock her world, Spike."

Pike snorted and disconnected the call. He tossed his phone on the chair by the window and padded to his closet to grab a T-shirt. But when he stepped out of his room, ready to block out all the information he'd learned—selfies, Instagram, Spike—in order to enjoy his date, he was greeted by a shriek instead.

Lark hadn't seen him come in because her gaze had zeroed in on a growling Monty.

"Give it back, you stupid mutt!" she yelled and jabbed a closed umbrella at Monty, catching him right in the side. Monty yelped.

"What the fuck?" Pike hurried forward and grabbed her wrist, stopping another poke. "What the hell's going on?"

She pointed at Monty, rage twisting her pretty face into something ugly. "Look at him! Your idiotic dog is eating my *Jimmy Choos*!"

She said it like Monty was murdering her kid. Pike glanced at Monty, who was in defense mode, baring teeth, two little paws on one of Lark's high heels. Pike shrugged. "Well, the brand does say *Choo*. Maybe he's just following directions."

Lark gasped and looked at Pike like he'd lost his mind. "Do you know how much those *cost*? What is wrong with you? Do something!"

The grating tone of her voice made his teeth clamp together. Being yelled at by anyone pushed his buttons. But messing with his dog pushed the ugliest of them. He took a breath, trying to keep his cool. "Do you know that my dog was *abused* as a puppy? And that jabbing him with a sharp object is fucking traumatizing to him? I'll buy you another pair of your goddamned shoes."

Her head snapped back a bit at that, and she had the decency to look chagrined. She glanced down at the umbrella still clutched in her hand. "Oh. Shit, I'm sorry. I didn't know."

And he didn't care. Abused or not, you don't poke an animal with something that could hurt them, especially over something as stupid as a shoe. He could put up with her using him for his fame or whatever. They would've both been using each other. They each knew the score. But he wasn't going to let anyone fuck with his dog.

"Monty, release," he said in the firm, dominant voice that worked best on the feisty dachshund/schnauzer mix. Monty looked up with big, sad puppy eyes and backed away from the shoe. But just when Pike was about to send him off to his bed, Monty trotted over to Lark and gave her the I'm-sorry look.

Lark's expression softened, and she reached down to pat his head awkwardly. "It's okay, buddy . . ."

Monty lifted his leg and pissed all over her bare foot.

"Monty, no!" Pike said.

But chaos ensued after that. Lark hopping and shrieking. Monty barking and spinning in a circle. And Pike doing his damnedest not to laugh.

He wasn't entirely successful, and that earned him a glare from Lark and a happy, yipping bark from Monty. Finally, he gathered himself together enough to direct Monty to go to his crate so he could help Lark.

He showed her to the bathroom so she could rinse her leg off in the tub, and he cleaned up the mess in the living room—after sneaking Monty his treat and a belly rub.

He was halfway through a beer when Lark stepped into the kitchen a few minutes later, wearing nothing but a pair of lacy pink panties and a bra that made her breasts look like icing-covered cupcakes. His dick jumped to attention—the response automatic.

She leaned in the doorway, posing like she was at a Victoria's Secret cover shoot, and gave him the inviting smile she'd given him from the audience tonight. "Sorry about all of that. How about we start over and get back to why we're here, hmm?"

Pike still had the bottle of beer pressed to his lips. He lowered it and set it on the counter.

Lark's smile spread wider and she sauntered over with a heavy sway in her hips. She pressed her hand to his chest. "I have all kinds of ways we can apologize to each other. For getting mad at your dog, I was thinking this would make it up to you."

She dragged her hand down his chest and lowered to her knees. Pike stared down at her. She looked like a fucking porn star at his feet—pouty lips with a fresh coat of pink lipstick, blond hair flowing down her back. A wet dream of a woman. But when she put her painted fingernails to the zipper on his jeans, he put his hand over hers. "Stand up."

She blinked, the sultry look shifting to a perplexed one. "Huh?"

He helped Lark get to her feet. "Be right back."

Her smile returned, though it had a confused tilt to it. "O . . . kay."

He headed back to his bedroom for a minute then returned to

the kitchen. She was drinking his beer, putting lipstick marks on the bottle. He draped her dress on one of the barstools, set a pair of his flip-flops on top of it, and handed her a few hundred-dollar bills. "For the shoes and a cab."

She stared down at the money in her hand. "What?"

"This isn't going to happen tonight."

"Wait, you want me to *leave*? But I thought—"

"It's time for you to go." He was tempted to take a co-selfie with her. Hashtag: *HookUpFail*.

She stiffened like a rod had been shoved up her back and she made these little sputters of disbelief—like she was trying to come up with a really good insult but couldn't think of any.

When she obviously couldn't string anything worthy together, she shoved on his flip-flops, which looked like flippers on her small feet, and yanked her dress over her head. "I can't fucking believe this."

He dumped the beer in the sink, bored.

His lack of response brought a new level of hatred glowing in her eyes. "Is this about the dog? Because that's just stupid. How was I supposed to know he was abused?"

He walked to his front door and pulled it open. "You never know where anyone's scars are hiding. Doesn't mean you get a pass to hurt them."

She reared back like he'd slapped her. Then her lips pressed together, and she flounced out the door, muttering something about hoping that the dumb dog kept him warm tonight.

He shut the door without watching her go and leaned against it, absorbing the quiet of the condo, relief instead of disappointment settling in. Hookup fail, yes. But even he had standards. He'd rather fuck his fist than spend another second with Duckface the Puppy Poker.

A year ago, he might've just written it off and taken her to bed anyway. What did it matter if a woman was shallow? It's not like they'd be seeing each other again. Plus, he'd always hated sleeping alone in a house. But now he couldn't stomach the thought of spending another moment with a woman like that.

Maybe he was getting used to being by himself. After his room-mate, Foster, had moved out to live with his girlfriend last year, Pike had felt that old need to always have people over. Mostly of the naked female variety. But for the last few months, he'd been so busy with band stuff and working at his music studio in between that he hadn't sought out that brand of companionship very often. He hadn't even gone to The Ranch, the kink resort he and his friends belonged to, in at least three months. Tonight had been the first night he'd done the hook-up-after-a-show thing in a while.

Now he remembered why he'd backed off from this kind of thing. He had no issue being someone's one-night stand. Most of the time, he preferred things that way. But now that he'd seen how Foster and Cela were together, how explosive the chemistry could be when two people connected like that, he could see how superfi-cial this other shit was in comparison. Women fucked his type. The bad boy. The drummer. Whatever. They didn't fuck *him*.

And he'd been guilty of the same. He'd fuck the groupie, the model, the B actress. If not for Monty chewing Lark's shoe tonight, he would've never known that the woman was capable of hurting a dog for something as inconsequential as a shoe. Because he didn't *know* her.

For some reason, that dug into him like a burr, annoying the shit out of him.

He sank onto his bed and Monty jumped up to join him. He scratched behind Monty's ears. "Good job, Monts. You're making me grow a goddamned conscience."

Monty licked his chops. There were pieces of red shoe leather stuck in his teeth.

Pike chuckled and kissed the top of his pup's scruffy head. Monty rewarded him by releasing some noxious gas and dog-grinning at the effort.

"Jesus, Monts." He put his hand over his nose and mouth. "Take that stuff somewhere else."

Monty, of course, took that as his cue to settle next to him on the bed. Pike waved the poisonous fumes away, coughing, and grabbed his cell phone.

Gibson answered on the second ring. "Please tell me you last longer than that because, seriously, any thoughts of going gay for you are definitely out of the question otherwise. I require stamina."

Pike let his head fall back to the pillow. "Shut the fuck up and stop flirting. It's not going to work."

"So you kicked her out?"

"Yeah."

"Good. You're better than that," Gib said, no sarcasm in his voice. "You need to stop dipping into the groupie pool, anyway. You're too old for that shit. Find yourself some normal women your own age."

"Normal women have too many expectations."

"What? Like remembering their names and calling them the next day?"

"Exactly. Plus, I'm best in limited doses. I'd send normal women running for the hills after too long."

"I don't know. You haven't scared off your friends yet. I mean, yes, I thought you were an egotistical douchebag when I first met you, but now you've grown on me. Like a fungus."

"So you're saying I should try to infect some normal woman with my fungus? Good talk, buddy. Good talk."

"Dr. Phil gets all his best stuff from me."

"Just tell me about this charity thing so I can get to bed and think about the sex I won't be having tonight."

Gibson paused as if ready to push the topic, but then relented. "Fine. The charity project. It would involve music."

"Excellent."

"And would be helping my lovely sister-in-law out."

"Making sexy Tessa happy. Good."

"You'd be working with kids."

"Aaaand . . . I'm out."

Gibson scoffed. "You have something against kids?"

"I'm inked up, curse like a convict, and have piercings in questionable places. Parents don't want me near their children, and kids freak me out."

"Bullshit. How can you be freaked out? You're one of them."

"Sorry, Gib."

"Are you being serious right now?"

"I'm not a kid person." He could still smell the stench of the house he'd grown up in. The overstuffed diaper pails. The spoiling government-issued baby formula. His younger siblings seeking him out when their mom had to work or when her boyfriend of the month was in a vengeful mood. That deep, terrifying feeling that lived in Pike that he was in over his head. That he'd never be enough to make it okay for them.

And he'd been one hundred percent right on that.

"This would be the older group, not the little ones."

The dredged-up memories sent a sick feeling rolling through him, making his skin go clammy. "Can't I just write a check or donate proceeds from a show or something?"

Gibson blew out a breath. "No, they need your expertise not your money. Just hear me out. Tessa has a great idea for a fundraiser, but she needs someone with experience in producing music. All the money would go toward the college fund and resources for the after-school program. You know what the charity's about. These kids don't have a lot, man. You and I both know what that's like."

Fuck. "You're really going for the jugular here, Gib."

"Just speaking the truth."

Yeah, that, and Gibson was a brilliant PR guy who knew how to pitch things. Monty laid his head on Pike's chest, and Pike scratched behind Monty's ear. "You've even got my dog giving me the don't-be-a-bastard look."

Gibson chuckled. "I sneak him treats when I'm there. He's on my side."

Pike ran a hand over his face. This was a bad idea. But even he wasn't a big enough asshole to turn his back on kids who needed help. It was places like Bluebonnet that had helped his family when they needed it. He and his siblings probably never would've gotten a Christmas gift or decent coats if not for community programs. What kind of hypocrite would it make him if he said no? But the thought of working with children made him want to run for the damn hills. "What exactly do they want me to do?"

He could almost hear Gibson's victory grin over the phone. "It won't be a big deal at all."

Pike closed his eyes. Famous last words.

THREE

Oakley fought to keep her eyes open as she transcribed information from the millionth file of the day and added it to the new thirteen-page government form that Bluebonnet Place needed to keep on every child. She polished off the rest of her coffee and glanced at the clock. Only half an hour before she got to take a break from the office work and go have her session with the kids. She could make it without a refill. Maybe.

She traced her finger down the convoluted form, trying to figure out where this information should go. *"If yes then go to line 7B. If no, go to line 10A.* If neither, rip up this frigging form and forfeit any remnants of your sanity."

"You know, I've always wondered if the people who create government forms spend their free time tying people up and torturing them."

Oakley's skin prickled at the low, smooth voice, the melodic sound like a soft stroke to the back of her neck. She spun in her office chair, poised to say *Excuse me?*, but nothing came out when her gaze collided with her visitor. At least six feet of lean, tattooed, blond bad boy was lounging against the counter and looking straight at her.

The guy gave her a conspiratorial smile and leaned a little closer, cocking his head toward her pile of papers, his eyebrow ring glinting underneath the lights. "I mean, only a sadist would make anyone try to fit letters into those little boxes."

He was talking about documents, but he may as well have asked her if she'd like to go out back and get naked for the way her body responded to the comment. Oakley swallowed past the dryness in her throat, trying to regain her professional composure despite her rogue hormonal reaction to the man's presence. This guy clearly was in the wrong place. Who walked into a children's charity and started making jokes about tying people up? Maybe he wanted the tattoo shop down the street. Though there didn't seem to be any spare spots on his arms to fill with ink. "Can I help you, sir?"

Yes. Good. That sounded calm and professional. Go her.

"No need for the sir." His lips tilted, mischief sparking in gold-green eyes. "I didn't say *I* was a sadist. But yes, I bet you can help me."

Yes, she could. Right out of that tight T-shirt.

No, no, no. Stop. What the hell was wrong with her? Hello, libido, meet Mr. Not My Type.

The man kept close, like this was some secret conversation. "I'm here to talk to the leggy blonde who runs this place. She here?"

The words snapped Oakley out of her lust haze. Leggy blonde? Oakley straightened, affronted on behalf of her boss. "If you mean *Mrs. Vandergriff,* she has a parent in her office right now. Name, please."

He tilted his head at her cool tone. "Did I say something wrong?"

"Name, please."

He rose to his full height and hooked his thumbs in his pockets, vague amusement on his face. "Pike."

She was about to ask his last name, but with a name like Pike, she doubted it was needed. "You can take a seat, and I'll let her know you're here when she's done."

He glanced at the row of chairs in the small lobby. "Or you could take a break from the torture and give me a tour of the place. I'd like to know what I'm signing up for."

She lifted a brow.

No way did he have a kid who qualified for services here. She'd taken a good long look at him now that he'd given her some breathing room. His worn jeans and vintage Dead Kennedys T-shirt may look thrown together, but she recognized expensive threads when she saw them. She'd taken that course in looking artfully casual once upon a time. Plus, imagining him with a kid just didn't compute. He looked like the guy you'd try to keep your kids away from.

"You do realize that you or your child have to be under eighteen to sign up for anything? And we don't give tours. We protect children's privacy here."

He grinned, undeterred. "I can see why Tessa puts you at the front."

Oakley straightened the file on her desk and gave him a tight smile back. "Because I'm so welcoming and warm?"

"Exactly." He eased forward again, challenge dancing in eyes framed by sooty lashes. "What's your name, o' powerful gatekeeper? Something about you seems so familiar."

Her fingers tightened around the file, his nearness and evaluating look making her heart skip a few beats, but she kept her reaction off her face. It was near impossible that anyone could recognize her these days. She'd changed her hair color from blue back to the natural dark brown, was a decade older, and at least fifteen pounds heavier since she'd been anyone worth recognizing. "Oakley Easton."

His eyes narrowed as if trying to place her. The name wouldn't be familiar to him even if he were close to the mark. But he gave up soon enough. "Guess we haven't met."

"I just have one of those faces."

"No, you don't," he said, his gaze drifting over every inch of her features. "I'd remember your face. I think it might be your voice. There's something about it."

Oh. Shit. She swallowed hard. No way Pike could be one of her callers. She didn't know much about him, but she had all the information she needed by looking at him. Tall. Confident. Sporting a body that made her want to stand up and hang over the desk so she could get a better look. He could walk into any bar or club and make panties drop with a smirk and a head nod. This would not be a guy who'd pay per minute for phone sex.

She attempted an air of nonchalance. "Lots of people have similar voices."

"True. But I have an ear for them. And yours is unique—smoky with some rasp in it. I like it."

Somehow the simplest, most innocuous words sounded illicit rolling off his lips. *I like it* sounded like *I'd fuck you* in her head. Paired with his intent focus, she was fighting hard not to squirm in her chair. She cleared her throat. "A voice fetishist. That's new."

The words slipped out before she could stop them. Dammit. Nighttime Oakley was not supposed to make an appearance at the day job. She worked hard to keep them separate.

Pike chuckled, the sound rich and full, like cashmere brushing over bare skin. "Maybe I am. Kind of comes with the territory."

Territory? That's when it clicked.

She should've pinned it from the start. Tattoos. Piercings. Attitude. She'd known enough of the type to last her a lifetime. Distaste filled her. "You're a musician."

He eyed her. "Wow, clearly, you're impressed. You look like you just smelled something bad."

"It's not . . ." But it was, and she didn't know how to finish the sentence without sounding even ruder. She picked up her phone and hit a button.

Tessa answered on the first ring. "What'cha got for me?"

"Was just checking to see if you're done with your meeting. There's a guy here to see you—a mister . . . Pike."

"Seriously?" Tessa said, triumph in her voice.

"Uh . . . yeah."

"Amazing. Bonus points to my brother-in-law. He actually got him here."

Pike reached over the counter and plucked a butterscotch from Oakley's candy dish. She gave him a you're-invading-my-personal-space brow lift, but Pike only grinned and dragged the wrapped candy between his teeth to suck it out of the cellophane. Obscene. Especially when he didn't look away from her the whole time. Her body stirred in a way it hadn't in longer than she could remember. Very, very stupid thoughts entered her mind.

She smoothed her lip balm and tried to tamp down her body's ridiculous response. Maybe she had some genetic malfunction. This was exactly the type of guy who shouldn't flip her switch. She'd already been burned by this kind of wildfire. No, not burned. Incinerated. "Would you like me to send him back?"

"Sure, that'd be great," Tessa said, the sound of shuffling papers in the background. "Is Ella coming in to relieve you this afternoon?"

"She should be here any minute."

"Great. Because there's something I need to run by you after my chat with Pike."

"No problem. I'll be in the music room when you need me."

She exchanged a quick good-bye with Tessa and set the phone in its cradle. Pike was still half-draped on her counter, making everything smell like butterscotch and male arrogance. Damn but she needed to get this man away from her.

"Mrs. Vandergriff is available now. I need to get a copy of your ID before you can go back there, though."

"Yes, ma'am." He pulled out his wallet and handed her his driver's license. Pike Ryland. So he did have a last name.

She ran it through the small desktop scanner and handed the card back to him. "Just go through that door. Her office is the last door on the right."

He tucked his wallet back into his pocket, which made that worn T-shirt stretch tighter across his lean chest. "You're not going to escort me back there? I may get lost or violate privacy laws or something. Plus, you never gave me that tour."

His tone was teasing, playful, but there was a dare in those wicked eyes. She pretended to busy herself with the papers in front of her. "I can't leave my desk until someone else covers it."

He glanced behind him. "It doesn't look like there's a line forming to get in or anything."

"Someone could come in."

He rolled the candy in his mouth. "You always so strict about following the rules, *Miz* Easton?"

"Yes." She didn't know why she was being so bullheaded about it. She could leave her desk for a few minutes if she needed to. One of the volunteers could watch the front. But Pike's presence had her off balance, and she didn't want to extend that feeling any longer.

"Mmm, shame." He cocked his head toward the door. "Then go ahead and buzz me in, Lady Gatekeeper. I wouldn't want to get anyone in trouble."

"I have a feeling that's not true at all."

He laughed. "Touché."

She hit the button under her desk to unlock the door, and Pike gave the counter two raps with his knuckles, like a warning that they weren't done here, before disappearing into the hallway.

She sagged back in her chair and expelled a breath she'd been holding. Then as soon as she determined he was safely ensconced in her boss's office, she opened up a search box on her computer, typing in *Pike Ryland*.

A page of results filled the screen in an instant, including a short line of thumbnail images. *Pike Ryland, drummer of the hard rock band Darkfall.*

Ha. She should've known. He had drummer written all over him—cut biceps, lanky frame, that I-own-the-world swagger. She had yet to meet a humble drummer. You had to be a big personality to make your presence known when you were stuck behind a drum kit and the rest of the band on stage.

Unable to resist, she clicked through a few of the images. Pike on stage. Pike shirtless, dripping with sweat, as he banged the drums. Good God. She shifted in her chair and clicked some more.

But the next few featured Pike with a rotation of supermodel-gorgeous women on his arm at parties and events. *Ugh*. That effectively cooled her jets.

She clicked on the Wikipedia entry. The page listed two albums and a gold single from a few years ago. She vaguely recognized one or two of their songs. Hard rock really wasn't her musical poison of choice. But everything she read and saw in the photos confirmed why she'd gotten that bitter taste in her mouth when she'd figured out he was a musician.

They were all the same. And it only got worse when they had some success.

She closed out all of the windows and went back to her forms, vowing to not give Mr. Ryland another thought. If nothing else she'd learned a few things this afternoon.

Good news: Her libido was not dead after all.

Bad news: It still had destructive taste.

And like a recovering alcoholic, she knew to stay far, far away from that brand of temptation.

FOUR

"Local children's theatre?" Pike settled back in the chair, focusing on Tessa and trying to ignore the raucous sound of children playing in the yard outside her window. He tugged at the collar of his T-shirt. After his run-in with the hot, uptight receptionist, he'd almost managed to forget what he was walking into. Now it felt like the walls were closing in on him. "No offense, but you're not going to make much money from that."

Tessa frowned from behind her desk. "The guy we were supposed to be working with—the one who had to back out—was going to mentor the kids and polish them up musically. He said if we did a couple of shows, charged ticket fees, it could be good."

"I don't see that happening. The only people who will want to see kids sing live are their parents." Pike hooked his ankle over his knee. "And I know that most of the families you're working with don't really have the money to pay a high ticket price. It'll be a waste of time."

Hers. The kids. And most of all, his. Maybe he could get out of this after all. No use helping with a dead-on-arrival idea.

"You'd make a lot more holding a benefit concert again and having some local bands play. I could get the guys to do a show, and I could reach out to a few other bands in the area."

Her frown stayed in place, and she tapped her fingernails on her desk, thoughtful. "We could do that, but I was hoping to do something where the kids are more involved this year. It's their college funds at stake. I think it means more if they feel like they've had a hand in earning it."

"Have them work the shows, sell tickets."

A line appeared in her forehead. "These kids have talent, though." His eyebrow lifted.

"Yeah, yeah, I know I'm biased." She gave him a what-can-ya-do smile. "But we've got some strong singers, a couple of guitar players, and a burgeoning drummer. Plus, the woman I have working with them is amazing. She's helping them to write their own songs and has really invested her time with them. I want to see the kids share what they're creating with the world."

The earnestness in her voice was killing him. He didn't know Tessa all that well. He'd only been around her when she was with her husband, Kade—and then it was usually at The Ranch where she was in submissive mode. But he could tell this wasn't simply a job for her. Lord knows she didn't need to work. Kade was a god-damned mogul. So this was all heart for her. And it was making him feel like a dick for wanting to get out of it.

He sighed, an idea coming to him that could be a perfect solution but a pain in the ass. "Having a performance at the children's the-atre isn't sharing it with the world. Maybe you should think bigger."

"Bigger?"

He shifted forward, bracing his forearms on his thighs, trying not to talk himself out of what he was about to say. "I don't know if Gibson told you, but I've opened up a small studio in town. It's kind of a side project for me when I'm not doing Darkfall stuff. I cut demos for people and have started to produce some local start-up musicians."

"Yeah, he said something about it. Aren't you working with Colby's boyfriend?"

"Keats? Yeah, talented kid."

She smiled, her amused gaze flicking over him. "I didn't know you were into country."

"I'm into good music, regardless of genre." Plus, if Pike wanted to make a real go of producing in the future, he needed to attract talent now, get some buzz going. Keats had a real shot at breaking out.

"So what does this have to do with the kids?" she asked.

"Well, I'm thinking that if you want the kids to be heard, maybe that's the way."

"Meaning?"

"There's no bigger world stage than the Internet. I help them cut a record. They can put a few tracks together and put them for sale online. The proceeds could go to the fund. Then once the songs are out, maybe they can put on a small show to promote it."

Her eyes lit. "You could do that? They could have real-deal songs out there?"

Fuck. Me. He forced a smile. "If they have enough material and patience to put together a track or two. Recording can be tedious."

She clapped her hands together. "Oh my god, that would be fantastic. They'll think they're stars! Imagine how proud they'll be to have an actual song out that people can buy. I love this idea."

Great. Fantastic. *Shoot me.* All he could picture was little kids running around his studio, screaming into the mics and climbing all over the expensive equipment. "How far along are they with having a full song ready to go?"

Tessa rolled her chair back. "Why don't you go see for yourself? They're working on it now in the music room."

"We don't have to—"

But Tessa was already cruising around the desk and grabbing for his hand. "Come on. They'll be thrilled to meet you. They were so bummed when the other guy had to bail. But now they get to work with a genuine rock star!"

He snorted. "Marginally popular at best."

And if his band didn't get it together soon, they would be candidates for *Where Are They Now?* shows in the not so distant future.

His stomach knotted as Tessa led him down a hall filled with colorful drawings and finger-painted artwork pinned to the walls. He rubbed the back of his neck, finding sweat there. This was so not his scene.

But when they rounded the corner and Tessa stopped in front of a window that looked into a wide room, he forgot his discomfort for a minute. Ms. Uptight Receptionist was sitting in the middle of a circle of older kids, strumming a guitar and singing something. He couldn't hear anything from outside the room, but the way her fingers moved over the strings was all confident elegance. Huh. The woman who had sneered at the idea of him being a musician appeared to be one herself.

And the tight-lipped, steel-spined posture she'd maintained during most of their conversation was gone, replaced with this sexy sway and bright-eyed smile. He let his eyes linger on her profile then travel down, watching the way her throat worked when she let out her notes and the way the swells of her breasts rose and fell with her breath. He adjusted his stance, willing his body not to react. Then Tessa cracked open the door, and Oakley's sultry voice hit him in the gut—smooth water over jagged rocks. Every ounce of his blood traveled straight south.

Goddamn. If a voice could be fuckable, hers was. And the woman attached to it wasn't hard to look at either. Dark hair and eyes that went cat green when she was annoyed—which had been about ninety percent of their interaction. He'd wanted that tour more than he'd let on just so he could keep teasing her and making those pink lips of hers purse. He put a hand on Tessa's shoulder. "Don't interrupt her."

Tessa looked over at him with a knowing smile. "I told you she was pretty amazing."

"Is that who I'm going to be working with?"

"Mmm-hmm. She works reception in the mornings, but once the kids get here after school, she helps out with them. If we do this project, I'll find someone else to cover the desk so that she can take this on fully."

"We met up front. I don't think she likes me very much," he said, keeping his voice low and his eyes on Oakley.

"Let me guess. You flirted with her."

He glanced over at Tessa, feigning an innocent Who-me? expression.

Tessa sniffed. "I knew she sounded weird on the phone. You Ranch boys are a menace."

"Hey, you're married to a Ranch boy."

"I stand by my statement." She glanced at the room and the woman in it. The singing had stopped and Oakley was directing the kids on something or other. "If you want to get along with Oakley, lay off that kind of thing. She has a lot on her plate and likes to keep things professional. She doesn't strike me as someone who's looking for a walk on the wild side, anyway."

"Who says I'm the wild side?"

Tessa gave him a withering look.

"Fine. If she wants to keep things professional, I can do that." Mostly. Maybe.

Tessa's eyes narrowed for a moment, but then she shook her head. "Come on, let's go in and do introductions so y'all can start planning."

When they walked in, the kids were all chatting at once. But one voice rang above the others.

"I swear to God, if she mentions another One Direction song, I'm going to puke," said a young girl with short-cropped black hair and a Runaways T-shirt. "That's all we did last week. Their songs make me want to punch someone in the face."

Pike had to bite his lip to keep from laughing.

"Reagan," Oakley said sharply. "That isn't how we share our opinions here. Be respectful."

Mini Pat Benatar turned her green-eyed gaze to Oakley. A little bit of a staring contest ensued, then Reagan finally gave in and turned to the girl she'd been addressing. She let out a heavy, dramatic sigh. "I'm sorry. One Direction songs make my stomach hurt, and I would really like it if we could do something different."

She punctuated the sentence with a toothy, plastic smile.

Pike instantly liked her.

The boy-band fan clearly did not, though. The blond girl crossed her arms and sneered. "At least it's not as bad as your weird music. No one's even heard of the stuff you like."

"Okay, let's get back on task," Oakley said, a tired edge to her voice.

Tessa stepped forward out of the shadowed back of the room. "Sorry to interrupt, guys. But I wanted to introduce you to someone."

Oakley turned and her gaze landed heavy on Pike. For a split second he caught her raw reaction—lips parting, gaze flicking down the length of his body as if she couldn't resist a full look. But as quickly as it was there, she reeled it in. Wariness descended over her face, but like the younger girl, she managed to fake a smile, clearly more for the kids' behalf than his. All the other heads in the room turned toward him, too—most of the kids staring at him with open curiosity. Tension coiled in his neck and shoulders.

"Everyone, this is Mr. Ryland. He's going to be taking Mr. Gull's place and has kindly offered to help with your song project."

"You're in a band," Reagan blurted out. Not a question.

The outburst startled Pike out of his stiff posture. Oakley turned to correct Reagan. But he interrupted her before she could. "How'd you guess? You know Darkfall?"

Reagan crossed her arms, her eyes not meeting his but looking at the rest of him instead. "No. But your ears and eyebrow are pierced and you have lots of tattoos. Some have music notes and drumsticks in them. It'd be pretty dumb to get those if you weren't in a band."

His lips tilted up. "Yeah, I guess it would be."

"My mom says all tattoos are pretty dumb, though."

"Reagan," Oakley corrected, pressing fingers to the spot between her eyes.

He laughed. He liked that the kid didn't mince words. Plus, the fact that this girl had plucked out details from his intricate full sleeve tattoos from across the room was pretty impressive. "I guess your mom would think I was a big dummy then."

Some of the kids in the group giggled and others started to announce who had tattoos in their family.

Oakley shook her head at the quickly deteriorating order in the group and then clapped her hands. "All right, all right. Let's get quiet so Mrs. Vandergriff can talk."

The kids settled after a few more seconds, and Tessa went on to explain what Pike had proposed—making a real record. Controlled chaos broke out again after that, the kids cheering, tossing out suggestions on songs, and planning their mansions in the Hollywood Hills for after they became famous. The only ones who weren't bubbling with excitement were Oakley and Reagan. Reagan was sitting quietly, a thoughtful, intense expression on her face. And Oakley looked as if she'd just been told she had a meeting with an executioner.

"Ms. Easton, can we steal you for a minute so we can work out some details?" Tessa asked.

Oakley instructed the kids to gather into two small groups and to brainstorm on what songs they wanted to work on the most, then she headed over to where Pike and Tessa were.

Tessa put a hand on Pike's shoulder. "Oakley, I know you two have already met at the front, but I wanted to officially introduce you. Pike's a good friend of Kade's brother, Gibson, and he's also the drummer in Darkfall."

Oakley didn't look a bit impressed by this news. She stuck out her hand formally. "Nice to meet you."

Pike took her hand. It was ice cold as he wrapped his fingers around it. She tried to pull back quickly, but he wasn't letting her get away with that. He rubbed his thumb along the back of her hand. "Likewise, Ms. Easton."

He released her hand when she gave another minuscule tug and flashed a warning with her eyes.

"Pike is doing us a huge favor to take time out for this," Tessa said. "So I really need you to help him in whatever way you can on this project."

He smiled. He could think of some interesting ways she could help him. Oakley wouldn't look his way.

"This will be our flagship project this year," Tessa continued. "And it'd be great to unveil at least one song at the annual benefit dinner. It's important for those who donate to us to see what we can do."

Oakley nodded. "Of course. I'll do whatever I can to help."

"It may take extra hours," Tessa said, looking over at the kids and missing the barest wince from Oakley.

"Extra hours?" Oakley asked.

Tessa nodded. "I was thinking you can make use of your time in the mornings. I'll find someone to cover the desk in the meantime. But I have a feeling this will end up being a lot of informal time not here at the office since, Pike, I'm assuming your schedule is a little erratic."

"It's not nine to five, for sure," he said, watching Oakley shift and her shoulders droop. The woman did look tired. Maybe extra hours were a hardship.

"I figured. So, don't feel like you have to keep everything here at the office within a certain time slot. You two do what you need to do to get this done on a schedule that works best for you. Let me know whatever overtime you log and keep me up to date."

Oakley gave a curt nod and smile to Tessa. "Of course. I'm sure I can get most of it done on my own and won't have to bother Mr. Ryland too much."

He smirked. So she was trying to get rid of him already. And though when he walked in, he would've happily taken the opportunity to have as minimal a role as possible, now he wasn't so sure. "It's not a bother at all. I'm looking forward to working closely with you. No use of bringing me in if you're not going to take advantage of my skills."

Her small smile radiated sarcasm, but she managed not to say anything snide in front of her boss.

"Fantastic," Tessa said, oblivious to the silent exchange. "Well, I'll leave you to it. And dinner's on me. Take tonight to make up a rough plan of what needs to be done and when and we'll go from there."

Oakley's gaze darted back to him. "Tonight?"

But Tessa was already strolling out the door.

Pike hooked his thumbs in his pockets. "Guess it's a date, then."

Her lips thinned. "Not a date. Work."

He grinned, unperturbed by her chilly response. "How can you not like me already? Usually it takes women at least a time or two to give me that look. And usually they get something out of the deal first."

She blinked, then that cat-eye green came back into her eyes. "You really have to ask?"

"Yeah. I'm asking. What did I do to you?" He leaned a little closer. "Well, besides make you think really impure thoughts at work. Because let's face it, that totally happened. It may be happening right now. With children present, no less. Are you thinking impure thoughts, Ms. Easton? You can tell me."

"Does wishing bodily injury upon someone count?"

He laughed. "Kinky."

She stared at him for a long second, looking as if she may maim or dismember him, but then she blew out a breath. "Look, I'm sure you're having fun, but I'm not playing this game. You're here to volunteer. Great. The kids are going to love it."

"But you're not."

"Doesn't matter. It's not about me."

"You're saying you don't need the help?"

She glanced over her shoulder at the kids, her expression softening before she turned back to him. "We always need the help. Sure. But this job means a lot to me. These kids mean a lot to me. And to be frank, I don't have time to cater to some celebrity who's here to put in time with the poor kids for the sake of a press clipping."

He frowned, all playfulness draining out of him. "You think that's what this is about?"

She shrugged. "Why else would you do it?"

He opened his mouth but then shut it again. If he said he was doing it for the sake of the kids, that'd be a lie. It's not like he would've strolled down here on his own out of the goodness of his heart. But he sure as hell wasn't doing it for the press. "I couldn't give a shit what the media says about me."

She crossed her arms, unconvinced.

He ran a hand through his hair. "I'm doing it as a favor to my friends, all right?"

She considered him a moment longer then gave a brief nod. "Fair enough. You really want to help, then I'll be done at six. We can go to the Italian place on the corner. But I need to be home by eight."

"Hot date?"

She leaned closer than he would've expected, right near his ear. "Yeah, with my daughter."

She gave him an angelic smile when she stepped back, then turned on her heel to head back toward the kids, leaving him staring after her. When she passed mini-Benatar, who was cross-legged on the floor, she ran her hand over the child's head and smiled down at her.

Well, hell.

Oakley had a kid.

At least now he knew which mom thought tattoos were dumb.

FIVE

Oakley smiled to herself as Pike rattled off timelines and tasks in between bites of calzone. He'd been all business since they'd sat down in the back corner of the little dive restaurant. Her tactic had worked. It usually did. Childless men found out she was a mom and ran away like their ass was on fire.

Pike seemed to be no exception. Since she'd informed him that she had a daughter, he'd turned off the flirt. A small, selfish part of her was disappointed. Not that she had any interest in pursuing anything with anyone right now, especially with someone like him, but it had been kind of heady getting that kind of attention thrown her way. If nothing else, it had reminded her that the sexual part of herself wasn't totally dead. Even now, that warm energy hummed through her as she surreptitiously watched Pike lick a dollop of red sauce off his thumb. He had a pouty bottom lip that would look feminine if not for the hard angle of his jaw and the scruff. She kind of wanted to bite it—see if it felt as plump as it looked.

He glanced up, caught her staring, and smiled. "So, wanna screw in the bathroom?"

She startled and stiffened, instantly yanked out of her less-than-PG thoughts. *"What?"*

He leaned back in his chair, vague confusion on his face. "I asked if you wanted to keep working in that back room? We could rehearse at the studio once they're close to being ready to record.

But until then, it's probably more trouble than it's worth to cart everyone over there. It's not that big of a place."

"Rehearse in the back room?" she repeated, running the words back in her head to make sense of them. "Oh, right, yes, that's fine. I'm sorry. I thought you said something else."

She eyed the small Bellini she'd ordered with her meal. Maybe that had been a bad idea. She was hearing things now.

Screw in the bathroom? How the hell had she gotten that out of what he'd said? Of course, now all she could think of was him doing just that—taking her by the elbow and leading her to that dark alcove at the back of the restaurant, pushing her up against that wall with the faded Italian flag on it, and putting his hands all over her. She licked her top lip, tasting the sweet remnants of her drink. *Pull it together, woman.*

Apparently, once her libido had been brave enough to peep its head out, it had decided it was Groundhog Day and needed to run around, declaring spring was coming early. She hated to break the news, but nothing and no one was coming anytime soon.

"What did you think I said?" Pike took a long sip from his drink, his snake-charmer eyes never leaving hers.

She followed suit, hoping the fruity drink would cool off more than her throat. "Doesn't matter."

His lips twitched. "You're all red."

"I think it's the Bellini. I don't drink very often."

"No way." His expression turned smug. "You thought I said something dirty, didn't you?"

"Huh?" She smoothed her napkin in her lap, trying to loosen the tightness in her voice. "No. Why would I think that? You've been very professional since we got here—which I appreciate, by the way."

His gaze slid lazily down her body, like butter melting over toast, and goddamn it all to hell, she could feel her nipples go hard and obvious beneath her bra. No wonder he'd figured it out. Her body was waving all kinds of flags in his face. *Hey! Over here! Horny girl, booth eight!*

"I am capable of being professional, you know," he said, but his tone was all sex and sin. "I'm also more than happy to turn that off when the occasion calls for it. So why don't you tell me what you thought you heard and why it's gotten you all flushed and nervous?"

"I'm not nervous."

He grinned.

Dammit. She schooled her face into a stoic expression. "The music is too loud in here. I thought you propositioned me to defile the restroom."

His eyebrow ring twitched. "Now you're just trying to turn me on with those big, stiff words of yours."

All she heard was *big* and *stiff* at first, but she managed to rein in her temporary insanity. "We're so not going to do this."

"Well, probably not here, you're right. I saw those bathrooms. But—"

"No, I mean, any of this. Flirting. Teasing. Whatever this is."

He leaned onto his forearms, looking all too pleased that he'd gotten a confession out of her. "You got a guy?"

"No," she said before she could get wise and fib.

"Then why can't we do this?"

"Because I'm not interested."

"Liar."

She huffed. "Are you always this cocky?"

"No, it's dialed down right now. I can get way worse."

She stirred her drink. "Not. Possible."

His lips spread into a menacing smile. "Challenge accepted."

"No, that's not—"

But he was already getting up from his side of the booth. He slid smoothly into the spot next to her on the cracked vinyl seat. He put his arm along the back of the booth, near to touching her, and leaned in close. "I dialed it back because what I could've said was how if you heard what you heard, it must've been on your mind already. That those pictures must be there in your head. Were we in a stall? Or bold as you please up against a wall?"

"Stop," she said softly, somehow frozen in place, the clean

scent of his shampoo mixing in with the heavy oregano smell of the restaurant and making her head spin.

"So that was it, huh? Against the wall where anyone could've walked up and seen? That would've been hot. Legs wrapped around my hips. I could've unpeeled all these layers you've wrapped yourself in." He touched the collar of her blouse but not skin. "I could've also said that I saw the want in your eyes before I knew what question you'd thought I'd asked. That your body jumped to attention like I'd stroked you. That you can tell me no and to shut the fuck up. But you can't tell me that you're not interested because I can see that truth all over you."

She swallowed hard, fighting her body's response as he let his gaze drift down and over her curves. No way was she going to let him get to her like this. She did this for a living. She talked dirty to men every damn night and they talked dirty back. But never had words rushed through her system like these. Every part of her was now achingly aware of just how long it'd been since she'd let a man touch her. But there was no way she'd allow herself to act on it with him. She cleared her throat.

"Does this usually work for you? A little dirty talk whispered in a woman's ear and she's all over you? Or maybe you just tell them you're in a band and that's enough." She turned to send Pike a frosty look. "Back off, Mr. Ryland. You've entered a restricted area."

His eyes flared with heat, like her attitude only turned him on more, but he moved back and gave her space. "If you think that's dirty talking, you've been seriously deprived."

She pointed. "Back to your side."

He raised his palms. "Not a problem. All I want to know is why not?"

Because attraction clearly wasn't the issue. Her traitor body had announced that loud and clear to him.

"Because this is my job, and this project is important to me. I'm not going to muddy the waters by crossing any lines with you. Plus, I'm a mom."

"So? I've heard rumors that moms get lives, too."

No, they didn't. Not really. Not when there was no dad in the picture, two jobs, and a kid with special needs.

She barely resisted rolling her eyes. "Come on, Pike. I know we don't know each other yet, but why in God's name would you come barking up this tree? The groupie business running low? You've got to have women with much simpler lives who want to play the hookup game with a big-time drummer."

His jaw tensed, expression darkening.

She sighed. This was probably about ego, challenge, and all that male bullshit. If she let him take her to the bathroom and do what he suggested, he'd be over it by the time he got home. And then everything would be weird between them for the rest of the project. She needed to clear this air and move on. Tessa had told her this afternoon that there could be a promotion in her future—project coordinator. A job that would allow her to quit the night gig. But it hinged on how well she did on this major project. She wasn't going to let some misguided attraction on her part or bruised ego on his part thwart that.

"Look, Pike. Yes, there's attraction. Maybe an inappropriate thought or two crossed my mind, but this has to stay professional. I don't have time or interest in anything outside of that."

Especially with a musician. Hell. No.

His gaze held hers for a moment longer, and she almost got lost in the mix of ambers and greens in his hazel eyes, but finally he dropped the eye contact and slid out of her side of the booth. "Okay, then. Let's get back to hammering out a rehearsal schedule. I have to be honest, your drummer needs more than a little work."

––––––––

Oakley seemed startled by his quick acquiescence and shift in subject, but he'd heard the message with ringing clarity. If he'd learned anything in life, it was how to not linger where he wasn't wanted. And really, Oakley had been one hundred percent right. What business did he have chasing a woman like her?

She lived a normal life, had responsibilities, and a child to worry about. She'd want some guy who fit into that—a nine to fiver with a steady job who played golf on Saturdays and went to church on Sundays. A guy who wouldn't show up at her place and make all the people in suburbia whisper about his weird haircut and his inked skin.

This was why he tended to stick to the twentysomethings who hung around after shows. Those women knew what they were getting into with him—sought it out. He was the thrill. The dare. The shocking story to tell to their girlfriends after they've settled down behind their white picket fences and are remembering those crazy days right out of college.

Oakley was a grown-up. She knew he had nothing to offer her beyond a hot night or two. Smart.

Didn't make him want her less.

"So just like that, you're going to drop it?" she asked, not answering his question about rehearsal schedules.

He shrugged. "I always respect a no."

Her gaze shifted to her food. "Well, that's something."

The words had been muttered to herself, but he'd heard them well enough. He frowned. "I'm not going to force anything, Oakley. Contrary to popular belief, I'm pretty harmless."

She glanced up, sardonic smile returning. "Now there's a lie if I've ever heard one."

He pointed at her. "Nope. I'm a lot of things. But not a liar."

"Oh, really? Mr. Honesty, huh?"

"Try me." He took a bite of his calzone.

Her Bellini must've been fully settling in because she asked him something he never would've expected. "So have you really done it in a public bathroom before?"

He smirked. "A few times. Taking a chance in a place where you might get caught can be really hot. Though, bathrooms aren't my preference. And never, ever try in one of those portable ones at music festivals. Learned that one the hard way."

She blanched. "I don't even want to pee in those."

"Wise girl. So what about you?"

"Me?"

"Ever in a bathroom?" He picked a pepperoni off his plate and popped it in his mouth.

Her gaze skated away. "Once. But it was one of those private single ones."

Based on her tone that was not a pleasant memory. "If there's no chance of discovery, you only get partial credit."

Her expression turned grim. "Believe me. That whole relationship was about trying not to get discovered. I should get all kinds of points."

He wiped his mouth on his napkin. "How so? Married guy?"

"God, no. I would never." She looked back to him, guarded. "I was young. He was a lot older."

"Ahh. I've had one of those, too."

Her mouth flatlined at that. "How nice for you."

The shift in demeanor surprised him. Only after a few seconds did he catch why she'd sent such a cold front his way. "Oh, shit. No, that's not what I meant. I haven't been with too young of a girl. I'm not a creep. All I meant was that I had one of those forbidden relationships when I was young. Lost my virginity to one of my high school teachers."

She lowered her glass without sipping. "Seriously?"

"Looking back, I realize it was a pretty messed-up thing on her part. But at the time, I was all for it."

He'd been young and dumb and horny as shit. His history teacher had been hot and still in her twenties. And he'd much preferred stopping by her house on the way home to get his education on the female form instead of going back to his own family's chaos.

He laughed when he saw Oakley's still-shocked expression. "And hey, let's pick Things You Shouldn't Tell Complete Strangers for five hundred, Alex."

A small smile finally broke through. "Sorry. It's just, I'm a mom. I'm horrified at the thought of a teacher taking advantage of a child."

He shrugged. "Like I said, I know now it was screwed up. Back then, I thought I was the man."

"I see life hasn't cured you of that last condition yet."

He cocked an eyebrow, enjoying this relaxed version of her. Alcohol was good for the uptight receptionist. "Touché, Ms. Easton."

"See, now you say the Ms. thing and it sounds dirty."

He smirked. "She let me call her by her first name. But be warned, I can make anything sound dirty."

"I'm noticing that. It's quite a gift."

"Absolutely." He had the suspicion that she'd have that gift, too, if she wanted it. Just listening to that low, husky voice talking about mundane things had made him hot earlier. But having an R-rated conversation with her now—well, he was halfway to hard already. If they kept it up, he'd have to order the cannoli just to prolong the time he could keep his lower half hidden under the table.

But before he could ask her anything else, she excused herself to go to the restroom. He asked her if she wanted him to join her, but she rolled her eyes and told him, "No, it's only going to be me and the pride of Italy."

He watched her walk away, enjoying the way her black slacks highlighted the curve of her ass. She had a nice swaying walk—one that would look downright decadent without the business clothes in the way. His phone rang, interrupting his appreciation of the scenery.

He reached for it without looking and slid his thumb across the screen to answer. "Yeah?"

"Uh . . ." asked a hesitant male voice. "Is this Sa—"

The phone cut out for a second. "What? I'm having trouble hearing you."

"Is this Sasha?"

"Who? No. I think you've got the wrong number, man."

"No, I mean, it's not. I have it programmed on my phone." There was a pause as if the guy was checking his screen, then he was back. "It's the right number. I reserved a call at eight. Am I going to get charged for these minutes? Where's Sasha?"

Pike frowned and pulled the phone away from his ear to check the caller ID, but when he did, he realized the phone in his hand didn't have a black cover like his. It had a bright blue one. *Shit.* He'd answered Oakley's phone.

But the dude was asking for a Sasha and the caller ID said Private Number. He put the phone back to his ear. "Wires must be crossed, dude. Wrong number."

"No, but—"

Pike hung up the call and dropped the phone back onto the table next to his own. Same brand and model. Same standard ring. *Motherfucker.* If Oakley realized he'd answered her phone, she'd be pissed. And have good reason to be.

But it had been a wrong number, so maybe it wasn't too big a deal. It hadn't been some boyfriend calling or a family member. Nothing that could cause any problems. Maybe he should just mention it to her, and they could laugh off the mix-up. It was a weird enough call.

The guy had wanted a Sasha . . . who he'd reserved at eight and had on speed dial . . . and would get charged minutes for.

He snorted when all the information locked together. Shit, had he intercepted some random 900-number call? Hilarious. Oakley would get a kick out of that.

Oakley hustled up to the booth, a frantic edge to her movements. "We've got to go."

"Hey, what's wrong?"

"I just saw what time it is. I can't believe we've been here that long." She reached for her purse, which she'd left on her seat. "I have to get back home—like now."

"Oh, yeah, sure," Pike said, pulling money from his wallet to toss on the table. He hadn't realized how much time had passed either.

"Tessa said she'd cover this. I have the company card."

"No, it's fine. You're in a hurry. I've got it." He scooted out of the booth.

Oakley's phone rang again. Private Caller flashed on the screen.

Oakley's gaze darted toward it, slight panic crossing her face. She swiped the phone from the table. "Crap, I need to take this. Sorry, I'll be right back."

"But—"

She turned in a flurry and put the phone to her ear, leaving Pike standing there in confusion. But before she got far enough away, he heard the hello, the name Sasha, and the utterly cock-hardening downshift in her voice.

He plunked back down in the booth.

What.

The.

Hell.

SIX

"Mom . . . Mom . . . MOM!"

Oakley jolted awake, almost rolling off the couch, and blinked in the bright lamplight. "Huh, what?"

Wispy threads of her dream clung to her brain like spiderwebs— something where Pike was sweaty and shirtless, like that photo of him drumming but with no drums involved.

"Why are you sleeping?" Reagan asked. Oakley's vision cleared and she stared up at Reagan's big, worried eyes. "It's only six thirty. Are you sick?"

Oakley yawned and sat up. "Oh, no. I'm sorry, baby. I'm fine. I guess that show was just really boring."

Little frown lines appeared around Reagan's mouth—her thinking face. Reagan didn't like when things didn't go according to her expected schedule. A few years ago, something like Mom falling asleep before bedtime would've probably freaked Reagan out enough for a tantrum. But thankfully, they'd moved past the tantrums with age and the help of Reagan's therapists. Her little girl was learning to cope in quieter, more effective ways. *High-functioning.* That's what went on all the reports now.

Oakley thanked the universe every day for those simple words. It was far beyond what she'd hoped for when she'd brought her mute three-year-old into a clinic and they'd given her the autism diagnosis. At twenty, Oakley had barely been keeping her head above water with single motherhood. The word *autism* had felt like a death sentence for them both. How was she going to handle something that big on her own?

But she had. *They* had. Her and Rae together. Day by day. Hour by hour. Sometimes in the worst times, minute by minute. Now she had her smart, quirky, beautiful eleven-year-old girl to show for it. They'd both learned how to work with each other and how to accommodate the needs Reagan still had. Not every day was a good day, but they far outweighed the bad now.

"What have you got there?" Oakley asked, noticing the papers clutched in Reagan's hand.

"Did you write these?" She held the pages up like an accusation.

Oakley rubbed her eyes and leaned closer. The handwritten title "Dandelion" stared back at her. Crap. "Where'd you find those?"

"In the garage. I was looking for some paint for a project and found a box of papers and sheet music."

"You're not supposed to be digging through stuff in the garage without my permission."

She cocked her head in that way Oakley knew would only grow more sarcastic as she closed in on the teen years. "You were sleeping. How could I have asked permission?"

Oakley sighed. Reagan was going to be a demon on the debate team one day. "Then you wake me up or wait. Did you dig through any other boxes?"

"No. They were labeled with boring stuff."

Thank God. She'd managed to keep her past tucked away from Reagan this long, she didn't need it coming out now. Good thing she hadn't labeled any of the boxes "Remnants of a Failed Teen Pop Star." One day she'd tell her the story of how Mommy was kind of famous once upon a time. But not now. She wasn't ready for the questions that Reagan would have yet.

"So are these yours?" she asked again.

Oakley took the pages from her. "Yes, I liked to write songs when I was younger."

She still did. Her feelings tended to come out in lyrics, and she couldn't turn that nozzle off. But now they were messy words scrawled on sticky notes or in her journal. Words that had nowhere to go except into the silence of ink on paper.

"Could we use some of these for the Bluebonnet songs? I like the one about wishes. How does it sound on the guitar?"

Oakley smiled. "Wait, Ms. Punk Chick likes 'Dandelion'?"

Reagan lifted her bony shoulder, a little sheepish. "I like that part about people's wishes floating in the air. That seems kind of cool. And the other girls will probably like it because it's about flowers. Even though it's really about wishes and not flowers."

"What about the boys?"

"Who cares what they like?"

Oakley laughed. "You'll probably care one day."

"Not today."

Oakley reached out and ruffled Reagan's pixie hair—a cut Rae had insisted on despite it drawing some teasing from the other girls at school. Short hair was a no-no in tween land, apparently, but Reagan wasn't one to take polls of popular opinion—a blessing and a curse. "Go and get my guitar, and I'll try to remember how this one goes so you can decide if you really like it."

Reagan's face lit up and she ran off to get the guitar. Oakley reached for the watered down Coke she'd left sweating on the side table and swigged it for the caffeine more than the taste. She was going to have to find a way to grab some more sleep. Last night, her regular eight o'clock Wednesday caller, Edward, had been more than a little put out by the fact that she hadn't been able to talk to him at the scheduled time. He said he'd called first and had gotten redirected to the wrong number and then when he'd called a second time, she hadn't been able to talk yet.

She'd almost died on the spot when the phone had rung in front of Pike. On Wednesdays, her brother kept Reagan overnight to give Rae a chance to visit with her cousin Lucas and to give Oakley a night to herself. But instead of relaxing, she typically used it to log more hours on the line and earn extra money. So she had her account set to sign in automatically at eight. And Edward was used to getting his call at that time every week.

She'd apologized profusely, not wanting to lose one of her most steady and decent customers, and had agreed to give him time off the clock late last night after she was done with her other calls. So he'd taken full advantage of that time. He liked to talk to her like she was his girlfriend. So though it always led to sex stuff in the end, he first had conversations with her about life, things going on in the news, the weather. She had to make up things about her job and life, keeping everything confidential, but he seemed to enjoy the relationship-y parts as much as the hot stuff. It was the behavior of a lonely guy, but he wasn't demeaning and he talked to her like she was a normal person.

She'd gladly take ten Edward calls a night than the rest of the stuff. Talking about the weather felt decadent after a night of being called a dirty little slut for the hundredth time.

Her phone buzzed from the coffee table and she grabbed it. *Unknown Caller.* It was too early for any calls to be forwarded from the service. She put it to her ear. "Hello?"

"I have two pizzas, a free night, and a lot of ideas. But I need your address in order to deliver these wondrous gifts."

"Who is this?"

"Well, someone has a lot of guys calling her and offering free food."

"Ryland."

"Give the lady a prize. So what do you say?"

"Pike, it's a weeknight and Reagan's here and—"

"This is strictly business. We didn't get to finish up last night and I'm booked up this weekend, so I figured we could squeeze in some planning tonight. Plus, what kid doesn't like pizza?"

"She's already eaten. And I didn't say we could have meetings at my house."

"Come on. I figured that'd be easiest on you since you wouldn't need to get a babysitter. And I really am harmless. Ask Tessa. You think your boss would let me work around the kids if she thought there was anything to worry about?"

Oakley blew out a breath. Of course Tessa wouldn't. The background check process was extensive. Oakley had almost backed out of the job when she'd realized she'd have to reveal the truth about her past to Tessa in order to get hired. But Tessa had thankfully been very understanding and hadn't brought up anything since.

Regardless, did Oakley want Pike at her house? She only had a little while before she'd need to put Reagan to bed and get on the phone. Last night had already been too close of a call.

However, the work had to get done and if he was going to be gone all weekend, they'd be even more behind next week when she had to report progress to Tessa. "Fine. But you can only stay a little while."

"Deal."

She rattled off her address, hung up, and glanced down at what she was wearing—a worn-out Mickey Mouse T-shirt and yoga pants. Very sexy. She ignored the ridiculous instinct to rush to her room and put something more flattering on. If he wanted to stop by last-minute, then he could deal with the true-to-life version of herself. Plus, she could use all the armor available to her. This outfit said loud and clear that this was not anything more than a planning session.

Now if she could just convince her racing heart of that.

―――――――――

When Pike walked up to the door of Oakley's small clapboard house, music drifted through the slightly open window. He tilted his head, recognizing the dulcet tones of Oakley's voice singing along with a guitar. Nice. He closed his eyes, straining to pick out the words.

Take my wish, pluck it from the air, plant it with your hands, and let it bloom . . .

The song was upbeat but had a yearning to it that made it almost sad. Wistful.

Blow it away, blow me away. Watch us fade away.

Pike hummed along with the chorus, picking up the pattern of notes quickly, and inserting a matching drumbeat in his head. Huh, the song was a catchy little thing. Sweet and raw. Like a Jewel tune with an updated rhythm.

He hated to knock and interrupt, but the next-door neighbor had stepped onto her porch and was sending him an evaluating glare. He was used to that look. He'd gotten it as a kid when he'd walk through his friend Foster's gated neighborhood. The blond kid with the thrift store clothes and the punk rock hair *did not belong*. He resisted the urge to lift the pizza boxes to neighbor lady and let her know he wasn't there to steal or pillage anything but to deliver gifts.

The music stopped and Oakley answered the door a minute later. Her dark hair was piled on her head in a haphazard bun and her T-shirt looked liked it'd seen better days—probably in the nineties. But she looked ten times sexier than she had in that boring work outfit. Now he could see the details of the tempting curves beneath the thin shirt and yoga pants—all woman. All the way down to the bright pink polish on her toes.

"I didn't realize I was supposed to dress for a slumber party," he said, allowing himself another head to toenail perusal. "I would've brought my footed pajamas."

"You come to my house after seven. This is what you get."

"Well, lucky, lucky me."

She shook her head. "I swear, you could flirt with a tree stump."

He handed her the pizzas. "Why do that when I can have fun annoying you?"

With a sigh, she opened the door wider and let him come inside. He shut it behind him while Oakley handed Reagan the pizza boxes. "Baby, you remember Mr. Ryland?"

Reagan nodded and shifted her weight to the other foot. "Hi, Mr. Ryland."

Her gaze was so serious, so . . . adult. Those old soul eyes made him forget how uncomfortable he was around kids. "If it's okay with your mom, you can call me Pike."

Reagan looked up at her mother and Oakley nodded. "That's fine."

"Why are you bringing us pizza, Mr. Pike?" Reagan asked. All bluntness.

He didn't bother correcting her that he'd meant she could drop the mister. "To get on you and your mom's good side."

Reagan's lips twitched into a little smile. "You'd have to bring dessert for that."

He laughed. "I'll remember that for next time."

"Can I eat another dinner, Mom?" Reagan asked, clutching the pizzas like she was afraid she'd have to give them back.

"Sure. Why don't you bring them in the kitchen and get out some paper plates? We'll be there in a minute."

Reagan hurried off, and Oakley grabbed her guitar to slip it into the case.

The living room was small and lived in, the furniture and carpet worn but not in disrepair. Nothing fancy, but Oakley's place had a cozy, welcoming feel to it.

"I heard you playing when I walked up. Great song."

She latched the case. "Thanks."

"Who's it by? I haven't heard that one before."

She glanced over at him, wariness putting lines around her mouth. "No one. It's just a thing I tinkered with a long time ago. Reagan found the lyrics and wanted me to play it."

"Wait, you wrote that?" He moved closer without realizing he was doing it. That was *her* song? "What's it called?"

" 'Dandelion.' It was just a stupid teenage thing I scribbled down." She gave him a dismissive wave of her hand. "Reagan wanted to change some of it around and maybe use it as a starting point for one of the songs for the group."

"Oh, hell no."

She set down the guitar case next to the TV and peered back over her shoulder. "What?"

His mind was already working, grabbing onto thoughts and running with them. "I only heard a little bit of it, but that's not a kid's song. Too much yearning in it for that. And that's a one-voice song. Besides adding in some drums and a bass track, it didn't sound like it needed to be messed around with. Maybe you could play the whole thing for me?"

She crossed her arms. "We're here to work, not to waste time serenading you with my teenage ballads. Plus, I don't play my own stuff for other people. I only did it because Reagan asked."

"Hold up. You have more stuff?"

A smile finally broke through at that. She tilted her head. "What's with you? You look like a beagle who just got offered a rack of ribs."

What was with him was that he had been trying his hand at producing for the last year, and he hadn't had a song hit him with that kind of gut-level force since he'd heard Keats. He was still new to this producing thing, but his instincts on what was good hadn't let him down yet. "Fine. We'll eat pizza and work. But before I leave, you're going to play that song for me."

"I will n—"

He raised a finger. "Remember, I am selflessly donating this Thursday night for the good of *children*, Oakley. I provided dinner. And I am mostly keeping my eyes to myself even though you are parading around in that enticing ensemble. All I'm asking in return is a song."

She snorted and looked down at her shirt. "Mickey Mouse does it for you, huh?"

"His ears are very strategically placed. Not that I've noticed."

She narrowed her eyes in playful warning. "Okay. I'll think about it. One song. But only if we get this plan hammered out before ten."

"I will accept this deal." But there she went with the time limit again, which had his mind chasing that bunny trail from last night.

After their dinner the night before, he'd gone home and had tried to talk himself out of his crazy theories about the phone calls. He'd ruled out the most ridiculous one first. No way was Oakley a call girl or escort. She had a kid and wouldn't be able to get away that much. Plus, during their conversations about the bathroom, she'd blushed. A hooker doesn't blush.

So there were only a few other possibilities he could think of. One was that she was seeing a guy who liked to role-play. Pike liked those kinds of games himself, so he'd been down that road of false names and such. But Oakley had said she wasn't seeing anyone and he believed her. Then he'd thought it could be an online relationship thing—pretending to be someone else and hooking up via the Internet. But really, why would Oakley need to catfish anyone? The woman was hot.

So then he'd landed on the last theory. That she was some kind of phone-sex operator. That would explain the guy mentioning minutes.

But maybe he'd heard it all wrong and was chasing crazy ideas. First, did people still call those old-school lines when every porntastic thing imaginable could be found on the Internet? And secondly, after replaying the scene, he wasn't one hundred percent sure that she'd said Sasha to the caller when she'd walked away. Maybe he'd heard wrong. The music had been loud in the restaurant.

And as he followed Oakley into the kitchen to share a pizza with her kid, he couldn't wrap his head around the idea that this doting mother who worked at a non-profit could flip the switch and play filthy phone-sex girl at night. He'd called those lines when he was a teenager. He'd lift credit card numbers from his mom's boyfriend and charge the calls that way. And he'd gotten quite an education when he'd found there was no limit to what those women would talk about. He had a hard time picturing Oakley saying "fuck" much less describing sex acts in explicit detail.

However, once they were in the kitchen, Oakley turned to him and asked him what he wanted to drink, and that voice hit him again right where it counted. That tone, dropping half an octave, and pressed close to the phone? It could probably make a guy hard before a dirty word was ever spoken. It'd be lethal.

He liked Oakley a lot already but had accepted yesterday during dinner that he was too far from her type to get anywhere. She wasn't looking to sow some bad-boy oats. She'd moved beyond that phase of life. But if the lovely Ms. Easton wasn't as buttoned-up and conservative as she was portraying, if she was up to some naughty, secretive business behind closed doors, that put a whole new shine on things. Because nothing was hotter to him than a woman who had her shit together during the day but who could also let loose and play dirty at night.

Maybe that had been part of what had gotten him in trouble with his teacher. She'd been strict in the classroom, so put together. But one day he'd walked up on her in between classes. She'd been bending over to get something on the floor and had stumbled, giving him the glorious sight of her lacy red thong before she could right herself. After that, he'd lost hours in that class imagining what she was like outside of school, picturing what happened when she took the pins out of her hair and stripped off that stern expression. And one day when he'd run into her in town on a weekend, he'd found out.

But that had been his young infatuation and a raging libido at work there. He'd been dumb and eager. She'd been lonely and recovering from an abusive relationship. Looking back, he'd been the epitome of non-threatening, which is why she'd probably crossed lines that should've never been crossed. He hadn't known what to do with that kind of situation then.

But now the thought of discovering a woman who had that ability to play both sides of the line had his mouth watering. The girls he usually hooked up with wore their sexuality on the surface. One-dimensional. Like the one he'd kicked out the other night. Physically, she probably would've been game for whatever he suggested. But it often lost its punch when a girl was doing something simply to impress him—to win the I'm-the-hottest-girl game. To play the porn star to his rock star.

So much of it was pure bullshit.

But a woman who wanted to do things because it would make her feel good, because she craved it? Well, that'd be an altogether different rodeo.

"You look lost in thought over there," Oakley said, sliding a glass of tea his way.

He took a long sip from the glass.

"Nickel for your thoughts?" Reagan said, mouth half full of pizza. "And if you say them, Mom actually pays you a nickel. I've got a big jar of them. I have lots of thoughts."

He nearly choked on his drink. His thoughts were *so* not kid-friendly, and he had a feeling it was showing on his face. He needed to pull it together. Here he was sitting in a kitchen with Oakley and her daughter in the middle of suburbia eating pizza and spinning some bent fantasy that the woman in the Disney shirt was secretly a phone-sex operator. He was an idiot. "I was thinking you should tell me what kind of music you like."

Reagan's face brightened like this was her favorite topic in the world. "Have you ever heard of punk rock?"

He laughed. "A time or two."

Oakley slid onto a stool and grabbed a slice of cheese pizza. "Reagan is *very* into the eighties."

"Is that right?" he asked, directing the question to Reagan. "How'd that happen?"

"Because Mom's a whore."

"Reagan!" Oakley said.

Pike spit out his drink.

Reagan's eyes went wide as she looked between the two of them. "What's wrong?"

Oakley looked like she'd swallowed a porcupine but managed to lower her voice, replacing it with a terse but calm one. "Where'd you learn that word? That's not a nice word."

"Whore?" she asked, all innocence and doe eyes. "On TV. How is it bad? It just means you like to keep a lot of stuff. That's how I found all those records and magazines from the eighties."

Pike bit his lips together, trying not to laugh as Oakley pressed her fingers between her eyes and rubbed. "It's *hoarder*, baby. Hoarder. That's the correct word. The other one means something different."

Reagan seemed undeterred. "What does the other one mean then?"

"It's an ugly word. We'll talk about it another day. Finish your pizza. You need to be in the bathtub in fifteen minutes."

Reagan didn't look as if she wanted to let it go. But after a few seconds she rolled her eyes, muttering a "whatever," and went back to her meal.

Pike had grabbed a paper towel and was dabbing at the spray of tea he'd sent flying. He cut Oakley an amused look.

She shook her head in kill-me-now chagrin, but the humor in her eyes warmed him right to his toes. Vixen or not, this woman was beautiful.

She pointed a finger his way. "Not a word from you."

He raised his hands. "I didn't say a thing."

But boy was he thinking them.

Many, many things.

SEVEN

After tucking Reagan in for the night, Oakley plopped down on the couch, settling against the side farthest from Pike. Like that would help. The guy had a gravitational field like a black hole. She could feel the force of it dragging her toward him, threatening to consume her completely if she let her guard down for one second. "All right, she's zonked out. We're good to go until ten as long as we keep our voices down."

"Then you turn into a pumpkin?" he asked, looking up from the legal pad he had in his lap.

"Got to get my beauty rest."

"Yes." He nodded gravely. "Very important for a whore."

She grabbed a throw pillow and tossed it at him. "Hey, only eleven-year-old kids are allowed to call me that."

And almost every single caller every freaking night. She'd nearly died when the word had rolled off Reagan's lips. For one panicked moment, she'd thought Reagan had somehow broken through all of Oakley's safety measures and had discovered what Mom did at night.

"She seems like a sweet kid," Pike said, glancing in the direction of the stairs. "And surprisingly knowledgeable about bands that existed decades before she was born. Good taste, though."

Oakley tucked a leg beneath her. "That's her thing. When she finds something she likes, she obsesses about a subject and wants to know everything about it. Wants to live and breathe it."

"Nothing wrong with passion. I was a lot like that when I started getting into music. Though, I was a little older than her when I got to the obsessive phase."

Oakley smiled. "I love that she's passionate and smart. But it doesn't win her many favors socially. She struggles with the group stuff, so I'm hoping this project will be good for her. At her school, she's in really small classrooms with specialized attention. Bluebonnet's where she gets a dose of the real world."

"What school does she go to?"

"The Bridgerton Academy."

"Whoa. That's the fancy one downtown with all the ivy on the fences, right?"

"Yeah. She has a partial scholarship. It's still crazy expensive, but it's the best thing that ever happened for Reagan. She has some extra needs, and she's made so much progress since I moved her there. She's finding her confidence."

"That's awesome." He shifted on the couch to fully face her. "So ready to get this stuff done or do you want to sing for me first?"

She grabbed her cup of coffee and lifted it in a toast. "Work comes first. This caffeine's only going to last so long."

"I see how it is. You're into making a guy wait."

She smiled sweetly. "Endlessly."

He narrowed his eyes at her and stretched his arm across the back of the couch. "Sadist, huh? I can work with that."

"You're flirting again."

"So are you."

"Am definitely not." She totally had been. It was like a goddamned reflex around him. "Talk to me about rehearsal schedules."

"Slave driver."

They worked for a little over an hour, Pike talking fast and her jotting down as many of their half-formed ideas as she could manage. Once Pike got started, his brain seemed to work faster than his mouth. Full-on creative mode. The energy rolling off him infected her, too, getting her heart beating quicker than the coffee ever could. This was the part she missed about the industry she used to be in.

She didn't miss the bullshit, the business, or the backstabbing, but she missed being around artistic people who ran on the fuel of their ideas and passions. She missed being in that flow with others and creating art. Music.

"Maybe we could see how expensive it'd be to get the rights to record some cover songs. If we tell them it's for charity, we might be able to get permission," Pike said, almost talking to himself. "Or maybe the kids want to do all originals. I guess that depends on how strong the originals are. We'd need at least one anchor song that has solid hit potential. Something people can really sing along to. And we could do a YouTube video with the kids—something fun. Morning shows will eat that up. And how many kids are in the program, not just in the music one, but all of it? A choir of kids in the background of a song can sound killer. You know, like the kids in John Lennon's 'Happy Xmas' or even like the crowd singing in 30 Seconds to Mars songs. It makes it anthemic. Or—"

"Whoa, slow down, speed demon," she said, raising a hand and forcing Pike to take a breath. "You're spinning ideas faster than I can write. I should grab my laptop."

He nodded. "Yeah, do that. We can share notes better that way anyhow."

She went into her room and unhooked her laptop from the docking station, double and triple checking that the window for the call service was closed, and then brought it into the living room.

Pike continued bouncing ideas with her, and the clicking keyboard filled the spaces between sentences. But she was watching the clock closely. When it hit 9:50, she set the laptop aside and stretched her arms above her head. "I think we've gotten more than enough done for tonight. Next week, we can look at the songs they have already first, and you can see what direction we need to go."

Pike pulled his phone from his pocket. "Is it that late already?"

"'Fraid so."

"Damn. Well, guess it's time for you to sing for me."

She shifted on the couch cushion. No way was she singing that song in front of him. It'd be like standing in front of him naked. "It's too late. Maybe next time."

"Come on, I'm sure you can stay up a little past your bedtime? It's just one song."

His tone was gentle, cajoling. Part of her really wanted to give in to him. But that was the same part that also wanted to crawl across the couch and run her hands up his T-shirt while she discovered what his mouth tasted like. She knew not to listen to that part. "I really can't. I have some other stuff to do before bed."

He frowned, considering her. "The same stuff that made you run out of the restaurant last night?"

Her heart ticked up a beat.

"You know how I said I have a thing about honesty?" he asked, setting aside his pad and pen.

The question caught her off guard. She swallowed past the tightness seizing her vocal cords. "Yeah."

"Well, I have a little confession to make. Last night when you left the table, I accidentally answered your phone."

Her stomach dropped right through the floor. Boom. Crash. Catastrophe. "You *what*?"

His gaze didn't waver. "It was a complete accident, and I'm really sorry. We have the same ring and I wasn't looking. I just grabbed it. A guy asked for Sasha."

Her pizza was going to make a reappearance. She could feel it burning the back of her throat. "So a wrong number."

"Was it?"

She'd gone clammy all over, like all the interrogation lights in the world had just turned onto her, glaring in her face. "Well, that's not my name, so yeah."

Pike blew out a breath and rubbed his palms on his jeans. "Okay. I just wanted to let you know that it happened. I'm not into secrets."

"I—I appreciate you telling me," she said, her words coming out as nervous as she felt.

He stood and she followed suit. But instead of turning toward the door, he stepped over to her, standing far closer than any two co-workers had any business doing. He put a knuckle under her chin to guide her face up to his. "Also, I'm not into judging. Or telling other people's secrets."

His eyes were going to be the death of her—those long, dark lashes framing eyes that changed color with his moods. Right now they were golden brown, penetrating. But she couldn't give him the honesty he wanted. She gave him a tight smile, ignoring her twisting insides. "Good to know."

After a long few seconds, where he held her solely with the power of that searching, steady gaze, he stepped back and grabbed his keys from the coffee table. "I left a name and number on the kitchen counter. You call that guy and tell him I sent you. My band's playing a big festival in Fort Worth next Saturday and he'll get you tickets. You and Reagan should come. I think she'd like it—even if my band's a little more hard rock than punk."

Oakley opened her mouth to protest, but he was already at the door.

He turned back to look at her, as if he wanted to say something else, then his gaze flicked to the coffee table where her phone sat. He put his back to her again. "G'night, Oakley. Don't stay up too late."

When the door closed, she sank back onto the couch, head in her hands. It would be so easy to call him back in. So. Easy. She could tell him about her secret job, unload that burden. She doubted Pike would care. It's not like he wanted to date her. He wanted to sleep with her. Who cared what she did for a living?

He could be in her bed tonight and sneak out by morning before Reagan woke up.

But then what? Awkwardness and hurt feelings, probably. She'd learned early on that she sucked at casual. Maybe it was her conservative upbringing, but she had trouble separating out feelings from sex. She didn't have a ton of experience, but when she let someone inside her body, it left a mark.

She didn't need any more marks. Especially ones meted out by fly-by-night musicians who bedded women for sport.

Her life was complicated enough.

So what if her libido had decided to make an appearance after a long hiatus? That didn't mean she had to appease it with the nearest willing heartbreaker. She didn't need some guy to fix it.

Tomorrow, she'd take a trip to one of those stores with the suggestive names and tinted windows. She'd handle this herself.

But for now, she had other people's libidos to satisfy.

Her phone was ringing before she shut her bedroom door.

"Hello, this is Sasha . . ."

EIGHT

By quarter to one, Oakley was running on fumes. She'd taken seven calls tonight and the last had been a guy who'd wanted her to humiliate him pretty much non-stop. She'd had to pull out all her reserves to find creative enough insults because he'd complained that other women he'd called only said things like "You're such a naughty boy." He needed more than that. He wanted to be verbally assaulted. That took energy.

She let her head sag onto her pillow, her headset like a weight pressing down on her brain, and waved the white flag. She'd planned to work until one but she didn't have it in her tonight.

After yawning loudly, she sat up and reached for her laptop to sign out of her shift. But before she could hit the button, the phone rang.

"Son of a bitch." Once a call was in her queue, she had to take it.

She clicked the Sign Out icon on her laptop so she wouldn't get another call after this one and slammed her laptop shut, then she sank back onto the pillows and hit the button on her headset to answer the call.

"Hello, this is Sasha. Ready for a fantasy night?"

God, she hated that cheesy scripted intro the service required. It made her teeth grind.

The caller cleared his throat on the other end.

Great. A breather. "Hello?"

"I'm here." The voice was quiet, still.

She closed her eyes, willing herself to put some effort into it. "Well, hi there, handsome. How you doing tonight?"

A few seconds passed, and she thought maybe the call had dropped, but then he spoke. "You sound sleepy. Are you in bed?"

"I am. All alone. How about you? You want some company?"

"I want you."

The words were ones she'd heard a thousand times before, but for some reason these sent a bloom of heat through her. Her body prickled with awareness. Huh. Weird. "Well, I'm right here for whatever you want."

"I just got what I wanted."

She frowned. "And what's that?"

"To hear your voice one more time tonight."

Her eyelids blinked open. "I'm sorry, I didn't get your name, have we already talked?"

The sound of sheets rustling filled the phone as he apparently shifted in bed. "Yes. And I'm still waiting for you to sing to me."

Her heart jumped into her throat, time slowing around her and alarm bells blaring in her head. She grabbed her cell phone from the nightstand and flipped it over. A name she'd programmed into it only tonight showed on the screen.

Pike Ryland.

She hadn't checked the phone before she'd hit the button on the headset. She'd been so tired she'd forgotten to look. Who the hell called after midnight? *Fuck. Fuck. Fuck.* Her hands trembled, adrenaline chasing her panic. "You must have the wrong number, sir."

"You know I don't," he said, his voice slipping into his normal tone now that he knew she'd figured out who it was.

"I'm sorry, I have to—"

"Oakley, take a breath. It's okay," he said, his words gentle. "I'd already pretty much figured it out. It's why I thought I could get away with calling you so late. I knew you'd be up."

She pressed a hand to her forehead. "Pike, I— We— No one can know I—"

"Shh, hey, calm down. I told you tonight I'm not into telling other people's secrets."

"This is— No one knows this, Pike. No one *can* know." She closed her eyes. "God, this is mortifying. You must think—"

"That it's incredibly hot? That the woman who I thought probably said *fudge* instead of *fuck* actually has the ability to talk dirty enough to get paid for it? Yeah, that's exactly what I think."

She groaned, tapping the back of her head against her pillow. "Of course that's what you'd think, isn't it? Guys are so ready to buy into the fantasy. You probably think I'm dressed in a silk nightie and have come seven times for my seven callers tonight."

He laughed. "Oh, no. We allow ourselves the illusion, but most of us know that we're probably talking to a Chris Farley lookalike who's watching infomercials on mute while she talks to us about how bad she wants us to give it to her."

"Sounds like you have some experience."

"Totally. Fourteen-year-old Pike was a big contributor to the Dial-A-Girl industry."

"Oh, God. Don't say that. I need to have my own illusions that the measures they have in place to keep kids from calling me actually work."

"Sorry. You'd probably be able to tell. They'd just want to talk about feeling up your boobs."

"Ha. Welcome to half my callers."

"Really?"

"No. That'd be too easy. Most require more effort than that."

He got quiet for a second. "So do you get into it? I mean, it's got to feel kind of powerful knowing you're turning someone on."

She blew out a breath. "We're so not going to talk about this."

"Aw, come on. I want to know."

"No, Pike. I do it for the cash. My position at Bluebonnet is great and I'm hoping for a promotion, but I could never afford Reagan's schooling on a receptionist salary alone. I do this because it's good money that I can earn from home. It doesn't turn me on.

If anything, it numbs me. Makes me immune to things most people would find sexy."

"Well, that would explain how you've so easily resisted my undeniable charms. But sexually immune? No fucking way."

"Believe what you want."

He sniffed. "I saw how you looked at me in the restaurant, Oakley. That look did not come from a woman who's numb."

"That look is called shock. I thought I heard something I didn't. And seriously, how do you and your ego fit in the same room?"

"We work it out. And that was more than shock. You wanted me."

"Whatever." Great. Now she was sounding like the kids she worked with.

"Close your eyes, Oakley."

"What? Why?"

"Humor me."

"We're not going there, Pike. I was not issuing a challenge."

"Come on, close them. What can it hurt? I'm all the way across town. You're safe from me."

Lie. Lie. Lie. She closed her eyes. She couldn't help it.

"Are you still wearing what you were earlier?" he asked.

"Oh my God. Seriously? The what are you wearing question? You could at least—"

"Tell me."

"Ugh. The shirt but not the pants. Super hot."

He made some sort of pleased sound on the other end. "Good. That's exactly how I'm picturing you now."

"Fantastic."

"And though you didn't ask, I'm wearing nothing. Just my sheets. I like the way they feel against my skin."

She rolled onto her side and pressed her face into her pillow. Shit on a stick. Pike was naked. This was a stupid, stupid idea. She needed to hang up. She adjusted her headset. "You are making crap up right now. I know this game way better than you."

"Don't taunt me, mama. I'm not above sending you a dick pic."

"Don't you dare."

"Play nice then. Now, where were we?" he said, in a sleep-soft, sexy voice—all cool sheets and hot skin and long nights. "Right, you on your bed in just a thin T-shirt and panties. I bet you've taken your bra off, too."

She had, but she wasn't going to confirm it for him.

"Mmm, I can imagine that shirt is pretty see-through with nothing else beneath it. I wish I was there to brush my fingers over the front of your shirt, see your nipples rise against the cotton so I could put my mouth on them."

"Are you charging me by the minute?" She kept her voice even, but her hand had drifted to her breast. She drew her fingertips over her nipple, casually at first, then with more purpose, sending a hot bolt of sensation down through her belly. Her toes curled.

God, what was she doing? She went through this scenario all the time with callers and never once had the urge to actually participate.

"First call's free." She heard the glide of sheets again. "Especially since I'm going to enjoy this, too."

She clamped her lips together. She would *not* ask him if he was touching himself. Would. Not. Ask. And she would *not* picture what he might look like laid out naked, thighs spread, cock in hand.

She shuddered and the spot between her thighs pulsed with awareness. "I'm going to hang up now."

"Don't. You don't have to pretend to hate this. I told you I'm honest. Do me that courtesy, too. This is a no-risk proposition. We don't even have to talk about it face to face. Work is work. Fine. This—this is just a no-pressure, late-night anonymous phone call. Give yourself a break, mama. Indulge a little."

She let out a long breath, the weight of her limbs pressing into the bed. It'd been so long since her body had tingled and ached, so long since she'd fantasized about a man. The offer was so damn tempting.

"I'm hard for you, Oakley."

Well, *hell*. That fucking did it. How was she supposed to stay cool after that? *Hard*. It was such a filthy word when he said it. She licked her lips, tried to find her voice. "Is that right?"

"Have been since you answered the phone. Your voice does it for me. I keep hearing your song in my head and picturing you in nothing but a T-shirt. If I were there, I'd peel it off of you and tie your hands with it so I could taste your skin and feel you against my tongue, watch your green eyes go black with want."

She let out a soft, needy gasp. One he had to have heard. But she couldn't help herself. Those sinful lips of his running over her body, tasting her? The image was too decadent to block.

"Still with me, Oakley?"

"I'm here." It was all she could manage to say without totally giving herself away.

"Are you wet for me?" he asked, shameless and bold. "Because I'm leaking for you. You should see how slippery the head of my cock is getting just thinking about you."

God bless America. A rumble of need moved through her like a possessed freight train, gears that had long gone rusty coming to life and spinning too fast. She could see him there, fist around himself, thumb rubbing the fluid over the tip, making his erection glossy and flushed. Could imagine being there with him, lowering her head and swiping her tongue across that little slit. She could almost taste the salt of him. "This is such a bad idea."

"My favorite kind. What are you thinking about, baby?" he asked, voice gruff. "Don't censor, and I won't either."

She swallowed past the tangle of protests in her throat. She could do this. Hell, she did this every night. She'd just never said the words and really meant them before. "I was imagining what you'd taste like."

He groaned, and that gave her a strange thrill of satisfaction. She was getting to him, too. "Answer my other question. I want to know."

She knew the answer but let her hand slide down her belly anyway. Her fingers dipped beneath the band of her panties and found the slickness waiting there. She stroked a finger over her clit, the simple touch making her thighs clench. "Yes. I'm wet."

"Fuck," he said in a strangled whisper. "You're touching yourself, aren't you? I can fucking hear it in your voice. God, you're driving me crazy. Hold on."

Something squeaked on his end of the line. "What are you doing?"

"Grabbing lube out of my drawer," he said bluntly. "I want to imagine how sexy and slick you'd feel around me."

"How very prepared of you," she teased, her words getting looser the more she stroked herself. "Were you a Boy Scout?"

"Not in this lifetime or the last, mama, but I'm always prepared to get off." Mattress springs creaked as he got settled again. "Ah, fuck, yes. That's better."

"Tell me what you're doing," she said, reaching down to slide her panties off and to turn off the bedside lamp. Darkness enveloped her, keeping her safe, secret. This wasn't really happening if it was in the dark.

"I'm on top of my sheets and have my hand tight around my cock, rubbing slow and teasing myself, losing myself in your voice and imagining what you're doing right now. Help me fill in the picture."

"I'm in the dark and have a headset on so my hands are free. I've taken my panties off and am touching myself."

"No," he said, gravel in his voice. "Use the words for me. I know you're not that polite on your calls. You don't have to pretend with me."

She inhaled a long breath, trying to find the courage. She said filthy things to men every night, but they were just words to strangers she'd never have to face. That was Sasha. She'd never gone there as Oakley. This felt altogether different—vulnerable. She'd have to see this man again, have to own this part of herself in front of him. She released the breath. Jumped off the cliff. "I'm pushing my fingers inside myself and rubbing my clit. Everything feels tight and achy, like I could come at any second. My pussy is clenching around my fingers just from me thinking about what you'd feel like inside of me."

"Fuck, yes, baby. You're perfect. And don't deny yourself. Get a toy and give yourself more than your fingers."

Her back arched, the pleasure building fast. It'd been so long since she'd done anything but snag a cursory orgasm in the shower. "I don't have any toys."

"What? I thought all women had a stash."

"Not numb ones."

"You're not numb, baby." She could hear his slick hand moving steadily on his end of the line. It was a familiar noise, but it'd never sounded so damn lewd and sexy. "Feel how hot and slippery you are against your hand. Feel it all. How awake and alive you are. How much you want this."

She moaned, unable to stop the sounds now.

"If I were there, I'd fill you up. Give you more."

Her fingers were pumping, pumping, pumping now but instead of the empty darkness of her bedroom, she saw Pike looming above her, his cock pumping into her, those inked arms sweating and flexing as he drove her into the bed.

"Oh, God." Choppy, choked sounds spilled out of her—so different from the practiced, porny noises she made for calls. Raw. Real. She'd forgotten what that sounded like.

"Yes," Pike said, his voice broken with sharp breaths. "Take it. Feel me there with you. Come for me, mama."

The command was unnecessary because she was already tipping over, her hips lifting off the bed and her free hand grabbing her breast with a too-rough touch. She cried out, turning into her pillow to muffle the sound. Light exploding in the darkness.

Grinding, erotic noises filtered through the phone—*unh, unh, unh*—as Pike fucked his fist. Oakley only sailed higher. And when Pike cried out, she saw it all in her mind. His head tipped back in ecstasy, his cock pulsing in his hand, fluid painting streaks across his chest. She'd never wanted to transport herself somewhere else so desperately.

But, of course, she wasn't there. And he wasn't here. When they both panted their way down from their orgasms, chilly reality settled in around her like a wet blanket.

She was alone. And she'd just exposed more than one secret to a man she'd promised to keep at arm's length.

Pike let out a long breath on his end. "Wow, that was . . ."

"Something we can't do again."

"What?"

She closed her eyes, tried to slow her heartbeat. "I expect you to honor your promise and not bring this or my night job up ever. When I see you again, we won't talk about this."

"I'll keep my promise, but Oak—"

"Good night, Pike."

She yanked off her headset, her blood still rushing through her ears and her body having aftershocks, and threw the damn thing against the wall.

Stupid, stupid Oakley.

NINE

Oakley stared at the collection of *personal massagers* in the Wicked boutique, already overwhelmed by all the choices and the prices. How could they possibly be this expensive? She'd had a makeshift vibrator once before, but it'd been a simple massage thing she'd bought at the drugstore. One that she could pass off as a non-sexual device. Back then, she'd been young and convinced everyone was staring at her while she made the purchase. Now she honestly didn't care. But how the hell was she supposed to know which one to pick? It's not like she could return it after trying it out if it was no good. And after the other night with Pike, she definitely needed one. Pent-up lust made her do idiotic things. She wouldn't allow herself to be that desperate again.

"Need some help?"

She glanced toward the end of the aisle to find an impossibly good-looking golden-haired guy sending her a friendly smile. Jesus, what was it lately with the hot blonds?

"I, uh . . ."

He cocked his thumb. "Or if you'd prefer, I can get my assistant out of the stock room and she could help you. Get a woman's opinion."

"Um, no, that's fine. I mean, yes, I guess I need help. But no, you don't need to bother your assistant." She could handle a ridiculously hot guy talking to her about vibrators. Sure. She was totally cool with this. Not awkward at all. Nope.

"Great." He sauntered over and stopped a few inches from her to turn and face the rack she'd been staring at.

Suddenly, the words *clitoral* and *G-spot* and *anal* seemed to go neon on the packages, screaming at them in the silence. The tips of Oakley's ears burned. She could talk dirty at night, but put her in the daylight and her conservative upbringing came back to haunt her.

"So have you narrowed it down any yet? Any features you're really after?" he asked, relaxed as you please. Like they were discussing which coffeemaker to purchase.

She cleared her throat and peeked his way. His name tag said *Jace Austin, Owner.* Okay, well if he owned the place, this probably *was* about as interesting as picking out a coffeemaker. "Nothing too fancy, I guess. I just—there are a lot of choices."

He pulled one from the display. "This is your most basic bullet vibrator. It can be inserted, but generally, it's used for external stimulation. This brand has a few different speeds and the most intensity. It's one of our bestsellers. And I think if this manufacturer stopped making it, my wife would picket the factory."

Oakley laughed, some of the awkward tension draining out of her at the word *wife*.

Somewhere behind her, the bell on the door announced someone else had entered the store. Jace glanced up briefly in what was probably an automatic gesture, but returned his attention to her.

"There are also your multitaskers." He grabbed a box off the top shelf. The picture of the device looked like a C. "This one can be inserted to hit the G-spot and will press against the clitoris simultaneously. It also allows for intercourse while inserted, which can give your partner some fun, too."

Well, that sounded interesting. But there was no partner involved for her. She shook her head.

"Then there are anal—"

"I think the first one will probably be fine," she said quickly.

He smiled good-naturedly and grabbed the one she'd selected. "Excellent. And I'd be a bad business owner if I didn't mention that this one works great in tandem with one of our realistic dildos, which are twenty-five percent off today."

She laughed at the bizarre conversation. "I feel like I'm in some X-rated infomercial. Buy a vibrator and get a fake penis for only nineteen ninety-nine!"

He chuckled. "Welcome to my life."

She shook her head, any awkwardness she'd had early on fading now. The guy seemed well-practiced at putting a woman at ease. "Thanks. I'll go take a look and see if there's anything else I want."

"Holler if you need me."

She turned her back to him to wander over to the next aisle and look at the display of colorful dildos. It's what Pike had suggested the other night—something more than her fingers. She'd avoided the aisle because she hadn't wanted to give in to his suggestion. Hadn't wanted to think about Pike. But now it seemed stupid not to get one while she was here. Plus, they were on sale. If she was going to take care of herself, she might as well do it right.

She heard Jace greet the other customers and then tuned them out, picking up an entirely too big hot pink rubber dong and wagging it in her hand.

She pressed her lips together, stifling a giggle at the wonky swinging motion. You could pound a chicken breast flat with the thing.

No, thank you.

Pike waited until his best friend, Foster, had exchanged a half-hug and slap on the back with their buddy, then he put his hand out to Jace. "How ya doin', man?"

Jace shook his hand in a firm grasp. "Oh, you know, crazy in the best way possible."

Pike stepped back. "Yeah, I haven't seen you around much lately."

Meaning he hadn't seen him at The Ranch. Jace was a regular

with his wife, Evan, and his husband, Andre—the threesome a fixture at the kink resort they all belonged to. But Pike couldn't remember the last time he'd seen the three out and about.

Jace crossed his arms, light in his eyes. "Yeah. Fatherhood is keeping me busy. Lucy's started to crawl and is attempting to disassemble the entire house. But we've got Foster and Cela lined up to watch Luce soon so we can get a little grown-up time."

Pike turned to Foster with a raised brow. "*You're* babysitting?"

Foster tucked his hands into his slacks, a smirk on his face. "Unlike you, I don't have baby-phobia."

"Since when?" Pike asked.

Foster shrugged, all cool businessman.

"Fuck me, y'all are all going over to the dark side," Pike said, shaking his head. Jace having kids. His best friend setting up house with his woman, and babysitting. "The Ranch is going to have to open a daycare."

Jace snorted. "Don't put it past Grant. If he knocks up Charli, which I'm pretty sure he's trying to do on a regular basis, I guarantee you, he'll have five-star nannies on-site."

Pike sighed dramatically. "I guess that'll leave all those lonely, single women at The Ranch to me and Gibson. We're going to have to play relay to keep up."

The guys laughed, but Pike didn't really have any excitement at the thought. He had his fun at The Ranch, but he hadn't hooked up with anyone the last few times he'd gone. He'd watched, but no one had caught his interest. The problem was that he didn't fit into a neat category like his friends.

Foster and Jace were both sexual dominants. The Ranch catered best to those who fell into those roles—dominant or submissive, masochist or sadist. People wore their labels there with pride. But Pike couldn't slap one of those stickers on himself. Like most things in his life, he didn't quite fit in. All his edges were messy, the wires tangled.

Once upon a time, he thought he'd become a dominant. He certainly could enjoy tying a woman up and playing some obedience games. He also didn't mind dishing out a little pain. There wasn't much out there hotter than his bright red handprint on a beautiful woman's ass. But he'd lived with Foster for many years and had shared women with him. He'd seen his best friend when the suit and tie came off and the dominant sadist came out. Dominating a woman was like breathing for Foster—natural and absolute.

Pike had never felt it in his blood like that. He didn't need the dominance to get off. And frankly, he knew if a woman wanted to turn the tables and tie *him* to the bed and beat on him for a while, he could have fun with that, too. Shit, he'd done it before.

Bottom line: He liked sex. He liked it rough and tumble without a lot of rules. And he'd try almost anything once. A sexual omnivore.

But that didn't fly as well at The Ranch because he couldn't give a true submissive what she'd need long-term and he couldn't give a dominant that either. So he hung out in purgatory—comfortable with his preferences but vaguely jealous of those who had discovered so clearly what would light them up. He knew for a fact he'd never tapped into that level that Jace and Foster had reached with their partners. He'd watched both of them scene and that shit looked transcendent.

"So what are y'all doing here? Need some supplies?" Jace leaned against the checkout counter.

"We were in the neighborhood for lunch. But Foster wants to buy a violet wand and needs you to swear that you won't tell Andre."

Jace sniffed. "Andre can't throw stones. He's a big fan of the violet wand."

"Not for his baby sister," Foster said. "He still winces anytime she mentions The Ranch in front of him. If I give him any more reason to think too hard about what I'm doing with Cela, he's going to beat me with his nightstick."

Jace sniffed. "The sadist in me wants to tell him he needs to get over himself. But I promise I won't say anything and will leave him in his state of semi-denial for now. Come on, they're over here."

Jace led Foster to the back corner of the store, and Pike took the chance to browse around. He hadn't been in Wicked for a while and always liked seeing what new, perverted things Jace stocked. Even with his dirty mind, Pike usually found something that surprised him.

But when he turned the corner of the third aisle, he stopped cold. Because hanging out at the other end was the biggest surprise he'd ever gotten in any store ever. The woman he'd left in a Mickey Mouse T-shirt last night was standing there with one hand on her hip and the other holding a giant rubber cock.

He must've made some sound of surprise because she turned his way. The impassive expression on her face shifted in an instant when she recognized him—from shock to horror then to outright red-faced mortification.

Of course, he should probably leave her to it. He should give her privacy. Everyone had a right to buy their sex toys without someone gawking at them. But all he could do was grin and cross his arms over his chest. "Well, hello there."

She glanced down at the dildo in her hand. He expected her to shove it back on the shelf, but instead she poked out her chin, held on to the thing like she was proud to be wielding it, and straightened her shoulders. "Hi."

He strolled down the aisle toward her. "Looking for a self-defense weapon?"

She blinked, clearly not as devil-may-care as she was trying to appear. "What?"

He nodded at the pink monster dick and imitated a batting motion. "You could take someone out with one swing. Or intimidate every guy who comes near you."

He flicked his finger against the head of the toy and it swayed back and forth in a rude, lumbering display.

She pressed her lips together, her cheeks still stained pink, but laughter entered her eyes. "I think this one is a little out of my ballpark, but they're twenty-five percent off if you want one."

"Nah, I'd break the bank buying enough lube to manage that one. I'll stick with the small ones that vibrate."

Her mouth went a little slack at that, but he figured the best

way to fight off her potential embarrassment was with his shame-
lessness. And by the look on her face it'd worked. A brief flash of
heat had lit her eyes. Good. She was probably picturing exactly
what he'd do with one of those. Dirty girl. He'd happily demon-
strate in person if she wanted a show. Or better yet, try one on her.

"Is that what you're here for?" she asked in an apparent attempt
to sound casual.

"Vibrating butt plugs? No. Not today. My toy box is fully
stocked. I was just stopping in to say hi to a friend. The guy who
owns the store is—Well, this is going to sound complicated, but
he's married to my best friend's girlfriend's brother."

Oakley's forehead scrunched like she was doing advanced math
in her head. *Two point three, carry the one.* "Wait, the owner is
gay? He said he had a wife."

"He does. And a husband. They're a triad, poly, whatever
you'd like to label it as. Basically, three people in love and married
who have a kid."

"Wow. That sounds . . . complex."

He shrugged. "Not for them. They're like those ridiculous people in romantic movies—so shit-faced in love you want to vomit a
little when you're around them."

She laughed and put monster dong back on the shelf. "My
brother and his husband are like that. Unbearably happy. Even
when they were going through the stressful process of adopting
their son two years ago, they stayed so upbeat and supportive of
each other. It's freakish how well-adjusted they are. Jace seemed
nice, by the way."

"You met him?"

"He, uh, helped me earlier."

Pike lifted a brow and leaned against the shelf. "Yeah? What'd you
need help with? I could certainly offer a few opinions. Or we could
just ditch the toys, and I could take you into his office to provide you
with the real thing. Though, fair warning, I can't compete with Mr.
Pink here. I'm a lot warmer, though, and have better moves."

Desire flared in her eyes for the briefest of seconds, boiling his blood, but she quickly covered it with a sardonic smile. "Now you've moved from flirting to outright propositioning. Not appropriate workplace behavior, Mr. Ryland."

"You're not on the clock right now, *Miz* Easton."

"Ryland," Jace called out from the end of the row, Foster at his side. "No hitting on the customers. My store is a safe zone."

"What if I already know her?"

"Ma'am?" Jace asked, firm tone. "Tell me if you want him to go away, and I will take care of it."

For a moment, she looked tempted, but she waved him off. "No, thank you. It's fine. I do know him."

Jace gave Pike a warning look that said *don't fuck with my customers*, and Pike blew him a kiss.

Pike caught Oakley watching Jace and Foster walk away with a little too much appreciation. He shook his head. "They're both taken, mama. You can stop staring now."

"Are all your friends that hot? Maybe I was too quick to limit our time together. You should introduce me to more of them." She said it so completely deadpan that he had no idea if she was fucking with him.

"Yeah? Which one does it for you? Mr. CEO or Mr. Blond Bisexual? I have a lot of friends. It'd be helpful if I could narrow down your type."

She tapped a finger to her chin and now he knew for sure she was fucking with him. "Well, I do love a man in a suit. And dark hair really does it for me. The clean-cut type is really hot. And no tattoos because, you know, they're dumb."

He narrowed his eyes at her. "Which aisle has the floggers? I'm feeling a little violent all of a sudden."

She put her hand to his chest and leaned close to him. For a crazed second, he thought she might kiss him, but instead she pressed her lips close to his ear. "The truth is . . . my type is sitting on that shelf. That's all I'm looking for right now."

His heart was beating too fast at having her hand on his chest and the smell of her grapefruit shampoo in his nose. She stepped back and grabbed a different flesh-toned dildo off the shelf. One, ironically, he'd estimate to be about the size of what was currently pushing against his zipper.

He looked down at the package in her hands. "So all you want is the fantasy? Nothing real?"

Her smile was resigned. "Ding. Ding. Ding. Give the pretty boy an A plus."

The words stung more than they should.

She walked toward him, and her shoulder briefly touched his. "And for the record, your two friends have nothing on you."

The words moved through him, stoked the fire.

"Oakley—" He spun toward her.

But she was already walking to the register, her faux lover in her hands.

She didn't look back. And she didn't say good-bye.

After she'd checked out and left, Foster and Jace found him scowling at the front window.

"Who the hell was that?" Foster asked.

My torment. "No one. Just a mom I'm working with on that charity project."

Foster's smile was wry. "Uh-huh. You normally get hard-ons for moms you work with? New fetish?"

"Shut the fuck up."

But Foster only grinned wider.

Jace leaned against the windowsill, looking just as amused. "A mom, huh? That's not usually your style."

"What else did she buy besides the dildo?" he asked, turning fully toward Jace.

He arched a brow. "Customer purchases are confidential."

The hell they are. Pike didn't hesitate. He dodged to the left, skirted around Jace, and jogged to the checkout counter. Jace realized a second too late what Pike was doing and couldn't beat him to the register. Pike rolled the receipt paper back.

The dildo and some kind of vibrator.

Jace scowled at him. "You can be a hardheaded asshole sometimes. She didn't buy anything exciting. Vanilla basics. You're sniffing around the wrong tree, brother."

"That doesn't mean vanilla. It might just mean inexperienced with toys or unexposed to other things. She's got this buttoned-up thing going during the day, but I know that's not all there is to her. I can tell. Did you hear that voice? That voice is not PG. And neither is that walk. Did you see how she walks?"

As he was babbling like an idiot, Foster leaned back on his heels, grinning. "Aw, fuck, this is going to be fun."

"What?" Pike asked.

Foster tilted his head to the side and cupped his ear. "Jace, did you hear the same sound I did?"

"Hmm, I think maybe I did. Did it start with *timber*?"

"I believe it did." Foster reached out and slapped Pike's shoulder. "Hope you enjoy your downfall, brother."

Pike stared at his friends, then provided them with the backside of his middle fingers. "Fuck the both of you."

Their idiotic smiles didn't falter.

Pike stared for a few long moments then yanked his wallet from his pocket and tossed his credit card at Jace. "Here."

"What's this for?"

"Open a tab. I've got a care package to put together."

"For a certain mom?" Jace asked, always one to rub it in. "Good choice. Nothing says *I really like you a lot* like a box o' kinky filth."

"That should be your slogan," Foster chimed in.

Pike turned his back on them. "You're both fired as friends. Fucking sadist motherfuckers."

"Motherfucker? Isn't that what you're trying to be?" Foster called after him.

"Fired!"

TEN

Oakley stared at the open red package she'd set on her bed. It had arrived on her doorstep this afternoon with instructions not to open until she was alone, Pike's slashy, masculine signature on the note.

She'd had no theories about what could be inside, but she definitely wouldn't have guessed this. She'd thought this whole Pike detour had been effectively shut down. They'd worked together a few days this week at Bluebonnet and he'd been nothing but professional. He hadn't so much as hinted at their late-night phone call or the run-in at Wicked. He'd respected her wishes to keep all of it confidential, and she'd figured he'd moved on just as she would've expected him to. He'd gotten a little something out of her and was over it. Bored. They could go on as co-workers.

Based on this box, she'd been wrong.

Inside were things from almost every aisle in Wicked. Vibrators of varying sizes, plugs, clamps of some sort, lubricant—the works. He must've spent a small fortune.

"You've got to be kidding me." Hello, most inappropriate gift ever. What in God's name was Pike thinking?

She removed all the items and dug through the black satin everything had been wrapped in. A card was tucked into the very bottom along with a longer envelope. She pulled them out and opened the card.

If all you want are fantasies, you should at least make them really dirty, well-equipped ones. Hope you enjoy what I picked out for you. Best, Pike.

She ran her fingertips over a dildo made of smooth glass, a shiver moving through her at the thought of Pike hand-selecting things that would bring her pleasure, things that would be inside her. What had he imagined when he'd picked out each thing? Her neck went hot and her sex pulsed with a dull ache.

P.S. There's a key taped to the bottom of the box. You can lock this stuff up so Reagan doesn't find it.
   P.P.S. I included four passes to the show tomorrow. Don't deny yourself the joy of watching me bang on things.
   P.P.P.S. I did not include Mr. Pink. Unrealistic expectations are unhealthy.

She snort laughed and put her face in her hands. Who was this guy? She reached back, grabbing her phone off her bedside table, and typed out a quick text.
   Oakley: Thank u 4 the gift, but u know I can't accept this.
Pike responded within a minute.
   Pike: No returns on that stuff—already licked each piece to make sure.
She snorted.
   Oakley: U r a sick, sick man
   Pike: PSA—silicone is not tasty.
   Oakley: The more u know . . .
   Pike: Tonight, on a very special episode of Family Ties . . .
She groaned and fell back against her pillows. He wasn't supposed to be funny. Slick, she'd expected. Charming, yes. But funny was like her kryptonite.
   She tried to think of how to respond to cut things off before they went too far, but he messaged her first.
   Pike: U busy? I could come over after rehearsal and show u how they all work ;-)

She closed her eyes, breathed through the urge to be reckless and say yes.

Oakley: I'm always busy.

Pike: The scandalous night activities of Oakley Easton . . .

Oakley: You mean Sasha

Pike: I'm not interested in her. Is Oakley taking calls tonight?

Oakley: Good night Pike

A few long seconds passed before he responded.

Pike: Sleep well, mama.

She sighed and tapped the phone lightly against her forehead. This guy was good. And so. . . . damn . . . dangerous.

She needed to shut this speeding train down because she was losing control of its direction. Despite her best intentions, she found herself flirting back with him, playing the game, encouraging him. He made it too easy to let down her guard. And that night on the phone made him too hard to forget.

But it was all fantasy. She had to remember that.

Pike was not some single dad down at the PTA meeting. He wasn't some guy looking to date her and see where things went. He was a drummer in a successful band. A guy who toured the country and most likely the beds of many, many women.

She had to get that message through to her misguided libido. It was easy to trick herself into thinking Pike was some normal, dateable guy because she was seeing him out of his element. Hanging out at her house, eating in dive restaurants, volunteering at a charity. But this wasn't his life. This was a small diversion in between his real-life activities.

This needed to be a strictly professional relationship. Tomorrow, she'd take Reagan to his concert. Reagan would love it, of course, but Oakley was going for herself, too. She needed to see the real Pike, remind herself what that world was like. This had already gone way too far. And it probably had less to do with Pike and more to do with the fact that she'd shut down this side of herself for so long.

Now that interest was stirring again, maybe she needed to open herself up to dating. Regular dudes. Guys who would take her to dinner and a movie. Ones who would bring her flowers—not send her a box of nipple clamps and butt plugs.

She inhaled a long breath, feeling better now that she had a plan, and sat up to shove all the toys back into the box. Tomorrow she'd fix the Pike situation. Tonight she'd take a necessary leap.

She grabbed her laptop from her desk and sat on the bed. She had a little while before she needed to sign in for her shift, so she opened up a site she'd never thought she'd visit. Perfect Match. She'd seen the commercials enough times to know it was a pretty popular one. Before she could let herself chicken out, she opened up an account, uploaded a pic, and filled out the profile information. When she was done, her finger hovered over the button that would make the profile active.

Nerves crawled up her throat. She'd never truly dated in the normal sense. The only long-term relationship she'd ever been in had been bent from the start. And after that, she'd been a teen mom. Not exactly the type who'd be hot on the dating market. She'd tried a few years ago to go out with a guy she'd met at the grocery store. Things had gone well for a while, but then he'd asked about her night job when her schedule kept interfering with dates. She'd been dumb enough to think honesty was the best policy. He'd been so disgusted, he'd left her in the restaurant to finish her dinner alone.

Hell, maybe she wasn't even capable of sustaining a real dating relationship. She had no idea. But she only had five minutes before she needed to take a call, and this was how people did it now, right? She closed her eyes and hit the button. A perky dinging sound let her know her profile was live.

She kind of wanted to vomit.

But she didn't have time for a full-scale freak-out. Work awaited. She closed the window for the dating site and signed in for her nightly shift.

Strangely, there was some comfort in putting on her headset tonight. This was predictable. Safe. Once she was on duty, the only men she needed to worry about were the ones who were paying.

They could be annoying and needy and misogynistic, but at least they couldn't rip out her heart when the line went dead.

Oakley eyed the concert tickets she'd set on her bedside table as the first call connected. She'd take care of everything tomorrow night. Life would get back to normal.

Whatever that was.

———

Oakley squinted through the orange rays of the setting sun, keeping an eye on the two kids in front of her. Reagan was bouncing on the balls of her feet and rapidly talking with her younger cousin, Lucas, as the stage crew turned over the set between bands.

"Mom," Reagan said, peeking back at her and talking too loud, "I can't believe you've never taken me to one of these. This is awesome!"

Oakley pointed to her ears. "You still have your earplugs in, baby. You're talking loud."

"What?"

She waved her hand. "Never mind."

Reagan gave her a toothy grin and turned back toward the stage.

"She really loves this stuff. It's like she's on some music high," Devon said from beside her. "You used to be like that. Remember when you had that complete breakdown after Mom found your Alanis Morissette CD and confiscated it? It was like you'd lost your religion."

Oakley tucked her hands in her back pockets and smirked at her older brother. "And she made me go to church every day for two weeks to pray for forgiveness. I didn't really know what most of those songs were talking about at the time, but I felt them in my bones. I knew I needed to write music like that."

"You were an angst factory for sure. I think Mom still blames Alanis for your defection from the righteous path."

"Yeah?" She bumped his shoulder. "And what does she blame your defection on?"

"Group showers at church camp? George Michael?"

She rolled her eyes. "Right."

Devon shrugged, his blue eyes shifting toward the stage. "Nah, she only blames me. And maybe Jake Walton, the neighbor she caught me making out with behind the cow pasture when I was sixteen."

"God, I had such a crush on him. He had these lips . . ."

Devon smiled broadly, adjusting his baseball cap over his dark hair. "Yes, he did."

"It's not nice to gloat. And good thing Hunter isn't here. You look a little too wistful about young Jake Walton."

"Nah, Hunter wins on every level. But you never forget that first one, that first time."

Oakley went cold at the words and wrapped her arms around herself. Not everyone remembered their first relationship so fondly. "Yeah."

Devon made a sound under his breath. "Damn, sis, I'm sorry. I didn't think . . ."

She put her finger to her lips and shook her head, reminding him that Reagan was only a few feet away. "It's fine."

Devon was one of the few who knew the whole story. The ugly one. The one she hoped she'd never have to tell her daughter. Of all of her six brothers and sisters, he was the only one who she trusted to love her no matter what, to listen without judgment. Her other siblings were good people, but they hadn't strayed from the very conservative lifestyle that her parents had raised them in. Homeschooling. Church. Unbendable rules about right and wrong.

Most of them still lived within a hundred miles of her parents' farm in Oklahoma. Only she and Devon had bailed. Devon had gotten a scholarship to attend college in California and had moved out before her parents could realize that whole kissing-a-boy thing hadn't been a drunken whim but a life plan. And Oakley had followed him out to California shortly after when she'd gotten discovered at fifteen by a music producer while singing in a local Christian group. She'd moved in with Dev until Pop Luck had gotten popular and started touring. He'd been her closest family since.

"So," Devon said, obviously searching for a change in topic, "you know a guy in the next band?"

"The drummer. He's the one helping out with that music project at Bluebonnet. He gave us tickets, thought Reagan might have fun."

Dev's eyebrow arched. "Right. Because he thought your kid might have fun."

"It's not like that."

"Uh-huh."

Guitar chords blasted through the speaker for a moment as the crew on stage did the sound check. Oakley turned her head as the big screens on the side of the stage lit up with a publicity photo for Darkfall—the wind making the screens ripple and the bodies in the picture come to life. The crowd cheered.

"Look, Mom!" Reagan shouted back at her. "It's Mr. Pike!"

"I see, baby." Boy, did she. The larger-than-life image had Pike staring down the camera with his bandmates. Badass. Tough. Beautiful.

"Which one is he?" Devon asked, following her gaze.

"The blond."

"Whoa," he said low enough for the kids not to hear. "You had that guy over for pizza and managed to keep your clothes on? You have more restraint than I do."

He had no idea. "I have no interest in being a groupie."

"Can I be one?"

She shoved his shoulder. "You're such a tramp. I'm so telling Hunter when he gets back in town."

"Tell him. He'd agree. But seriously, is the guy a jerk? He looks like he has high potential to be an egomaniac. I don't want that kind of guy around my baby sister and niece."

She frowned and dragged her eyes away from the picture. "Oh, he's got an ego, all right. He's entirely inappropriate most of the time and a shameless flirt. But I wouldn't say he's a jerk. He's kind of, I don't know, weird and manic and . . . funny."

Devon tipped up the bill of his hat, eyeing her with a sly smile. "Oh, so we have a mad crush then?"

"What? No."

"Oak, you're here in the Texas heat at a hard rock festival. You don't even know these bands. And a few weeks ago, when I asked if you wanted to take Reagan to see that eighties cover band, you told me she was too young for concerts."

Oakley crossed her arms. "Rae has since proven her maturity."

He smirked. "Bull. Shit. You've got the hots for this guy."

"He's not my type."

Dev shook his head and draped his arm around her shoulders, pulling her close so the kids couldn't hear. "Come on, don't freak out about it. You work too hard and spend too much time alone. This could be good for you."

"An ill-advised hookup with a drummer who will drop me as soon as he gets bored could be good for me?"

"Exactly. Look, I know I'm your brother and shouldn't be saying this, but there's nothing wrong with finding yourself a hot, temporary fuck buddy."

"Dev!"

He laughed. "Oh, don't be such a prude. I mean, yes, you're right. The guy's probably not boyfriend material. But you're a grown woman and deserve some fun. You know we're always happy to have Rae over if you need a date night."

"I think you just flunked big-brother school."

He gave her shoulder a pat. "Okay, fine, want responsible brotherly advice? Use a condom. And don't let him take video."

She poked him in the ribs. But before she could respond to his comment, the lights on stage began to flash and the crowd surged forward, excitement like a contagion moving through them.

"Come on, Mom! Let's get closer." Reagan grabbed her hand and dragged her with the flow of the crowd.

They'd already been pretty close to the stage, thanks to the special passes Pike had sent, but now they were only ten or twelve rows of people back on the far left side of the stage. Bodies pressed close to them and she couldn't help but get caught up in the fervor of the crowd.

She pushed onto her toes, knowing the drummer was almost always the first one to come out.

"Is that him?" Dev asked.

"Where?"

Devon pointed to the other end of the stage, and Oakley froze up the moment her eyes landed on Pike. Tight gray jeans, combat boots, and a black sleeveless T-shirt that showed off his ink. All swagger and sex and guyliner. Pike waltzed onto the stage like it'd been built just for him. He lifted his hand in greeting, earning screams from the audience, then hopped behind his drum kit. He put in his earpiece, raised his drumstick, and leaned over to his mic with a cocky smile. "Y'all ready for us, Dallas?"

The crowd erupted. Sound exploded from his drums.

And Oakley forgot to breathe.

Good. God.

The rest of the band ran onto the stage, adding guitars and vocals to Pike's heavy rhythm, but Oakley barely heard the words.

All she could do was stare. Pike took command of the drums like he had a personal vendetta against them, banging hard and violent but with a sharp-edged grace that made it look like moving art. Every part of his body worked in perfect rhythm—muscles flexing, tattoos dancing, sweat flying—and the expression on his face wasn't far from what she'd imagined he looked like in the throes of sex. He was taking the songs in his fists and making them his with every swing of his drumsticks.

Oakley swayed on her feet, the pounding beat taking on an erotic edge, vibrating through her and invading her like a drug.

He looked possessed.

He sounded amazing.

And she was toast.

She felt the urge ride up her throat and she couldn't stop it. Her hands went up with the rest of the crowd and she screamed Pike's name like a goddamned groupie.

Fucking. Toast.

ELEVEN

Pike tugged off his shirt and used it to wipe the sweat off his face. His heart was still pounding and the adrenaline pumping hard after the set. *Boom. Boom. Boom.* His body felt ready to fight or fuck. They hadn't played for that big of a crowd in a while, and the effect was potent. He'd missed that kind of energy blasting his way; made him feel like he could fly.

He snagged a bottle of water off one of the tables backstage, trying to cool down, and exchanged high fives with the guys along the way. Then he thumped Braxton, Darkfall's lead singer, on the back. "You fucking killed today, man."

Brax tapped his throat. "Felt good. Almost like the old days."

"Glad to hear it."

Braxton had gone through vocal cord surgery after their second album, which had screwed up a major tour and the publicity for the record. Nobody's fault, but it had halted their ride to the top they'd been on after the first album. Then Geoffrey, their lead guitarist, had fallen off the wagon and ended up back in rehab, which had delayed things further. Now they were on the hunt for a big-time band to pick them up for an opening act—something that would give them a shot at arenas again. The local shows and festival circuit were cool, but if they wanted to break through to the next level, they needed more exposure than what they were getting here.

They had a few feelers out and their manager was hopeful. But if nothing else, at least all the guys were getting back into some sort of groove on stage. Things were gelling together again.

Pike moved through the crowded backstage tent, letting his eyes scan over the area. They had the usual suspects milling around—other bands who'd performed today, crew, spouses and girlfriends, promoters, and of course, the women they'd let backstage. Well, women *and* dudes. One of the other groups performing this afternoon was The Boys Club, which was an all-female band. They had their own groupies.

But Pike wasn't looking for any of the people he saw. He'd given Oakley backstage passes with her tickets and was hoping she'd use them, but he had no idea if she'd made it to the show at all. After last night, he may have scared her off with the gift. The only hope he held on to was that Oakley would want to give her daughter a fun night, so would come even if she hadn't wanted to see him.

"Hey there, gorgeous," a redhead said, putting her hand on his arm as he passed through the crowd. "Where are you off to so fast? I wanted to tell you how much I liked the show."

An automatic smile jumped to his lips—the politician face, the face for fans. His eyes flicked over her. Model pretty. Enhanced rack. Edgy look. Vaguely familiar.

"Hey, thanks. Glad you liked it . . ."

"Holly," she provided, conspiratorial smile touching her glossed lips. "We met at a Houston show a few years ago. I hung out with you and Eddie Duff."

By hung out, she probably meant slept with. He scanned his memory bank. Eddie was the lead guitarist in Crucial Madness and they'd done a show out there together. But memories of what had happened afterward were vague. Back then, Pike and pretty much everyone he surrounded himself with had been on a rotation of trying out every illegal substance known to man.

"Right, yeah. Good to see you. You look great."

She gave him an of-course-I-do smile and gave his arm a squeeze. "So do you."

He moved out from beneath her touch. "Thanks. And I'd love to catch up, but I need to find someone."

"Maybe you've already found her."

Fuck. Normally he liked a forward girl. No use wasting time playing coy games when both people knew what the end result would be. And all the adrenaline coursing through him had his dick on a hair trigger. He could tug her in a back room, hike up her skirt, and be inside her in five minutes. But he couldn't muster up any real interest. He knew he should tell her he wasn't feeling it. But he didn't have time for any drama, so he pulled a douche move instead. He leaned over and kissed her cheek then whispered, "Maybe later, sweetheart."

She smiled. "I'll hold you to it."

He moved past her and continued his search of the crowd, but after twenty minutes passed, he'd given up. Oakley either hadn't come to the show or she'd skipped the backstage tour.

He was disappointed. And pissed at himself. Why did he give a fuck if she showed up or not? He sank onto one of the couches and grabbed a beer. This was so not his style. If Oakley wasn't interested, then that was her prerogative. He didn't chase women. They chased him. He could have two back at his place before he finished this beer if he put the barest amount of effort into it.

This whole thing had been ridiculous from the start anyway. He had no business messing around with some soccer-mom type— even if she did have an X-rated job at night. What the hell had he been thinking? He leaned back and rubbed his hands over his face.

"This seat taken?"

His eyelids snapped open. He'd know that voice anywhere. He lifted his head to find Oakley staring down at him, looking altogether uncomfortable . . . and altogether lickable. She'd donned a pink tank top, a white pair of shorts, and her hair was pulled high into a ponytail. The glisten of sweat and the rosy glow from a day outdoors clung to her. No sign of the buttoned-up work outfits or oversized T-shirts. Just lovely, luscious curves and sure-to-be-salty skin.

"I was saving it for you," he said, forcing the flirt out past his suddenly dry throat and patting the couch cushion.

"Liar." She sat on the chair catty-corner to the couch instead of taking the spot by him.

"I didn't think you were coming. Where's Reagan?"

"I sent her home with my brother. She had a great time, but I wasn't sure if backstage would be kid-friendly."

He shrugged. "Things will be pretty tame back here since it's a daytime all-ages show. A few guys brought their kids. Any debauchery will happen in the buses or hotel rooms."

She glanced toward the rows of tour buses parked behind the tent then back to him, her eyes briefly dipping down to his naked chest. "Is that where your harem awaits?"

He smirked. "Nah, I waited too long to gather them up. Most have already found their prince for the day."

She frowned, something flashing in her eyes. "Right. If candidate A isn't readily available, they'll find candidate B."

He rubbed the back of his damp hair, her comment landing squarely. Wasn't that the truth. People came backstage to fuck a band member. As long as the guy was halfway decent looking and willing, in the end, it didn't matter who they ended up with. The sentiment was the same from the other side, too, though. Pretty groupies were just as mix and match. "It is what it is."

Her expression was wry but grim. "I'm aware."

That's when he realized he shouldn't have invited her back here. Even if he wasn't partaking of anything, it highlighted exactly how different their worlds were. Sometimes he forgot this wasn't normal. He could see her opinion in the vague disgust on her face.

"So how'd you like the show?" he asked, pulling her focus away from the scene around them. He hated that he felt the urge to ask, probably sounded like he was fishing for compliments. But for some reason, her opinion mattered to him.

She leaned back in the chair, considering him. "Your guitarist is crazy good. *Crazy* good. And hot."

He sniffed. "Is that why you're back here? Want me to get his phone number for you?"

"That'd be great. Is he single?" she asked, all wide-eyed eagerness.

He gave her a stony look.

Her mouth tilted into a pleased smile. "You're kind of cute when your ego is bruised."

"Wonderful. You know, I don't really need another sadist in my life. I've got enough of them."

She leaned forward, bracing her forearms on her thighs, unintentionally giving him a nice view of her cleavage. "Oh, get over yourself. You know you're a phenomenal drummer. Watching you is like falling into some voodoo spell. Arms and sweat and sticks flying. Even I had to fight the urge to throw my granny panties at you."

He laughed. "Granny panties?"

She patted the waistband of her shorts. "I'm all about the comfort, my friend."

A lightness filled his chest, his mood buoying. "So what you're saying is, watching me drum turned you on and now you must have my sweaty, dumbly tattooed body or you'll just die of lust."

She gave him a droll look. "What I'm saying is that I came back here to be honest with you. You have a thing for honesty, so it's only fair I give you some of mine."

His eyebrows lifted. "All right."

"Yes, I'm attracted to you. In truth, I couldn't tell you what your guitarist looked like because I never took my eyes off of you."

Pike leaned forward, his blood stirring.

"But this can't happen. I know I've given you the wrong idea with the phone call and all, but you need to hear this. I'm the kind of woman you most fear. The relationship kind. I don't do casual hookups."

He shifted on the couch, the word *relationship* making his skin prickle. "What's so bad about casual?"

"I have a daughter to worry about."

He released a breath. "I get that. Believe me."

"Do you?" she asked, clearly unconvinced.

He glanced around, making sure no one was in earshot. "Yes. I do. My dad walked out on us when I was five and left us with jack shit. After that, I can't tell you how many 'friends' my mom brought home to play daddy and help pay the bills over the years. I hated those guys. Hated those men who used my mom and acted like they had some say over me and my brothers and sisters. I'd never want to be that guy."

He could still remember the first boyfriend—Louis. Pike had been young and gullible enough to let himself get attached to that one. Louis would play baseball with him sometimes, so he'd thought he was a good guy. But he'd been a petty criminal with a mean streak and had disappeared after getting in a bar fight that left a man with a brain injury. His mom had been pregnant at the time. That had started the pattern of the many dangerous, destructive men who would come into his family's life, wreak havoc, and bail without looking back.

Oakley frowned and he braced himself for the trite sympathy. Why the hell had he let himself tell her that? No one besides Foster and Gibson knew about his background. Even the band had a false bio for him.

But she didn't do the oh-you-poor-thing routine. She simply nodded. "So you get it, then."

He shoulders loosened. "I get why you need to protect her. But I also get that there are ways around it. She doesn't have to know. You've kept your night job private. We could keep this private."

She sighed. "It's not that simple."

It was. It could be. He eyed her. "So this isn't just about Reagan, then. This is about you."

A wrinkle appeared between her brows. "Maybe."

"Because of the relationship thing? You want that?"

"I—" She frowned in frustration. "I don't know what I want. I mean, we're doing the honest thing, right?"

He nodded.

"Good. Then I'm not going to be a bitch and lie about the night on the phone. That was great. I needed that. God, did I need that.

But I know myself. The minute I take this a step further, my emotions are going to get involved. I'm not—" She looked around at the others backstage. "I'm not like these women. I don't judge them for taking what they want and having a good time, I just can't relate. I had a kid when I was still a kid. I didn't go through the stage where you layer up that tough skin, where you can just hook up for fun and move on. I tried it in my early twenties and I sucked at it. I'm not built for what you'd want from me."

"I think you're a lot tougher than you give yourself credit for," he said, not trying to push her but sharing his honest opinion. The girls he'd met backstage city after city had nothing on Oakley. She'd raised a kid on her own, was holding down two jobs, and had no qualms about laying out what she needed from a guy. Potential. A relationship. There was no apology there. No game. He liked that.

Even if he wasn't the guy who could fulfill it.

He opened his mouth to say something, but before he could get it out, long, bare legs appeared in his periphery. He turned right as Holly lowered herself into the spot next to Pike. Her hand went to his knee. "I'm about to head out. You ready?"

Oakley seemed to grow in height as her spine stiffened in the chair.

A flash of anger whipped through Pike at the interruption and uninvited touch. He put his hand over Holly's and moved it off his leg. "I was in the middle of a private conversation."

"No, it's okay," Oakley said, moving to get up, her voice tight. "I need to get going anyway."

Holly smiled, victory in her eyes.

Fuck. Pike stood. "No, Oakley, don't. Please stay."

Her jaw twitched as her gaze slid over to Holly. "It's okay. I think three's a crowd."

"Doesn't have to be," Holly said, suggestion in her tone.

Jesus Christ. Pike swiped a hand over his face. "Holly, give us a few minutes."

Holly shrugged, but didn't look too perturbed, probably because she figured he was going to work out a threesome with Oakley. She stood and gave his shoulder a squeeze. "I'll just go and grab a drink."

She sauntered off, her heels clicking on the concrete in a slow, purposeful beat. Pike moved closer to Oakley. "I'm sorry about that. I—"

"Don't worry about it," she said with a dismissive lift of her shoulder. "It's fine. I know how all this works. That's why I can't be a part of it. I'm not built for this. For you." She cocked her head in the direction Holly had gone. "You don't need to waste your time talking to me. You've already got someone who can give you what you want tonight."

He frowned. "So you think it's like that? Women are interchangeable."

She smirked. "Aren't they?"

The blow stung. Mainly because it was mostly right. Until now. For the first time in longer than he could remember it wasn't about getting laid in general. This was very, very specific. And he had no idea what to do with that.

"I don't want Holly or any of the rest of them. I want you."

"And if I say no?"

"I go home alone."

She scoffed. "Sure you do."

He stared at her for a few long seconds, feeling the distrust roll off her. She truly thought that the minute she walked out, he'd bed Holly or some other random chick. He had no idea how to prove otherwise because she certainly wasn't letting him go home with her. And it's not like he could lie and say he was looking for a relationship and maybe they should give it a try. He slept with a lot of women but never under false pretenses. He couldn't give her what she needed.

At least not in that way.

But . . .

"Give me your phone," he said, holding out his hand.

"What? Why?"

"Can you trust me just a little?"

She pressed her lips together and he waited for the no, but finally she dipped her hand into her purse and slapped the phone into his palm.

He smiled and took it over to the couch.

"What are you doing?"

"Shh. I'm working here." His thumbs moved over the on-screen keyboard.

"Pike."

After a few minutes of typing and clicking, he stood and handed the phone back to her.

"What did you do?"

"Just added a few of our songs to your playlist. At least I can go home with you that way." He leaned close to her ear. "Have a good night, Oakley."

He kissed her cheek and walked away.

"So we're done here?" she called to his back, confusion in her voice.

He smiled and waved.

Oh, we're so not done here.

TWELVE

Oakley hated that she was listening to the music Pike had added to her phone. What was she? Twelve? A mixtape should not get her going like this. But lying on the couch in the dark with her headphones on, hearing the songs he'd chosen drift through her ears, had this intimacy to it, like a private conversation.

He'd chosen a mix of songs, some from his band, most from other artists. All had a dark, sexy edge to them. Visceral beats. Nothing romantic. If dirty, sweaty sex could be put into music, this was the soundtrack. And her body hadn't missed the memo. With every heavy, pulsing beat, her blood pumped and her skin tingled.

Reagan had gone to sleep over at Devon's place after the concert, so Oakley had the house to herself. It'd be easy to take advantage of the solitude. So simple to call Pike. But she hadn't been lying to him backstage. She couldn't let herself get involved with someone like him. Plus, Pike was probably wrapped up in the model-thin legs of that redheaded chick by now. Oakley's stomach twisted, but she tried to ignore the kick of jealousy. The fact that she was feeling that emotion at all proved why she needed to keep her distance with Pike. She was already getting attached.

The current song ended and one by Darkfall started. It was the one they had opened the show with. She closed her eyes and let herself fall into the rhythm of Pike's bass drum. *Thump. Thump. Thump.* She could still see him there, biceps flexing, knees bouncing, confidence bleeding through every moment, could feel the sound vibrating through her bones, his music curling inside her. She pressed her thighs together, warmth building there.

Her phone dinged, interrupting the music and her daydreaming state. Her eyelids fluttered open. She hadn't signed in to take work calls tonight since she'd needed a break. But who else would message her this late? Worry that something was wrong with Reagan was her first instinctual response, but when she lifted her phone to look at the screen, it wasn't Reagan or a work message, it was a calendar reminder. All it said was, Open me.

What the hell?

She pressed the notification and the calendar page opened up. The words on the screen danced in her vision.

It's bedtime for you, Oakley. Time to have some fun.

Make sure Reagan is in bed, then do the following.

Her heartbeat ticked up a notch. She scrolled down.

Find the gift of glass that I gave you and put it in a bucket of ice water. Don't question it. Just do it. You can back out of the game at any time but don't stop before you try. (Allotted time: 5 minutes) Go.

She stared down at the words as she sat up on the couch. What. The. Fuck. Pike had obviously been doing way more than adding songs to her playlist. The message glared at her, daring her. Just do it. The gift? Only one thing had been made of glass. She wet her lips. This was ridiculous. Pike wasn't even texting this in real time. This was some sort of game he'd set up on her calendar. She should ignore it.

But she found herself climbing off the couch and heading to her room anyway, strangely compelled. Her fantasies had already been running rampant while listening to the music, and this felt like it was still part of that dream. Not real. A distant voice of a mystery lover telling her what to do. What could it hurt to do this one thing? He wouldn't even know if she'd done it or not.

The locked box of toys was in the bottom corner of her closet. She grabbed the key off a high shelf and unlatched the lock. Right on top sat the clear glass dildo, an erotic piece of art daring her to touch it. She let her fingertips run over the smooth surface. What would it feel like ice cold? A shiver raised goose bumps on her skin.

Before she could talk herself out of the ridiculous move, she grabbed the thing and brought it to the kitchen. The freezer blasted her flushed cheeks with cold air and she filled a wine chiller with ice then brought it to the sink to fill it with water. She plunged the glass toy into it.

Another ding came from her phone.

Good girl. I know you did it for me. Now reward yourself with a hot, relaxing bath. Use your best stuff. Scrub your skin until it's rosy and nothing of the day is left. But don't touch yourself. That's off limits. For now. (Allotted time: 30 minutes)

She closed her eyes and tried to breathe through the rush his words caused. She should be irritated that he was arrogant enough to think she'd follow some arbitrary instructions—especially after she'd told him they couldn't see each other. But her body was already warm and needy, her thoughts and logic blurring from the arousal. She peered toward her bedroom. Pike *was* keeping his word. This wasn't *seeing* him. He could be sleeping right now for all she knew or out with friends or . . . no, she wouldn't let her mind go down the groupie route again.

She went into her room, set aside the bucket of ice water, and headed to the bathroom to turn on the faucet. It'd been at least a month since she'd even used the tub. A quick shower in the morning was about all she had time for these days, so she had to dig deep in her cabinet to find bubble bath. But once the tub was full, the air scented, and the mirrors steamy, she sunk into the fantasy again.

She set her phone on the edge of the tub and submerged herself in the water, the heat gliding over her skin like a lover's touch. Was Pike thinking about her right now? Was he picturing her sinking into the tub? There was something kind of hot about him being out wherever he was, going about his business but knowing that somewhere across town, she was getting naked at his command.

A wave of arousal went through her and she groaned.

The man was a hazard.

She needed to stop.

But she was too curious to see what was next.

———

Pike propped his feet on the coffee table and tried to concentrate on what Gibson and Foster were discussing. His two friends had shown up at Pike's place after the show with takeout and his favorite beer. A Rangers game was on the TV, but Pike had barely glanced at it. All he could focus on was the damn clock. Was Oakley getting his messages? Would she follow them?

"So she thought his name was Spike!" Gibson concluded, his triumphant voice breaking Pike from his obsessing for a moment.

Foster laughed and peered over at Pike. "Wow. That's a new one. Remember that chick who kept getting our names mixed up and finally just gave up and called us both sir? I thought that was bad."

Pike took a sip of his beer and smirked. "Not her fault. She barely knew her own name by the end of that night. I blame you and that flogger."

Foster smiled, unrepentant. "Subspace is a beautiful thing, my friend."

"Yeah, it is. You don't miss that life?" Gibson asked Foster. "You two had a pretty good setup going."

Foster leaned back, blue eyes crinkling. "Nah. Those days were fun at the time, but they're nothing compared to what I have with Cela. Having someone play submissive to you for a night is one thing, but having the woman I love surrender all to me?" He shook his head. "Fuck, I can't even tell you what that's like. That absolute trust. It's like the scariest and hottest thing I've ever experienced. You can't get to that place with someone you're just scening with for the night."

Gibson frowned. "I'm not sure I'd want that much trust from someone, that kind of responsibility. I just like having a good time. That level seems . . . heavy."

"It is." Foster shrugged. "But it's the ultimate drug. At least for a dom."

Pike watched Gibson's expression change, the downshift, the

doors closing. He should ignore it. He didn't. "Maybe you just don't see it that way because the dominant thing isn't really your drink of choice, Gib."

Gibson shot him a murderous look.

But Pike had a few beers in him and wasn't in the mood to play nice, especially after Gib had taken so much glee in telling the Spike story. "Whatever happened to that chick you were subbing for—Sam? Wasn't she Tessa's friend?"

"I wasn't subbing for her. I was helping her with her training."

"To be a domme," Pike clarified.

"I was teaching her how to top." Gibson's jaw flexed and he ran a hand over his dark, curly hair. "And it didn't go further than that. We didn't hook up. She needed a real bottom."

"Mmm," Pike said noncommittally, which, based on Gibson's expression, pissed his friend off even more.

"Nothing wrong with switching," Foster said, either oblivious to Gib's tension or ignoring it. He reached over to scratch a napping Monty on the head. "Or bottoming. That girl you were with was a firecracker. I saw her at The Ranch the other day. She's been topping Julian."

"Julian?" Gibson looked like he could gnash rocks with his teeth. He gulped his beer instead. "Fantastic."

Pike shook his head, but before he could annoy his friend more, his phone beeped. He'd included himself on the appointments he'd made for Oakley. He reached forward to grab his cell but Gibson swiped it off the coffee table first.

"Let's see what's going on in Pike world."

"What the fuck, man?" Pike stretched toward Gib. "Give me that."

"Are we keeping you from something? All this beeping. Sounds like you're real busy," Gib said, mischief in his eyes, revenge in his grasp.

Pike pushed himself off the couch to go for the phone but Gibson was already reading the screen. " 'Get out of the bath and put on something sexy. Allotted time: ten minutes.' "

"Give me the goddamned phone." He yanked it from Gib's hand.

Gib was already laughing. "What the hell? You reminding yourself to get pretty for us tonight?"

Pike flipped him off and sat on the arm of the couch.

"Or wait," Gibson said, eyes alight. "Maybe all this talk of subbing is because *you're* the one answering to a domme this evening."

"Fuck off, Gib. Unlike some people, I've got no hang-ups about playing on that side if I get the itch."

"No," Foster said, leaning forward, shit-eating grin on his face. "That's not it. You've been distracted all night. *You're* the one telling someone else to do that, aren't you?"

Pike didn't respond.

"Is it that woman we saw at Wicked?"

"Wait, what woman?" Gib asked.

Foster's smile went smug. "Pike's got the hots for a mom at Bluebonnet Place. Sent her a big box of sex toys for a how-ya-doin' gift."

"Wait, *what*? You're sleeping with someone who works for Tessa? Dude. Not cool."

Pike scowled. "Hey, weren't you the one who told me to find a normal woman?"

Gibson gave him the are-you-kidding-me glare. "Not one at the charity, idiot. I told Kade you'd be—"

"Look, I'm not sleeping with her, all right? Haven't even kissed her. I'm just . . ."

"Telling her what to do and when to do it," Foster said, his mouth tilting up at the corner. "Didn't know you had it in you."

He didn't either. Though he'd topped women at The Ranch on occasion, it was all just fun and games, not the real dominance people like Foster wielded in the bedroom. That always seemed like too much work. Why waste all the energy on building trust with someone you'd only be with one night? But he couldn't deny that the thought of Oakley doing exactly as he instructed had left him fighting a hard-on all night. "I have my moments."

Gibson looked back and forth between the two of them. "So you're seeing her tonight?"

"No. She— Look, I'm not going to talk about this with you two dickheads. It's between me and her. All you need to know is that it's late and it's time for you to leave." He stood.

They followed him, but as they moved out of the living room, Foster's eyebrows were up near his hairline and Gibson didn't look at all ready to let the conversation go. Probably because Pike had called him out about his crush on Sam the feisty domme. Luckily, Foster stepped up and clapped Gibson on the back before Gib could say anything else. "Come on, man. I need to get back home anyway and I think I've had one too many. You can drop me off."

Gibson frowned and met Pike's gaze as he grabbed his keys off the kitchen counter. "Look, you know I'm not going to get up in your business. But don't fuck up anything at Tessa's place. My brother will kill me if you cause Tessa or any of her employees grief."

Pike tucked his hands in his pockets. "Understood."

Gibson seemed appeased by that. He walked by Pike and thumped him on the back. "Break hearts somewhere else, brother. I'm sure there's a line of willing victims waiting somewhere."

Pike knew he was supposed to laugh, but the jab dug into his ribs and twisted.

Gibson didn't notice but Foster did. They'd been friends too long for him to miss much. Foster let Gibson head out the door before he said to Pike. "You good, man?"

Pike's hands curled in his pockets. "I'm fine."

"You into her?"

He shrugged. "She doesn't do casual. She's got a kid. Not my type."

"That wasn't my question."

"Too bad, 'cause it's the only answer you're getting."

A knowing smirk touched Foster's lips. "Don't forget to give her a safe word."

"It's not like that."

Pike's phone beeped in his hand.

"Uh-huh." Foster nodded at the phone. "Sounds like the girl

you're *not* seeing is done with her bath and dressed for you. Your move, Master Pike."

"Good night, asshole."

Foster gave him another clap on the back and slipped out the door.

Pike sagged against the counter once the door shut and lifted the phone. He knew the next instruction that would be on his screen. Get in bed and turn the lights low. Now it's your turn. To get your next instruction you have to call. (Allotted time: 5 minutes.)

He rubbed his hand over his eyes. Was she there? Was she between her sheets, thinking of him? Or had she blown off the whole thing?

She'd told him today that this couldn't go any further. She'd told him and he hadn't accepted it. She'd probably gotten the first message and blocked his number.

He punched in five minutes on the microwave timer and hit Start. The time seemed to slow as he watched the numbers count down, and the silence of the kitchen turned oppressive. Four minutes. Three minutes. Two minutes.

Monty wandered in, tiny nails clicking on the wood floors, and stared at up at Pike, a question in his eyes. *What the hell are you doing standing here?*

He was wondering the same thing. He punched Clear on the timer, the last thirty seconds disappearing, and turned to go to the bedroom.

"Come on, Monts. We're done here."

Twenty minutes later, the phone sat silent on the bedside table. Pike crawled into bed and turned out the lights.

He told Oakley he'd always respect a no.

Now he just needed to learn how to accept one.

THIRTEEN

Oakley stared at the ceiling, her body on fire and her mind on high-speed blend. She'd followed Pike's instructions word for word, had tried hard not to think too much but to act instead. It had worked until he'd turned the tables. Now she was lying in bed in a silk cami and lace panties and panicking.

He wanted her to make the next move. To call. But she knew what would happen then. They'd do what they'd done the other night. She wouldn't be able to resist. Her libido would steamroll her good sense. It already had.

No. She couldn't call. She would take care of this herself. Beyond the stuff she'd bought at Wicked, she now had an arsenal of things to satisfy her needs. She would shut her phone off and test a few out. As soon as she got an orgasm out of the way, this insanity would abate. This was simply hormones. They made her daring, reckless, stupid.

She glanced at the clock. The five-minute time limit had long passed. If Pike had been waiting, he wouldn't be anymore. This would effectively end their—well, whatever this was. Nice and clear message. Thanks but no thanks.

She let her hand drift down to the band of her panties. Her skin was fever hot beneath her fingertips and her clit pulsed, her entire body growing more and more impatient. But when she touched where she most needed, instead of providing relief, it only sent a frisson of restlessness through her. Frustrated, she grabbed the little bullet vibrator from her bedside drawer and flicked it on. At the first touch of it, she flinched, the stimulation almost too much. She eased back, trying to find the right speed and angle. She sighed into the pleasure of it. Okay, this would work. She closed her eyes and tried to fall into the sensations. But she couldn't keep her focus, and after a few minutes, she felt stuck at the same plateau—feeling pleasant but too distracted to get to where she needed to go. She stroked a little harder and closed her eyes. But it was useless. If anything, she felt the release sliding further away from her. Dammit.

What would Pike have given as the next step? What would he have had her do? And how much different would all this feel with his voice in her ear?

"Fuck it." She turned off the vibrator and tossed it to the side. Her other hand closed around her phone. She flipped it over and pressed what her thumb had been hovering over for almost an hour.

He picked up on the second ring and cleared his throat. But no greeting.

"Pike?"

"You're late," he said. No accusation there, just observation and sleep-softened words.

"I'm confused."

He made a sound under his breath. "Join the club."

"Yeah?" She splayed her hand over her stomach, reveling in the sound of his voice in the dark, enjoying the way her breath automatically quickened. Somehow when they were like this it seemed okay. A fantasy in the night. Only a dream. "I'm not interrupting some wild night with a groupie?"

"Always thinking the worst of me, huh?" he asked, his tone teasing. "For the record, I turned down three different offers after the show because all I wanted to do was come home and imagine you following my instructions."

"Rock-star fail."

He laughed, low and soft. "So was I wasting those thoughts?"

She closed her eyes. "Meaning?"

"Did you follow my instructions?"

She wet her lips and took a deep breath. "I shouldn't have."

She could almost hear his slow smile over the phone. "Ah, but you did."

"If I died of a heart attack right now, the paramedics would find a glass dildo chilling in a wine bucket. The papers would have a field day."

"Mmm, is it bad that imagining that is making me hard?"

"My death turns you on. Noted."

"I'm kinky like that."

"Are you?" she blurted, then cringed when she realized how it sounded. "I mean, not the death thing, but, in general?"

His bed springs creaked. "I'm not vanilla."

"Right. I was just wondering. With all the instructions, you know. I've done some calls with people into BDSM stuff."

He didn't respond for a few seconds, and she realized she hadn't technically asked a question, but then his voice came through the line again. "Some of my friends are deep into the lifestyle. The guys you met at the store are two of them. I'm only telling you that because I know they don't care who knows."

"And you?" she asked, unsure of what answer she was hoping for.

"I belong to a kink resort where BDSM is the primary focus. But I don't label myself a dom or a submissive if that's what you're asking. I like to experiment, push limits. That kind of thing."

She digested that. A kink resort? "Gotcha."

"That bother you?"

She considered the question before answering. "No. I can actually see the appeal in the power-exchange part. Following your instructions tonight has made things . . . interesting. But I guess I asked the question because I just had a caller the other night who asked me to verbally humiliate him. I was able to do it, but I felt drained afterward. I don't think I'd get into doing that in real life. And to be honest, I've had enough guys call me ugly names to last me a lifetime. So I can't see enjoying the reverse either."

He blew out a breath. "Humiliation isn't my kink. And it seriously stresses me out that you have to do that shit if you don't want to. I mean, if that's what gets you going, that's one thing. But to be forced into it . . ."

"I'm not forced," she said, rolling onto her side. "I could make money other ways, I'm sure. Just not as fast. And not from home. I'd rather be called a dirty slut a few times a night than have to clean grease traps at a fast-food restaurant and leave Rae with a babysitter."

He was quiet for a few long moments. "I get it. Believe me. I've always been of the do-what-you-need-to-do school of getting through life. But if you get that promotion from Tessa, would you be able to quit the night job?"

"It would depend on how much she offered me, but yeah, I think so."

"All right, we'll make that happen. But until then, how about I just call you every night and pay for all those minutes?"

He made it sound like a joke, but she had a feeling he wasn't kidding. "I'd kill you."

"Oh, really?"

She sighed and flipped onto her back. "I can be everyone else's hired whore. I don't want to be yours, too."

"You're nobody's whore, Oakley," he said, a quiet firmness in his voice. "Don't ever let yourself think that. You're acting in a role just like I am on stage. They can't touch you unless you let them in."

"Do you? Let them in?"

"No."

"Ever?"

He sighed. "You saw what it's like backstage. They want the rock-star drummer. That's what they get."

"Is that who you are right now?"

"I don't know."

She pulled the sheets around her. "Tell me something about you that isn't part of that image."

"Okay." He considered the question for a moment. "I'm a nutcase about my dog—like two steps away from buying him outfits and carrying him around in my bag."

She laughed. "You're kidding."

"Nope. Crazy about him."

"What else?"

"Hmm, let's see. Horror movies scare the shit out of me. If I watch one, I can't sleep for days."

"Really? I love scary movies. What about things like *Scream* where it's kind of funny, too?"

"That one has a guy in a mask. Fuck that."

She laughed. "Are you trying to be adorable? Because you're being kind of adorable right now."

"Oh, Jesus Christ. Adorable is definitely not what I'm going for." He let out a beleaguered sigh. "You've completely lost your erection haven't you?"

She smiled into the darkness. "Quite the opposite actually."

"Is that right? Well, then adorable is exactly what I'm going for," he said, that deep voice all playful and sexy. "I also like bunnies and romantic comedies starring Meg Ryan."

"God, I'm getting so hot now."

"Oh, no you don't. No Sasha for me. Only the real Oakley."

She shifted under the covers. "It's not entirely a lie. Some crazy man sent me instructions all night. I've been tortured with hot baths and silky clothes and sex toys on ice."

"Mmm, this guy sounds exceptionally crafty and smart. Tell me more about this silk."

She let her fingers play along the edge of her camisole. "I'm in bed in a purple cami top with lace edges and a matching pair of bikini underwear. How about you?"

"In bed, just a pair of boxers. The lights are off and Monty is snoring in his bed in the corner."

"Did you think about me tonight?"

"Every damn moment," he said on an exhalation. "My friends came over to watch the game and shoot the shit and all I could think about was what you might be doing. *If* you were doing it."

"I did. Every step."

"Why?"

She watched the blades of her fan go round and round, her

heart a steady beat in her ears. "I don't know. Why'd you set up the messages?"

"Because you said you needed what we did the other night. I know I can't be the kind of guy you're looking for. But I can give you this. I want to give you this."

"What's in it for you?"

"You are."

Her breath stalled. "I can't give you much, Pike."

"All I'm asking for is your trust. Trust me to give you this kind of escape. I'm not asking for more than that."

"Pike . . ."

"Take off your panties for me, Oakley. It's time for your next instructions."

Her body went from hum to full buzz, the quiet command in his voice like a physical touch.

"You want to stop, you tell me so. *No* is all it takes with me."

She stayed quiet.

"Lose the panties and spread your legs, mama. Time to try out my gift."

She bit the inside of her cheek and grabbed her headset from the bedside table to switch to that then shoved off the sheets and tugged off her underwear. In the black quiet of her bedroom, she lay back and let her legs fall open. Cool air moved over her exposed skin. "Okay."

"You did it?"

"Yes."

"Good girl," he said, a caress in his tone instead of the patronizing one that usually accompanied those words. "Tell me, Oakley. Are you natural down there? Smooth? What would I feel if it were my fingers rubbing your pussy right now?"

The words sent a hot shiver from the crown of her head down to her toes. She swiped her tongue along her lower lip. "Trimmed."

A pleased sound rumbled through the phone. "Gorgeous. I'm there with you now, baby, inhaling your scent and feeling how aroused you are against my fingers. You feel me?"

She let her fingers slide along her flesh. "I feel you, Pike, can imagine you inside me."

"Fuck," he breathed. "Get rid of your top and then take that glass dildo off the ice. Bring it with you to the bed."

Her blood pumped harder. She wanted to keep stroking herself, already a hundred times closer to release than she had been when she'd tried on her own the first time. But she also wanted this game, wanted to obey him. She rolled out of bed to tug off her cami and grab the toy out of the now melted ice. The water was still freezing cold though and the minute she had the glass in her hand, goose bumps broke out on her skin. She heard movement on his end of the phone.

She lay back down on the bed. "I've got it."

"Hold it above you and let the water drip onto your nipples," he said, his voice like warm, stroking hands against her.

She hesitated for a breath. Tomorrow she'd probably regret this. But right now, her hormones were overtaking her logic, her nipples going hard and achy at the thought of the stimulation. She lifted the glass above her and fat, freezing droplets splashed onto her chest. She arched and her breath caught. "God."

"Feels almost painful against your hot skin, doesn't it?" he asked, grit in his voice. "I grabbed an ice cube from my water glass and am doing the same thing."

She squeezed her eyes shut, imagining him there, dragging ice across his chest, those tan, flat nipples glistening. If she were with him, she'd chase the drops with her tongue, lap at his skin, nibble at that muscular torso of his.

"You know what's next, baby. I want that smooth cock inside you."

She groaned. "It's freezing cold."

"That's the idea. Spread your legs and push it in slow. I want to hear you, want to picture how sexy you look sliding it in."

Oakley was burning with a steady heat now, but not from shame or embarrassment. Those emotions had exited the building a long time ago with her good sense in tow. No, this was pure anticipation and arousal. She brought the toy down between her spread thighs and touched it to her clit. She gasped at the bitter cold.

But it wasn't painful. Just shocking, sending all of her senses on high alert. She dragged the head of it lower and found her entrance. The contrast of heat to cold made her muscles clench. "It's going to burn."

"Take it for me, mama. Heat it up inside you. Let it make you feel good."

After forcing herself to breathe and relax, she pushed the toy into her cleft, the slickness of her arousal easing the way. She cried out at the icy invasion.

"Fuck, fuck, fuck," she panted, all the while easing it deeper, her nerve endings lighting up and sending sensation radiating through her body.

Pike groaned. "That voice of yours is going to kill me. You're driving me crazy."

Her body stretched and protested. It'd been years since she'd had anything bigger than her fingers inside herself. She'd had yet to try out the dildo she'd bought. But God, the cold lit her on fire in the best way possible. Everything coiled, alive and awake, her nipples straining and her thigh muscles tensing.

"Tell me how it feels," Pike said, his words strained enough to let her know he was touching himself as well.

She breathed through the initial wave of sensation, pumping the smooth glass inside her. "It's waking everything up. It feels . . . damn. Painfully good."

"Stroke your clit, baby. Take everything you need to make it feel good."

She didn't need to be told twice. "Tell me what you're doing."

"The ice is melting on my chest, making a mess, and I've got my fist around my dick with my other hand stroking my balls."

"You like them played with?" she asked, her words choppy as she brought herself right to the edge of orgasm and held there.

"I do. I like it kind of rough. Squeezing, tugging, dragging your nails over them. When you suck me off, feel free to explore. Nothing's off limits."

She smiled even as her head tilted back, release hovering. "So sure I'm going to have your cock in my mouth one day, huh?"

"A boy can dream."

Pleasure was making her near delirious. She focused on the images he was painting. Him cupping and tugging his balls as he jerked off. Thighs spread. All that maleness on display. "Do you really own plugs for yourself?"

It was a question she wouldn't have had the guts to ask a few minutes before, but her filter had disintegrated into a pile of ash.

He grunted. "Freak you out?"

"I think it's hot."

And she wasn't lying. A straight guy who had made no apologies about indulging in that kind of pleasure? There was something unbelievably sexy about that.

"What does it feel like?" she asked.

"Mmm, never tried it yourself?"

"No."

"You're missing out, mama. Hard to describe. Want me to grab mine?"

She bit her lip, her hand still working the toy. "Only if you want to."

"One sec. Keep doing what you're doing." There was the drag of a drawer on his end then he was back. "Haven't done this in a while, but I like that the thought is making you hot. I like this dirty side of you."

Her hips undulated forward, the pleasure building and building inside her. "Tell me what you're doing."

"I've lubed up the plug and now I'm stroking my cock while I work the plug in with my other hand."

Her eyelids squeezed tight. The vision of Pike penetrating himself with something was making her inner muscles clench and sending desperate need rolling through her. Never before had she considered that something like that would do it for her. But Christ the image was hurtling her toward release.

Pike let out a low groan. "Fuck, that feels good."

Oakley pressed against her clit, trying to hold off her orgasm as long as she could. "Tell me."

"The plug's inside and vibrating. It's making everything feel full and tight, and every stroke I give my cock feels more intense. I want to come, but I'm stroking slow, teasing myself, thinking of you here, your fingers on the plug, my cock in your mouth. The scent of you in the air."

"God," she whispered.

"Maybe I'll try this on you sometime. Fuck you while you have a toy in your ass, my fingers stroking your clit. You'd feel so filled up, baby."

She moaned, the image almost too much. "I'm close."

"Take it, baby. I want you fucking yourself good and deep. Let me hear you come around that hard, cold cock."

She lost it then, the dildo buried deep and her fingers working. She cried out freely, no one home to hear. "Pike!"

"Fuck, yes." Pike's grunts filled the phone line, and she could hear the slick pace of his fist even as she gasped her way through her orgasm—light breaking behind her eyes. Pike came with a shout and a string of curses. But before he finished, she heard her name on his lips. Over and over again.

Oakley, Oakley, Oakley.

Not Sasha. Not baby. Not some filthy name. *Oakley.*

It'd been a long time since she'd heard her own name said in the heat of passion like that. She liked it. More than she probably should.

She pulled the toy from her body and collapsed back into her pile of pillows in a panting heap. After they'd both been quiet for a few moments, listening to the pounding of her heart in her ears, she found her voice again. "Wow, maybe I should be paying you."

The chuckle on the other end was sated and sleepy. "The feeling's mutual. Plus, don't bother. You couldn't afford me."

She smiled as she set the toy aside and pulled the sheets over her body—the cruise down from the orgasm letting reality slide in. Awkwardness would soon follow. Then regret if she didn't hurry this along. "Well, I guess we better get some sleep."

"No, don't hang up yet."

"Why?"

Sheets rustled. "Because if I was there, I would never let you sleep alone after that. I'd be curled around you, taking up all the room in the bed and stealing the covers."

"Pike."

"Shh, we don't have to talk. Just picture me there with you. That's what I'm going to do."

"But—"

"Sweet dreams, mama. Get some rest."

She waited for the dial tone but none came. She heard a few quiet movements, maybe him cleaning up. But then the bed squeaked again and a few minutes later, steady breathing.

She listened to him for as long as she could, falling into the soothing pattern of his breath. But soon her own lids were drooping. She pulled her headset off, left her phone on speaker, and closed her eyes.

When she woke up the next morning, her phone was dead. But neither of them had hung up.

The man on the phone had stayed the night.

No one had ever stayed the night.

FOURTEEN

Oakley walked into the main office at the Bridgerton Academy, hair dripping and the bottom of her pants soaked. Her shoes squeaked on the floor as she made her way to the desk.

Mrs. Daley, the secretary, lifted her head and got to her feet when she saw Oakley's state. "Oh, you poor thing. Let me take your jacket." She grabbed Oakley's windbreaker and now-useless umbrella and hung them on a peg by the door. "Do you want me to grab you a school sweatshirt or something? You must be freezing."

Oakley waved her off. "Thank you, but I'll be okay. The umbrella flipped inside out halfway across the parking lot."

Mrs. Daley frowned at the scene on the other side of the glass doors. "Another half hour of this and the street is going to flood."

Oakley lifted her leg and pointed at her black slacks. "Already about three inches deep in the lot."

"I'm so sorry we had to call you out in this. But—"

"It's fine," Oakley said quickly. "I want y'all to call me when she gets like this. I can deal with the weather."

To get to her kid, she'd take a damn canoe here if she had to.

Mrs. Daley nodded. "I understand. She's in Mr. Craig's office. She's settled down a lot since the lights came back on."

Oakley thanked her and headed toward the back where the offices were. Sure enough, when she entered the school counselor's office, she found Reagan curled into a chair, headphones on and eyes closed. Her small fingers were interlocked and flexing, the only outward sign that she wasn't as peaceful as she might appear.

Mr. Craig looked up with a sympathetic smile. "She wasn't up to talking, but she's done a good job calming herself down in the last half hour or so. The music does help."

Oakley nodded. "Thank you for letting her take a break in here."

"My door's always open for her. It was an unsettling day for all the kids with the lights flickering and the tornado siren going off."

She appreciated his attempt to make her feel better, the sentiment being that if the typical kids had been affected, Reagan wasn't all that different. But Oakley knew that the level of anxiety was not near the same. With Reagan's sensory issues, alarms and sirens hurt her ears in a physical way. And ever since Rae had seen a documentary about a destructive tornado in Oklahoma years ago, she'd held a deep-seated phobia of bad weather.

Oakley crouched down in front of the chair and touched Reagan's knee. Reagan jumped and opened her eyes. Relief filled her reddened eyes. "Mom."

"Hey, baby."

Reagan hit Pause on her iPod but didn't take off the headphones. "Is it still raining?"

"It is, but the worst is past us. No more sirens. Just a lot of rain."

She chewed her lip. "There's a front coming through. More storms could pop up. I heard the weatherman say that last night."

"That part's done. I promise." She gave her knee a little squeeze. "Classes are almost over for the day. I thought I'd bring you to Bluebonnet instead of riding the bus today. How's that sound?"

She glanced toward Mr. Craig then back to Oakley. Oakley could tell Reagan was having that debate between two things that stressed her out—facing the rain, which would mean breaking her routine, or being left here to ride in the storm on the bus alone.

"I'll go with you."

Oakley nodded. "Okay, baby. Let's get your bag and head out. I know the kids at Bluebonnet will be ready to start working on the new song once school lets out. You can get a jump start."

Oakley helped her gather her things, but Reagan wasn't giving up the headphones. She wanted them just in case any sirens went off while they were driving. And when they left the offices, Reagan made Oakley walk to the other side of the school to exit through the doors she'd normally leave out of to get to the bus. On a different day, Oakley may have urged her daughter to try to go against the routine, to go out a different door. But Rae was so on edge already, it was worth traipsing a few more yards through the flooded parking lot to avoid the added stress or possible meltdown. She'd learned to choose her battles.

Luckily, besides the rumbling thunder, the drive to Bluebonnet was quiet. Reagan listened to her music and kept her eyes closed. Oakley prepared herself for a trying evening. Once Reagan had a bad episode, the rest of the day was usually a loss, leaving her emotional and edgy. The only Reset button was a low-key evening and a good night's sleep. But they wouldn't get to that part until after rehearsals at Bluebonnet with Pike.

Pike.

Oakley rolled her shoulders to try to loosen some of the tension. She hadn't talked to Pike much over the last few days. He'd been busy and any exchanges had been texts about the project. But he'd promised to be there this afternoon to help get one of the original songs the kids had chosen in shape.

The kids would be excited, but nerves had her gripping the steering wheel harder as she got closer to the center. Her and Pike's last night on the phone had been more than a silly fantasy thing like the first time. Way too intimate and personal. They'd slept together over the phone. How was she supposed to face him after that?

She didn't have any extra time to prepare for it, though. Because when she walked into the music room, Pike was already there. Bradley, their aspiring drummer, was sitting in front of the drum kit, and Pike was instructing him on how to loosen his arms so he could move from snare to cymbal more quickly. Bradley, normally Mr. Tough Guy, looked ready to pee his pants. Guess she wasn't the only one nervous around Pike.

Pike glanced up, noticing her for the first time, and for half a beat, there was a flare of naked, open desire. She sucked in a breath, but as soon as the look was there, it was gone. A good-natured smile replaced the heat. "Looks like Noah's Ark dropped y'all off."

Reagan didn't say anything. Instead, she clutched her iPod to her chest and walked away to sit against the back wall, separate from everyone else.

Pike frowned and stepped away from Bradley to meet Oakley by the door. "Something I said?"

Oakley sighed and set her bag and keys on a chair near the door, then made sure none of the other kids were close enough to hear the conversation. "She probably didn't even hear you. She had a rough day at school. Storms upset her and sirens set off her sensory issues."

"Poor baby." He crossed his arms and peered over at Reagan. "Anything I can do to help?"

"Just leave her be. Sometimes she needs to check out to get herself calm. So if she wants to join us, she can. If she wants to stay over there, let her."

His eyes met hers. "And you? Anything I can do? You look cold and stressed."

God, he smelled good. Like summer and spice. She could think of more than a few things he could do to warm her up. But beyond the normal dirty thoughts he inspired, she had this ridiculous urge to hug him, to feel his arms wrap around her, to feel comfort after a shit day. Stupid. She cleared her throat. "The rest of the kids are going to be here soon. Can you get them started so I can run home and get a change of clothes? I won't be long."

A panicked look crossed his face. "Wait, you want to leave the kids alone with me?"

"You were doing fine with Bradley."

"Yeah, but he's one kid and we were talking drumming. I'm not—I'm not good with kids. I don't know—"

She smiled and lifted a brow. "So my kid has a storm phobia and you have a child phobia?"

"It's not—"

She reached out and grabbed his shoulder, giving it a squeeze and trying not to notice how muscular it felt. "You'll do fine. All kids want is to be treated like people. Don't talk down to them. Be a good listener. And be confident when you're in charge so they don't try to get one over on you."

"That last part is what I'm worried about."

"You have no problem with confidence." She leaned closer. "And I've heard you're pretty good at giving instructions."

His smile went lazy at that. "I thought we weren't supposed to talk about such things face to face, Ms. Easton."

She shrugged, nonchalant. "I don't know what you're talking about, Mr. Ryland."

"Well, if that rule's not in place right now"—he turned his back to the kids, facing her fully—"then let me say that the other night hasn't left my mind all week. That every time I think about it I get hard. And that it's taking every bit of restraint I have not to find the nearest storage closet and peel these clinging, wet clothes off of you."

Her body surged with heavy, hungry desire, and her breath left her for a second. Hearing it on the phone was one thing. Hearing him say those kinds of things face to face—complete with those chameleon eyes and pirate smile—was like plugging her system into an electrical socket. Everything lit up. Buzzed. Her gaze darted toward the two kids in the room. "Pike."

"Don't tell me you haven't thought about it."

"We can't talk about this here."

His eyes darkened—spun gold rimmed by green. "Maybe we've done enough talking. Maybe the next conversation shouldn't be across phone lines. Maybe those instructions should be whispered in your ear while I—"

"Pike—"

But before she could get another word out, a group of kids bustled through the doorway, chatting loudly and breaking the moment. Oakley stepped back, putting more distance between her and Pike.

"I'll be back in twenty minutes. Get them started on the chorus of the song. If you need help, call for one of the volunteers."

Pike gave her a quick up-and-down perusal, as if he were saving the picture to his permanent file. "To be continued."

She shook her head and turned away before she could get herself in trouble. She needed to get some breathing room. Pike was exciting on the phone, sexy and daring. But she could handle him in that venue. There was space, safety. But in person, the man was a full-frontal assault on her senses. Every part of her yearned to touch, to taste, to bury her nose in the crook of his neck and absorb his scent. To lick his tattoos, to bite that muscular curve of his shoulder, to glut herself on him like a starved person at a buffet. She'd always rolled her eyes at the women swooning in those Regency romances she read, but now she understood the definition. The man could knock her on her ass with a look and a few well-chosen words.

She grabbed her bag and slipped out the door, inhaling the cool air of the hallway and trying to quell the flush that had surely crept up her face. She hurried to the door that led to the back parking lot, actively avoiding any of the other staff, and pushed back out into the rain.

The storm had waned from torrential downpour to steady shower, but at this point, she was soaked anyway, so what did it matter? She jogged to her car, sloshing through the puddles, and dug into her purse for her keys. But the outside pocket she normally kept them in was empty.

"Shit." She plunged her hand into every corner of the pocket then opened up the main zipper to see if she'd dropped them in there.

"Looking for these?"

She glanced up. Pike stood there in the rain, her keys hanging from his finger, raindrops landing on his skin and eyelashes

"You left them on the chair," he said, slicking his hair back as he took a step closer.

Her tongue felt glued to the roof of her mouth. The guy was unfairly beautiful. Drenched in rain he looked even better. "You're getting wet."

The corner of his mouth kicked up. "Isn't that my line, Ms. Easton?"

She laughed, feeling ridiculous and a little embarrassed. "We're not supposed to talk about those things."

He took another step, his eyes not leaving hers, and she backed up until her backside bumped against her car. He took her hand and unfurled her fingers, his touch like a branding iron on her chilled skin, then placed the keys in her palm. He didn't move forward. He didn't cage her in. He simply held her in thrall with his presence, raindrops sliding over his skin and dripping off the ring in his eyebrow, and kept his hand on hers. His thumb traced over her knuckles. "Then let's not talk."

Four simple words.

That was all it took. Well, that and how irresistible he looked with rain running down his face and promise in his eyes. Every mooring inside her broke free in that one ill-advised moment. All the good intentions, all the logic, all the sense she thought she possessed drained from her. His name passed her lips, the keys hit the ground, and then her mouth was on his—hands gripping fistfuls of wet T-shirt and toes pushing off the ground.

Even though he'd been the one to throw down the challenge, he stiffened as if surprised. But as soon as her lips closed over his, he snapped into action. His hands moved to her waist and he pressed her fully against the car, taking control of the kiss. His mouth tasting and taking, his fingers biting into her sides like he was half a second from ripping her shirt from her skin.

She moaned into the kiss, and his tongue dipped into her mouth, stroking hers with blatant erotic rhythm—making promises. She could almost hear those promises as if he'd whispered them into her ear. *This is how my hips will move against yours. This is how I'll lick you. This is how slow my cock will grind inside of you.* Everything inside her went bright and electric. She yanked him closer, aligning her body with his and rubbing against him like a shameless, desperate thing. She couldn't help herself. The dam had cracked. It all felt too good. Too hot. Needful in the best way.

Pike's hand found her hair, and he laced his fingers in the damp tresses, angling her head to deepen the kiss. She answered his urgency stroke for stroke, and he groaned and shifted his position, letting her feel his erection against her hip. Her sex clenched, the intensity of her arousal making her breath catch. She wanted to climb him, wrap her legs around him, beg.

But he wasn't letting her out of the kiss. He swallowed her gasp and bit at her bottom lip, which only made her whimper again. All their movements were frantic and jerky, like bulls waiting to go into the ring and thrash everything in sight, thrash each other. He said her name and his other hand slipped beneath the hem of her shirt, grasping at her rain-slicked skin as if he couldn't get her close enough. She let her fingers trail upward, tracing the muscles beneath his T-shirt and then curling into the hair at the nape of his neck. She gripped hard, ready to let him absorb her completely.

But when he lowered his arms to grab her thighs and bring her legs around him, seating him exactly where she most craved him, some of her brain cells sparked back to life.

They were in the parking lot of her job. Any co-worker or child could walk out the back door. And she was about to dry hump the one guy she'd sworn she'd steer clear of for all the world to see.

She broke away from the kiss, panting. "Wait. Stop."

Pike blinked, his eyes as lust-drunk and hazy as hers probably were. "What's wrong?"

She shimmied out of his hold. "We can't. My job."

Full sentences wouldn't come to her, but he got the message. Awareness came back into his eyes, and he jerked back. He glanced toward the door and ran a hand over his face. "Shit. That—it wasn't supposed to—"

She smoothed her shirt, her hands shaking, and bent down to swipe her keys out of the puddle they'd fallen into. "It's okay. I— that was my fault. I need to go."

"Oakley."

"Get back to the kids. I'll see you in a few."

Pike frowned but didn't make a move to stop her. "Right. Yeah. The kids."

"Great." She climbed in her car and didn't take a breath until he'd headed back inside. When the door shut behind him, she rested her head against the steering wheel and screamed in frustration.

Her lips were tingling, her body pulsing, and her brain blitzed. What the hell was she doing?

Of all the impulsive, stupid, ill-advised things . . .

And she couldn't even blame Pike. *She'd* kissed *him*!

The move had been hers. She'd been a minute away from finding a way to get it on in the parking lot. She was no better than one of his groupies looking for a quickie backstage.

She stabbed the key into the ignition and turned it. She had twenty minutes to get herself back together.

Twenty minutes.

It would never be enough.

FIFTEEN

Pike had to look twice when Oakley came back into the music room because at first he'd mistaken her for another teenager. She had her hair pulled into a haphazard knot and wore a Bluebonnet Place T-shirt and gym shorts, her long legs bared. Damn. All that skin conjured some really inappropriate thoughts.

He dragged his gaze back up to her face and frowned when he noticed how drawn she looked. *Pissed*, he'd been expecting. The kiss in the parking lot had freaked her out. Shit, it'd freaked him out—how easily he'd lost control, how quickly it had gotten out of hand. How much he'd wanted to take her over and carry her off. But he hadn't expected her to look so downtrodden.

He got up from the circle he'd been sitting in with the kids and walked over to her. "Everything all right, mama?"

"Don't call me that here."

He lifted a brow. Not here. But maybe somewhere else. Good to know. "You were gone awhile. We're about to wrap up."

"Sorry." She sighed and flicked a stray hair away from her face. "My street is flooded. They've blocked the roads."

"Shit."

"The cops told me all the houses on the street are fine. But they're not letting anyone through because there are a few downed power lines close by and they have to secure the area." She spread her hands out. "Hence the makeshift outfit. Tessa had to lend me clothes."

"Damn. Did they tell you when you could go back?"

"Probably not tonight. And even if I could, the lack of electricity would freak Reagan out too much."

"You've got somewhere to go?"

"My brother's. But he's hosting business associates for dinner tonight and I don't want to interrupt. He'll probably be done by nine."

Pike glanced over at Reagan, who had finally joined the group in the last half hour. He'd been happy to have her back in the circle, but her normal spark definitely wasn't there. "How's Reagan going to deal with all that?"

Oakley closed her eyes and rubbed the spot between them. "I can't tell her about the house. She's already had a bad day. And if I do, every storm that comes from now on, she'll think the house is going to flood and lose power. She's got enough to worry about. I think I'll just tell her we're going to have a sleepover at Uncle Devon's. And take her to dinner or whatever in the meantime."

"Or you could just come to my place."

Her attention turned back to him at that. "What?"

He shrugged. "Reagan said she wants to see my vintage album collection. We could grab takeout. It might distract her until it's time to head to your brother's."

"Pike. I—we can't. I mean, I don't want to confuse things or give Rae the wrong idea."

"You mean give *me* the wrong idea," he said with a smirk.

"That, too."

He lifted his palm like he was swearing in at court. "Seriously. It'll be completely innocent. Just one friend helping out another. It's not like I'd make a move on you with your daughter there, anyway."

She lifted a brow. "I doubt you have ever in your life been completely innocent of anything."

He grinned and pointed to a spot above his head. "Come on, can't you see the halo?"

"Yes, your horns are holding it up."

"Now you're just hurting my feelings," he said, putting his hand over his heart in mock despair. "Come on. There's a kickass Greek restaurant down the street from my condo. Gyros for us all. And homemade pita. Reagan can dig through my record collection. We can talk about project stuff."

"Why?" she asked, a wrinkle appearing between her brows. "I mean, why would you want us there? I'm sure you have your own things to do tonight. It's Friday."

Why? Good question. One he didn't have an answer for. This wasn't his game. He didn't bring women back to his place unless it was to get them into his bed—which would definitely not happen in this situation. But he found himself excited about the possibility of having the two of them over anyway.

Bizarre. He rubbed the back of his neck. "We're friends. Don't overanalyze it. I don't have plans. You need a place to kill time. I have one."

"Mom, why are you wearing *that*?" Both he and Oakley turned toward the new voice. Reagan stood a few steps from them, staring at her mother's outfit with a vaguely horrified expression. "Those shorts are *short*."

"Yes, they are," Pike agreed. "So very short."

Oakley shot him a look and, turning away from Reagan, he mouthed, *I love them.*

Oakley narrowed her eyes in warning for the briefest of seconds then smiled at her daughter. "Ms. Tessa lent me some clothes since my other ones got wet."

"Can we go home? I'm tired."

Oakley sent a wary glance Pike's way. "Not yet. Mr. Pike thought we might like to go over to his place and see his album collection."

Reagan perked up like a flower finding sun. "Really?"

"Would you like that?" Pike asked. "I have a whole punk section."

"Best. Idea. Ever," Reagan said, expression comically serious.

Pike grinned. At least he had one Easton girl on his side.

Oakley shook her head and told Reagan to get her things. As soon as she was out of earshot, Oakley stepped in front of Pike and pinned him with a look. "No crossing the line, Ryland. No kissing or comments or grabby hands or sexy looks, nothing."

His lips curled. "That's what you're picturing isn't it? Getting Reagan occupied with something then me sneaking you into a room, pushing you against a wall, sliding my . . ."

Her hand flew up to cover his mouth. "Stop."

He maintained his smile behind her fingertips.

"There are two Oakleys," she said, her voice firm and quiet. "Sometimes you get to say those things to the other one. Not this one. This one is off limits."

He nodded and she lowered her hand. He peeked over his shoulder to make sure the kids were still occupied. He turned back to her, meeting her eyes. "All joking aside, I would *never* disrespect you or your daughter that way. My mother didn't give me that courtesy. Our rental house was small. I saw way more than I should've ever seen between her and her boyfriends. I wouldn't do that to someone else's kid."

Oakley's stern expression softened. "Thank you. I'm sorry you had to go through that."

He shrugged, uncomfortable with the sympathy. "What can you do? Some of us don't win the parent lottery. I survived."

Barely. If he hadn't finally bailed at seventeen after his mother hooked up with yet another guy who liked to take out a bad day by pounding on Pike, he'd be dead or in jail. Pike had thought Red might be different. Unlike the other boyfriends, Red had money, a house, and a good job. The guy owned a successful car dealership, and he'd seemed like he'd be the prince to pull Pike's family out of their hand-to-mouth existence. But the guy had wanted the picture-perfect family. The younger kids and his mother had been able to fit into that mold. Pike with his Mohawk, piercings, and fuck-you attitude hadn't fit. And in the end, it turned out his mother had a type. Red was just better at hiding that penchant for violence and justifying it when it flared. And though his mother was sometimes in the line of fire, Pike was Red's favorite target by far.

The last beating he'd taken from Red had ended with Pike pulling a gun on the guy. Pike had gotten caught trying to sneak out with the car for the night, and Red had slammed Pike's hand in the car door, breaking the delicate bones in one swift crunch. The pain hadn't even registered at first. All Pike had seen was bright red rage. One of his hands—the only fucking thing about him that was special, the thing that was going to get him out of this hellhole existence—was now crushed. How the fuck was he supposed to drum one-handed?

Without thinking, he'd grabbed the gun from the glove box with his good hand and jumped out of the car. He'd shoved Red against the wall and had held the gun right to his head, his finger twitching to squeeze the trigger. And when Red had smirked, grabbed Pike's nuts, and told him he didn't have the balls to do it, Pike had pulled the trigger and braced for the blast. Nothing had happened. The gun hadn't been loaded. But before Pike could even register how completely crazy he was being, his mother and younger brother had come out, seeing him with the gun.

He'd dropped the thing like it was on fire, but the incident had sealed his fate with his family anyway. If Pike ever had any doubt, he'd learned that night where his mother's loyalties lay. She'd been hysterical when she'd come into the garage. Pike's hand had been a mangled, swelling mess. But she hadn't listened to his side of the story. And instead of carting him to the ER for his hand, she'd listened to Red and had told Pike to get out for good.

Pike had considered going to the police about his hand. But he knew no one would buy that the punk teenager hadn't been the one who started it. So after a night sitting in the free clinic to get his hand looked at, he'd officially moved in with Foster, cutting his mother and Red out of his life. Unfortunately, he'd lost his siblings in the process, too. Red took out a restraining order and forbade the family from talking to Pike. And Pike's mom hadn't protested the edict, too far under Red's thumb or too enamored with her new suburban life to bother fighting for her first child. Red paid the bills. He won. Pike was cut out. Dead to them all.

Pike hadn't slept for weeks after he'd left. He'd always tried to act as the buffer between any of his mom's boyfriends and the younger kids, so he knew it'd only be a matter of time before one of his siblings became Red's next target. He made anonymous calls to CPS and tried to get the asshole caught, but his mother and Red were too good at putting on a show and faking it for whoever investigated.

By the time his younger siblings were old enough to make up their own minds, they'd only known what they'd seen—a brother who'd abandoned them—and what they'd been told—that Pike was some psycho asshole who almost killed Red. Pike couldn't deny the charges because they'd been true. The gun hadn't been loaded. That's all that separated him from being a murderer.

Reagan ran up to them, breaking Pike out of the old memories and dragging him back to the present. She bounced on the balls of her feet. "I'm ready."

Her enthusiasm and bright smile hit him in the gut. His brother, Tristan, had been just a little older than Reagan last time he'd seen him. Tris had been his constant shadow back then. And the one he'd worried about the most when he'd left because he was the obvious choice for Red to move onto once Pike had left. Pike had always sworn to Tristan that he'd keep him safe, and he'd bailed. Thinking about that had given him daily nightmares. He'd known Tris was too sensitive and gentle of a kid to survive the stuff Pike had been through. Tristan was a kid who bottled everything up and let it eat at him instead of exploding in anger. But when Pike had tried to sneak over and check on him, Tristan had run from him—betrayal in his eyes. They'd all counted on Pike and he'd let them down.

He'd tried to call Tris one night a few years ago when he was having a particularly rough night on tour. Right before Christmas. Alone. He'd been fucked up with pills eight ways to Sunday, and he'd pulled out the number he'd tracked down months earlier. He'd been closest to Tris since they were the only two boys, and for some reason, he'd felt this need to connect with someone who shared his blood. He'd barely been able to string words together, and when Tris had realized who it was, he'd hung up on him. Pike had tried to call him back a few days later when he was clear-headed, but he hadn't answered. Message clear: *I don't want to know you.*

Then a year later he'd gotten the news that Tristan had been killed in a car accident in Austin. His car had wrapped around a tree, and there'd been speculation that it might've been a suicide. Pike had been torn to shreds at the news and had gone to the funeral. But a security guard had met him at the door and told him he couldn't go in.

He'd never gotten the chance to say he was sorry. The kid he'd helped raise was gone.

Pike rubbed the heel of his hand over his chest where that hurt still burned bright and dragged his gaze away from Reagan, the memories still too hard to think about.

Oakley gave him an odd look, like she'd caught his shift in mood. "You okay?"

"Fine. Just getting heartburn."

She didn't look like she bought that one bit, but she cocked her head toward the room. "Rae, why don't you help Mr. Pike get the room straightened and I'll walk the rest of the group back to the activity room? We'll head out after that."

"'Kay."

Pike lifted his head, the simple act of Oakley trusting him to be alone with Reagan both surprising him and helping him pull out of that dark cave in his mind. Usually being alone with a kid was not something he'd want, but Oakley's endorsement buoyed him. "You sure?"

"I'll meet you out front."

Oakley rounded up the other kids and guided them out of the room. There wasn't much to clean up, but there were instruments to put away and chairs to move. The mindless work helped Pike come back into himself, locking that ugly stuff away again.

Reagan seemed perfectly content to do the work in silence, and Pike found it to be a comfortable quiet. She wasn't like the other young girls who needed to fill all the blank spaces with chatter.

He stacked a few chairs and Reagan grabbed potato chip bags and granola bar wrappers off one of the tables. Then in the quiet, he heard her soft voice as she sang to herself. He pretended not to notice, not wanting to make her feel self-conscious, but the notes were hard to ignore. Her voice was pure and strong even at low volume, like a lonely bird in a still night. He slowed his movements, recognizing the chorus of Christina Aguilera's "Beautiful." A sweet eleven-year-old girl singing about words not bringing her down. His chest tightened.

He stacked another chair and glanced over at her. "You have a pretty voice, Reagan."

She ducked her head and went over to the trashcan to dump the wrappers. "Thanks."

"No, seriously, you've got something special there. You should use it in the group." He didn't add that her voice was heads above the girl they'd chosen to do the solo parts on the first song, but it was the truth.

"I'm not a singer. I just want to play guitar."

"How come?"

She shrugged. "Mom told me playing an instrument is better."

"Who says you can't do both? Braxton, the lead singer in my band, also plays bass."

She toyed with the headphones hanging around her neck as if she were considering blocking out the conversation. "I don't think Mom likes my singing."

He frowned. "I can't imagine that. I think your mom loves everything about you."

She tilted her head, her expression turning thoughtful. "No one loves everything about anyone. That doesn't make sense."

"Why not?"

"Because no one is perfect. Being friends or family is liking someone even when they have stuff about them that you don't like."

"Is that right?" he asked, impressed by the mini-philosopher.

"Yep. Like Mom thinks tattoos are dumb, but she still likes you."

He laughed. "You think so?"

Reagan nodded seriously. "She smiles at you a lot. And she let you come to our house. And she listens to your music all the time now."

Pike's eyebrows rose. Well, then. "That's good to know."

Reagan put her hand on her hip. "So how many albums do you have at your house? Any Patti Smith?"

He pretended to think, tapping his chin with his finger. "Hmm, I may have a slightly scratched copy of *Horses* in the mix."

"Really?" Reagan's blue eyes went big. "We're done cleaning up, right?"

He slid the last chair in place. "Looks done to me."

She gave him a crooked grin, lighting up every part of a face that had been drawn and dark when she'd come in earlier. "Let's jet, Mr. Pike."

He chuckled as she ran toward the door. An eleven-year-old who got giddy about Patti Smith. That was definitely a first.

Seems the Easton girls were full of surprises.

SIXTEEN

Oakley put a blanket over Reagan and got an annoyed huff from Monty for disturbing his position curled up by Rae's side. The dachshund/schnauzer mix had taken an instant liking to Reagan and had followed her around most of the night like her personal mascot. He apparently was not relinquishing the position anytime soon.

Rae nestled her head deeper into the throw pillow but didn't wake up. Oakley smiled. Poor Rae. She'd been all excited about staying up late, but she'd zonked out right after finishing *Willy Wonka & the Chocolate Factory*—a movie she'd chosen from Pike's DVD collection and declared "weird but kind of awesome."

Pike sauntered into the living room, his feet bare and his jeans and T-shirt replaced with blue plaid pajama bottoms and a white undershirt. Something about seeing him in sleep clothes, sauntering through his personal space—a beautiful but not ostentatious modern condo with a killer view of downtown—did something to Oakley.

"She's out?" he asked. "I was about to dish up some ice cream."

"Yeah, she had a long day. Usually she has trouble sleeping anywhere but home or at my brother's, so she must've been wiped." Oakley rolled her neck, the stress of the day trapped there in her muscles.

A loud snore came from the couch—the dog's, not Reagan's. Pike laughed. "Monty must've had a rough one, too. All that chasing birds from window to window."

Oakley's mouth curved. "He's adorable."

"You don't have to be nice. He's obnoxious. But we get each other, so it works."

"Because you're both adorable and obnoxious?"

"Precisely." He nodded toward her kneading hands. "You know it feels way better if you let someone else do that for you."

She lowered her hands from her neck. "I'm good."

"Come on. Sit on the floor, and I'll help you out."

"Pike."

"Don't get all excited. I didn't say there was a happy ending involved." He gave her a playful waggle of his eyebrows. "But do you have any idea how strong a drummer's hands are? And this one's been shattered and rebuilt into a bionic one. There's magic in these here fingers, woman."

"Your humility overwhelms me."

He pointed to the floor. "Sit."

She checked her phone. Her brother would be calling any minute to give her the green light to head his way. What could it hurt? She lowered herself to the floor. "Fine. But hands must stay above collarbone."

"Yes, mistress. I like it when you get bossy."

She rolled her eyes. "Did you really break your hand?"

"No. My mom's boyfriend did it for me." He said it offhanded, like he was announcing he'd fallen off his bike as a kid or something. He climbed over the back of the love seat and settled in the spot behind her, his knees on each side of her head.

"Jesus."

"Yeah, I told you my mother's taste in men sucked. She was like catnip for assholes. But in the end, the injury altered my drumming style, which gave me a unique technique and made me stand out. So screw him."

"That's awful." Her stomach wrenched at the cruelty. A child's hand—shattered. She wasn't naive enough to think those things didn't happen. She'd seen her fair share of stuff working at Bluebonnet, but her heart broke for that young version of Pike nonetheless.

He put his hands on her shoulders. "I survived, mama. Don't stress. And it gifted me with excellent massaging ability. You don't realize how lucky you're about to get. Just sit back and behold the greatness."

She could tell he was deflecting, changing the subject. She let him. She had a feeling he hadn't meant to share that much.

"I will do my best to behold." But she didn't have to try hard. The minute his hands squeezed her shoulders, she groaned aloud.

"Damn, woman, you're like stone." He ran his thumbs over her knotted muscles, sending hurts-so-good sensations through her. "You sure you're not moonlighting as a linebacker?"

"You know what I'm moonlighting as." She closed her eyes. "And that feels amazing."

"Don't say that in that sexy voice," he warned, leaning close to her ear. "Makes me think about other ways to get you to say those words. Because it would be amazing. So. Amazing."

"Pike, you promised," she said, but there wasn't much oomph behind it. His massaging fingers were too good, making it hard to muster up any annoyance. The simple indulgence of being touched by a man intent on making her feel good was pleasure in and of itself, making her acutely aware of how little physical contact she had with anyone outside of Reagan these days.

He traced his thumbs along her spine to the nape of her neck, making small, wondrous circles along the way. "I know, but I think we have an issue that needs to be discussed."

She let her head loll forward. "What's that?"

"After what happened in the parking lot today, I think we both need to admit that the phone calls aren't working for us."

"Mmm," she said, losing herself in the bliss of loosening muscles. "Yes. We need to stop doing that."

"Agreed. Wholeheartedly."

She lifted her head, a little surprised at his emphatic agreement. After the kiss, she'd been planning to tell him that they had to quit messing around, that it was getting too intense, but she hadn't expected him to be the one to bring it up first. "Well . . . good, then. We're on the same page."

His fingertips made their way into her hair, kneading her scalp with near-orgasmic results. "Yep. We definitely need to do this in person."

She straightened and whirled around, his fingers knotting in her hair for a second. She pulled free. "What?"

He sat back, his expression frank. "That's not what you were going to suggest?"

"No. You know it wasn't."

He shrugged. "Look, I'm a believer in the get-something-out-of-your-system method of dealing with cravings. People fail on diets because they deny themselves what they really want. But if they had a few bites of the chocolate cake they want instead of sucking on sugar-free candies as a replacement, they wouldn't fall off the wagon so easily."

"What does that have to do with anything?"

He leaned forward, cupping her jaw, and ran his thumb over her lips, a feather-light touch that sent swirls of smoky need curling through her. "Don't you see? The phone calls are our sugar-free candy." His thumb paused at the plump part of her bottom lip and his gaze moved there. "I always knew it wasn't enough for me. But after that kiss, I know it's not enough for you either. You want me."

She felt the urge to pull the warm tip of his thumb into her mouth, to taste the salt of his skin. But she turned her face away from his touch, trying to find her voice. "I told you why we can't."

"But you can't stop thinking about it, right?" His voice was a hypnotic song in the quiet of the condo—beckoning, tempting, a juicy apple dangling at the edge of her fingertips. "What it would be like? How it would feel? I know I can't get it off my mind." He captured a lock of her hair and wrapped it around his finger then let the hair unfurl slowly from it. "My fist has gotten quite a work-out over you, Ms. Easton."

Her eyes were locked on his hand, that strong, talented hand that had just released her hair. And she couldn't block the images from coming. Pike in the shower, head tilted back, fist wrapped around his cock, soap sliding over his inked skin as he stroked himself.

"I—" Her lips parted as words failed her, arousal washing over her like a rising tide.

He tucked the lock of hair he'd played with behind her ear, his gaze holding hers. "I can't be the kind of guy you're looking for. I'm not going to bullshit you and say that I am. But I also know that we're driving each other to distraction and there's one easy way to fix it."

She closed her eyes, her head automatically moving in a *no* motion.

He brushed his lips along her jaw, his breath hot on her neck. "Let me have one night, Oakley. One night and I can give you what I can't over the phone." He pressed a kiss to the spot behind her ear—a barely-there touch that lit her aflame. "Let's eat the cake, baby."

A very pointed ache settled between her thighs, and she inhaled a ragged breath. How was she supposed to think with him so close? With the scent of him filling her head.

He nuzzled her neck. "We'll do it right. I'll take you out, get us a private table at Barcelona, maybe go dancing at that new club downtown, then I'll show you what I've been wanting to do to you since that first time we talked."

She swallowed hard, trying to quell the instant reaction his nearness and words were giving her. But she couldn't block out the images his invitation incited. One night. Pike naked and braced above her, glistening with sweat as he pumped inside her. Pike laid out on twisted sheets as she explored all the places her eyes hadn't been privy to. Hers for the night. An indulgence to fill the near obsessive craving she'd developed for him. A purging.

Was it really such a terrible idea?

Her biggest fear about sex with him was that she'd develop feelings for him, but if she kept up this game of talk-but-don't-touch much longer, she'd be in trouble anyway. The effect he had on her was potent and dangerously all-consuming. The dating profile she'd set up in defense had gone untouched. Every time someone tried to chat with her, she couldn't help but compare them to Pike. Since when had he become her measuring stick?

So maybe the best thing would be to take away the temptation.

Have the forbidden thing and move on. Grab that chocolate cake by the handfuls and lick it from her fingers. She was a big girl. She could handle it. Pike couldn't hurt her, not if she didn't give him the power to. This was sex. Primal. Basic. Physical.

A need they could meet for each other. Simple as that.

She raised her head, meeting his eyes. "Okay."

His gaze darkened, black eating up the green-gold. "Yeah?"

Just the look had her ready to drag him into the bedroom right now. If not for Reagan on the other side of the room, she might have done just that. "Next Saturday night Rae's going camping overnight with my brother's family. I'll have the night to myself."

"Perfect."

She sat back a little, trying to catch her breath and regain some use of her senses. "But nix the wine-and-dine date."

His pierced brow arched.

"I appreciate the offer, but I don't want or need the rock-star treatment. I'm already a sure thing."

He frowned. "That doesn't mean I don't want to give you a nice night."

"I know. It's just—" She sighed, trying to put her feelings into words. "I'm not one of those women you need to impress with VIP tables and five-star dinners. I don't want the image, Pike. I just want you and a bed and maybe a little adventure."

Something flickered over his expression, something unpleasant, but he covered it quickly. "Adventure?"

She gave him a half-smile and met his eyes. "I talk a big game on the phone, but I'm pretty damn vanilla in real life. I like that you've pushed my boundaries."

He considered her for a moment then nodded. "How about this? I'll take you to The Ranch, that resort I belong to. We'll have as much privacy as we want. But we'll also have all kinds of things at our fingertips if you want to seek out some adventure."

The kink resort. Exciting. Terrifying. She licked her lips. "All right."

Pike's hand wrapped around her neck and drew her closer, his thumb mapping the hollow of her throat and his position over her making her feel small. "Then Saturday, you're mine."

The words held both promise and warning in them, making her heart beat faster. But before she could respond, her phone beeped and broke the spell.

Pike released her and sat back. "Your brother?"

She grabbed her phone and checked the screen. "Yeah. His dinner party's over. I better get going."

"Or you could stay."

She sat on her calves. "You know I can't."

"You and Reagan can take my bed. I'll take the couch. You shouldn't disturb her if you don't have to."

She glanced over at her sleeping daughter. The snoring was now two-fold between her and Monty. Carrying her downstairs and putting her in the car would wake her up. And she was more than a little cranky when awakened in the middle of the night.

"I hate to take your bed."

He smirked. "You're always welcome in my bed, mama. Even if I'm not going to be in it with you tonight."

She eyed him for a long moment, tiredness and practicality eventually winning out, and then typed out a message to her brother.

Oakley: Going 2 stay at Pike's.

Devon: What???

Oakley: Totally PG, Rae sleeping, don't want 2 wake her

A few seconds passed before her brother responded again.

Devon: Use condoms.

Oakley: Dev!!!

Devon: ←Responsible big brother

She laughed and rolled her eyes.

Pike smiled. "What? Your brother headed over with a shotgun?"

"No. He told me to make sure I use protection."

"I like this brother."

"I think he likes you, too. You know, in *that* way."

Pike grinned, unrepentant. "Ah, good taste then, too. Is he hot?"

She shoved his leg, relieved that the consuming tension from a few moments before was dispelled. She could breathe again. They'd made a decision. They could handle it. "Oh, I see. You don't care the gender as long as the person provides proper adoration?"

He chuckled. "You haven't Googled me and learned all about my steamy gay affairs?"

She blinked. "There've been steamy gay affairs?"

He glanced toward Reagan's sleeping form and cocked a thumb toward the kitchen. "Ice cream. Then I'll answer any sordid question you have."

"Good plan." She knew Rae slept like the dead once she hit the snoring stage but better not to risk it. And really, she didn't care if Pike was bi, but she was damn curious now.

When she was perched on a stool in the kitchen with a bowl of fudge ice cream in front of her a few minute later, Pike hopped up to sit on the counter across from her. She lifted her brow in silent question.

He shrugged. "I've tried almost everything to be honest."

"So, guys?"

He swallowed a bite of his ice cream. "No, not in the way you're thinking. My best friend, Foster, and I used to live together, and there were rumors out there for a while that we were secretly in a relationship. Why else would two men who could afford their own places many times over choose to be roommates?" He shook his head. "Neither of us bothered to dispel the rumors because— well, fuck them. Being gay shouldn't be a scandal. But even though we weren't together like that, there was a relationship of sorts. We were single and kinky and shared women more often than not."

Oakley tried to school her face into an impassive expression. "Oh?"

"Yeah, so to answer your question. Have I been naked in bed with a guy? Yes. Have I had sex with one? No. Not my deal."

She took a second to absorb all of that and to get the images out of her head. "So is that why y'all lived together? The threesome thing?"

"Nah. That was just a side benefit. Foster and I became friends when we were in junior high. I met him when one of my mom's boyfriends was doing work on Foster's family mansion and brought me along to help. It was a weird match. Richie Rich hanging out with the punkass kid from the rough neighborhood. But we both had crap home situations. His parents were never around and mine was best avoided. So we clicked and ended up being each other's family in a lot of ways, taking care of each other like brothers." He smiled, a wistful touch to it. "And we take that bond seriously.

"When I got home from my first tour, I was a fucking mess. I'd found out my brother had been killed in a car accident, and my recreational substance use had turned into the dangerous kind. Dumb, grieving kid meets endless supply of drugs, booze, and women. It wasn't pretty." He gave her an uneasy look like he wasn't sure he wanted to talk about this stuff. "Foster saw how strung out I'd gotten, so he dragged me to his place and set me straight. I stayed for a few years after that because I didn't trust myself to be alone and left to my own devices."

Her stomach dipped. She'd seen addiction and the ugliness of it when she'd been in the business. One of the other girls in Pop Luck had gotten hooked on heroin after one little sample at a party. Insidious stuff. Last Oakley had heard, Collette was on her fourth stint in rehab. "And now?"

"I'm good. I got lucky and managed not to get hooked on anything except the chaos. Took a while to purge myself of that. But now I'm older. Smarter." He nodded toward the living room. "Plus, Monty keeps me in line."

She smirked. "I bet he does."

He scooped another bite of ice cream and waggled his eyebrows. "So now that I've told you my sordid *Behind the Music* interview, what about you? Any girl-on-girl episodes in the life of Oakley Easton? Scandalous sexcapades?"

He was obviously teasing, but her lungs cinched anyway.

"Whoa, what's that look for?" he asked, his smile dropping. "Some chick break your heart or something?"

"No, nothing like that." She tapped her spoon on the side of her bowl. *Shut up, Oakley. Just make up something and shut the fuck up.* But her pep talk did no good. The words fell out of her anyway. "I kissed a girl a few times. But it was . . . for show."

He tilted his head. "To impress a guy?"

Yes. Just say yes.

"Sort of." Fuck. She stirred her ice cream into a soupy mess, fighting with herself on how much to tell him. Her past was something she never discussed, but annoyingly, Pike's honesty about his own background and the open, nonjudgmental expression on his face were hard to lie to. He was like some damn truth serum. "I was on stage. It was a publicity stunt."

His spoon paused halfway to his mouth. "A publicity—on stage?"

She gave him a grim smile. In for a penny. "Remember that thing you said about not telling other people's secrets? Does that still hold true?"

His forehead creased. "Of course."

"Would you believe me if I told you that once upon a time, I was doing exactly what you do? Touring, performing, living that life."

Pike set his bowl aside, his focus completely on her. "What the hell are you talking about?"

"Ever heard of a girl group called Pop Luck?"

His lips parted, his eyes widening. The expression would've been comical—GIF worthy—if not for the pit the whole conversation was causing in her stomach.

"Imagine me many years younger with blue pigtails and a schoolgirl skirt. I used the name Krissy Crow."

A few long, tortuous seconds passed. Then it was as if the sun had dawned on his face.

"Jesus fucking Christ, I *knew* I'd heard your voice before!" He slid off the counter. "I had that CD. I used to have the hots for the one with the pink hair."

"Brianna," Oakley supplied, smirking. "You and the rest of the male population."

"Shit, sorry. That was the wrong thing to say. But—God, I'm trying to remember what you looked like."

She lifted a shoulder. "Easy to miss me. My voice sounded too old to sing lead in any of the teen pop songs, and I got tall and awkward fast so I stayed mostly in the background."

Pike still looked stunned. Then he snapped his fingers and pointed at her. "Wait—that song about broken butterflies."

" 'Wings.' "

"Yes, that one. The bridge was you, wasn't it?"

She glanced down. "Yeah. Brianna sang that part in the video, so everyone assumed it was her."

"But it was you. I can hear it now. Your voice was sick on that part—throaty and edgy. It was my favorite song of the record."

His praise and the fact that he remembered the one song they'd actually given her a lead vocal on pleased her more than it should. "Thanks."

His exuberant expression at remembering faltered a bit. "But the group had a few big hits. What happened? I mean—"

"Why am I living in suburbia, working two jobs to make ends meet?"

"I didn't mean it like—"

"I was kicked out when I got pregnant." That wasn't the total truth. She'd been told to go home and get an abortion then to come back. "That kind of behavior was breach of contract because it would mess with the image. We were supposed to be young and sexy and available. They replaced me. I didn't own rights to anything—crap contract that favored the guy who put the group together. So I moved to Texas with my brother, had Reagan, and started a new life."

Pike raked a hand through his hair and sagged against the counter. "Wow. That's—why didn't you tell me before now?"

She rubbed her lips together. "I don't want people to know. I— Rae's father is out of the picture, and I need to keep it that way. I don't want any press or any of the shit that comes along with being a has-been. Those years were some of the worst of my life. It's a chapter I've happily closed."

"Does Reagan know?"

She shook her head. "No. I'll tell her one day. She'll romanticize it if I tell her now. I tried hard early on to lead her in any direction but music because of it, but she found her way to it anyway."

The corners of his mouth dipped down. "Is that why you don't like her to sing?"

"What?"

"This afternoon she was singing while we were cleaning up. She has a gorgeous voice, Oakley. But she said you don't like her to use it."

Her chest squeezed. "God, is that what she thinks?"

"Seems so."

She sighed. "I don't want her to think that. It's just—I was that kid with the outstanding voice. It got me all kinds of attention growing up. Then it ruined everything. I'm terrified she's going to want to follow in my footsteps. It's an ugly, soul-sucking business. My baby doesn't need to be exposed to any of that."

Pike braced his hands on the counter in front of her and nodded. "I totally get that. But even I can see how much she loves music. I know that no one would've been able to talk me out of it once I got the bug. And no one should've. What kind of life do we have if we can't chase our passion?"

She pushed away her bowl, the conversation making her lose her appetite. "You can take a different path and be happy. Just because you're passionate or good at something doesn't mean it has to be your destiny. I managed to give it up and not look back."

His eyes held hers, evaluating. "Have you? You don't crave that high of being on stage and creating music? I mean, I don't know what I'd do if I wasn't making music. You were just able to drop it all?"

She traced a line in the granite countertop with her fingertip, his words prodding deep. Did she miss it? She rarely let her mind go fully there. When she'd gotten pregnant, she'd shut that door without looking back. It had hurt too much to think about *what-ifs* because that would mean she was regretting Reagan—and she never regretted having her daughter. The circumstances, yes, but not her baby girl. Rae was her world. And God knows where Oakley would've ended up if she'd gotten rid of the pregnancy and stayed with the group. The rest of the girls hadn't fared very well. But making music . . .

"I don't miss the stage. Honestly, I would've been happier singing on a stool in a coffee shop, playing my guitar. The joy I got was in the song creation—the writing. I loved that process."

"Based on what I heard at your house that night you sang to Reagan, you're good at it, too," Pike said, no bullshit in his tone. "Do you still write?"

She sniffed. "Only if writing lyrics on napkins and the back of take-out menus counts. When I'm stressed, that's how my thoughts come out—in poetry, lyrics."

"Totally counts. Some of the best songs out there were probably scribbled first on a bar napkin." He lifted his palm, where she could see minute print along the fleshy mound beneath his thumb. "I'm partial to the writing-on-my-hand method when I get inspiration."

She laughed and grabbed his hand, turning it so she could read the slightly smudged words. *Bread. Beer. Cheese.* "This is your grocery list."

He grinned. "It's a multipurpose notepad."

She lowered his hand but didn't let go of it.

He curled his fingers around hers. "So what's it going to take for me to hear some of those songs you've written?"

"Not gonna happen."

"You know," he said, undeterred. "There's this great guy who has a studio. He's very good-looking and wildly talented. He'd probably be willing to cut you a deal to make a few demos."

She gave him a small smile and shook her head. "I appreciate that. Really. But I have no interest in resurrecting my singing career."

He rubbed his thumb over her knuckles. "What about trying a new one as a songwriter?"

"Pike . . ."

"No, I'm serious. You could put together a few demos, try to sell the songs to a publisher. It's always a long shot, but if the rest of your stuff is anything like the song I heard, you have a solid chance. Even the songs we're working on at Bluebonnet are strong, and I know they're based on melodies you originally came up with."

She blew out a breath, the offer tempting in that way going on a trip to the moon was—fantastical but impossible. "I appreciate the offer, but I'm past the point of having time to chase a pipe dream. I've already got two jobs. I don't need another—especially one that may never put food on the table."

He put his hands back on the counter and eyed her. "Come on, Oakley, that's bullshit and you know it. You're writing the songs anyway. Laying down a couple of tracks wouldn't take long. What could it hurt to try?"

There was no censure in his voice, but his earnestness was prodding at things she didn't want poked, stirring up hope that she'd long put to rest. She had to remember that it was easy for someone with a pile of cash in the bank to spout off about chasing your passions and dreams, but Pike didn't live in the real world. She did.

She slid off the stool and walked around the counter. He turned to face her, and she put her hands on his shoulders, meeting his eyes. "Pike, I'm willing to go away for a night with you. I'm looking forward to that and I like working with you at Bluebonnet. But this—my life, what I do with it, how I handle my daughter—is not your territory. So, back off."

His expression fell then darkened, but he didn't say anything.

She pushed up on her toes and pressed a kiss to his cheek. "It's late. I'm getting Rae and going to bed. Thank you for letting us stay."

He didn't kiss her back and he didn't touch her. His open expression had closed fully—a tightly sealed door. "Good night, Oakley."

She walked out of the kitchen and didn't look back. She didn't want him to see the tears that filled her eyes.

Stupid tears.

Ones that shouldn't be wasted on long-dead dreams.

She got Reagan settled into the big bed in Pike's room without waking her, curled up in sheets that smelled like him, and let the old, familiar grief drift away.

She'd gotten good at saying good-bye to that dreaming girl.

That girl had no place in her life anymore.

SEVENTEEN

Pike watched Braxton's face change from intense and serious to a wide smile as the phone conversation went on. Pike and the guys had been rehearsing in the studio for a few hours, bouncing around a few new song ideas, but all had come to a halt when Harlan, their manager, had called.

The interruption was welcome. Pike had been having trouble concentrating all afternoon. Tonight was the night with Oakley, and he had no idea how to feel about it. Part of him couldn't wait to get her out to The Ranch so he could finally touch her and not have to worry about who saw. But he couldn't help being bothered by the line she'd drawn between them the other night. First, she'd turned down his offer to take her on a date. Then she'd shut him down when he'd tried to talk to her about pursuing her song writing. So it was okay for them to fuck but not to discuss real life stuff.

He should've been relieved. The woman wasn't looking for more than a hot time in bed. That was how relationships usually worked for him. But hearing it from Oakley had stung. She'd said she didn't want the rock-star treatment, but she'd lied. Maybe she didn't want to have a flashy date, but she wanted the one-night stand. She wanted to treat this like some anonymous hookup after a show.

That sucked.

He'd been tempted to call her out on it. But he'd told her upfront that all he required was honesty and she'd given it to him. It was his problem if he didn't like how the truth sounded. He needed to accept it. The only other option was to walk away. And screw that. He wasn't that noble. No way was he turning down the opportunity to be with Oakley tonight. If what she wanted was a hot night in bed, he was more than game for it. She wanted an escape, a wild time—fine. She picked the right guy for it. He'd bring his A-game.

Pike peered toward the far side of the room, watching Brax's lips move on the other side of the soundproof glass. He couldn't decipher the words but based on Brax's expression, it was positive news. Geoff set his guitar aside and waggled his brows at Pike. "Think Harlan landed us a spot on a tour?"

Pike got up from his drum throne, spinning one of his sticks in his fingers, nervous energy coursing through him. "Could be. There are a lot of summer tours being put together. Now would be the time."

"Might snag a festival. The Manic Five just got a spot at Edge Fest."

"That'd be good, but we need more than onetime gigs if we want to get any traction. Otherwise, we're going to end up on another club tour when the next album drops."

The thought of that made Pike's head hurt. He loved performing, and club shows used to be fun—the energy, the intimacy of the crowd. But it was a grind, too, because in order to make any money, you had to book three times the number of shows you'd have on a big tour. He'd paid those dues and didn't relish going that route again. Plus, he had bad memories from the club tours. The endless travel on the bus, the long nights of partying, the *Groundhog Day* life. He'd nearly killed himself on that first tour, trying every illegal substance he could get his hands on and drinking his way down from the highs. He'd come back a fucking disaster.

Foster had kicked Pike's ass when he'd returned so strung out. Pike hadn't jonesed for the drugs so much but he'd craved the constant companionship and partying. The mayhem. He spent the first few weeks back home, fighting off panic attacks anytime he was alone in the quiet and going out to clubs to get lost in the crowd. He didn't realize then that he'd never learned how to be alone. He'd jumped from big family to living with Foster to touring. When Foster had found him one night, blitzed out on too many antianxiety meds and in danger of overdosing, Foster had dragged him back to his place. That's when they'd become roommates again. Foster knew Pike had no family looking out for him and took on that role instead.

Of course, that meant Foster had turned into a complete pain in the ass for a while afterward—making Pike get up and go to the gym, setting him up with a therapist, forcing him to work on new songs. Looking back, he knew now that Foster had just put that dominant side of his to use—taking control when Pike was unmoored. But it'd been ten kinds of annoying at the time. He probably would've bailed if Foster hadn't eventually introduced him to The Ranch. That's when things had started to settle inside of him. There was a place to push the edge without having to party or get high every night. There was a place he could be himself.

And since then, he'd managed to quell that need for chaos. The fact that he now lived alone—and enjoyed it—was testament to that. So even though he wanted nothing more than to see his band reach the next level, he dreaded life on tour. Yes, he missed performing. It was his first love. But he liked coming home every night to his own place and to Monty. He liked working with emerging artists at the studio. Hell, he was even enjoying the charity project. If they landed a tour, he'd have to drop all of that for months or even a year, depending on how big of a tour it was.

But he wanted the band to succeed. He wanted arenas. He wanted his mother and that fucker Red to see he was more than a piece of trash to be discarded. He wanted to build that mansion on the hill and then not invite them to dinner. The desire was ugly, but he couldn't help that it was there. That fire had gotten him this far, and it still hadn't gone out.

So he'd do whatever it took. He just prayed that Darkfall got an opening spot on a bigger tour instead of the club circuit. Fewer shows, more people, more exposure. Maximum impact.

Braxton tucked his phone into his pocket and headed back into the studio space. He was grinning wide.

"So?" Geoff asked.

"We got a spot at Voodoo Fest in New Orleans in October. Early time slot, but lots of big names on the same ticket."

Pike tucked his hands in his back pockets and smiled. "Sweet."

"And," Brax said in his wait-there's-more voice, "we're one of three opening bands being considered for Wanderlust's summer tour."

"Wanderlust?" Geoff asked, impressed. "Shit, they're blowing up right now. That could be huge."

Pike's smile went wider. "Well, hot damn. That fucker Lex Logan might pull through. Guess lead singers aren't as unreliable as I thought."

Braxton looked over at him, ignoring the dig. "You have something to do with this?"

Pike shrugged. "I called Lex a few months ago. Even though his band's a big deal now, Lex hasn't forgotten that we all started in the same place, played some of the same shows. He likes our stuff and knows we hit a rough patch that was out of our control. I didn't want any pity, but I wanted to let him know that if they were ever looking to fill a slot to look us up."

"Fucking A," Geoff said, standing and stretching his neck. "It'd be perfect. Their music is sick. And can you imagine the prime level of ass they must get backstage at their shows?"

Pike sniffed. "Glad to see it's all about the music for you, man."

Braxton rocked forward on his toes, looking almost giddy. "Harlan said there are two other bands they're looking at, so it's not a done deal. But he's going to send them a few videos of our recent performances so they can see for sure that my voice is back."

"Awesome. We've been killing it lately. They watch those videos, we've got this," Geoff said.

Pike smirked. "You don't even know who the other two bands are."

He shrugged and pushed his shaggy dark hair behind his ears. "Doesn't matter. We're fucking Darkfall!"

Pike laughed and bumped fists with the other two guys. "Damn straight."

Brax checked the time on his phone. "Hey, we should go out and celebrate. A girl I met the other night is having a big birthday bash at a club downtown. She said the whole band was invited. She's a model, so I bet her friends will be hot, too."

"Sweet. I'm in," Geoff said without missing a beat.

Pike frowned. Geoff was a few months out of rehab, and as much as Pike didn't want to be *that* guy, he also didn't want another setback for Geoff or the band. "Dude, that doesn't sound like a great idea."

Geoff snorted. "Don't worry, Dad. I'm not going to fuck things up this time. I've become friends with club soda and lime. I'm going for the girls not the booze."

Braxton clapped Geoff on the shoulder. "Yeah, and if I catch you with a drink, I'm punching you square in the nuts and dragging you to your sponsor. None of us are going to screw this up. Not when we're this close again."

"Noted." Geoff looked to Pike. "So, you game?"

"Nope." Pike twirled his drumstick between his fingers. "I've got plans."

"With your dog?" Braxton asked.

Pike tossed the stick at him. "Fuck you. And no, I've got a date."

Braxton knocked the stick away before it hit him. "That brunette I saw you with backstage the other night?"

"Yeah. She's meeting me here in a little while."

"Nice. Well, let's keep working out that bridge then. You should look as badass as possible when she walks in."

"Good idea. You need all the help you can get," Geoff agreed solemnly. "I heard that actress you took home a while back shut you down, that you couldn't close the deal. There were tweets. Lots of tweets."

Pike gave a derisive sniff and shoved past the two of them to get to his drum kit. "Fuck you both."

"You might have to. Might be your only options left."

"Just get back to work, jerkoffs."

Braxton grabbed his bass and blew a kiss Pike's way. "And a one, two . . ."

Oakley sat behind the control board in the studio, unnoticed for the last few minutes, as she watched the guys of Darkfall jam. The music was coming through the speakers, filling the small space and wrapping around her. She hadn't heard the song before but liked it already. It was slower than most of their other tracks, with a heavy, thudding beat, and the steady bass was working to soothe her jumbled nerves.

She'd been looking forward to tonight since the moment Pike had suggested it, but now that she was here with an overnight bag packed in the car, she wondered if she was out of her depth. Pike looked like a beast behind his drums, arms rippling, eyes closed, drumsticks twirling. He emanated this raw sexuality that both turned her on and intimidated the hell out of her. How was she going to match up with that?

She'd been with exactly two guys in her life. The first—Reagan's dad—had been a fucked-up situation from the start. He'd been Pop Luck's manager and twelve years older than her. At sixteen, she'd thought she must be special for an older, sophisticated guy like Liam to take an interest in her. She'd never considered how wrong it'd been for him to be putting moves on a minor.

And convincing her into his bed had been like a series of well-calculated chess moves—him playing on her insecurity and inexperience and teaching her "what guys liked." He'd been handsome and charismatic, so she'd fallen into the trap easily. He started her slow, like he was just helping out the poor sheltered girl from Oklahoma get used to her new life in California. Then the compliments and attention had started, and she'd fallen under the spell. *You're the most beautiful girl I've ever met. I can show you how to kiss. I can take care of you better than guys your age ever could.* Until finally, they'd fallen into a physical relationship and he'd told her he loved her.

It still made her stomach turn to think of it. She'd bought it all. He'd been wildly jealous and had kept male fans away from her. He'd made her promise not to tell her brother because Devon would break them up. She'd seen it as protective. He'd dictated where she went, what she wore, how she acted. She'd thought he was keeping her safe. And in a way, she'd liked that he seemed to care that much. There'd been some comfort in that role.

Then she got pregnant. And the real Liam had shown his face. She wasn't his one and only. It wasn't love. She was disposable. And replaceable.

Her other encounter had been the guy she'd tried to date when Reagan was younger. The sex hadn't been anything extraordinary, but he had seemed to enjoy himself, and it'd been nice enough for her—well, until he'd dumped her over her night job.

But she had a feeling with Pike, she was entering a whole different arena. The phone sex alone had been way hotter with him than any in-person encounters she'd ever had. Plus, he belonged to a sex resort for God's sake. What did that even mean?

She put her hand to her forehead. Hell, she was having freaking stage fright over sex. This was ridiculous. It's not like sex was some mystical process. Pike was a guy. She talked to guys every night on the phone and handled herself just fine. What turned them on was pretty easy to decipher.

The music stopped and she looked up. Pike was smiling her way through the window. "Looks like it's quitting time, boys."

She shook her head then searched for the button on the panel that would let her talk to them. The control board was different from the ones she'd seen back when she was in the business, and there were way more computer screens going.

"The orange button," Pike said.

She found it and pressed. "Don't quit on account of me. I'm fine listening."

But the guys were getting up from their spots anyway and putting their instruments away. Pike came through the doorway first, sauntering in like sex appeal personified in his heather gray V-neck T-shirt and black jeans. He grabbed her around the waist and gave her a quick kiss. "Hey, mama. Glad to see you didn't chicken out."

"Thought about it," she said, breathless at his nearness and open affection.

He smiled. "But you didn't. That's all that counts."

He let her go when the other guys strolled in, and he made introductions. Geoff and Braxton shook her hand, and though they were subtle about it, they both clearly gave her a once-over. She fought the insecurity that tried to well up at their perusal. She doubted she looked anything like the type Pike and these guys usually hooked up with. But she wasn't going to feel bad about not being twenty-three and stick thin. This was who she was. If Pike wasn't into it, he wouldn't have asked her here tonight.

Pike nodded at her. "Oakley came to the festival to see us play."

"Y'all were great," she said. "I couldn't get the songs out of my head for days."

"Yeah, and if I remember right, you thought Geoff was ridiculously hot on stage," Pike offered, mischief in his eyes.

Her neck went hot when Geoff grinned wide, but she wasn't going to let Pike get the last word. "I did say that. You free tonight, Geoff?"

Braxton let out a bark of a laugh and Geoff winked. "Totally. Let's get out of here, sweetheart."

Pike's mouth flattened, and he put a hand on Geoff's chest when he tried to step toward Oakley. Pike sent her a look. "Well played, Ms. Easton."

She smirked.

"On that note," Braxton said. "We're out of here. I don't want your girl to realize she's getting stuck with the ugliest member of the band."

Oakley laughed. Truth was, all three of them were pretty damn gorgeous—the other two dark and scruffy to Pike's platinum— Braxton lean and long and Geoff broad-shouldered and built. But neither of them drew her eye like the blond, tattooed drummer who was currently giving her a you're-all-mine look.

The guys exchanged their good-byes and headed out, leaving Pike and Oakley facing off in the control room. He gave her skirt-and-flowy-blouse combo a slow, rolling once-over. She crossed her arms, feeling self-conscious.

He reached out and unfurled her arms. "Please, don't hinder the view. I've never seen you with a low-cut top. I may need a minute here to ogle. Christ."

She laughed. "This old thing? That I just bought yesterday."

"That shirt is a gift. I thought the guys' eyes were going to roll out of their heads when they saw you."

"I just thought it was the shock of seeing real boobs," she teased.

He narrowed his eyes and stepped into a space. "Mmm, they are a rarity these days." He lifted his hand and brushed the back of it oh-so-gently over the curve of her breast, bringing her nipple to an instant point. "I might have to dedicate part of tonight reacquainting myself with such a luxury."

Shivers traced over her skin from where he'd touched her. "I won't oppose this plan."

He wrapped his arm around her waist and drew her against his body. The hard heat of him made her tongue press to the roof of her mouth. She'd told him early on that she'd gone numb to sex. And she had been. But Lord, her libido was making up for lost time now. She couldn't even pretend to be unaffected. "So, ready to get going?"

He brushed his mouth over hers—a tease. "Yes. After you pay the price of admission."

She let her hands slide along his waist, the warmth of his skin bleeding through the thin material of his shirt. "And what might that be?"

He touched his forehead to hers. "You're going to sing for me."

"What? No, Pike," she said, stepping out of his embrace.

He cocked his head toward the studio. "Come on, mama. No one's here to listen but me. I want to hear you."

She shook her head, her stomach tightening. "I don't sing those songs. They're too . . . personal."

The songs she'd written after her years in Pop Luck were hers, her private thoughts and scars. Singing them was like standing naked in front of someone. And though she was willing to physically bare herself in front of Pike, she wasn't ready to do it emotionally.

"Songs aren't worth shit unless they're personal. And if we're going to go to The Ranch, I need to know you trust me." He closed the space she'd put between them and took her face in his hands. "Play for me, Oakley. I'll even back you up with drums so you don't have to feel like I'm watching. I want to hear you."

She closed her eyes, the gentle plea in his voice hitting her right in the chest. "You're hard to say no to."

"So don't."

She swallowed hard. What could it hurt? It was just an old song sung in an empty studio. It didn't have to be a big deal. She lifted her head. "Fine. One song."

The smile that broke over his face was genuine and breath stealing. "Thank you."

Without another word, he led her to a stool in the studio and set her up with a microphone and an acoustic guitar. She took the instrument and stilled. "Holy shit, is this a Martin?"

"Yep, D-42. Geoff insisted we have one on hand even though we don't record a lot of acoustic stuff."

She stroked the neck of the instrument with more than a bit of envy, taking in the ebony fingerboards, the gold tuning gears, the gorgeous inlays. She loved her beat-up Yamaha. She'd had it long enough for it to feel like a family member, but she couldn't help but covet the gleaming, high-end instrument. "She's beautiful."

"You look beautiful with it."

That brought her back to earth, the anxiety rushing back. She was about to sing. For Pike.

Pike must've noticed the fear on her face because he dimmed the overhead light, making everything feel more private, intimate. He took the spot behind his drums and gave her a nod. "You start whenever you're ready, and I'll find the beat and jump in."

She took a deep breath and closed her eyes. Her fingers hovered over the frets, trembling. But after another few seconds, she mustered up enough nerve to pluck out the opening notes of "Dandelion." The instrument was unfamiliar in her hands and took some getting used to, so she let the intro go long, not adding words yet and letting Pike get a feel for it as well. In a matter of seconds, he was tapping out a beat in time with her—subtle but rich.

The old lyrics came to her like they'd been burned into her skin, and she began to sing. The first few lines were shaky but as soon as she hit the chorus, her mind went to that place where it was only notes filling her head and fingers on strings and words pouring out of her. Pike's drumbeats pulsed through her, deepening the original song, and the emotion behind the lyrics welled in her. She angled her head back and let her voice off the leash, allowing the song to sweep her away. She'd written the song after she'd left the group and Liam. But the song wasn't about him. It was about the dream for her life exploding around her, her wishes for her future slipping away like dandelion seeds on the wind.

"Blow it away, blow me away. Watch us fade away."

When she hit the final lines of the last verse, she didn't even notice that Pike had stopped playing until she felt his lips on the back of her neck. Her fingers strummed and her voice sailed, a deep, cleansing ache in her chest. She didn't stop until she'd come to the end of the song, but her body became liquid with each soft caress of his mouth.

When the studio was silent again, Pike slipped the guitar strap from around her neck and set the instrument aside, then his arms wrapped around her from behind, anchoring her. "Baby, I don't even know what to say. I felt that all the way down to my gut. You're . . . spectacular. So soulful."

She looked down, her heart pounding behind her ribs. "Thanks."

He pressed his nose to the nape of her neck, inhaling her. "Sing me something else."

"What?"

"Anything. I don't care what it is as long as it's in your voice." He pushed her hair all to one side and nipped at her ear. "Sing for me, Oakley."

Twining threads of need and adrenaline snaked down her body and wrapped around her mind, holding her spellbound. She didn't know what song to pick so she sang the first thing that came into her head—"Wicked Game." It'd been a song she'd slowed down and revamped when Pop Luck was planning on doing a cover album. But she'd left before that album had come out and her song had been cut.

So as Pike kissed down her neck, she sang about the world being on fire and how no one could save her but him. But when he stepped around her, all hungry eyes and dark looks, and opened the top buttons on her blouse, she couldn't hear the words anymore. Her voice switched to autopilot as her body went up in flames.

"Don't stop," he whispered before kissing along her sternum and palming her breast.

She continued to sing but with him sliding his thumb over the lace of her bra and nuzzling the curve of her breast, she kept going off key. Then he lowered to his knees.

She gasped into the microphone when he inched up her skirt and slipped off her panties, but she didn't stop singing. The singing was anchoring her, weaving the spell around them, holding them hostage. She held on to the side of the stool and closed her eyes as he spread her knees apart. All of it seemed to be happening in a dream—the low lights, the song in her throat, the big, warm hands on her thighs. It'd been years since she'd been touched by anyone but herself, so she was half-convinced the man kneeling in front of her was pure fantasy. She'd wake up soon and he'd vanish like a specter.

But Pike wasn't going anywhere. Her stomach muscles quivered as he moved closer, his breath balmy on her damp skin and anticipation a living, pulsing thing inside of her. He kissed her inner thigh and her voice caught on a word, but she swallowed past it and kept singing. Kisses trailed higher and higher, and his teeth nipped at the sensitive flesh. As he reached the apex of her thighs, her fingers curled against the wood of the stool and her breath went choppy. His tongue glided along her sex, grazing her clit, and she lost all sense of her place in the song.

"Keep going," he said softly, his words punctuated with teasing licks against her flesh. "I want to hear that voice while I taste you. If you stop, I stop."

Her pussy throbbed, and she whimpered. Fucking whimpered. "God."

"What's the matter?" he asked, drawing the tip of his finger over the lips of her sex, teasing her.

"I sound like one of my callers—panting and whining."

"You sound fucking hot. Don't be ashamed of that." His fingers dipped into her heat and sent frissons of need through her. "Now sing to me while I lick this gorgeous cunt."

Damn. The crude words didn't shock her. She heard them all the time on the phone. But hearing Pike say them only made her desire burn brighter. He wasn't talking to Sasha, he was talking to Oakley—inexperienced Oklahoma girl who'd grown up in a house where saying *hell* outside of Bible study would get you grounded. That girl went molten at the sexy, forbidden words.

She took a shaky breath and started the chorus of the song again—her voice wobbly but back in tune. Pike moved his mouth against her again, and his talented tongue lashed at her most sensitive spots while his fingers curled inside her. She arched on the stool, her arousal going to Spinal Tap eleven. The man's mouth was a weapon of mass destruction—teasing and hot, confident and precise. No matter how advanced sex toys had gotten, none could stand up to this—teeth grazing, lips sucking, and tongue lapping at her like she was ice cream melting in the blazing sun.

Pike sucked her clit between his lips, and she lost her place in the song again, her body shifting all resources to the orgasm that was rushing toward her. But he wasn't cruel enough to stop this time. Instead he hooked her legs over his shoulders and spread her wider, sliding his tongue inside her and letting his nose rock against her clit. Every one of her muscles tightened, all of her senses going on high alert, taking it all in—the scent of her arousal in the air, the sweat gathered on her neck, the erotic sounds of Pike's mouth devouring her. Wet and crude and totally obscene.

She moaned, her eyes squeezing shut and her arms shaking from her stranglehold on the legs of the stool. Then every molecule in her body detonated at once. *Boom!*

She shouted Pike's name, her voice blasting through the quiet of the studio, and rocked her hips against his mouth with jerky, involuntarily movements as she rode the wave of her release.

Pike didn't let up until she was gasping for air and nearly falling off the stool. He eased back and rocked to his feet, keeping his hands on her waist so she wouldn't fall, then he was gathering her to him.

She pressed her face into his shoulder, breathing hard and trembling from the aftershocks. "Jesus Christ."

"Amen and hallelujah," he said, a smile in his voice.

"That was—"

"My pleasure," he finished.

She shifted against him, and his very prominent erection brushed against her belly. Her stomach fluttered. Normally, after an orgasm, she was set for a while, but the ache inside her pulsed anew at the thought of feeling Pike inside her. She tucked her hand between their bodies and curled her hand around the outline of his cock.

He groaned.

"Your turn now," she said, giving him a stroke through the denim.

He leaned back and smiled down at her. "This isn't about tit for tat. I can wait until we get to The Ranch. I just couldn't resist you once you started to sing. I had to taste you. Had to hear you come."

Oh, was that how he thought this was going to work? She pulled off her unbuttoned blouse and unhooked the clasp of her bra, channeling that place inside her where the confident Sasha and the real Oakley collided. She'd been bold on the phone with him. She wouldn't chicken out in person. She let her bra fall to the floor. "No, Pike, this can definitely be about tits. And there's no way I'm going to make it through the hour drive without having you inside me first."

He groaned as he coasted his hands up her rib cage and cupped her breasts. "Fuck, baby. This isn't how I planned to have you the first time, but you're killing me."

She sank into the touch, the feel of his callused thumbs grazing over her nipples. "So stop planning."

He growled under his breath and put his hands beneath her thighs to wrap her legs around his hips. "Quick and dirty it is then."

"Yes. That." Her heartbeat picked up speed and she looped her arms around his neck.

He carried her a few strides and pressed her back against the window that separated the control room from the recording area. The wide ledge of the window took a little of her weight, but he kept an arm around her while he flicked the button on his jeans and opened the fly.

Taut belly appeared behind the zipper, no underwear between Pike and his jeans, and Oakley's fingers itched to touch. Pike dipped his hand in his pants and freed his erection. He swiped a bead of moisture from the top and drew it down his length, giving himself a slow stroke. "This what you want?"

Another flood of arousal hit her. Fuck, he was beautiful. That snug T-shirt hugging his abs, his arm muscles flexing beneath his tattoos, and that long, thick cock promising erotic oblivion. She could watch him all night. "This view is so much better than what I imagined on the phone."

He smiled and let his gaze travel over her naked torso and spread legs, her bunched up skirt providing no modesty. "Same here, beautiful. This is going to feel a lot better than our hands did, too."

He moved closer and drew the tip of his cock along her outer lips, teasing her and sending a bolt of need straight to her core. She wanted to reach out and guide him inside her, fill the desperate ache, feel that hot silken skin against hers with nothing between them. But she couldn't afford to be reckless. And she hoped to God he was prepared because her supplies were in her bag in the car. She licked her lips. "Please tell me you have a condom."

He grinned, reached into his back pocket, and handed her his wallet. "Outside compartment."

"Thank God," she said on an expelled breath. She fumbled with the wallet for a second but managed to get the condom out and rip it open. She tossed the wallet and wrapper to the floor. Pike was still holding her up against the wall with one of his arms, so she reached out to roll it onto him. She'd never actually done that for a guy before, but he put his hand over hers and helped her smooth it down his length. The feel of his erection in her hands and his fingers pressing over hers was surprisingly sensual. She wanted to explore more, to get on her knees and touch and taste him. But there'd be time for that later. Right now, she needed him inside her.

She leaned back against the glass and hooked her arms around his neck again. "Fuck me, Pike."

His lips curled wide at that. "Dirty words rolling out of your sweet mouth are becoming an addiction for me."

"That's why I make the big bucks."

He ran his fingers over her wetness, making her writhe. "Yeah, but when you say them to me, I know you mean it." He took his slick fingers and swiped them over her mouth. "And that makes all the difference."

He took her mouth in a heated kiss, sucking and licking her arousal from her lips, and she moaned into the connection. He stroked his tongue against hers and shifted forward, spreading her thighs wider and pushing the head of his cock against her entrance.

That desperate ache surged in her and her arms tightened around his neck. Then he was easing inside her, stretching her and hijacking her breath. Her body fought to accommodate him.

He groaned into the kiss. "Fuck, baby, you feel so good around me, but I don't want to hurt you. Try to relax and let me in."

She pressed her forehead to his, her blood pumping in her ears. "You won't hurt me. I'm okay. It's just been a long time since I've done this with another human being."

He lifted his head to look at her, his eyes searching. "How long?"

"At least five years."

If he was shocked, he hid it well. He gave her a devil's smile. "Well, we need to fucking fix that right this minute. Breathe for me and let's make up for lost time."

She took a long, expansive breath, focusing on relaxing her

muscles. She'd used the toy so she knew this wasn't about any-thing but nerves. But when she met Pike's eyes, saw the inferno burning there, the need, her body gave up the fight. She pulled him closer and he entered her.

He made a grinding noise of pleasure as he sank deep, and a whole body quiver went through her. She tilted her head back, that full, decadent feeling overtaking her. "God, yes."

Pike's fingers dug into her hips as if he was taking a moment to regain his composure, and then he started to pump into her. The sounds he made were better than any he'd given her on the phone. Low and masculine noises that said everything words couldn't. And his eyes . . . they never left hers. His look said, *Pay attention. I'm the one making you feel like this. I'm the one who's going to drive you out of your fucking mind.*

"You're so goddamned sexy," he murmured. "Can't get you out of my head."

The words hit her in a soft spot, one she didn't want prodded. "Better fuck me out of your system then."

Her response was blunt, but she needed to remind both of them why they were here. This was their one night together. They were eating cake. That's all this could be.

His eyes flared, but he set his jaw and picked up speed. The window rattled behind her with every hard thrust, and he dipped one of his hands between them to stroke her.

Soon, any errant thoughts or worries slipped from her mind, and all she could do was hold on and feel the pleasure of it all. He knew exactly how to angle himself, how to rub inside her in a way that let her feel every bit of him, every ridge and swell.

Sweat beaded on his brow. "Come for me, Oakley. Let me see how much you love being fucked against a wall, how bad you needed my cock."

The command zipped through her, pressing her hot buttons and assuring her that they were on the same page. This was sweaty, dirty sex. Period. End of sentence.

And they were going to make it the hottest and dirtiest they could.

One night.
One night.
One night.

The mantra floated through her head until her orgasm whipped through her like a maelstrom and emptied her brain.

Pike called her name and rammed into her with abandon as she gasped her way through her release. The window rattled louder, his shirt knotted in her fists, and she lost all sense of place, nearly sliding off the windowsill. But he didn't let her fall and soon he was flying alongside her, his neck muscles straining with the force of his orgasm. The ecstasy plain on his face.

Beautiful, wicked perfection. She could drown in it.

She nearly did. Her muscles went loose and her body lax as he took the last bit of his pleasure in a few short, hard thrusts. But he never let her go.

When they'd both given everything they had, he gathered her to him and they slid to the floor. She sat astride his lap, his cock still buried inside her, and they kissed until they couldn't breathe.

So this was what sex was supposed to be like.

She'd told Pike it'd been five years.

Now she realized that had been a lie.

It'd been a lifetime.

This—she'd never had.

EIGHTEEN

Pike parked Oakley's car in the garage behind the studio before helping her to get into his truck. She hadn't said much since they'd put their clothes back to rights and locked up the studio, but as she settled into the seat, she seemed at ease, everything back in place.

Good thing she was put back together because he certainly wasn't. He'd only planned to convince her to sing, to show him some piece of herself, some trust, so that he could feel good about taking her to a place like The Ranch. Then when he'd approached her while she was singing, he'd only meant to take the edge off, indulge his desire to finally touch her. But the plan had gone off the rails almost immediately. The way she'd responded, the physical abandon, the sound of her singing while he tasted her. She'd been so ready for him. Wet and hot and bold. Fuck. He hadn't been able to hold back.

But he'd also gotten the sense that she was working hard to make it all about sex, blocking out anything else that might creep in. She was white-knuckling this. When he'd told her he hadn't been able to stop thinking about her, she'd flinched like he'd pinched her. The girl was scared.

But he couldn't bring himself to do the cool, detached thing with her even though he could tell that was what she wanted—no dates, no emotions, just sex. Usually, he was fine with those boundaries. Sex was sex. As long as everyone had a good time and was safe about it—game on. But for some reason, he didn't want to be that guy with Oakley. She deserved better than that from him and from herself. Hell, she'd gone five years without sleeping with someone. If all she wanted was sex, she could've gotten that long ago without much effort. The woman would have no problem finding an interested guy at any bar or club in town.

Instead she'd picked him to break her dry spell. Why? He wasn't sure, but he guessed that on some level she trusted him, liked *him*. Not Pike the drummer, Pike the man. And that was kindling something inside him, something he'd heard his friends talk about but had never experienced himself. Oakley had high walls that fortressed her in her protected world. Even in the throes of passion, she'd kept him outside those gates. He understood why, but the fact that he didn't have a key to get in was poking at him, rousing an unfamiliar need.

He didn't want to only be inside her body; he wanted to be in her mind as well. He wanted to climb over those walls and see what she was like when she let go of it all. He wanted to take her to The Ranch and strip her in every sense of the word, to earn her trust completely.

Fucking hell. He wanted to dominate her.

The urge was so goddamned foreign that he had to stop himself from texting Foster to ask what the hell he was supposed to do with that. Sure, he'd watched his best friend dominate women. And Pike had been a member of The Ranch for a while, so he'd seen everything and had taken the training classes. He'd even used much of the equipment and topped a few women, but never with real intent. Always playfully. A game.

But that wasn't what he craved with Oakley. He wanted to evoke real emotion from her, for her to give him control, to be vulnerable with him. To show him what hid behind that all-is-well facade. To look to him to keep her safe while her walls were down.

He wanted to be more than a random hookup. He needed her to feel something. Shit, *he* wanted to feel something.

And he had no idea what the fuck to do about that. She'd agreed to one night. She was here for the sex. If he brought her to The

Ranch and asked her to play submissive, she probably would. And he could pull off the role of cool, unfazed dominant. That was the fantasy newbie women often came to The Ranch with. Mr. Mystery Man who would use them and bring them pleasure, all the while never revealing anything to them beyond his stoic facade. Pike could do it. But it'd be the game, a fun night, not anything real. It'd allow Oakley to cast him in a role. Her fortress would stay firmly in place.

That held no appeal. Plus, it wasn't who he was. This wasn't about flogging and restraints. Though that could be fun, that's not what was making his blood pump harder. He wanted that barrier-bashing shit that he'd seen between Foster and Cela. That rawness. The stuff that required real trust.

But he had no idea how to get that from Oakley. Or if he even deserved to have it.

He climbed into the driver's seat and glanced over at his date, taking in the flush of her cheeks and the way her hair had curled around her temples from the exertion of their interlude. The only signs that he'd at least gotten to her a little. But the staid smile she sent him said her armor was firmly in place.

That wouldn't do. Not at all. No polite stranger smiles for him. He pushed the ignition button, an idea popping into his head. "Ready for the best dinner of your life?"

Her smile faltered. "I told you I didn't need the fancy night on the town."

He smirked. "We both need to eat. And I promise this will be the opposite of fancy. Ashamed to be seen with me in public?"

She scoffed. "Shut up. You know that's not it."

"Good. Because I'm not putting out again until I'm fed. I have standards, woman. Don't make me feel cheap."

She snorted like it was no big thing, but she shifted in her seat, clearly uncomfortable that he was doing anything date-like. Well, she'd just have to deal with it. Because he figured the only way to get rid of her stranger smile was to stop being a stranger to her.

If he wanted her to give him a peek past her gates, to trust him, maybe he needed to give her a look past his.

Oakley peered out the window as they drove toward the outskirts of Dallas. Rain had fallen earlier, and the streetlights reflected off the pavement, throwing orange light in random patterns. Her thoughts were as scattered as the reflections. She smoothed her skirt and then tucked her hands beneath her thighs so she wouldn't fidget.

After their tryst in the studio, every part of her felt sensitive and electric. The sex had been amazing—everything she could want from an adventurous night out with a smoking-hot guy. She'd loved that Pike hadn't held back with her or treated her like she was someone's mom. He'd been down and dirty and unapologetic about it. He'd made her feel like a woman. Basking in that had been downright heady.

But now that she'd drifted down from the high and Pike had insisted on taking her out to eat, her worries had reappeared, nipping at her like an annoying school of fish.

She'd *sang* for him. At first, it had been stilted and awkward but then she'd fallen into it. Her voice had soared and along with it, her spirit. Singing hadn't felt like that in so long. Sure, she played for Reagan and the rest of the kids sometimes, but she never let herself get swept away by songs anymore, that transcendent feeling of becoming part of the music. Tonight she had. Because Pike had been listening. And it had felt like the song mattered to someone besides her. He'd wanted to hear it.

She blew out a breath. "Thank you for earlier."

He glanced over at her with a hint of a smile. "For which part? Orgasm number one or number two? No, that's a stupid question. Number one was strong, but I thought I really nailed it on that second one."

She laughed, some of the tension she'd been holding in her posture releasing. "Oh, you definitely nailed it. But I meant for pushing me to sing the song. It felt good to be behind a microphone again and really punch the gas."

His expression warmed, and he switched his focus back to the road. "I'm the one who should thank you. You're a fantastic musician. Plus, I totally recorded your song and will soon be selling it for millions of dollars."

She sniffed. "Yeah, right."

"No, really. It recorded."

She turned her body toward him. "Hold up. *What?*"

He chuckled. "Don't freak out. The mics were still live when we started playing, but I won't be sharing the recording with anyone."

She blinked. "The mics were—oh my God. So . . ."

"Yeah. There will be quite the X-rated soundtrack recorded afterward." He sent her a don't-kill-me look. "But don't worry. The file is in my private account and protected. I only wanted to record your song for you. I thought you might like to have it or maybe share it with Reagan. I didn't plan for everything else that happened afterward. I'll edit the other stuff out when I get back to town."

"And delete the rest."

He shrugged. "Or save it for my own listening pleasure. Or sell it to TMZ for a Where Are They Now."

Her mouth fell open, and she shoved his shoulder, trying not to laugh. "Extortionist."

He grinned as he turned off onto a side road. "Totally. I'm holding the tape hostage tonight until you have lots and lots of hot, kinky sex with me."

"Lucky for both of us, I accept these terms."

"Excellent. But that will have to wait because right now, we must eat tamales."

Oakley looked up as gravel crunched beneath the tires of the truck. Over the last few minutes, they'd driven to a part of Dallas that she wasn't familiar with. But as promised, it was definitely the opposite of fancy. All the storefronts appeared in need of a nip and tuck, the roofs sagging and the pastel paint peeling. But the restaurant they'd just pulled in front of seemed to stand proud among the rest of the block. The building was a bold robin's-egg blue and *Flora's* was painted in bright yellow on the side.

Pike cut the ignition and climbed out of the truck. When he

came around and opened her door, he gave a sweep of his arm Vanna White style. "Welcome to my 'hood."

She lifted an eyebrow as he helped her out. "Pike, I've seen your neighborhood, Mr. Uptown."

"You saw where I live now. This is where I'm from. Well, this is the nice part. This was uptown for me when I was a kid." He cocked his thumb to the left. "The rental house I grew up in is about five blocks that way."

She peered in the direction he was pointing, then back to him. "Do you still have family out here?"

He tucked his hands in his pockets, his smile sagging and his posture stiffening. "I don't think so."

"You don't know?"

"It's complicated."

"Sorry. I wasn't trying to pry." He'd already told her he had a shitty childhood. It'd been a stupid, automatic small-talk question. "You don't have to say any more."

"No, it's fine. It's just an ugly answer." He rolled his shoulders, seeming to shake himself free of something. "The night Red, my mom's boyfriend, broke my hand, they kicked me out."

"Wait. They kicked *you* out? You were the one who got hurt."

He wet his lips and looked into the distance. "I pulled a gun on the guy when he hurt me that night. Kind of lost it. My mom walked in on that part. She wasn't going to risk anything that messed up her situation with Red since he was paying the bills. I was a risk. So I left and haven't seen either of them since. But they were living in a nice part of Lewisville by that time. They may still be out there."

"God, Pike. How old were you?"

"Seventeen."

She frowned. "I'm so sorry."

"It's okay. My life got much better after I was out of that hell-hole. Once upon a time, my mother had her good points. I got my love of music from her. But she had damaging tastes in men and a codependent personality. Bad combination. I just wish I could've taken my younger brother and sisters with me when I left."

"Do you have relationships with them now?"

His expression darkened. "No. My brother died in a car accident a few years ago. And the girls were too young when I left for them to really have memories of me, so all they know is what my mom and Red have told them. I've tried to reach out, but they're not interested in knowing me."

Simple words, but she could see how deeply they affected him. Happy-go-lucky Pike had retreated for a moment, exposing a stark sadness in those green-gold eyes. She reached out and pulled his hand from his pocket, then she laced her fingers with his. "I'm sorry."

The smiled returned, though a little strained. "Hey, how'd we get into this heavy conversation? I brought you here for killer tamales, not to unload my Jerry Springer family drama on you. Come on. Let's eat."

She gave his hand a squeeze and let him lead her inside.

Mariachi music and the smell of roasted chiles filled the air as Pike held the door open for her. She inhaled the decadent scent. "Okay, now I'm officially starving."

"Right? It's like they lace the air with crack," he said, his tone much lighter now that they were inside, the somber conversation abandoned in the wet streets outside.

She grabbed a paper menu from the slot by the door. "So what's good here?"

Pike's lips parted, but before he could answer, another voice sounded from her right. "Paco!"

Pike turned, a grin breaking over his face, and guided Oakley toward the main counter where a young guy with dark eyes and a devil-may-care smile was waving them over. Pike let go of her hand briefly to step around the counter and give the guy a one-armed, thump-the-back man hug. "Emilio, *qué onda?*"

"*Qué onda?*" Emilio repeated. "You ask me what's up? I live. I work. The news report isn't all that exciting. But what about you? We haven't seen you in months. Mamá was worried."

Pike slipped back to the other side of the counter and took

Oakley's hand again. "I know. Things have been crazy. But I couldn't go another day without Mama Flo's food in my belly."

"She'll be happy to hear it." Emilio stuck his head through the doorway to the kitchen and yelled something in Spanish.

Oakley leaned over to Pike. "Do you know what he's saying?"

Pike smirked. "He's telling his mother that her ungrateful boy, Paco, is here and that he's looking too skinny and needs her help. And that's he brought a pretty girl with him."

"Paco? Her boy?"

He chuckled. "The Rivera family lived on my block when I was a kid. I was friends with Emilio's older brother and every time I went over to his place, his mom would tell me I was too thin and would feed me. She didn't speak English and my Spanish was spotty at the time, but I got the gist, especially with her pinching my arms and then heaping beans and rice on my plate." His face took on a pensive look. "She figured out my home situation was screwed up and took me in like a stray even though they barely had anything themselves. A neglected, underfed kid was a cardinal sin in her book. I knew a good thing when I saw it, so I hung around as much as I could until my mom hooked up with Red and moved us to the suburbs. But I was around enough that Emilio started calling me Paco. He said if I was going to be part of the family, I couldn't have a ridiculous *gringo* name like Pike."

Oakley smiled, the affection in Pike's tone making her love this woman and her family already. "She sounds kind of amazing."

"She's a force to be reckoned with for sure. And now that she knows I've brought a girl, I'll give her three, two . . ."

As if on cue, a petite older lady with silver-threaded black hair burst through the doorway from the kitchen. She wiped her hands on her apron and made a beeline for Pike, wagging her finger. Her words were in rapid-fire Spanish, but Oakley got the sense they were firm ones. The smile didn't leave Pike's face, though. He let her have her say. Then she smacked his arm with her dish towel and hugged him.

He hugged her back, speaking fluent Spanish back to her—tone apologetic and soothing, but amused at the same time. He sent Oakley a wink over the woman's head.

"Mama Flo," Pike said, extracting from the hug. "This is my friend Oakley."

When Flora turned around, her perturbed expression had been replaced by a beatific one. She flipped her dish towel over her shoulder and took Oakley's hands in her callused, warm ones. "Flora Rivera. Nice to meet you. I'm so happy my Paco finally thinks my food is good enough to bring a woman here."

Oakley lifted her eyebrow at Pike.

Pike put his hands on Flora's shoulders. "Flo, I haven't brought a girl by yet because none have been worthy of your food. You're my best-kept secret in Dallas. I can't just share you with anyone."

Though Pike's tone was light, the fact that he'd never brought another girl here to meet people who were clearly important to him registered with Oakley. She didn't know whether to be pleased or worried.

She squeezed the woman's hands. "I'm glad I get to be the lucky one to eat your cooking."

She nodded. "I'll make you both a plate."

"Can we have the number three?" Pike asked. "You know it's my favorite."

She let go of Oakley's hands and waved Pike off. "You get what I serve you. No plain tamale plate for a date. I made my best mole for today's special." She poked his side. "And you getting too skinny again."

Emilio shook his head. "He's busy being important, Mamá."

"*Importante*. Bah." She sniffed, letting them all know that this was no excuse.

Pike lifted his palms to her. "We're in your capable hands. Fatten me up."

She left them with the look of a woman on a mission, and Emilio told them to grab whatever table they wanted and he'd bring over a couple of beers. Oakley and Pike settled at a table by the front window that gave them a view of the rain-slicked streets, and Emilio dropped off two Negra Modelos, a basket of fresh tortilla chips, and two kinds of salsa—one red, one green, which he identified as "kinda hot" and "the one that made Paco cry."

Pike flipped Emilio the bird and then went straight for the dangerous green one. "This stuff is amazing. But they served it to me when I was a kid, and I scooped it on a chip like it was Pace Picante. I thought I was going to die in the middle of their kitchen. I ended up eating ice cream out of the container by the handful to cool my tongue. It's taken years to build up a tolerance to the heat."

Oakley laughed. "I like spicy, but now you've scared me."

"My advice is dip, don't scoop." He grabbed a chip and dunked the edge into the green salsa then handed it to her. "And be brave. That's our theme for the night anyway, right?"

"Is it?" She took the chip and eyed it warily.

"Of course." He held up one finger, counting off. "One, you sang in front of me. Two, you agreed to spend the night with me." He leaned forward, wicked smirk touching his lips. "And three, I fucked you against the wall of my studio. I'd say you've been pretty brave."

She glanced toward the counter to make sure no one was close enough to hear that last part. The few patrons in the place were seated on the other side of the restaurant, and Emilio had his back to them. She turned back to Pike. "Maybe. But how is it *our* theme? I'm guessing your night hasn't been all that out of the ordinary."

She popped the chip in her mouth and her tongue lit afire. She coughed but managed not to spit out the chip. Pike's lips curled upward, and he pushed her beer closer to her. "Just chew, it gets better."

Her eyes were trying to water, but she continued chewing, and the heat gave way to the flavors of lime, cilantro, and tomatillos. She swallowed the bite and took a swig of beer, then another, waiting for the flames to cool. "Wow. That is impressively hot. But tasty."

"Like me."

She snort-laughed at that one. "I need Flora's dish towel so I can smack you with it."

"Sounds kinky." He leaned back in his chair, his gaze analyzing her. "But back to what you said about being daring, why would you think tonight is par for the course for me?"

She focused on the bowl of chips and shrugged. "You're living the wild, single life every day. That's all I'm saying."

He reached out and tapped the top of her hand, making her look up. Lines appeared around his mouth. "No, you're saying I fuck random girls in random places, so you're just another one on the list, right? Another night."

She winced. "I didn't mean—"

"You did."

She sighed. "Fine. Maybe I did. I'm not saying I have a problem with it."

His jaw twitched. "Let's get something straight, Oakley. If I wanted a random fuck tonight, I would've had one—at the party the guys invited me to, at The Ranch if I went solo, at any club downtown. But that's not what I wanted. I wanted to be with *you*. You think I haven't taken risks tonight?"

She stuck another chip in her mouth, fighting the images of Pike going out and picking up some other girl.

"So that's a yes." He let out a frustrated breath. "Look, you can believe what you want, but I've never done anything with a woman at my studio. I've never brought a date here. And I definitely don't talk about the shit that happened when I was a kid to anyone. Even the record company has a fake, generic bio for me just so I can avoid talking about it altogether. So stop thinking you're just some piece of ass, all right? I'd like to think we're friends and that I'm treating you as such—regardless of whether or not we're sleeping together."

She frowned, his words stinging. Had she been treating him like that? Like she was just a fill-in lay on his calendar? Maybe. Yes. No matter how much she liked Pike, she kept reminding herself that he was who he was. Screwing women was sport to a guy like him. Keeping that at the front of her mind helped her keep her head straight about all this. But the hurt hovering in his eyes hit home. "I'm sorry. You're right. I didn't mean to imply that. I'm glad we're . . . friends."

He grabbed his beer and took a sip, brooding.

"And the childhood stuff . . . I know you didn't have to share that with me."

He shrugged. "I should've never said anything. Nothing ruins a fun date faster than some poor-me sob story. It just slipped out. That was my bad."

"No. I'm glad you did," she said, reaching out for his hand. "I . . . I like getting to know you. Even the ugly stuff. We all have it. I mean, in a lot of ways, I can relate."

He looked up, clearly still annoyed but curiosity sparking in those green-gold depths.

She let go of his hand and took a long sip of her beer, trying to find some bravery so she could be open with him like he had been with her. "I didn't struggle in the same way you did. In a lot of ways, my childhood was ideal. We didn't have a lot of money, but my parents owned a farm, so we had space and I had a lot of brothers and sisters to play with. We were homeschooled so there was a lot of flexibility."

Pike nodded but didn't say anything. He was probably afraid to spook her off talking.

She picked up her butter knife, turning and turning it to give her hands something to do, the memories of her childhood rearing up and punching her in the chest. Sometimes she forgot how good things had been in those early years when her parents were heroic and infallible in her eyes. "Things were happy for a long time. But my parents had strict views on religion and life. They supported my singing career when I originally got signed to a Christian group at fifteen, but when that didn't work out and I landed the Pop Luck gig, things became strained. They let me continue with it for a while because the family could use the money. But when I got pregnant, they told me I couldn't come back home unless I married the father or placed the baby for adoption. I wasn't willing to do either, and they cut me off. Just like that. Like we hadn't had this whole life of being a family together. I moved in with my brother permanently after that."

He grimaced. "Wow."

"Yeah, they're good people in many ways. I never wanted for

love when I was a kid. But they're neck deep in very old, strict beliefs that they won't ever shake. They eventually forgave me for the premarital sex and the fact that I didn't marry the father, because they wanted to see their grandchild. But Devon was cut out completely once he came out to them."

Pike shook his head. "Sad."

"I probably would've never talked to them again if not for Rae. I don't want her to not know her grandparents, aunts, and uncles, so I make an effort to go up to the farm on holidays. But it's tense and awkward. And I spend the whole time pissed because they don't let Devon come. I mean, I can't imagine Rae doing anything—outside of murdering someone—that would make me cut her out of my life. How does a parent do that?"

Pike took another swig of his beer, eyes stormy. "It's fucked up. But it happens all the time. Your parents chose their beliefs over you and your brother. My mom chose her boyfriend and a nice house over her son." He grabbed another chip. "It's one reason why I don't want to have kids. I don't trust that I'd be one of the good ones."

She tilted her head. "Why would you say that?"

Emilio served their plates, interrupting the conversation. He slid two steaming hot dishes in front of them. "*Pollo en Mole Poblano*, Mamá's specialty."

Oakley leaned over her plate and inhaled the fragrant steam, picking up some savory combination of chiles and cinnamon. Dark sauce covered bone-in chicken, and fried plantains and rice completed the dish. "This smells like hours in the kitchen."

Emilio smiled proudly. "Days. Mamá's sauce takes days to build up all that flavor."

"Well, tell her I can't wait to try it," she said.

Emilio made sure they didn't need anything else and then left them alone. Pike tucked into his meal as if she hadn't asked him something right before the food had arrived.

She lifted a brow at him. "Not going to answer my question?"

He chewed his bite of chicken and gave a half-shrug. "I'd suck as a parent. My band is my life. I travel all the time. I'm a selfish fucker. And no one needs me as a role model, believe me."

"Right. Someone who came from nothing and made his dream come true. You're a totally lame role model."

His lips smoothed into a straight line. "That life's just not for me."

"Yeah, well, I would've said the same thing back in the day. Music was my only true love. But sometimes life has other plans."

She cut into her chicken and began to eat, lost in thought. When she was a teenager, she'd balked at the idea of growing up and doing the mom thing. Her mother's whole life was her kids—taking care of them, feeding everyone, cleaning the house, home-schooling. She'd never seen the woman have an identity outside of that. Her mom didn't seem to mind. She was one of those people whose life mission was to be a mother. But Oakley had never imagined that to be her own future. She still felt woefully unequipped most of the time with Reagan. She'd never be Super Mom. She'd never have that sparkly clean sink.

"Must've been terrifying to find out you were pregnant that young. I had a scare with a girl right after I finished high school and I fucking panicked. I knew then that I wasn't meant for parenthood because all I wanted to do was run."

"You wouldn't have been the first guy to do it."

"Is that what happened with Reagan's dad?"

The delicious food turned bitter in her mouth. She stabbed a plantain with her fork and looked up. "How about we talk about this place you're taking me to?"

He smiled, chagrined. "We're ruining the date again, aren't we? God, you'd think we could just shut the fuck up and talk about all the sordid things I'm going to do to you tonight."

"We suck."

"Yes, there will be that. Lots of sucking."

She laughed and threw him an are-you-twelve? look. "Seriously, what am I getting into? I read those papers I had to sign. The contracts. Seems like there's lots of . . . things to try."

He leaned onto his elbows, considering her. "We'll have everything at our fingertips. It just depends on how brave you're feeling. Technically, you have to go in as my submissive. That's how I'm getting you in without you having a membership. And that will also make it clear that no other members should approach you for play."

The word *submissive* sent a little shiver through her. "But it's just a technicality because you're not a dominant, right?"

He lifted his beer, his eyes never leaving hers while he sipped. "I don't pick a label. Doesn't mean I can't take control."

She licked her lips. Pike was a playful guy. She'd fully enjoyed their give and take in the studio. But she couldn't deny that the thought of him taking the reins intrigued her. The night he'd given her instructions on the phone had been intensely erotic, knowing she was doing his bidding, that she could just let go and follow the steps without all the analyzing that usually accompanied her every move.

"Do you like doing that? Being in charge?" she asked carefully.

He leaned forward and covered the hand she had on the table with his. "In life? Yes. In the bedroom? I'm usually more flexible. But I have to tell you." He flipped her hand over, exposing her palm, and ran a finger down the center of it. "It's all I've been able to think about since I first touched you tonight."

The words crawled up her spine, wrapping around her body and washing over her breasts and neck, making her aware of every one of her erogenous zones in one swift rush. She took a deep breath. "Why is that?"

His finger continued to caress her hand, but his eyes held her gaze. "Because you're so put together, so self-contained. I got glimpses of what's behind all of that on the phone, but tonight I saw what you're like when you let go, when you give in to your desires. Thinking of you putting your pleasure completely in my hands, trusting me to take care of you tonight?" He shifted. "I'll get hard as fucking stone just thinking about it."

The flush in her upper body ventured south—the *pulse, pulse, pulse* of awareness settling between her thighs—but she tried to keep her voice even. "I can see the appeal in that."

"Yeah?"

"I never would've thought I'd say that. My ex—Rae's father—he was into having all the control."

Pike frowned. "Was he a dom?"

"No, he was an asshole," she said flatly. "I was too young. I let him control things in my life, including the bedroom. But it wasn't BDSM. I think he got off on my innocence, so he played the romantic role, the gentle lover, the man who would show me the way."

Lines appeared around Pike's mouth. "How old was he?"

"Twenty-eight. He was my manager."

"Christ, Oakley. He—"

She put her hand up, not wanting to travel too far down that road. "I'm only telling you because I know you can probably understand better than most since you had that relationship with your teacher. His control was laced in sweet words and dressed up with romantic notions. It turns my stomach to think about how easily he manipulated me. So I have no interest in ever handing over that kind of control again. But the dominance/submission stuff . . . well, that seems a lot more honest and upfront. You've got me thinking pretty hard about it lately."

He stared at her for a moment longer, appearing to debate whether he was going to prod more of her story out of her, but eventually he let the intense scrutiny ease and he softened his expression. "So I'm wooing you over to the dark side?"

She smiled. "Maybe. I don't know if the formal stuff would be my thing. If you made me call you *sir*, I'd probably want to punch you in the throat."

He laughed. "No worries. *Supreme Master of the Universe* would work just fine."

She snorted. "Of course. But now I'm starting to understand how the power-exchange thing can be exciting when done right. When clients call and want to play the master/slave role-play, I spend most of my time rolling my eyes at their commands. I've never found it sexy until . . ."

"Until what?"

"The night you put all the appointments on my calendar."

A pleased smile spread on his lips. "I've never wanted to give commands like that, but I nearly lost my mind that night wondering if you were following them."

"I did. I liked it. It was nice to shut off the busy part of my brain and just follow the directions. All my adult life, I'm always the one who has to be responsible, make the decisions, handle it all. Listening to you for a little while . . . it was like a vacation. A really sexy vacation."

Fire flared in his eyes, and he held her gaze. "Wanna take another trip then?"

"I don't want to force you into a position you don't want to be in . . ." She paused, considered. "Well, on second thought, that could probably be hot, too."

He chuckled. "Dirty girl."

"Definitely. It's in my job description."

"No." He shook his head. "This has nothing to do with your job. This is you." He laced his fingers with hers. "And I promise you, you're definitely not forcing me into a role I don't want. I want this—more than maybe I ever have. You seem to inspire that side of me. But I'll make you a deal. If you're really interested in exploring both sides, next time I'll be yours to do with what you will. Your personal slave boy."

The offer sent her nerve endings tingling and X-rated pictures flashing through her head, but she frowned. "This is only supposed to be one night, Pike."

He leaned closer, all swagger and sex appeal, and a slow, confident smile curved his lips. "Baby, you're not going to want to walk away after what I do to you."

Her breath left her for a second, and the restaurant seemed to fade around them as their gazes locked. She swallowed hard. "Well, someone's confident."

His eyes creased at the corners. "Gonna find out if I can back it up?"

She didn't break the eye contact. It felt like they were squaring off in a ring, challenge hovering between them. She'd promised herself this was a one-night getaway, but the thought of her and Pike trading power back and forth, pushing each other to new edges—no, she couldn't think about that right now. That kind of temptation was dangerous. "Guess I am. For tonight."

He looked like he may argue the one night point with her again, but then his expression smoothed and he gave a small nod. "Pick a safe word, Oakley. One that you can remember easily."

The command startled her for a second, sent her thoughts scattering, but her body's response was instant. "Why do I need one of those?"

"Because I'm not going to ask your opinion on our activities tonight. This isn't going to be a negotiation. But I also want you to let me know if we're about to cross a line you're not willing to cross."

She could feel her heartbeat in her throat. They were going to do this. She was going to give him the control tonight. If the theme of the night was bravery, she was about to bungee jump off a rocky cliff. She wet her lips and gave him the first word that came to mind. "Oklahoma."

His brow arched.

"It's where I'm from."

"Okay. Use that word if you want anything to stop at any time tonight. But only use it if you truly want to pull the eject cord. You'll enjoy this a lot more if you trust me to take you outside your comfort zone. Understand?"

"Yes."

"And you understand that for the rest of the night, I'm making the decisions? The only control you have is that safe word."

Blood rushed through her ears. "I do."

"Excellent. Now"—he released her hand and slouched back in his chair, legs wide in that cocky man way—"let's see how much you mean that. The restroom is in the back right corner of the restaurant. Go in there and take off your panties."

"What?" She'd heard him, but the knee-jerk reaction was impossible to stop.

He seemed unmoved by the shock in her voice. He pitched himself forward and crooked a finger at her. She leaned in close, their lips a hairsbreadth apart. He kept his voice low. "You heard me just fine. It's a clean, private, one-person bathroom with a lock. Take the panties off, put them in your purse, and then slide your fingers into your pussy until you're good and wet for me. I want you slick and ready. Once you've done that, you can come back out here and finish your dinner."

She blinked. "You're serious."

He pressed a soft kiss to her mouth. "You have five minutes, gorgeous."

Her face had to be red as a tomato. Hopefully, the other patrons in the restaurant would just assume she'd eaten too much green salsa. She'd been down with playing submissive at The Ranch where that kind of thing happened. But here? Now? "Pike, I—"

"Just don't think too hard about it," he said, his tone like a caress and his hand coasting over her knee beneath the table. "Trust that I won't put you in a situation that would compromise your reputation or hurt you. You'll be safe with me. You have my word."

She rubbed her lips together, his promise resonating. She hadn't known Pike for long, but all her instincts told her that he was telling the truth, that he wouldn't do anything to put her at risk, and that his word meant something. She nodded and pushed back from the table. "Okay."

The desire that sparked in his eyes when he saw that she was complying nearly had her stumbling in her heels as she stood. Prickling awareness tracked over her body as his gaze dragged along every inch of her.

"I'll be back in a few minutes," she said, managing to keep her voice steady.

He lifted his hand and wiggled four fingers. "You're down to four minutes. Don't make me wait longer than that. Can't have our food getting cold."

The sexy half-smile he gave her nearly undid her. Despite the shift in his tone, the playfulness she loved about him danced in his eyes. She had a feeling with that smile, he wouldn't have a hard time getting her to do most anything.

He wanted to play.

And she was ready for the game.

NINETEEN

The drive to The Ranch was too fucking long on a good day. On a day with a pantyless Oakley in his car, it was goddamned torture. And of course, a misty fog had rolled in, slowing the drive even more. The subtle scent of Oakley's arousal taunted Pike in the enclosed space, making his cock throb in protest. If it hadn't been Flo's place, he would've followed Oakley into the bathroom, propped her on the sink, and fucked her senseless. But he had too much respect for Flo to do that there.

Pike curled his fingers around the steering wheel and tried to concentrate on the dark road in front of him, but Oakley's presence was impossible to ignore. After she'd returned from the restroom—two minutes late, he'd noted—she'd had a high flush on her cheeks and a drunk-on-lust look in her eyes. She hadn't said a word about what she had or hadn't done, but he could tell she'd followed his directive. He'd had to adjust his napkin on his lap because he'd gone hard in an instant.

And now, in his periphery, he could see that she kept shifting in her seat and that her nipples were peaked against her blouse. He wanted to pull over to the side of the road and take them in his mouth until she was so desperate she begged for him to be inside her. But they were still a ways from The Ranch and he was trying to be patient.

"You were late coming back from the bathroom," he said, breaking the silence. "Got carried away in there?"

She turned her head and gave him a wouldn't-you-like-to-know smile.

"Don't tease me, mama. Tell me. In vivid detail preferably."

She pressed her lips together, humor in her eyes, and looked toward the road. "You sound like one of my callers."

"You're dodging my question."

She nodded. "A fair assessment."

"How come?"

She glanced down, a self-deprecating smile tugging at her lips. "It's silly, right? I talk sex for a living but when it comes to talking to you about it, I lock up like some awkward virgin. I had to fight it the first few times we talked on the phone. Now, in person, it's coming back."

He appreciated the honesty. "I get it. Everything's easier when it's a role. You talk sex as Sasha. But it's just you here tonight. Same for me. It's easier for me when I'm the drummer from Dark-fall. But the only person you've got in this car with you is James Pike Ryland. So don't feel awkward. We're on even ground."

She looked over at him. "Your name is James?"

"It was my father's name. But my dad walked out when I was five and I started going by Pike since my mom said she couldn't stand to hear his name in the house. I legally changed it when I joined the band to separate myself from my history, but for some reason, James still feels like my real name. It's what my brother called me."

She considered him. "So if I was in here with Pike Ryland, rock star, how would it be different?"

He laughed. "We are *not* going to discuss that. You would hate him."

She turned her body toward him, devious smile beaming. "Oh, no. We have to go there now. I think I got a glimpse of him the first time we met."

He rubbed the back of his head. How had he gotten trapped in this corner? "Fuck, all right. I do what's easy. I tell women what they want to hear. Most girls just want to know how hot they are, how great they look in whatever they're wearing. It's much more about them and the conquest of landing the band member than it is about me. I figured that out early on. Then it usually ends up with talk of who I know, where I've been, all that shit that makes me sound like a big deal."

Oakley bit her lip like she was trying hard not to laugh.

"What?" he asked, grinning. "That shit totally works."

"Oh, I have no doubt. I'm sure ten minutes of that and there's no more talking because the girl's head is bobbing in your lap. Frankly, I don't know why you even bother talking. I mean, looking at you is enough. You probably could just unbutton your fly and point."

His mouth kicked up at the corner. "Yeah? Would that have worked on you?"

"That would've gotten you a knee to the balls. And a thank-you for showing me where to aim."

He laughed.

She turned, peering out at the passing mileage signs. "Looking at you is no hardship. You know that. But talking to James Pike Ryland is what got me here. The other guy would've never had a chance."

The gently spoken admission thumped him right in the chest. He focused on the road, trying not to show on his face how the words had affected him. "Thank you, Oakley."

A few quiet seconds passed and then he heard the click of her seat belt. She slid across the bench seat and placed her hand on his thigh, the touch like a brand through the material. He didn't move, didn't look her way.

She dragged her hand higher and grazed his half-hard erection, tentative yet purposeful at the same time. "But if James wants to unzip and point, I may not oppose the suggestion."

He inhaled a slow breath at her touch and her offer, not to mention the sound of his given name on her lips. But he didn't turn to her or unzip his pants. As much as he wanted to know what her mouth would feel like around him—God, did he want to know—he recognized a bid for control when he saw it. He'd learned from Foster that a scared submissive's best tactic at getting a dom off track was playing to his baser needs—offering blow jobs being the top of the list. The conversation had gotten too personal, and she was retreating into the role she knew better. He wouldn't allow it. "Tell me what happened at the restaurant."

Her hand stilled on his thigh.

"I know you're scared to say the words, but you have to know there's no judgment here. You don't have to try to impress me with how you say it or make it like one of your calls. I just want you to tell me in your own words."

She listened, her shoulder rising and falling against his with her deep inhale. "Okay. I'll try."

"Go on, baby. I'm listening."

"I was late coming back to the table because before I got to the restroom, I ran into Emilio in the hallway and we talked for a minute."

That wasn't what Pike had expected. "Oh? About what?"

"He told me that you bought the restaurant for Flora after his dad died. That all she owned before was a food truck and they would've never made it on that income. He said you saved them."

Pike's jaw clenched. Emilio knew better than to share all that. Pike's role in the restaurant was supposed to be completely silent. The kid had probably been trying to help Pike look good to Oakley. "*Flora* saved them. Her cooking and business sense has made that place a success. I just got her the building to do it in. It was the least I could do after all she did for me."

Oakley squeezed his thigh. "It was still a pretty amazing thing to do."

"You're still avoiding telling me what you did, Ms. Easton," he said, peeking over at her. "Don't think I'm above pulling over to a secluded spot and turning you over my knee."

Her eyes blinked with surprise at that. Surprise and interest.

He smiled inwardly.

"Fine." She reached over and dug in her purse. She took his hand and unfurled his palm and placed the silky fabric in it. "First, I went into the restroom and pulled off these."

Pike glanced down at the flimsy red swath of cloth in his hand

and closed his fist around the panties. Fuck. They were still damp. "You were wet before you started."

"I've been like that since minute one tonight," she said, easing the material from his grip so that he could put both hands back on the wheel. "Even without any smooth lines or name-dropping, you seem to have that effect on me. Or maybe I'm just really hard up."

He sniffed. "Thanks. You're great for a guy's ego."

"I doubt yours needs help." Her fingers played along the waistband of his jeans. "By the time I was alone in the bathroom, I was distracted by the conversation with Emilio. So I had to get my head back into the right space."

He put his hand over hers, stopping her movements.

She licked her lips. "Can I touch you, Pike? Please."

At that, he relented. She'd asked and she knew it wasn't going to get her out of telling the story. He released her hand. "Yes, as long as you keep talking."

"Deal." She unhooked the button on his jeans.

He glanced down. Painted fingernails against black jeans, her delicate fingers tugging down his zipper. Fuck, yes.

"So I leaned back against the wall and imagined you were there with me, that you were touching me and trying to keep me quiet so that no one would hear us outside the door." Her fingertips teased the trail of hair below his belly button.

Pike rubbed his thumbs along the steering wheel, trying to keep calm and focused on the road. "You like the idea of that? That we could be discovered?"

She was quiet for a moment, her fingers idly stroking his abdomen, the *scritch-scritch* of her nails against the coarse hair erotic in and of itself. "In the right situation, I think it could be exciting."

He filed that knowledge away. "If I had been there, I would've turned you around, pushed up your skirt, and pressed you against the door with one hand over your mouth to keep you quiet and one between your legs to make you come."

She made a soft, breathy sound and he peered over at her. His eyes flicked down her body over the curves and to the soft material covering her thighs. There'd be nothing beneath that thin layer—just sweet flesh and heat. He reached out and traced the hem of the fabric. "Lift your skirt for me, Oakley."

He could feel her breath catch, her body going still against his side.

He gazed out at the highway, keeping his expression placid. "I want to see you. You're getting your own view. It's only fair I get one, too. Lift up your skirt and spread your knees. It will help me imagine your story better."

Her anxiety was a palpable thing. She was used to having the control. That's what she'd been taking by coming over and touching him. But he needed to remind her of who was in charge tonight. He waited to see if she would retreat now that he'd pressed his bet, but instead, after a few long moments, Oakley lowered her hands to the edge of her skirt and dragged it up her thighs.

It took everything Pike had not to immediately take in the sight, but he kept his eyes forward as if he were completely indifferent. "Now, go on with the story and feel free to touch whatever you'd like."

Oakley paused for a beat, but then after another deep breath, she folded back his fly to free his erection and wrapped the silky fabric of her panties around his cock. The smooth, rich material moved over him like liquid heaven, and he had to fight not to jerk his hips forward. He inhaled a ragged breath through his nose, finding some shred of inner calm.

Only then did Pike give himself permission to look at what Oakley had revealed to him. Goddamn. Her knees weren't parted wide but his angle gave him a view that could kill a man. The creamy, smooth skin of her thighs, the soft black fabric of her skirt bunched up, and the dark curls covering her pussy beckoned him. Not to mention those long, elegant fingers wrapped around his satin-covered cock.

He had to clench his teeth together not to groan. But his dick didn't bother hiding its appreciation. His erection swelled thick in her grip, and he had to steel his way through the flood of desire so he wouldn't wreck the damn vehicle. He cleared his throat. "So what happened next?"

Oakley polished the head of his cock with the soft material, a teasing, torturous stroke. "I imagined you touching me and then I moved my hand between my legs. I was already wet by then and knew I only had a few minutes, so I rubbed my clit. I thought about what we did at the studio, about how you felt inside me, and I fingered myself."

Pike lowered his hand to her thigh, letting it settle against that smooth skin.

"The more turned on I got, the bolder I felt. The nerves went away. So I opened my eyes and watched my reflection in the mirror."

"Fuck, baby. You're killing me." That was a picture. Oakley watching herself as she got off. Legs spread. Fingers buried in that hot little cleft. That would go in the fantasy arsenal next time he needed to jerk off. His fingers dug into her thigh. "Did you come?"

"No, I figured you didn't want me to take it that far. I saved that for you. But I was soaked and aching by the time I got back to the table."

He groaned, unable to hide his reactions anymore. "You did well, mama. Now I'm the one tortured."

She moved the panties downward, cupping his balls with them, then lowered her head and licked the head of his cock with a long, slow glide. The tires hit the rumble strip on the side of the road, sending loud vibrations through the truck, and he jerked the wheel back to center them on the road. She lifted off of him with a soft popping sound and gave him a siren smile.

Oh yeah, that girl had some sadist in her, too, because her pleasure in his discomfort was wickedly obvious. He smirked, knowing two could play at that game. He slid his hand to the apex of her thighs and dragged his fingers over her pussy, slick arousal greeting his fingers. Hell, yes. "You're soaked, baby. You like seeing what you do to me."

She closed her eyes briefly and rolled her lips together as he dipped two fingers inside her and stroked, her wet heat enveloping him. She took a deep breath and answered him. "Now you know what the rest of dinner felt like for me. I barely tasted Flora's meal. All I could think about was climbing across the table and straddling you in your chair."

He grinned, loving that as soon as she got really turned on, her shyness melted away. He had a suspicion that "Sasha" wasn't so much a persona as a secret, bold part of Oakley that she kept on a tight leash. "And what are you thinking about now?"

Her fingers curled around his cock like it was taking everything she had not to climb on top of him. "That straddling you while you're driving would be a road hazard."

He chuckled. "I could pull to the side of the road, but anyone passing by could see."

She didn't say anything to that, but he could feel her clench tight around his fingers. He glanced over at her, curious. Her eyes were still closed but something about her expression confirmed his suspicion.

"You wouldn't mind that, would you? That idea of being heard or seen does it for you." He drew his fingertips over her clit, knowing the touch was too light to get her off but had to be driving her crazy. Just like hers was doing to him.

She wet her lips and her head tilted back, exposing the length of her neck. "You're making it hard to put thoughts together right now."

He smiled. "Try harder, babe. Because there's no way I'm going to stop touching you and I expect an answer."

She lifted her lids and stared straight ahead at the road, like she was trying to focus on something to block out the way her body was reacting to him. "I don't know if I'd have the guts to do that kind of thing. But everything about my sex life from day one of it has been about hiding and being secretive. Even now. So there's something about the idea of just being out there that has its appeal. It's one reason why being on the phone with you was so hot. You were an observer to a private thing."

He shifted in his seat, absorbing that. So the lovely Oakley had an unexplored exhibitionist streak. He felt like he'd hit the lottery, because God knows he didn't have a problem doing whatever he wanted in front of others. It was one reason he craved the stage so much and why he'd liked the threesomes with Foster. Being watched could be a huge turn-on.

But Oakley had said she wasn't sure she'd actually be able to do it. Her pussy was clenching and wet around him just from the conversation, so at the very least she was attracted to the idea, in theory. But he was ready to find out how far she was really willing to go. He smiled as he pulled off the main road to the narrow country road that would lead to The Ranch. Luckily, he knew the perfect place to test out theories.

He would show the lovely Ms. Easton exactly why she wouldn't be able to walk away from him after one night.

Because that was definitely not an option.

One taste was supposed to satisfy the craving. But Oakley wasn't cake, she was heroin. And he was fucking hooked.

TWENTY

Oakley was so close to coming that if she rocked her hips and ground into Pike's touch, she'd go off. She'd already lost her ability to multitask, her intention to stroke Pike falling by the wayside as she was swept up in her own pleasure. But right as they pulled onto a different road, he moved his hand from between her thighs. She couldn't hold back the sound of frustration. She'd been keyed up since dinner, and her entire body felt like a coil ready to snap.

Pike smiled and casually put the two fingers he'd been using on her in his mouth. Shiny, long fingers disappeared between those sinful lips of his, and she had to groan again.

"Is your plan to keep me desperate all night?" she asked. "You know it's not nice to tease a girl who's been celibate for five years."

He smirked and pulled off the road without warning, the truck bumping on uneven ground. "You're absolutely right."

She glanced out the window. The fog hung low, but it wasn't blocking the fact that they were no longer on true road. Oh, shit. "What are you doing?"

He concentrated on the terrain in front of them, the natural grasses and shrubbery slapping at the base of the vehicle. A large Texas Ash tree loomed in the distance, its canopy seeming to hover above the fog like a leafy, green spaceship. As they got closer to the tree, Pike angled the truck toward it. Low brush surrounded the area, but Pike managed to find a clearing big enough to drive through. Once they were in the shelter of the Ash, Pike put the truck in park and cut the engine.

"Pike, what's going on? I was just talking. I didn't mean—"

He turned to her and cupped her chin. "I'm in control tonight, remember? And I'm not waiting another minute to get to The Ranch."

She opened her mouth to say something, but instead he brought his lips down on hers, and his palm slid to her breast with the urgency of a groping teenager but with the skill of a man who knew exactly what he was doing. All the words in her head evaporated. He tasted of Mexican beer and her own arousal, and she couldn't remember having ever tasted a sexier combination. Her eyes fell shut and she groaned as Pike gripped her neck and deepened the kiss.

Long, slow, and sensual, he took over her mouth and all of her senses. His scent, his taste, the way his five o'clock shadow scraped against her skin. Every part of her sprang to life, blood roaring in her ears like breaking waves. He seemed to fall into the moment with her as well, threading both of his hands in her hair, tugging and angling her just how he wanted. Like he wanted to consume her. Like he couldn't bear to be separated for even a breath.

So they were going to do this. Fuck in the front seat of his truck in the middle-of-nowhere Texas. Somehow she couldn't find it in her to protest.

He broke away from the kiss, panting, eyes like coal in the misty moonlight. "Hold that thought, gorgeous."

Then he was grabbing something out of the backseat and hopping out of the truck. Her head was spinning, her blood pumping, but nerves resurfaced. She shoved open her own door and leaned out. "What are you doing?"

He appeared on her side and put up a hand. "Don't get out. I'm going to carry you."

"*What?* Where? Why?"

He grinned and tucked his arms beneath her. "Don't forget *who* and *when.*"

He lifted her with ease even as her protests continued. "Is this the part where you admit you're a mass murderer and this is your favorite place to bury the bodies?"

"No, this spot would be too obvious." He bumped the door shut with his hip. "And I'm carrying you because it's too dark to be able to check for snakes and you've got open-toe shoes on."

"Snakes?! Pike—"

But he cut her off with a kiss again and carried her toward the back of the truck. He set her down on the open tailgate. A thick Mexican blanket had been double-folded and spread in the back, shielding her from the metal. That's when it finally sunk in as to what he was doing. What *they* were going to do.

"Oh, no. No way, Pike. We can't out here. We're not that far from the road. Anyone could see—"

"Take off your clothes, Oakley," he said, bracing his hands on each side of her. "I only want you wearing moonlight and fog."

Anxiety crackled through her, and she peered toward the path they'd forged through the brush. The canopy of the tree and surrounding shrubbery offered some cover, as did the low blanket of mist, but she could still make out the road from here.

"We can't—" But then she looked back to Pike and the words died on her lips. His mussed-on-purpose blond hair was bathed silver in the gleam of the moon, and his eyes were promising all of her dirtiest fantasies. She couldn't look away and she couldn't speak.

He leaned forward and brushed a kiss over her lips. "Trust me, Oakley."

She gave a mute nod, captured in his spell.

He leaned back and pulled off his T-shirt, exposing his honed chest and all of that inked skin. Jesus H. Christ. The man looked like some surreal being who'd emerged from the fog around them—an angel, a demon. Maybe some combination of both. She reached out and traced a vine tattoo that tracked over his shoulder. In this light, it was almost as if the twining patterns of his ink were breathing, all the colors swirling. Beautiful. And it was all wrapping up a package she was liking more and more. A *man* she was liking more and more.

He put his hand over hers, a quirk of a smile on his lips. "Exploring my dumb tattoos."

"I'm thinking of changing my stance on this whole ink situation."

The metal gave a groan as he climbed onto the tailgate with her then scooted her back into the bed of the truck. "Yeah?"

She pretended to consider the question. "I might have to taste them first. You know, to make an educated decision."

He moved his hands to her buttons and started unfastening them as he put his mouth on her neck, kissing a line along her throat. His hand slid into her open blouse and cupped her breast. "Good idea. You don't want to make a hasty judgment. You need to fully explore this new theory." He pushed her bra strap off and lifted the full weight of her breast in his palm, sending need sizzling down her nerve endings. "I'm not sure about my stance on pretty pink nipples."

Hot goose bumps chased over her skin. "By all means, do what you need to do to form an opinion."

He lowered his head and took her into his mouth. He sucked with surprising pressure, and it was as if a direct line connected that spot to her pussy. Her clit jumped to attention and Oakley moaned. Pike pressed his teeth into her sensitive flesh, and she gripped his head, her noises getting louder. Fuck, how could that feel so good?

"Mmm," Pike said against her skin. "Sounds like you like a little roughness, Ms. Easton."

She let her head rest against the truck's back window, lost in the laving of his tongue along her stinging nipple. "Or maybe I just like *you*."

The words slipped out, but she realized they had been the wrong thing to say almost immediately. Had revealed too much.

Pike lifted his head to meet her gaze, something intense burning there. Something tender. "I like you, too, Oakley. More than you want me to."

She closed her eyes and turned her head away. "Don't. Please. I'm not one of those girls who needs you to tell her what you think she wants to hear."

His grip on her tightened. "I know. That's why I told you what you needed to hear, not what you wanted to."

"Pike—"

"Take everything off. I need to see all of you when I fuck you."

The words were coarse, as was his tone, but it was exactly what she needed in that moment. Something to bring this back to what it was supposed to be. Physical release. Adventure. Nothing more, nothing less.

He backed away and she tugged off her top and bra. The night air licked at her skin, but she was beyond worrying about their exposed status at this point. She needed that edge. If she could focus on the thrill of it, the daring act, she wouldn't have to worry about the other stuff creeping in—her stupid instincts trying to attach some sort of significant feelings to someone she was sleeping with. It was just remnants of an upbringing that tied sex exclusively to lifelong love. This wasn't about Pike.

She kneeled up and tugged off her skirt, baring herself in full to him. He'd watched her every move like a jungle cat waiting to pounce and now he let his gaze travel over her with hungry interest. "You look good on your knees, mama."

"We could get arrested if someone catches us."

"Mmm-hmm." He stood, his heavy black boots clomping on the bed of the truck, and shoved his pants to his thighs, revealing that impressively hard cock. "Better try to be quiet then."

Good God. She licked her lips. What a view. Pike looming over her, cock in hand, tree branches swaying above him, moonlight gilding his cut shoulders—it was enough to send another rush of needy arousal flooding through her. Any errant thought or worries were forgotten. Never before had she seen the appeal in submitting to some guy, but right now, she wanted to worship.

His lips curled into a wry smile, mischief lighting his eyes, and he pointed to his dick with both hands.

She smiled back at him and rose fully on her knees. "Look at that. Guess it can be effective."

He slid his fingers into her hair and gripped. "Going to kick me, beautiful?"

The harshness of his grip made her nipples tighten, her body rev. Maybe he was right. The rougher he was, the more she liked it. It was so opposite from every other sexual experience she'd ever had. Liam had shown his ugly side after she'd gotten pregnant, but he'd always been gentle with her in bed, like she would break. Her youth and innocence his kink. Sick fucker. She licked her lips again. "No."

"What do you want then?"

The answer jumped into her head unbidden. She barely swallowed it back before she could say it. Where the hell had that urge come from?

Pike tilted his head, his eyes shrewd, evaluating. "What were you going to say?"

"Nothing."

"Oakley," he warned. "Tell me. No filters tonight. No judgment."

She couldn't break the eye contact. Her heart hammered, her palms went sweaty. But Pike's steady gaze and command had her good sense falling into the fog somewhere. "I was going to say maybe you should make me."

Desire flashed over his features like a starving man who'd had a steak waved in front of him, but his expression went instantly wary. "That's an intense game, baby. Be careful. Might not want to jump into the deep end right away."

"Have you played it before?" she asked, honestly curious.

He considered her carefully. "I've watched other people play it. Haven't done it myself."

She smirked. "Women can't even fake resisting you?"

The tilt of his mouth went wry. "Smart-ass."

"Come on, don't you want to see what it feels like to meet a little resistance for a change? I'm not some fragile thing. I know what I'm asking. Tonight's supposed to be our daring night, remember?"

He stared at her another long moment. "We're in the middle of nowhere. There's no one here to intervene. No dungeon monitor. No staff. You understand the situation you're putting yourself in?"

A tremor went through her hands at his serious tone. "You'll listen to my safe word if I need it."

"You trust that?" he asked, his grip tightening on her hair but something stripped and naked in his eyes.

"I do."

Some emotion moved over his face, an ache there, but he quickly smoothed his expression into something harder. "You gonna suck my cock, Oakley?"

She caught the change in tone, the shift in the air. Game on. She tilted her chin up. "Fuck off. Take me home."

He grabbed her skull with both his hands, stepping closer until the head of his cock brushed over her lips. She could taste the musk of his skin, smell the scent of sex. Her mouth watered. "You're not going anywhere until you give me what I want. You've been a fucking cock tease the whole drive over. Now you're going to deliver on that promise."

"You teased me first." She tried to turn her head away, but he held her fast.

"Oh, and I plan to deliver on that promise as well. Those pretty thighs are going to spread wide for me. But first you're going to suck me like you mean it. Use teeth and I will leave your naked ass out here in the woods with the snakes."

"Such a fucking romantic," she said, channeling some dark part of herself, falling into the role-play, feeling the freedom of it.

"Open," he said, nudging himself against her lips. "Do a good job and maybe I'll let you come when I fuck you."

She resisted for a moment, but then he grabbed her jaw and squeezed, making her open. He pushed the head of his cock in as soon as her lips parted. She choked for a second, the invasion sudden, but it only added to the illicitness of what they were doing. Her belly dipped and a rush of heat went through her.

He groaned as he slid along her tongue, seating deep. And she held back a moan at the feel and taste of him inside her mouth—

salt and smooth skin and man. She let her eyes open barely, unable to resist the intimate view of Pike. She wanted to map every part of him. His sac loomed heavy in her line of sight, obvious and masculine and fucking sexy. She'd always found that part of a man to be obscenely arousing—a secret fetish of hers that she could probably blame on discovering Devon's stash of gay porn magazines when she was a teenager. Stealing away to peek at those pages, she'd developed quite an appreciation for all the secret parts of the male anatomy. But in her brief sex life, she'd never let herself openly explore because it was hard to know what a guy would like.

But she'd talked to Pike on the phone, remembered what he'd said about how he touched himself, how he liked it. It was like a flashing green light to indulge. She knew she was supposed to be the resistant captive in this scenario, but the temptation proved too much. She lifted her hand and cupped him, letting the weight and heat fill her palm. Then she let her nails draw along the tender skin.

A pleased sound rumbled through Pike. "Fuck."

She rolled her tongue around the head of his cock, taking her time and enjoying the feel of him guiding her back and forth over his length. Then she let her fingertips trail under his scrotum to rub along the span of skin behind it.

Pike's knees flexed and drops of salty fluid touched her tongue. She lifted her gaze to him, needing to see for herself how this was affecting him. But when their eyes met, it left no question. The look he was giving her seared her like hot coals. He pulled her off his cock and got ahold of her hair again. "You touch something, you taste it. That's the rule."

Her pussy clenched as if he'd directly stroked it. He was giving her the go-ahead to explore. He took his cock in his free hand and angled it higher so she could have access to all of him. The view was all male and in full color. Pike kept things neatly trimmed, so she could see the details of every forbidden part of him. She let him guide her forward and she put her lips to his scrotum and then drew her tongue over the flush skin. He tasted of musk and heat, and some primal part of her wanted to bury herself in his scent.

He grunted and gave his cock a squeeze like he was staving off orgasm. "Don't be shy, baby. Let's not pretend you're a good girl who doesn't want it."

She dipped lower, taking his balls in her mouth and rolling her tongue around them. Then she drew her fingers over his perineum again and ventured farther back. She definitely had never dared to go that far with any other guy, but Pike had already told her he played with plugs sometimes, and she couldn't help her curiosity. She teased the tip of her finger lightly over his opening.

Pike's hold on her hair faltered. "Fuck me, you're going to be fun when we do role reversal."

She hummed against his skin, the words inspiring decadent visions of Pike restrained to a bed and spread out for her to explore and experiment however she wanted. Hell, he was doing what he promised, making her want another night already.

She let her lips kiss a path along the spot where thigh met pelvis and then licked across the knuckles of the hand he had wrapped around his erection. Finally, she kissed the head of his cock and sucked.

He tugged her away from him. "Enough. Hands and knees. Thighs spread, ass in the air."

"And what if I don't want to?"

He squatted down, getting eye to eye with her. "Tell me no, Oakley, and see what happens."

She narrowed her eyes. "No."

He grabbed his discarded T-shirt and gathered her wrists in his fists and wrapped the material around it, knotting it swiftly and efficiently.

"What are you doing? You can't—"

He grabbed her shoulders and spun her around, the blanket going with her. Then he splayed his palm on her back and forced her down until she was braced on her elbows, ass in the air. "I can. And I will. You're fucking mine."

He gripped her thighs and spread her knees wider, exposing

every bit of her to him and the moonlight. He dragged his fingers along the lips of her sex, which were embarrassingly wet by now.

"I can see how much you hate this. How much you can't stand the thought of me taking you. Look at you."

He rubbed her clit with rough fingers, the movement almost too much to bear. She didn't want to go off too soon, but everything felt on edge, poised to explode. She tried to squirm away, but he grabbed her hip and smacked an open palm right over her pussy.

She cried out, more from the shock than anything else, and vicious, aching need nearly steamrolled her. Holy shit. She pressed her forehead to the blanket and groaned. Arousal leaked onto her thighs.

He laughed low behind her, a smug, pleased sound. "It's a crime you've put yourself on ice for five years, baby. Look how responsive you are. Numb, my ass." He hit her again, this time on the spot where thigh met curves. Three sharp hits that sent her system reeling. "You weren't numb. You just needed someone who wasn't afraid to give you some bite."

She inhaled a deep breath, letting the reverb of the slaps move through her. He was so right. She'd been celibate by choice, convinced that her libido had faded, but that had been because sex had never been all that great for her. Decent, sure. But it'd all been soft and sweet and unremarkable. Never before had she felt so physically tuned in with someone else. Whether Pike was being gentle or rough, her body seemed wired for his touch.

He spanked her again, matching hits going from left to right. Her skin began to tingle, the moisture in the air clinging to her and mixing with a building sheen of sweat. She rocked in the position, tilting herself closer to him.

His callused hands moved over her skin with a gentling touch, hands that knew how to smash drums or make them softly rumble and could do the same to her body. "You make me want to turn your whole backside pink, baby. Look how hot and wet you're getting."

He pinched her thigh and she moaned. Hell, maybe she had some undiscovered masochistic streak. Or maybe it was just Pike. Anything he did to her seemed to be a turn-on. She was in so much damn trouble. But right now, she didn't care. She'd worry about that stuff later. Right now she just needed him. "Please."

"Please what?" he asked, gravel in his voice as he drew his fingers over her slickness, the sound of his fingers on her flesh obscenely erotic.

It was on her lips to beg him to fuck her, but then she remembered the game they'd started and wanted to finish it. "Get the hell away from me and let me go home."

He wiped her arousal onto the back of her thigh as if to show her just how turned on she was. "Is home Oklahoma?"

The question confused her for a second but then she realized he was checking in with her on her safe word, giving her an out in case she'd meant her words. "No, you know where I live. Now take me home."

He grasped her hips, fingers digging into her skin. "Not yet, gorgeous. Not until that sweet cunt of yours is squeezing my cock."

She made a half attempt to shift away from him, but he gripped the back of her neck with one hand, holding her in place while he used his other hand to get the condom.

The vulnerable position did something to her. She knew she should probably be worried that this was turning her on. But somehow being with Pike made her feel safe to explore even taboo stuff. There was this bubble around them—one where she trusted that he wouldn't really hurt her and that there'd be no judgment on either side. So she let herself fall into the moment—the tight bindings around her wrists, the cool metal of the truck against her arms, the naked sky above them, and the feel of Pike holding her in place. Surrender.

Pike released her neck and gripped her hips again. "You should see how goddamned perfect you look right now. All mine."

And without further warning, he plunged into her. The move was rough, but she was so turned on that he slid in without resistance—hot and thick and deep. They both groaned at the connection.

"You feel numb now, baby?" he asked, sliding out and thrusting back in.

"Totally," she breathed, her fingers curling into her palms.

"Oh, really?" His voice held a playful, goading tone. All part of the game. One that was working quite effectively on her.

"I don't feel a . . . thing." The catch in her voice made a liar out of her.

Pike's fingers dug into her hips with steely force and he pumped harder for a few seconds, making the blanket slide beneath her. The truck started to make metallic grinding sounds along with them. "Well, if that's the case, don't come before I do and you win the game. I'll take you home."

"Easy money," she whispered.

But then he slowed down his movements considerably and teased the flared head of his cock at her opening, in and out with light thrusts that lit up sensations she didn't know she was capable of.

Holy mother of God. She let out a whimpering noise, despite her best efforts to keep quiet. She could feel everything so intimately, each ridge and smooth part of him as he continued the shallow thrusting, awakening long-dormant nerves.

"Mmm, that's it, mama," he said, his voice like warm cider on a cool night. "Feel every bit of me stretching you, rubbing over that sweet pink flesh and making it feel good."

She didn't know how she was so close to the edge of orgasm already. He hadn't touched her clit, but the man knew how to manipulate her body and hit all the right spots.

He seated deep and she could feel his balls pressed up against her. For the first time, she wished she had her hands free so she could reach back and stroke him while he was inside of her. Maybe another night . . .

And there she went again. Thinking of more nights.

But Pike didn't give her any time to hold on to the worry. Because he reached around her then and found her swollen nub. The combination of his roughened fingers on her clit and his cock buried inside her was too much. She arched up, begging for him to move.

He draped himself over her back with a dark chuckle. "Begging words sound so pretty on you, baby."

"Next time I'll make you beg," she threatened.

He bit her shoulder with enough pressure to sting. "Looking forward to it."

That's when she realized he'd won. Not the game they were playing but the much bigger one. She'd just agreed to a next time.

Goddammit to hell.

But when he pressed her flat against the truck bed, his hand still on her clit, and started fucking her hard, she forgot to be mad. Because having him take her hard under the stars, his body challenging hers to unknown heights, was worth any price she was going to pay.

Probably.

Maybe.

She'd worry about it later.

Right now it was time to explode into a million little bits.

TWENTY-ONE

"Not even on the grounds yet and you're already breaking the rules."

The unfamiliar voice made Oakley jolt awake. Pike, who'd been holding her against him, broke away from her in an instant. "What the fuck?"

Oakley scrambled, trying to clear her head, and gathered the blanket Pike had draped over them around her naked body.

"Let me know when y'all are decent," the unfamiliar voice said.

Pike scowled and helped Oakley straighten the blanket then buttoned his open jeans. "Sorry, baby."

"What's going on?" she whispered urgently.

"It's all right. Give me a sec." He sat up in the bed of the truck and helped Oakley do the same.

All she could see was the back of a man in a long-sleeved shirt and jeans.

Pike leaned over and popped the guy on the back of the head. "What the fuck is wrong with you, Gib?"

The man turned around, moonlight illuminating dark, curly hair and bright blue eyes. He sent Oakley an apologetic look over Pike's shoulder. "Sorry to interrupt."

She had no idea what to say to that. She was still too startled that anyone was there at all. How had they let themselves doze off? One minute they'd been kissing and cuddling after their rocking orgasms, and the next she was waking up naked in the back of a truck with a stranger staring at them.

Though, the guy didn't seem to be a stranger to Pike.

"Then why are you here?" Pike asked, annoyed.

The man gave Pike an are-you-kidding? look. "You do realize this is part of Grant's property, right? Security cameras caught a truck veering off the main road. When it didn't return, they ran the plates in the database and figured out it was you. No one knew if you were in some kind of trouble or getting into trouble. I volunteered to come and check on you. Looks like it was the latter."

Oakley peered toward the road. In the distance, she could see a car with the headlights pointed this way.

"You could've called my cell, asshole," Pike said, but there was no ire behind it.

The man smirked, a dimple appearing. "I did. Twice."

Pike ran a hand through his hair and then reached for his T-shirt to tug it over his head. "Well, thanks for interrupting. We *so* appreciate it."

The guy grinned. "Happy to help. Don't want you to get eaten by coyotes or something." He lifted a hand to Oakley. "I'm Gibson, by the way."

"My former friend," Pike added.

She couldn't help but smile. The situation was so bizarre. "Oakley."

"Pretty name."

"Thanks." She narrowed her eyes. Something about him seemed familiar, nudged her memory. "Have we met before?"

"Don't think so," Gibson said.

Pike blew out a breath. "Gib is Kade Vandergriff's brother."

Oakley stiffened like she'd been pinched. *Oh, shit.* Kade's brother. As in, her boss's brother-in-law. That's where she'd seen him before. Tessa had a family picture on her desk. And now he was here, staring straight at her as she sat in the back of a truck, naked beneath a blanket, on the way to a sex resort. Fantastic. She wanted to climb into the glove compartment and die.

Pike eyed her. "Don't freak out. Rules here dictate absolute confidentiality. No matter what happens here, Gibson will act like he doesn't know you if you run into each other in the outside world."

Gibson lifted his brows in question.

"Oakley works for Tessa," Pike explained. "She's the one heading up the charity project."

"Ah, I see. Glad you took my advice." Gibson sent Pike a look but then gave Oakley a reassuring smile. "But yes, absolutely. Your secrets are safe. That's the beauty of a place like this. You can kind of exist in a vacuum once you're inside the gates. Plus, you have dirt on me now, too. *I'm* here at The Ranch as well."

"And for probably way more scandalous reasons," Pike said wryly.

"Right." Oakley put her hand to her forehead, her palm cool against her burning skin. Regardless of confidentiality, she was still mortified. How unprofessional did this look? Beyond the whole sex-resort thing, she was hooking up with a guy she was supposed to be working with.

"Well," Gibson said, all good nature and relaxed smiles, "I'll let you two get on with your night. Maybe we can all grab a drink later."

"That doesn't have the same ring to it when all they serve here is soda," Pike said. "But if you're not tied up at the time, maybe we will."

Gibson's dark brows lowered. "Watch it, smart-ass."

Pike laughed. "Have fun, Gib."

Gibson headed back to his car, and Pike sagged against the side of the truck.

"Well, that was embarrassing," Oakley said, releasing a breath.

Pike reached out and grabbed her hand. "Don't be embarrassed. Really. Gibson's not going to say anything to anyone. Most of my close friends are members at The Ranch. We've all seen one another in compromising positions at some point—believe me. It's all very open. I have more dirt on Gibson than could fill a dump truck, but we all trust one another to keep it private."

"What did he mean about not taking his advice?"

"Foster told him about us running into you at Wicked, and Gibson warned me not to mess with you. He's the one who asked me to take on the charity project, and he said his brother and Tessa would kill him if I caused any of Tessa's employees grief."

"Is that what you do? Cause women grief?"

He shrugged. "Well, once you sleep with me, you are pretty much ruined for all others, so I see where he's coming from."

She laughed and shoved his arm. "You're ridiculous."

"What? I can't help the facts."

Pike waved to Gibson when he gave them a honk from his vehicle, and Oakley watched his taillights disappear through the cloud of dust his back tires kicked up. "Have you shared women with Gibson like you did with Foster?"

Pike sent her a sidelong glance. "You making a request, Ms. Easton?"

A choked sound burst out of her. "What? No!"

Well . . .

No.

She shook those images from her head. "I'm just curious."

His mouth curled at the corner. "Good, because I'm not sharing you."

"But I thought you did that all the time."

He leaned forward and kissed her nose. "If that's really something you feel like you want to explore at some point, we can talk about it. But I have to admit, you bring out my selfish side, mama. I don't mind if others want to watch, but I want to be the one to touch."

Something pinged through her at that declaration and the *you're mine* in his tone. As curious as she may be about the whole threesome thing and as good-looking as Gibson was, something about Pike staking his claim settled something inside her, made her feel safe.

"And no, I haven't shared a woman with Gib. I've watched him scene a time or two, but he keeps most of his play here private."

"Is he a dom?"

"He's a lot of things."

The vague answer let her know that Pike wasn't going to share Gibson's secrets. In a way, that was comforting. Maybe her secrets were safe, too. "It's not weird knowing that much about your friends' sex lives?"

Pike handed her clothes to her, and she started to get dressed.

"At first it can be, but after you hang out around here for a while, it just becomes another facet of your friends. You know so-and-so likes to get tied up and whipped in front of a crowd. And that another friend likes to give his wife a male submissive to play with every now and then while he watches. Now Gibson knows we like to fool around outdoors. It just becomes another thing about them. The taboo aspect fades and it brings you closer."

"I can't imagine." She'd been raised in such a close-lipped environment when it came to sexuality that what he was describing was hard to wrap her head around. No one talked about sex aloud when she was growing up. No one. Her brother had once made a joke about "choking the chicken" and he'd been grounded for a month. So imagining such casual openness with friends blew her mind a little.

Pike helped her button her blouse. "The most honest version of ourselves is the one behind closed doors. I'm sure you see that with the calls you take. You probably know more about your callers' true selves than ninety-nine percent of the people in their lives. Sex and how we feel about it, what we crave? That's about as vulnerable as a person can get. So with my friends, instead of hiding it, we let one another see behind our closed doors. It's a privilege we don't take lightly."

"Sounds wonderful and completely terrifying."

He laughed and leaned over to kiss her lightly. "Yes. To both. But I think you're going to do just fine here."

"Oh?" she said, meeting his eyes and getting lost in them for a moment. "Why is that?"

"Because your time for hiding behind those doors is done, mama. What we just did out here proves that. You're fearless." He pushed her hair away from her face. "Tonight you're not the staid professional or the good daughter or the responsible mom or Sasha the sex-line operator. Tonight it's just you and me, whatever that looks like, whatever we want. Tonight all you have to be is mine."

She closed her eyes and pressed her forehead to his, letting the words sink in. This was their night. Her break from it all. Tomorrow her life would go back to normal. She didn't mind that. She liked her life. But she wasn't going to let anything hold her back from enjoying her time with Pike tonight.

She wasn't going to stress about her inexperience or the fact that this was not very mom-like. And though she'd sort of agreed to another time with Pike already, she knew she couldn't honor that. This one night had to be it and she was going to grab the most she could from it. If you knew you only got to go to the moon once, you wouldn't waste your time worrying about how you looked in your space suit or what other people thought of you for climbing on the rocket ship. You would keep your eyes wide open and drink it all in.

And she was definitely going to imbibe in every last bit of the beautiful man in front of her.

She looped her arms around Pike's neck and lifted her head to meet his eyes. "Let's get going."

But as soon as they climbed back into the truck and headed toward The Ranch, Oakley's phone rang.

When she saw the name pop up on the phone, she answered immediately. "Devon? What's wrong?"

"Don't freak out."

"Devon," she said louder, making Pike send a concerned glance her way.

Her brother sighed. "She's okay, but Rae may have broken her arm. We're at the ER."

"What?!" Oakley's stomach plummeted.

"I told you not to freak out. Look, she's all right. She took a fall when she and Lucas were riding bikes. She's being a trouper. But I knew you'd want—"

"Which hospital are you at?"

Pike immediately slowed the truck and pulled to the side of the road.

"Memorial."

"I'll be there as soon as I can, but we're at least an hour away," she said in a rush, adrenaline flooding her system. "Can I talk to her?"

"She's in getting X-rays right now, but I'll tell her you're on your way. You know how she is. She's being really stoic about it, but I know she'd feel better if you were here. I'm sorry to call you on your one night out."

"Don't even. You know I'm not going to be anywhere else but there. I'll see you soon."

They exchanged good-byes and Oakley let the phone drop into her lap.

"What's wrong?" Pike asked, tone urgent.

She rubbed her hands over her face. "Rae may have broken her arm."

"Shit." Pike put the truck in gear and made a quick, dirt-spraying U-turn on the road. "Is she okay?"

"Sounds like it. Devon's got her in with the doctor. But I need—"

"Where are we going?" he asked, purpose in his tone, all play-fulness gone.

"She's at Memorial but you can just bring me back to my car and I can head out from there. I'm sorry to screw up the night. But I can't—"

"Don't you dare apologize for that." He frowned her way. "And bringing you back to the studio is completely out of the way. We'll be there twenty minutes earlier if we just go straight there."

"But—"

"If you're worried about Reagan seeing us together, we can just tell her we were working on Bluebonnet stuff. Most important thing is we get you to her as soon as we can."

Oakley sagged in the seat at his resolute tone. It felt nice to have someone else handle things for a moment so she could get her nerves under control. Her mom panic was in full gear, but she'd heard Devon's tone. He wouldn't lie to her. If Rae was freaking out or in any true danger, he would've told her. A broken arm was awful but it was something that could be fixed.

She looked over at Pike. So much for their wild night. "Thanks for this. Welcome to the joys of dating a mom."

He gave her a quick smile. "So we're dating now? Excellent."

"Shut up," she said, a half-laugh escaping. "You know what I mean."

He reached out and gave her knee a squeeze. "I have a feeling there'd be a lot of joys dating you, mama."

There was no sarcasm in his voice, and the statement sliced her right open, making her want things she shouldn't. "You're not playing fair, James Pike Ryland."

He looked back to the road, a shuttered look on his face. "You should know better than to expect that. I don't play fair. I play dirty."

But the joke landed flat because there was none of his trademark humor in it. Unspoken words sat heavy between them for the rest of the drive.

Yep. She needed to end this quick.

It was starting to sting.

TWENTY-TWO

Pike kept his eyes on the road as Oakley dug through her bag and grabbed fresh clothes to change into. She wriggled into clean underwear and jeans and then pulled her post-sex hair into a ponytail. By the time they drove up to the hospital, she looked like nothing had happened between them tonight.

And maybe for her, the memory could be wiped away that easily. But for him, the events of the evening lingered, sinking into his bones and settling in. He and Oakley hadn't even made it to The Ranch tonight, but being with her had been like nothing he'd ever experienced. It had all been so easy, so effortless. They could joke and tease. They could be dirty. They could trust each other enough to indulge in a taboo fantasy.

He'd thought he'd feel like an absolute creep taking her up on her offer to play out that force fantasy. He never wanted to force a woman to do anything. But somehow it hadn't felt that way with her. Knowing she was getting off on the roughness had been the biggest turn-on. It'd sparked something inside him that had made him want to spank her, had made him want to hold her down and tease her.

For the first time in his life, he understood where his friends in the lifestyle were coming from. Pike had thought he knew what it was about, but tonight with Oakley had felt altogether different. They'd called it a game, and on the surface, it had been. But the layer beneath was real and honest. They'd tapped into some part of themselves that they didn't show the world. There'd been an undercurrent he'd never had before even when he'd done D/s scenes with others. And he knew there was more there, more to uncover and experience. But he had a feeling he may not get the chance because Oakley was going to run. When he'd said something about dating, she'd shut him down cold.

And he knew it wasn't fair to expect anything more from her. He was acting like a groupie who tried to change the price of poker after the hookup. Oakley hadn't led him on. She'd set up her parameters up front. But right now, he wasn't so ready to play by those rules.

Pike turned down an aisle in the parking lot of the hospital, looking for a spot. Oakley grabbed her bag. "You can just drop me off at the front. You don't have to get out."

He peered over at her, sending her his non-negotiable look. "I'm going in."

"But—"

"I want to see if Reagan is okay, too. And you're going to need a ride back to your car." He pulled into a parking spot.

"I can ride with my brother."

"I'm the only one who can get into the garage. I'm coming with you. Get over it, mama." He cut the ignition.

She blew out a breath. "This dominant thing is going to your head. But fine, come on. Just stick to the story that we've been working."

"Of course." He hopped out of the truck and went to her side. But she'd already gotten out before he could grab her door.

He wanted to take her hand as they walked through the lot, try to calm her. She had that frantic mama bear look on her face, but he knew his touch wouldn't be welcome here. He couldn't have her that way in real life. This was her family. He was the outsider.

They made their way into the waiting room and before Oakley could ask at the front desk, a man came striding toward them. He looked to be dressed for the outdoors—cargo pants, hiking boots, and an army green T-shirt—but somehow it all looked perfectly put together. Like he wasn't really going camping but modeling for a camping catalog. The only thing that looked off was the dark hair going every which way—like the guy had been raking through it repeatedly.

The man met Oakley with a big hug. "Jesus, you must've teleported here. You said an hour."

Oakley gave him a squeeze. "Pike was creative with the speed limit."

Oakley's brother stepped back and put a hand out to Pike. "Thanks for getting her here. I'm Devon."

He shook Devon's hand. "Pike. And no problem. We got here as soon as we could. How's Reagan?"

"Her wrist is broken."

Oakley winced, and Pike instinctively put a hand on her shoulder to give it a squeeze. Devon's eyes went to the touch, and Pike lowered his hand to his side.

"But it was a clean break," Devon assured Oakley. "They're putting it in a splint for now. Then in a few days when the swelling goes down, they'll cast it. A month in the cast and she'll be all fixed up. Hunter is in there with her. I had to stay out here since Lucas crashed half an hour ago."

Devon nodded his head toward one of the plastic waiting room chairs where a young boy was curled up and fast asleep.

Oakley let out a breath. "Thank God she's all right. Where is she?"

"Right through those doors. It's room B. Tell the nurse at the desk, and she'll get you back there. I know Rae will be relieved to see you, and the hospital needs you to sign some papers anyway."

She turned to Pike. "Thanks for bringing me."

He cocked a thumb to the waiting room area. "I'll be out here whenever y'all are ready to leave."

"Pike—"

"Let your brother and his family go home and put their son to bed. I can get you and Reagan home safely."

Devon put his hands on Oakley's shoulders and gave Pike a raised-eyebrow look from behind her. "We can bring her."

"I've got it," Pike said, voice firm.

Devon looked down at Oakley. "Oak?"

She sighed. "It's fine. You guys get back to your camping trip and get Lucas to bed. I'll send Hunter out. Thank you for getting her here and taking care of her."

Devon kissed the crown of her head. "Not a problem."

Oakley gave Pike a quick look and then she turned and hurried toward the double doors that led to the back. Once she was out of sight, Devon faced him. "Coffee? It's absolute shit here but you might be out here awhile. I saw the pile of paperwork she needs to fill out."

"Yeah. That'd be great."

"Keep an eye on my kid?"

"Sure."

Pike took a spot next to the sleeping child. The waiting room was pretty busy but as cold as a morgue despite all the people. Babies cried. People coughed. Parents soothed. The whole scene made him shiver. How many times had he been in places like this when he was a kid? They hadn't had insurance, so any illness or injury that came up had to go through the emergency room. He could remember long hours of sitting with feverish, crying siblings under florescent lights. And then there were the other times when he was the patient, his mother coaching him on what to say. *Say you fell. Say you got in a fight with another kid. Say you burned yourself with your own cigarette.*

That last one had been a fun one to explain. It'd been another of his mom's winner boyfriends. The guy had been drunk off his ass one night and had told Pike real men didn't cry. Then he'd proceeded to put a line of cigarette burns along Pike's inner arm to try to get him to cry. He hadn't stopped until Pike had vomited from the pain. Six burns. With his and his mother's lies, the doctors had labeled it self-harm. And maybe in a way, it had been. He'd wanted to prove he could take whatever the guy dished out. Now he had a phoenix tattoo on the inside of his arm that blended the burns into the feathers of the beast. It'd been his first major ink.

If only he could go back and tell the truth to those doctors and social workers, maybe his brother and sisters would've had a chance to get out of that family, too. But back then, he'd been only fourteen and the unknown of where all the kids would end up if taken away from his mom had been too overwhelming to think about. She wasn't great, but he'd known even then that things could always be worse.

He wondered how many children came through this very room with the same stories, with nervous mothers, and paper-thin lies. The thought made acid churn in his stomach. He leaned back in his chair, and Devon's kid slid his head onto Pike's shoulder as if sensing body heat was near. Instead of the urge to scoot away, he had to resist the instinct to touch the child's head.

"Sorry about that."

Pike looked up.

Devon handed him a steaming paper cup and then set his own down. "I can take that spot. Luc's a drooler."

Pike smiled and put his hand under the child's head so he wouldn't fall over during the transfer. Devon probably didn't want his kid leaning on a stranger. He didn't blame him. Devon slid into the spot and in an instant, Lucas slumped all the way down and put his head on his father's thigh and snored loudly.

The sight warmed Pike. At least this kid was safe. He only knew Devon through what Oakley had told him about her brother, but the guy had taken care of his sister when she needed help and was still doing it sometimes. He'd done what Pike hadn't for his own siblings.

"He's out cold," Pike said, trying to make conversation and block out the bad memories.

"I think all the excitement did him in. He and Rae are really close, and it was hard for him to see her get hurt. He thought it was his fault because he'd been the one who wanted to go ride on the trails. But it could just as easily have been him. Reagan raced ahead, and there was a fallen branch that launched her off her bike. We were only a few feet behind but couldn't get to her quick enough. I should've led the way."

"Sounds like he's not the only one blaming himself."

Devon gave him a chagrined smile. "I was the one in charge. Parental guilt is a wicked bitch."

"I wouldn't know." Pike sipped his coffee and tried not to make a face at the taste—warmed-over dishwater.

"Yeah, I guess having a family would be pretty tough with

your job." Devon took a long draw from his cup, but his eyes didn't leave Pike's.

Pike had the distinct impression he was being evaluated. "It's not ideal, no."

Devon nodded. "Which begs the question, why are you in the waiting room of a hospital, waiting for my sister and her daughter to get discharged so you can bring them home?"

Pike's attention snapped to him, gazes colliding. "Because I'm trying to help."

"She told you she didn't need it."

"Like she'd ever admit she needed help from anyone."

He smirked. "Point taken. Maybe you know her better than I thought. But you still need to tread carefully."

"Meaning?"

He shrugged, his hand idly stroking his son's hair. "Meaning, I'm all for my sister dating and letting new people into her life. She needs to take some time for herself. But—"

"But not with a guy like me," Pike said, unable to keep the sarcasm out of his tone. He could only imagine what he looked like to Mr. Put-Together Dad. Like danger and bad news and all the things one tried to keep their little sisters away from.

Small lines appeared around Devon's mouth—a restrained frown. "It's not like that. I actually encouraged her to pursue this thing with you. But for a fling." He looked toward the doors where Oakley had disappeared. "Flings don't sit in hospital waiting rooms. You're sending mixed messages, and I don't want anyone leading her on. She doesn't deserve that."

Pike crossed his arms. He didn't blame the guy for trying to protect his sister, but he wasn't about to try to define his need to be here to a stranger. He didn't quite understand it himself. "I don't lead people on. I want to be here for her, so I am. Simple as that. Your sister's a grown woman who can tell me if I'm crossing any lines."

Devon considered him for a long moment then seemed to relent—if only a little. "Look, you seem like a decent guy. Oakley wouldn't have let you be here at all if you weren't. But she doesn't need extra drama in her life. You and I both know your world is not going to mix well with hers. So don't give her the impression that whatever you have going on is something different than it is. It'll hurt her. And Rae."

"Oh, Christ, is he polishing his shotgun over here?" a deep voice said from behind Pike.

Pike turned to find a broad-shouldered man with shaggy black hair and a good-natured smile rounding their row of seats. Unlike Devon's polished camping look, this man looked ready to climb a mountain with his bare hands. He strode over to Pike and put his hand out. "I'm Hunter, Devon's husband, and the man who's going to save you from the third degree."

Pike shook his hand, the grip firm. "Pike Ryland."

Hunter tilted his head. "So you're the fabled Pike, the drop-dead-gorgeous drummer Oakley's seeing. Nice to meet you."

Hearing the words roll off the man's tongue sent Pike for a loop. "I know Oakley didn't say that about me."

He gave him a sly grin. "No, Devon did when he told me about you."

Pike sent a raised eyebrow look over at Devon. "Oh."

Devon shrugged. "It was an empirical observation."

Hunter patted the back of Pike's chair and looked toward Devon. "Don't mind him. He has a wicked protective streak when it comes to his sister. I'm still trying to convince him she's no longer sixteen."

Pike's muscles relaxed. "It's okay. Family's supposed to look out for each other."

Though his family never got that memo.

"Oakley and Reagan should be out shortly. She's just arranging payment and all that fun stuff." Hunter walked over and squeezed Devon's shoulder, the men a stark contrast to each other but somehow conveying their inherent bond with the easy way they looked at each other. "You ready? I have a feeling if we don't get back soon, all of our new camping gear is going to be gone. I'm sure that guy we asked to keep an eye on our stuff has gone to bed by now or is currently selling our shit on eBay."

Devon put his hand over Hunter's and gave it a pat. "Yeah. You want to grab Lucas? My leg's fallen asleep."

Hunter leaned over and massaged Devon's leg for a second then scooped up the child with ease. The scene was so sweetly domestic that it twisted something in Pike's gut.

Devon stood and nodded at Pike, expression serious. "Get them home safe. And make sure Oakley doesn't stay up all night hovering over Rae. Every time Rae gets sick, Oakley runs herself ragged and ends up sick herself."

"I'm on it."

"Or on *her* as the case may be," Hunter offered with a wink.

Devon groaned. "We're divorcing for that comment. Just so you know."

Hunter smirked Pike's way. "He divorces me every day. He likes the makeup sex."

"Kid is here, Hunter."

"Kid is snoring, Dev."

Pike chuckled. "Y'all have a good night."

The guys headed out, and about twenty minutes later, Oakley walked out of the big double doors, Reagan in tow. Reagan's left forearm was wrapped in an electric blue splint, but otherwise she looked no worse for the wear. When she saw Pike, a smile broke over her face. "Mr. Pike! What are you doing here?"

Her obvious delight at seeing him there tugged at him. He stood and met them halfway. "Hey, kiddo. You're looking pretty punk with that splint. Now you just need a blue Mohawk to match."

"Ooh," she said, looking to her mom. "That would be killer."

"Don't give her ideas," Oakley said, ruffling Reagan's hair.

Pike tucked his hands in his pockets to keep from taking Oakley's hand. "And I'm here to give you two lovely ladies a ride home. Your uncles had to get back to the campsite."

Reagan yawned. "I want to go back camping. I was supposed to sleep in a tent."

"Another time, baby. Let's get you home and into bed."

Oakley looked ten times more tired than she had before they

walked in, her makeup now smudged and her hair sagging out of her ponytail. But there was quiet beauty there Pike couldn't help but appreciate. The women he was usually with were the type to rush into the bathroom in the morning to make sure they had full makeup complete and hair blown out before he got up. Women who wouldn't go walk the dog without looking perfect. He loved that Oakley didn't need all of those things. Dressed up or down, she was all woman—strength and softness colliding.

Reagan led the way, and Oakley and Pike followed behind. He reached out and touched Oakley's elbow. "Everything okay?"

Oakley glanced over, weariness in her eyes. "Yeah. They don't think she'll need surgery, thank God. And she doesn't seem to be in much pain. She's got a high tolerance for that. But this hospital doesn't take my insurance, so that was fun."

He grimaced. "That sucks."

"I'll live. Nothing a few after-hours calls won't fix."

That made him grit his teeth. He wanted to give her the money right there. Whatever the bill was, he could take it off her plate. He didn't want her to have to make more calls. But he knew how that offer would go. She'd bite his head off and be insulted.

So he opted for reaching out and giving her hand a squeeze and dropping it before Reagan could turn around and see anything. She gave him an appreciative look. "Thanks for waiting. You mind dropping me off at home instead of picking up my car tonight? I want to get Rae to bed as soon as I can."

"No problem. I was going to suggest the same. If you give me your car keys, I can get one of the guys to follow me over tomorrow to drop it off."

"That'd be great."

They all climbed into the truck, and Reagan fell asleep against her mom before they even got onto the highway. Somehow even though they were in the same spots from earlier when they had their hot interlude, it didn't feel weird to have Reagan between them now. It felt comfortable and domestic. A few weeks ago if someone had asked him if he'd want to hang out with a mom and her kid, Pike would've balked. But these two didn't make him want to bail. If anything, he felt frustrated that he couldn't do more.

When they arrived at Oakley's house, Oakley touched Reagan's arm to wake her, but Pike put his hand over Oakley's. "Don't disturb her. If it's okay with you, I can carry her in for you."

She looked up at him, something unreadable in her eyes. "I don't know. She has personal-space issues with non-family members."

"I'll make sure I don't jostle her too much and wake her."

"You sure? I'd do it myself, but I feel dead on my feet and am not sure I could get her up the stairs. Tonight's been . . . eventful."

His lips tilted at the corner. "Hopefully not all bad."

"Not at all."

He climbed out of the truck to go to Oakley's side and carefully took Reagan from her. The poor kid was like a rag doll in the hand-off, completely spent, but when the night breeze gusted unexpectedly, she stirred. Her eyelids fluttered open and Pike stiffened, expecting her to freak out if she realized it wasn't her mom carrying her, but when she saw it was him, she snuggled up against his shoulder and let out a little mumbling grunt as her splinted arm bumped into his chest.

The easy acceptance from her hit him right in the sternum. She was okay with him being there for her. In that moment, he had this overwhelming protective urge rush through him. Like he wanted to hug her and keep her safe. Like he wanted to break the bike that had hurt her in two.

Oakley's eyebrows had climbed to her hairline as she watched, but she quickly smoothed her expression. "Well, that was a close one. I'll get the door. Her room is the second on the left at the top of the stairs."

He followed Oakley in and to Rae's room. Purple walls greeted him along with vintage music posters mixed in with more modern ones. On the corkboard above her desk, there was her festival ticket from the other weekend, a photo of her and her cousin at the concert, and two photos of Darkfall performing.

Oakley noticed him looking. "I think you landed a new fan that day."

"Only one?" he asked, lowering Reagan onto her bed.

Oakley tucked the blankets around her daughter and propped the splinted arm on a pillow. "Maybe two. I think my brother liked you."

He smirked. "Never an inch, huh?"

"If I give you one, you'll take a mile."

"I absolutely will."

Oakley clicked off Reagan's bedside lamps and turned on a baby monitor by the bed. When she saw Pike looking at it, she said, "It's like a walkie-talkie. Rae has a thing about not wanting to leave her room at night so this lets her talk to me if she needs something."

He nodded, the reminder of Rae's special needs leaving him even more in awe of Oakley. He couldn't imagine how hard it must've been for her to do this on her own all this time—especially so young. Reagan was a kick ass kid. But he had a feeling getting her to this point had been a hard-fought process.

He followed Oakley out of the room and stood by as she shut the door with a quiet click. She pushed a stray hair away from her face. "Thanks again for bringing us home."

"Happy to do it."

"Come on, I'll walk you out."

They headed downstairs, and he could tell by the slump of her shoulders that she was running on fumes. He reached out for her when they neared the door and pulled her close to him. "You gonna get some rest, mama?"

She wrapped her arms around his waist, coming to him easily. "The doc said to check on her every few hours to make sure she's not swelling too much beneath the splint, so I'll probably just grab a catnap."

He frowned.

"What?"

"I should stay."

She leaned back. "Pike, you know I can't—"

"No, hear me out. If I leave, you have no car. What if something goes wrong in the night? How would you get Rae back to the doctor? And you said yourself you're dead on your feet. You need to get some rest."

"I'll be fine. I have neighbors if I have an emergency."

He shook his head. "I'll sleep on the couch and leave before Reagan wakes up in the morning. I can even check on her arm if you want to grab a couple of hours' sleep. I'm used to staying up late."

She stared at him, dropping her arms from around his waist. "Pike."

He grabbed her hand and laced his fingers with hers. "Come on, mama. I want to help. You'll be better for Rae tomorrow if you get some rest. I promise the offer is totally without ulterior motives."

She considered him a moment longer then let out a breath. "I guess it would be risky to not have a car tonight."

He smiled, sensing victory, and leaned over to kiss her. "My night owl abilities are at your service. All I need is a blanket and a TV remote, and I'm all set."

She let him pull her into a full hug this time. She pressed her face to his shoulder. "What am I going to do with you, James Pike Ryland?"

"Lots of dirty, sordid things." He kissed the top of her head. "But not tonight. Tonight I'm your sentry. So try to control yourself."

She laughed against him. "I'll do my best."

He released her and put a knuckle beneath her chin. "Get to bed, baby. I've got you covered."

"Thanks. And by the way, you completely suck at this one-night-stand thing."

"I'll try to do better next time."

Because there would be a next time. As he watched Oakley head down the hallway to her room, he knew there'd be no easy walking-away from this one.

Devon had been worried that his sister and niece were going to get hurt, but Pike had a feeling the only one who'd end up with gaping wounds at the end of this was him.

TWENTY-THREE

Oakley leaned against the wall in the hallway, hidden by the pre-dawn shadows as she watched Pike come down the stairs. She'd heard him go into Rae's room on the monitor. Despite Oakley's absolute exhaustion, she'd woken each time the door clicked on the monitor. Too many years of being acutely attuned to her daughter's sounds had left her a light sleeper, so she knew that Pike had checked on her daughter every hour since Oakley had gone to bed.

Normally she would've never let someone else, especially a guy, go into her daughter's room at night. But every instinct she had told her Pike meant no harm to either of them. And each time he'd checked on her, he'd stayed all of ten seconds—long enough to eyeball the state of Rae's hand. So despite waking up each hour, she had been able to grab some much-needed sleep in between. And now, her sentry looked like he was fading. He stretched out on the couch, lying on his side, and flipped to the early, early news—the one only overnight workers and parents of newborns watched.

Seeing him there, putting himself through the trouble on her behalf, made something warm and powerful curl inside her. This guy was going to kill her. They weren't supposed to be doing this. The two spheres of her life were not supposed to collide. Pike wasn't allowed in this part of her existence. It made her feel things she shouldn't. Want things she shouldn't. At least things she shouldn't want *with him*.

But she couldn't help the feelings that were developing. As much as she told herself to shut off that part of herself, she couldn't. He wasn't letting her. Each time she thought she'd created some line between them, he did something that moved him back on her side of the wall. So though she knew nothing could come of this, she was tired of denying what was there. She'd feel what she wanted to feel and when it ended, she'd deal with it. She was a big girl. A little heartbreak wouldn't kill her. Hell, she'd probably get a notebook worth of songs over it. At least she wasn't numb anymore.

She padded into the living room on bare feet. Pike's eyes were closed, but his breathing wasn't even enough for sleep. She stepped around the couch and knelt down next to it then leaned over to kiss him on the cheek.

His eyes blinked open, and he gave her a lazy smile. "Well, hi there."

"I've heard this four A.M. news is very compelling."

"Mmm," he said, pushing himself on his elbow. "Couldn't take my eyes off it."

"You look exhausted."

"So, stunningly sexy, right? That's what you mean."

"Of course." She let her fingers trace over the phoenix tattoo on his arm. Small, smooth bumps moved under her fingers, surprising her. Her eyebrows scrunched. "You covered something with this one."

"Burns," he said, reaching out and tucking her hair behind her ear. "Compliments of another of the boyfriends."

Her chest squeezed. "God, how did you not murder somebody?"

"Almost did," he said, his voice quiet.

Her heart broke for the kid who'd had to deal with such horrible circumstances. How he'd made it out and become such a successful man, a *good* man, she didn't know. She leaned over and pressed a kiss over the first burn mark. His body went tense as a bow beneath her. But when she continued and trailed kisses along the path of burns, he cupped his other hand over her head and let out a slow breath.

She lifted her head and brushed a kiss over his mouth. "Come to bed, Pike."

His hazel eyes flickered blue in the light of the television. "What about Rae?"

"She'll be out for another few hours and won't come downstairs until it's light."

His hand slid to the back of her neck. "You sure?"

"Never more sure of anything."

A sleepy smile broke through at that. "Well, then I can't think of a better way to start the day."

"Not too tired?" she asked, climbing to her feet and taking his hand to pull him up from the couch.

He wrapped his arms around her and kissed her. "Unless I'm dead, I'll never be too tired for you."

She led him by the hand down the hall and into her bedroom. He locked the door behind them and before she could even get a lamp on, he had his hands on her face and his lips on hers. The kiss started off slow and languid, but as soon as their tongues twined and bodies pressed against each other, a spark ignited, chasing off the exhaustion. The kiss turned deep and breath-stealing, parched people drinking from the waterfall, and Oakley could feel their control breaking, any internal restraint giving way.

She gathered his T-shirt in her fists and backed them both toward the bed. His mouth went to her neck and his hands beneath her nightshirt. Cool palms on her sleep-warmed body. He cupped her breast and then lowered his head to take her in his mouth. She moaned and yanked at the button on his jeans, needing him skin-to-skin right now.

They fumbled and kissed, hands everywhere, like desperate teenagers who'd never gotten laid. The fact that they'd slept together twice in the last twenty-four hours didn't seem to matter. The need was just as acute each time. Maybe even more so now that she was letting herself off her leash and just indulging in every part of this connection, no walls erected.

The sound of fabric ripping filled the air. She felt her brand-new nightshirt drop off her body.

"Fuck," Pike said under his breath. "Didn't mean to do that. That looked new. I'll get you another one."

"It's just a shirt. I'd rip yours off if I had the strength."

He broke away for a second, yanking his shirt over his head and off. "You don't care?"

"About a stupid shirt? No."

He gave her an unreadable look in the darkness.

"What?" she asked.

"Nothing. I just love . . ."

Her heart stopped beating for a second.

"How you are."

She grabbed a breath. "And how's that?"

He hooked her around the waist and tossed her to the bed, following close behind. "Like no other woman I've ever met."

She didn't know what to say to that, but the statement rang through her like the reverb of a bell—radiating out and making everything hum.

He didn't give her a chance to process it fully though because he was kissing her again. She looped her arms around his neck and let him press her into the bed as he kissed the ever-loving sense out of her. Fucking with his mouth, that's what he was doing. Long, deep strokes and hot, quick nips and thrusts. Her body rocked against him, grinding against the open fly of his jeans. She wanted to fuse with him, to melt together and lose herself in the moment.

She got a handful of his ass and squeezed the firm muscle. "You need to ditch these pants."

He braced himself on his arms above her. "Undress me, then."

He didn't have to tell her twice. She yanked at his jeans and tugged them down and off. They hit the wall somewhere in the dark. And then it was hot skin sliding on hot skin, hard against soft. His cock ground along her slick cleft, grazing her clit over and over but not entering her. Then his mouth went to hers again as he slowly drove her wild with the stimulation.

He groaned into her mouth. "You feel so fucking good against me. So soft and wet. I bet I could make you come just like this."

"Don't you dare. You're going to fuck me, James. No getting out of it."

He laughed, and she could tell it did something to him to hear his first name. She hadn't even meant to say it, but when he was stripped down like this, that's how she thought of him. The rock star left the building. It was just the man.

"I promise to do just that." He moved his hand to the bed. "Fuck."

"What?"

"Please, please tell me you have condoms because I just realized we used my wallet stash already and my bag's in the truck."

"Shit. Check that bedside table. I think I might."

He reached over and yanked the drawer open. There was rummaging. Then: "Jackpot!"

Pike lifted the foil wrapper in victory like he'd found the coveted prize in the bottom of the cereal box. Oakley couldn't see it fully in the low light, but it looked to be a sample package the OB/GYN had given her on her last visit. Thank God for free samples.

Pike tore the package open and rolled the condom on. "Now, where were we? Oh yeah, you were demanding I fuck you."

"Yes, let's get to that part."

He leaned down and kissed her. "Definitely. But first, we're going to play with the other thing you're keeping in your drawer."

"What?" Her eyelids snapped open.

Pike held up the vibrating plug and small bottle of lubricant he'd included in his Wicked care package. "Tried this one out yet?"

Her face heated. "I was saving it for our next call."

His grin went wide in the dark. "Well, lucky, lucky me. I get to see it in person." He uncapped the bottle of lube and drizzled it onto his fingers. "Plus, it might've killed me to be stuck on the other end of the line imagining you sliding this inside yourself."

His fingers dipped low, moving toward that forbidden zone.

"Pike . . ."

But before she could protest further, he found her back entrance and stroked with the barest amount of pressure. Her entire body seemed to clench and ache at the same time. "Oh, God."

"See," he said, his voice all dark promise as the tip of his finger worked gently against the resistance. "Just relax and let me show you how good this can feel. Touch yourself while I do this. It will help."

She followed his instruction, lowering her hand between her legs and finding her swollen clit. Then she put all her focus on softening the tension in her body and breathing through the odd sensation that was some combination of discomfort and forbidden excitement. But when he managed to slip past the resistance and slid his finger fully in, the discomfort gave way to blunt-force need. Her back arched and she groaned. "Holy hell."

"Imagine how good it's going to feel when it's me here one day. I'll fuck you nice and slow, and I'll bury that glass dildo deep in your pussy at the same time. You'll be so full of me, baby." He eased a second slick finger inside. "I could come just thinking about it."

Goddamn, so could she. She slowed her own strokes, afraid she'd go over too quickly.

"Mmm, look at how beautiful you are. Fingers stroking that pretty cunt. My fingers buried in your ass. I can see how close you are already." He gently pulled his fingers from her and replaced it immediately with the cool silicone of the plug. The toy was bigger and firmer but her body was ready after his preparation. He slid the plug forward and seated it in place. Then he switched it on.

Her toes curled and her head fell back onto the pillows. "Jesus."

"See?" he said, his voice low against her ear now. "Now you know why I like to use them."

That image was almost enough to send her completely over. Imagining Pike shamelessly using a toy on himself, sliding a slick hand over his cock while a plug filled him up. "I'd like to see that one day."

He nipped her earlobe. "Maybe you could be the one to put it in me. I did agree to let you have control next time."

She moved her hand away from herself at that. She couldn't even handle the barest touch with those images dancing through her head. She loved that Pike was so comfortable with himself and his desires. Loved that he brought that out in her. "Pike, I can't take—"

"Shh," he said, shifting above her. "Neither can I."

His hands moved to the backs of her thighs and he lifted her legs, opening her fully to him. She glanced up, catching sight of his face as he looked at the view. No doubt he could see everything— how turned on she was, the base of the plug, every private spot of her. But where his gaze was glued was on her face. And the look he had on his—some pained expression—knife-edge desire and need of another sort almost broke her completely.

It was a look no man had ever given her.

He pushed inside her with one word on his lips. "Oakley."

The way he said it made her want to cry.

Or run.

Or fall.

She closed her eyes and pulled him down to her, letting the overwhelming physical sensations overtake any emotional ones. She fused her mouth to his, dug her nails into his shoulder, and made love to him with every ounce of her being.

Despite the urgent need both of them were fighting, Pike took his time, dragging himself in and out in a languorous rolling of his hips. His tongue matched his rhythm and soon Oakley felt herself falling, falling. The decadent feel of him inside her, the plug buzzing, the drunkenness of his kisses. All of it was too much, too good.

She came in a rush, biting his shoulder to keep from crying out too loud. But he just rode the wave with her and kept going.

"You're not done, gorgeous. Give me another one."

She didn't think she had anything else to give, but she held on, happy to be along for the ride until he reached his high. But before long, she felt the pressure building in her again, the tide washing out and rushing back in.

"Pike," she said on a gasp.

Then he had his hand tucked between them, stroking her clit, and she was shattering again. This time she couldn't keep her noises to herself. But before she could get herself into trouble, Pike's hand came up and clamped over her mouth.

He pumped hard into her, the seams to his calm control fraying and popping along with hers. Her headboard rattled, their skin collided with hard slaps, and she came hard and loud, screaming into his hand in a way she'd never screamed before. Guttural, primal, teeth clenched.

The sound seemed to send him over the edge and he buried deep and fucked into her with long, hard strokes as he tipped over into his own release. Everything about the moment was beautiful: the sweat on his skin, the straining muscles in his neck, the filthy words falling out of him. But most of all it was the way he didn't look away from her, the way he pinned her with his gaze and gave her everything in that look. No filters, no bullshit. Just him and what they were sharing together.

She wanted to drown in the moment, roll around in the feeling of it.

And in that brief stretch of seconds, she knew she would not run from this man. Not anymore.

Good sense be damned.

She was doomed.

She was falling in love.

TWENTY-FOUR

Oakley sucked in ragged breaths and reached for the vibrator's remote to shut it off as Pike draped over her, spent from his own release. She should be panicking now that she knew she'd developed feelings for this man. But she couldn't find it in herself to be scared right now. Everything tasted too sweet. Too perfect.

Pike buried his face in her neck. "God, you're the best girl *ever*."

She laughed at his exuberance. "That's what all the guys say when they have their dick parked in that particular girl."

He lifted his head and kissed her lips. "No, they say that she was the best sex ever. You've got the whole package, Easton. I like the woman, not just the raunchy sex. Although, that's a highlight, too."

She let her fingertips trace over the curve of his ass. "Well, I'm just with you for your body. Just so you know."

"I can live with that." He flashed her a grin.

"We should probably, like, get up and shower and stuff. Someone will be getting up soon." She traced his eyebrow with her fingertip, toying with the piercing there.

"Do I have to?" he said, turning his head and kissing her palm. "I think we should just stay like this for the rest of the day."

"Hmm. An interesting plan, but it could get sticky. You know, when that stuff dries . . ."

He chuckled. "Good point."

He pushed himself up on one arm. First, he gently slid the plug out of her. Then he reached down to grab the base of the condom as he slid out.

Oakley closed her eyes, enjoying the spent state of her muscles. A morning in bed would be lovely. Her and Pike naked all day, making love when they felt like it, getting take-out and watching movies. It was a nice fantasy. Maybe one they could indulge in when Reagan did her next sleepover at Devon's.

"Oh, shit."

The tone of Pike's voice cut right through that fantasy. Oakley's eyes popped open. "What?"

When Pike didn't answer, she rose up on her elbows. His whole face had gone a shade of pale.

Her stomach clenched. "What's wrong?"

Pike lifted the condom. No. He lifted the remnants of a *broken* condom.

Panic surged, and everything inside her went cold at the feel of warm fluid moving down her thighs. "Oh my God."

"Okay, okay." Pike wet his lips. "It's okay. I'm clean. I get tested regularly. And haven't been with anyone since the last test. And I always use condoms. So you're on birth control and haven't been with anyone either, so we're good."

No. No. No. Oakley's hands were shaking. This could not be happening. "Pike, we're not okay."

"What?"

"I'm not on birth control."

"*What?*" Now his face went truly white. "What woman isn't on birth control?"

The accusation in his voice made hers go shrill. "A woman who's been celibate for five years and can't afford an unnecessary prescription. What kind of question is that?"

"Shit. I'm sorry. I'm sorry." He was frantic now, tossing the condom to the side and raking his hands through his hair. "It's just—shit. Okay, we're still all right. They have those morning-after pills, right? I can go to the pharmacy and get you some. I can go right now."

He jumped up to pull on his jeans, his movements jerky.

But Oakley could only wrap her arms around herself, the room and moment moving too fast around her. She closed her eyes, trying to calm down. She could get pregnant. *Pregnant.*

Eleven years later and she was facing this blow-your-world-up thing again. She couldn't get pregnant. She was almost thirty. Pike was a fling. She was alone. She had a daughter she struggled to support already. She *could not* get pregnant.

"I'll be back in less than half an hour," Pike said, pulling on his shirt. "Just take a breath. It's going to be all right. You go shower, and I'll go to the store." He walked to the side of the bed and leaned over to kiss her quickly. He touched his forehead to hers, his hand trembling where he held her face. "We're all right, mama. These things happen. We can fix this."

Fix this.

They were words Liam had said to her once upon a time.

Fixing that would've meant not having Reagan.

Her insides wanted to fold in on themselves. She couldn't form words.

Pike was out the door before she even had the chance.

———————

Fuck. Fuck. *Fuck.* Pike had to go to three stores before he found what he needed, and by the time he got in the car with the package in his hand, he was sweating and felt like he was going to vomit. He leaned his head back against the seat and tried to rein himself in.

This didn't have to be a big deal. Condoms break. Shit happens. That's why there were backup plans. Hell, he was probably freaking out over nothing anyway. The chances of Oakley getting pregnant from one encounter were probably low. And this pill would be the safety net. But he still had this sinking sensation in the pit of his stomach. He couldn't get the look Oakley had on her face when he left out of his head. She'd looked . . . traumatized. And he'd hightailed it out of there like his ass was on fire.

Smooth. Real smooth. But he'd had a knee-jerk reaction. He was always so careful with women. He'd been warned early on in his career that some girls would take advantage of guys in his position by getting "accidentally" pregnant and then asking for money. And he'd certainly seen enough unplanned children in his own household growing up. The thought of it happening to him had sent sirens going off in his head. His reaction had been panicked and automatic.

He just needed to get back to Oakley and everything would be fine. He'd apologize for his reaction. They would handle it and move on.

But when he knocked on the door to Oakley's place, drugstore bag in his hand, Reagan was the one who answered the door. Her hair was sticking up on end, but she'd changed out of her clothes from last night into pajama pants and a Tegan and Sara T-shirt. "Hey, Mr. Pike. What are you doing here?"

He tried to school his expression into a jovial one. "Just wanted to stop by and see how you and the bionic arm were doing."

She raised her arm. "I'm okay. But I won't be able to play guitar for the Bluebonnet songs. Mom says I'm going to have to get a cast for a long time. It's not fair."

"That does stink, kiddo. But I bet we can find some job for you in the group."

She huffed a world-weary sigh. "I guess so."

"Where's your mom?" he asked, hoping his voice didn't sound as tense as he felt.

"Making farm breakfast. You want some? You should. It's really good." She gave a sage nod of her little head.

"Sure." He gripped the bag at his side and walked with Reagan to the kitchen. "What's farm breakfast?"

"All the yummy stuff. Bacon. Eggs. Cheese grits. She makes it every Sunday morning. No cereal allowed."

"Sounds great."

When they entered the kitchen, Oakley was at the stove, sporting jeans and a long-sleeved blue T-shirt. Her hair was drying in waves down her back, her feet were bare. From the outside looking in, she appeared totally at ease. A mom cooking breakfast on a slow Sunday morning. But when she turned and met his eyes, he could tell she was anything but. Worry sat heavy in her gaze. "Hey."

"Can Mr. Pike stay for breakfast, Mom?"

Oakley's attention shifted to her daughter. She gave her a tight smile. "Sure, baby." She turned her back to Pike, her hand stirring, stirring, stirring whatever was in the pan. "You like your eggs over easy or scrambled, Pike?"

"Either's fine for me. Do you need any help?"

"I've got it." Stir, stir, stir. Her movements were harsh, too forceful—the only outward sign that she was probably freaking the fuck out inside.

He wanted to go over to her and wrap his arms around her, assure her everything was going to be fine, but with Reagan sitting there he couldn't do any of it. He'd just have to wait for his chance to talk to her alone.

He did manage to walk over and lay the bag on the counter next to her. Her eyes slid to it. She grabbed it quickly and tucked it on a high shelf in the cabinet near the stove.

Reagan didn't seem to notice the exchange. She was busy pouring them all glasses of orange juice. And as soon as Pike sat down at the table, Reagan started chatting. She told him and her mom all about camping and her harrowing bike ride. And she got all excited telling them about building the campfire and how Uncle Hunter had almost set the whole forest on fire trying to get one started. And then there was something about a one-eyed deer sighting.

For a kid who'd spent the night in the ER, she seemed fresh and spry this morning. And in a way, Pike was thankful for the running commentary. It kept him from jumping out of his skin while waiting to talk to Oakley. They all tucked into their breakfast, but he noticed Oakley mostly pushed her food around her plate. He didn't have much of an appetite either, but he didn't want either of them to think he was ungrateful for the invite.

When Rae was finished with all of hers, complete with a second helping of cheese grits, she asked her mom if she could have her video-game time. Oakley sent her on her way, and Pike started clearing the dishes. The minute he heard the game blaring in the living room, he walked over to shut the kitchen door then went to Oakley, grabbing her elbow. "Hey, you okay?"

She stilled, a frying pan in her hand. "I'm fine."

"Look, I know it's been a stressful morning, but everything's going to be okay. You can take the pill now and you'll be protected."

She nodded. "Right."

"Do you want me to get you some water?"

She turned at that, jaw tight. "Why? Want to make sure I take it?"

"I—" He stumbled on his words, surprised at the bite in her voice. "I mean, I just figured you'd want to take care of it as soon as possible. I think it's supposed to be most effective within twenty-four hours."

She set the pan down and crossed her arms over her chest. The pose would've normally looked tough, but instead it looked vulnerable, like she was trying to hold herself together. And sure enough, her eyes went shiny when she tried to talk.

"Hey," he said, stepping closer, putting his hand on her arm. "What is it? Talk to me."

She lowered her head, pinching the bridge of her nose and breathing deep like she was trying to not fall apart right in front of him. "I can't do this, Pike."

"You can't what, baby? Can't deal, can't what?"

She shook her head. "I can't take the pill."

His stomach dropped and his throat went tight. "What do you mean? Are you allergic or something?"

She looked up, stark emotion in her eyes. Fear. Pain. "I mean I *won't* take it."

Everything inside him chilled, dread curling around his bones and gripping hard. "Oakley . . ."

She pressed her lips together, a tear falling over this time. She swiped at it roughly. "I was supposed to get rid of Reagan. When I found out I was pregnant, her father sent me home with a plane ticket and money for an abortion. I went to the clinic and was an hour away from doing it. If I hadn't panicked at the last second . . . if I'd gone through with it . . ." She looked toward the living room, a million unspoken words on her face. "I just . . . I can't."

He stared at her for a long second, the reality of what she was saying taking time to line up in his head. But when the words finally fell into order, he nearly bent over with the impact. "Oakley, you can't mean to risk . . . I mean, we can't, I don't—"

"It wouldn't be your problem."

He leaned back against the counter, gripping it for support. "*What?*"

"The chances of anything happening are slim. But it's my choice not to take the pill, so it will be my situation to deal with. I'm not going to expect anything from you, so you can relax."

"*Relax?*" he said, working hard to keep his voice down. "What? You get pregnant and then I just fucking brush off the fact that there's this kid out there who's mine?"

Kid. Mine. Jesus Christ. The world spun in his vision for a moment, and he gripped the counter harder.

She tipped her face toward the ceiling like she was asking for some divine intervention. "Come on, Pike. I know this situation sucks—it may not even *be* a situation. But if it is, what are you suggesting as an alternative?" She met his eyes. "All of a sudden you'd be down with being a father? How would that work? You'd stop in during tour breaks for a visit?"

He raked a hand through his hair, fisting the strands. Panic was rising to drowning level, stealing his air. "God, I don't know, Oakley. But what about you? You're not set up for another kid. You already have your hands full."

"I'd figure it out. I always do." The words were strong but her voice shook when she said them.

He looked at her then, really looked at her. Despite the fierce determination in her eyes, she was trembling. This was Oakley's brave face. He stepped forward, putting his hands on her upper arms and rubbing them, trying to comfort her in the midst of his own anxiety attack. "Baby, we need to take a breath here—both of us—and not let our emotions run away with us. I hear what you're saying about what happened with Reagan, I do. I hate that you had to go through that, and I want to beat down the guy who took advantage of you and put you through it. But this is a different situation entirely. I talked to the pharmacist. This just prevents the pregnancy from happening. It doesn't end one that's already there. It's not the same decision you were faced with back then."

Tears slipped down her cheeks, tearing his goddamned heart out, but he had to say his piece.

"I get that this is bringing up a lot of stuff for you, but think through this. Do you really want to take this risk right now? You're on the way to a promotion. You're getting settled into the life you want with Reagan. A pregnancy—a baby—would blow that up. Neither of our lives are equipped for this."

She looked down at the floor, her body still trembling beneath his hold. Her voice was soft when she spoke. "I'm giving you your out, Pike. Take it. This is your pill."

The words stabbed into him and twisted. That's what she expected him to do? If she got pregnant, she thought he was the type of guy who would walk away and leave her saddled with his child. Like he was no better than his father or the men who'd come and gone out of his mother's life.

He reached down and cupped her chin, lifting her face to him. "Is that what you really think of me? That if you went through with a pregnancy, I'd bail on my kid and leave you to foot the bill. Just go on with my life like it never fucking happened?"

She held his gaze, a slight wince crinkling her eyes, but she didn't refute the accusation.

That stung even deeper than he expected.

"Jesus, if that's what you think of me, I don't know why you'd let me in your house, much less your bed." He stepped back and crossed his arms, anger simmering up now. "Or maybe you just wouldn't want someone like me to be involved. I'm just supposed to be the hookup, right? The guy to get off with but not one you'd want around for too long."

"Pike . . ."

"You know what, screw it." He grabbed his keys from the counter. He needed to get out of there. The room felt too small, the air too stifling. "It's your body, your decision. But know that if you get pregnant, it's *our* baby. You'll have to deal with me for the rest of your life. No way my kid is going to lie in bed at night wondering why his daddy isn't around. I've been that fucking kid. It sucks."

Oakley stared at him like he'd spoken a foreign language.

"I'll drop your car off within the hour."

With that, he strode past her to the back door so he could avoid going by Reagan and stormed out of the house, his heartbeat booming in his ears. When he got in his truck, his lungs felt as if they couldn't expand and he was sweating all over. He drove to his studio, parked in the back, and let the full brunt of the panic roll through him, ugly, awful sensations choking him.

Worst part was he had no idea what was freaking him out more. That Oakley might become pregnant. Or that he'd just lost the one girl who'd made him feel something.

He rested his forehead against the steering wheel just as his phone dinged with a text.

He reached out and grabbed it, hoping it was Oakley, hoping that maybe this could turn around, but instead Braxton's picture was displayed. He clicked on the message.

Braxton: We landed the fucking Wanderlust tour! Scooooore! Call me.

Pike stared at the words, the news he'd so long awaited there on the screen. But he couldn't find an ounce of excitement in it.

He tossed the phone on the seat.

Maybe Oakley had been right. What the hell did he have to offer a kid? There were things he was good at. Staying in one place wasn't one of them.

Maybe he wasn't that different from his dad after all.

TWENTY-FIVE

Oakley tried to focus on the kids as they rehearsed one of the songs in Pike's studio. None of them could stay still or on key, the excitement of being in a real studio too much to contain. But they had limited time here today and needed to make the most of it. She had to take control and calm them down. But she was having trouble doing that when she couldn't calm herself.

Pike was there, helping with everything, guiding the kids, but she and Pike may as well have been strangers sharing the same room. They'd only talked once since that morning in the kitchen— and even then, it'd only been through text. He'd wanted to know when she would know for sure if she was pregnant or not. She'd told him at least two weeks. Now a week had passed and the only interaction they'd had was during rehearsals.

She'd pushed him away, so she wasn't surprised he was keeping his distance. She'd basically told him that if she got pregnant, the child didn't really need him in its life. She'd seen the hurt those words had inflicted. *You're not needed. You're not worthy.* That kid who'd been discarded by his family had surfaced. And she'd felt like an absolute bitch for doing that to him.

That hadn't been her intention. She'd wanted to give him his freedom. She knew her decision not to take the pill wasn't logical or fair to him. She'd taken the choice completely out of his hands, so she'd wanted him to know he still had one. But her words had come out all wrong.

She had expected him to be thankful for the out, to walk away with clean hands. But he'd declared the exact opposite. If there was a baby, he'd be involved somehow, a part of the child's life. She had no idea what to make of that, but it both comforted her and terrified her. She wouldn't be all alone this time. But she'd have Pike in her life indefinitely. She'd have to watch him live his life, date other people, move on. All while raising a new baby . . .

God. The thought of another baby had kept her awake at night for a week. She'd made double money at the night job because as long as she was taking calls, she wasn't thinking about everything else. When things got quiet, the blind terror came. She had no idea how she was going to manage a baby. Those first few years with Rae had been so impossibly hard.

But even knowing that, she couldn't bring herself to take that pill. She'd stared at the thing all that night, trying to talk herself into it, knowing it'd be the saner path. But then she'd flash back to when she'd been at the clinic at seventeen. She'd been way less equipped at that time than she was now. If that girl could handle an unexpected pregnancy, this one could, too.

And all the worry was probably for naught anyway. It'd been one broken condom. She was older, surely less fertile. She had friends her age who'd tried for months and sometimes years to get pregnant. It didn't happen that easily.

But the *what-ifs* were going to kill her.

Pike was going to kill her.

Sharing a room with him and not going to him was proving to be an exercise in torture. The drama between them hadn't quelled the effect their night had had on her. She'd fallen for the guy— recklessly and totally. Stupidly. She'd been halfway there already, but when he'd stayed up to watch over Rae, she'd been a god-damned goner. She'd failed the casual-hookup test spectacularly.

"Why don't you try to sing it, Reagan?"

The question broke Oakley away from the nonstop hamster wheel of her thoughts. She looked over at Pike, who'd positioned Rae in front of a microphone.

Rae glanced over at her, worry in her eyes. "I'm not the singer."

"I know," Pike said. "But Madison has a cold, and I think this song might be better suited for your voice. Just give it a try and see."

Reagan wet her lips, clearly tempted. The poor girl had been chomping at the bit since they'd gotten here, but her cast prevented her from playing her guitar and participating. "Mom, what do you think?"

Pike's eyes met hers.

Oakley's knee-jerk response couldn't be stopped. "I don't know, baby."

The thought of Reagan's voice being recorded and out in the world could open her up to all kinds of attention. Oakley knew her daughter had something special, and Oakley's instinct was to cocoon her from all that. She didn't want Rae to even have a chance at being sucked into that world like she was.

Reagan's head dipped. "It's okay, Mr. Pike. I don't think my voice is good enough for the song anyway."

Her daughter's response hit Oakley right in the chest. And Pike's words rang in her ear—*Reagan doesn't think you like her singing.*

God. The last thing Oakley wanted was for her daughter to think she didn't believe in her or see her talent as beautiful. Reagan stepped away from the mic, shoulders hunched.

"Wait." Oakley's voice came out too loud and all the kids turned her way, including Rac. She walked over to her daughter and put a hand on her cheek. She had to work to get the words past her tight throat, but she knew they had to be said. "No, you should sing it, Rae. You'd sound amazing on this one. I know you would."

Reagan's eyebrows knitted, suspicious. "Really?"

Oakley smiled. "Really. Give it a try."

In her periphery, she caught Pike's lips curling upward. He stepped closer, putting a hand on Oakley's elbow and squeezing as he moved past her. "All right, kiddo. Let's get your headphones on so you can rock this."

Oakley and the rest of the kids moved to the room on the other side of the glass, and Pike got Rae set up to record. Oakley grabbed a set of headphones so she could hear better and the music started. It was Oakley's original music and the kids' lyrics laid on top of it. But all of that faded into the background as her daughter began to sing.

She hadn't heard Rae really open up in longer than she could remember. So when the words came through, her voice clear and pure and stunning, tears jumped to Oakley's eyes. The voice she'd remembered as that of a talented little girl had morphed since she'd last heard it into one of an older-than-her-years songstress—rich and textured and effortlessly on key.

My God.

Pike's gaze found hers through the window. She shook her head in awe and he gave her a little nod. Not an I-told-you-so nod but a reverent one, like he agreed that they were both in the presence of something special.

The other children in the group had gone still and quiet around her as they shared headsets and listened in. It was no longer a question of who should sing this song for the group. They'd found their voice.

Rae had found her voice.

Oakley watched as Reagan, who was a few rows in front of her on the bus, chatted with one of the boys from the group. They'd wrapped up at the studio, laying down a rough version of the main song, and were headed back to Bluebonnet. Normally, Rae would've sat with her, preferring her mother's company to the stress of having to interact with other kids. But Rae seemed to be getting more and more comfortable with the group. She could bond with them over music and have a common topic to talk about. A few years ago, Oakley would've never dared to hope that her daughter could navigate being in such a group, but Rae was finding her place in the world and learning how to be in it in her own unique way.

Oakley leaned back, a small shred of peace coming over her, and she turned her attention to the evening traffic that crept past the windows. But the peace was short-lived. Her seat bounced and she turned to find Pike sliding into the spot next to her.

"This seat taken?"

His hazel eyes were golden in the muted sunlight of the bus windows. She could see the green flecks, the striations of color, could remember how dark all those shades went when he'd been perched above her in bed. She shifted in the seat. "You're already in it. Kind of late to ask."

"How about I ask for forgiveness instead of permission, then?"

She blew out a breath, knowing he wasn't talking about the seat. "You have nothing to ask forgiveness for, Pike."

He shifted his body to face her more fully, dipping his head so that none of the kids nearby would overhear. "That's not true. It wasn't right to storm out on you, especially not when you were so upset. It was a dick move. I'm sorry."

"Yeah, well, I said some things I shouldn't have, too. We were both freaking out in our own way."

His gaze held hers, searching. "How are you doing now?"

"Dealing. Working a lot of double shifts."

Lines appeared around his mouth, his jaw tightening. "You don't need to do that, Oakley. You know that if this happens, anything you need financially, I'll cover."

"I know," she said, not doubting that he would do just that. "But that's not why I'm working so much. It helps keep my mind clear, and I can only sleep if I'm completely exhausted."

He sighed and put his hand on the seat between them, next to hers but not quite touching. "You don't have to deal with it all alone, you know? You can call me. It's not like I'm not constantly thinking about it, too."

"Thanks, but talking about it is not going to do any good.

What's going to be is going to be. I'd rather not think about it until I know what I'm dealing with."

"So you're of the block-it-out-and-deny school of thought?" he asked, his mouth hitching up at the corner.

"Totally."

"And how's that working, Ms. Insomniac?"

"I'm not currently in the fetal position, rocking in a corner, so I'd say pretty well."

His amused expression fell at that, concern filling his gaze. "Baby . . ."

"Don't." She closed her eyes, her emotions riding dangerously close to the surface. "I can't."

His hand moved over hers, a gentle press of his fingers against hers. "I want to be there with you when you take the test."

"Pike . . ."

"Don't shut me out of this, Oakley." His fingers tightened around hers. "This impacts both of our lives. We should both be there."

She inhaled a deep breath, working to tuck her emotions back underneath the rug. She couldn't lose it here on the bus. One screw loosened and everything was going to spill out. But she also knew it wasn't fair to cut Pike out of things. If there was a child, it was his as much as it was hers. If he wanted to be a part of this journey, he had that right to be.

She slipped her hand from beneath his and tucked hers in her lap. When she opened her eyes, she dragged her calm mask back into place. "I'm planning on doing it next Saturday. First thing in the morning is supposed to be best."

"I'll be there."

She peered over at him. "And then what, Pike?"

He ran a hand over the back of his head, Mr. Unflappable finally showing a chink in his armor. "Then I guess we'll figure things out from there."

"You can still walk away," she said quietly. "I won't hold it against you."

His jaw twitched and he stared toward the front of the bus. "Then you need to raise your standards of what you expect from a guy."

The comment landed square, and her defenses rose. "Low expectations are better than getting blindsided later."

He looked at her then, his gaze burning into hers, but his voice was soft when he spoke. "I'm not him, Oakley. And you shouldn't let me be. You deserve better than that."

She rubbed her lips together, her patched-together facade fraying at the edges again. "I don't know what better looks like, Pike."

His eyes creased at the corners, empathy there. "I get that. Once I left home, I expected the worst from every person I met. I looked at people like they were all out to screw me. I know how hard it is to break free of that, to trust someone—especially to trust someone like me. But when I say you're not alone in this, I mean it. Whatever you need, I'm here."

She closed her eyes, letting his words wash over her. She wanted so badly to believe them. She wanted to hope that if this happened, it wouldn't be as terrifying as last time, that she'd have someone in her corner.

"Tell me what you need, Oakley. Name it and it's yours."

She shook her head, unable to voice what she wanted most. She couldn't ask that of him. Wouldn't. It was dumb to even think it. "I just need to get some sleep."

She could see him in her periphery, staring at her, evaluating. But finally he released a long breath and leaned back. "Okay, Oakley. I'll stop asking."

TWENTY-SIX

Oakley adjusted herself on her pillows, trying to keep some enthusiasm in her voice as her caller described what he wanted tonight. He was a talker, so he was making it pretty easy on her as he seemed happy enough with her interjecting *oohs* and *oh, yeahs* every now and then. His own talk was what was getting him riled up. The only problem was the steady cadence of his voice was making her mind wander. She rubbed a hand over her face, trying to refocus. Just a few more minutes . . .

"I would fuck you so hard, Sasha. We'd wake up my neighbors."

A quiet buzzing against her thigh made her jump before she could respond to Darren's dirty talk. She reached for her phone in the dark. A text message lit up the screen.

Pike: Open the door, mama.

What the hell? She glanced at the clock. Half past midnight.

Darren cleared his throat on the phone and she hurriedly said, "Maybe you could shove something in my mouth, keep me quiet."

"Oh, yeah," he said, then went on with his description of exactly what he would shove in her mouth.

She typed her reply to Pike.

Oakley: Working

Pike: I figured. Let me in anyway. I'll be quiet.

She stared at the phone. Letting him in was a bad idea. She couldn't cut off this call until it was done, and it was the middle of the night anyhow. But Pike was already at her doorstep, and she found herself moving that way despite her misgivings. Maybe he wanted to talk. Maybe he was having a rough night, too. He said he would be there for her. Maybe she needed to be there for him.

She made her way to the front door and unlatched it. Pike stood on her doorstep, holding a box of Krispy Kremes and giving her his trademark smile.

She put her hand over her mouthpiece. "What are you doing here?"

He shrugged and stepped inside like she'd invited him. "The Hot Donut sign was on. How could I pass that up? I thought you might like to share."

"I want you to lick my asshole," said the voice in her ear.

Oakley jolted at the intrusion. *Shit. Shit. Shit.*

"Would you do that to me, Sasha?" Darren asked, his voice husky. "I've always wanted a girl to try that."

She shut the door behind Pike and moved her hand away from the mouthpiece. "Yes. I'd love that."

Pike's eyebrows lifted, a mischievous glint she hadn't seen since everything had happened lighting his eyes. He leaned forward against the ear not blocked by the headset. "What would you love?"

She shook her head and mouthed *Stop it.*

"Tell me, Sasha," Darren whispered. "I want to hear you say you'd put your tongue there."

Oakley pointed that Pike should go into the kitchen, but he simply grinned and mouthed *No way* back to her.

"Sasha?" Darren asked.

She closed her eyes, pinching the bridge of her nose. "Yes, baby, I'd love to lick your asshole."

A choked sound came from in front of her. Pike had his hand over his mouth, clearly trying not to laugh. She gave him a narrow-eyed glare and pointed again to the kitchen, but he turned and went toward her bedroom instead.

Holding in a frustrated sigh, she followed him, ready to give him hell as soon as this call was done. He set the box of donuts on her desk and took one out. He studied the donut a little too closely, giving her a questioning look.

She knew him well enough to know where this was going. She put her hand over the mouthpiece again. "I swear to God if you mimic rimming with that thing, I'm going to personally injure you. I *cannot* laugh on these calls."

But despite her threat, a smile tugged at her lips.

He leaned forward, keeping his voice low. "How much longer do you think it will go?"

"He's pretty worked up. Give me a few minutes, and I'll get him there. He wants to hear me come first." She moved her hand off the mouthpiece for a second to talk to Darren, keep him going. "Ooh, I feel so dirty doing this, baby. You're getting me so hot."

She covered the mouthpiece again.

Pike smirked. "A gentleman, then. Nice. Anything I can do to help?"

"Go in the next room so I don't have to embarrass myself in front of you."

"No, I should stay because, let's face it, I've never heard a fake orgasm. I mean, there's never been a need."

She groaned. "Pike, stop, seriously."

He licked the inside ring of the donut in a lewd, slow glide despite her warning not to, and gave her an oh-yeah nod.

A full-bodied laugh threatened to burst out of her. She spun to turn her back to him, to concentrate on the job at hand.

"Tell me what you're doing, Darren. I want to know."

Darren moaned softly. "I'm jacking myself nice and slow, thinking about your tongue inside me."

Dammit. Nice and slow was not what she needed. She tried to ignore Pike's presence behind her. "I'm never going to last, baby. You've got me so turned on."

"Ah, you're so sexy. Tell me how wet you are."

She put her hand on her forehead, dying a little inside. "Soaked."

Heat pressed against her back and she stiffened. Pike slid his hands onto her waist, beneath the hem of her T-shirt and kissed the slope of her shoulder. His lips brushed against her other ear. "It's not nice to lie to the man. I can help."

She peered over her shoulder at him, taken off guard by the shift in his voice and the suggestion. She cupped the mouthpiece. "What is this, Pike?"

His fingers stroked along her hips. "I've missed touching you. It's hurt to be in the same room, knowing I couldn't have you. I can help you sleep."

She inhaled the words, an eddy of confused emotions swirling in her. "This isn't sleep."

He let his hands skate up her belly. "Then tell me to stop."

She turned her head, putting a hand to brace herself on the wall, her knees going weak from the rush of need his touch was inciting. She should tell him to quit. This was a bad idea on so many levels. They hadn't figured out anything between them. They couldn't just act on the lust that always seemed to simmer between them. Everything was so much more complicated than that now. Plus, she was on a work call.

But when he slid his hands upward and cradled her breasts in his big, warm palms, all that came out of her was a moan. And something that had been so tightly wound loosened just a little bit.

Darren made a pleased sound on his end. "What am I doing to you that's making you make that sound?"

Pike pinched her nipples and rolled them between his fingertips, sending pure, illicit sensations straight downward. She tipped her head back with another grunt. The combination of the stranger on the phone and Pike here for real was doing a number on her head. How was she supposed to talk to one guy while another made her feel good? "You're grabbing my breasts, pinching me."

Pike coughed.

Shit.

Darren was quiet for a moment. "Is someone else there with you?"

Crap. Crap. Crap. "I—"

Pike cupped her between her legs and drew his fingers along her clit through the soft cotton of her sleep shorts and panties. She gasped.

"No, I can tell by your voice. You sound . . . different." Sheets rustled on the other end. "Fuck, you have your boyfriend there with you or something, don't you?"

"No, it's—"

"That. Is. So. Hot," Darren said, a new interest in his voice. "What's he doing to you?"

She clamped her hand over the speaker. "He knows you're here."

Pike stilled. "Shit. Did I get you in trouble?"

"He thinks it's hot."

Pike considered that for a moment then a game-on smile slowly curved his lips. He kissed the shell of her ear. "Mmm, excellent. Then let's give him a show, shall we?"

"Pike," she whispered. But Darren was requesting her attention. She cleared her throat. "Yes, Darren. Sorry, my . . . boyfriend showed up unexpectedly. I can tell him to leave."

Pike moved to stand in front of her, lifting a pierced brow at the *boyfriend* word. But there was pure wickedness in his eyes. He leaned back against the wall, looking damn edible with his messy hair and black T-shirt, and slowly let himself slide down to the floor.

"It's okay. Let him stay," Darren said, excitement in his voice. "It will be like a threesome. This will be so much hotter 'cause I know it's real. Just tell me what he's doing to you."

She closed her eyes, taking a deep breath. "He just slid down to the floor in front of me."

She couldn't believe the truth had fallen out of her mouth. Was it fucked up that this was turning her on? It wasn't Darren. He was as generic as any of her other callers, but having anyone on the phone at all listening to her fool around with Pike had this element to it that was making her blood heat. Plus, the fact that Pike was so wholly unthreatened by her night job, that he had no problem making a move on her while she was working, did something to her. The only other guy who'd found out about her second job had left her mid-date in a restaurant, not even bothering to pay the bill. And she assumed most guys would react similarly. But not Pike. He just saw it as another adventure to be had.

Pike's fingers hooked the waistband of her boxers and panties and tugged down. "Tell him I'm about to lick your cunt until you're coming so hard, you won't be able to stay standing."

"Oh, fuck yeah," Darren said in her ear, voicing her own thoughts.

"He heard you," she said to Pike, her voice going raspy as Pike stroked over her slick flesh.

"Come closer." Pike dragged her forward to where he leaned against the wall. "You don't come until I say so. And he doesn't get to come until then either."

She shuddered at the command and wet her lips. "He said you can't come until I do."

Darren made a choked sound of assent, and she could hear his fist pumping in the background. Slippery, rude sounds filling her ear right as Pike grabbed her ass and dragged his tongue along her cleft.

Her entire body seemed to weaken in an instant. She braced both her hands on the wall and groaned.

"He gives orders. Does he dominate you?" Darren asked, breathless.

She swallowed hard. "Yes. He's a dom."

Pike looked up at that, something possessive flashing in his eyes. "And you do what he says?"

"Yes," she said, the word getting caught in her throat.

"Shit, that's hot. What's he doing to you?" Darren asked, a desperate edge in his voice.

Oakley tried to steady herself and she looked down at Pike, taking in the erotic show he was giving her. His gaze held hers as he circled his tongue around her clit, evilly slow, and then he nipped at her tender flesh with his teeth. The bite of pain sent her to a different place. Her mind blurred for a second. And though someone was listening on the phone, in that moment, it was just them—her and Pike channeling this crazy energy that seemed to flare anytime they were near each other. So when she spoke, it was for Pike and no one else. "He's making me feel so good. His tongue is hot against me and every time he licks, my pussy clenches and my clit throbs. And he's not afraid to bite. The man knows what to do with his mouth."

Pike held her gaze and slid two fingers inside her. Her body clamped down around the invasion and his callused fingertips brushed tender, needy places, bringing her right to the edge already. She bit her lip hard, trying to reel herself in.

"Talk to me, mama," Pike said softly, his fingers moving inside her. "Tell me what I do to you."

She eased one of her hands off the wall and reached for Pike, letting her hand slide into his hair. "He's got two fingers inside me, rubbing just like I like it—kind of rough but never too much. He knows exactly how to keep me riding the edge, how to torture me with the wait. And the way he looks at me . . . like he's going to do everything in his power to fuck me senseless, like he owns every piece of me. I could get off just from that."

Darren groaned in her ear. But she barely heard him now. Pike's hazel eyes had gone dark and held her in his spell as his fingers and mouth worked her over. Her thigh muscles started to quiver from the sensation of it all. She gripped Pike's hair tight and kept her other hand braced on the wall, afraid she would collapse any minute.

"Tell me how bad you need his cock," Darren said, panting.

The request jolted her for a second, but she was too far-gone at this point. All of her filters had broken down the minute Pike had gone down on her. So words rolled freely out of her mouth. "I need it so bad. He's long and thick and when he's inside me, I can barely breathe because it feels so good."

Pike was the one to groan this time. And the sound vibrated against her flesh, nearly sending her over. Pike reached down and undid his pants. She couldn't see what he was doing, but she heard the belt and zipper, and could imagine him taking his erection out, stroking a hand over it—which only made her body throb more, her own need coiling to the breaking point.

"Come for me, mama," Pike said, keeping his voice low and intimate as he dipped his fingers deep inside her, mimicking the slow, tortuous pace he'd fucked her with once before. "Let's give him the real thing."

Pike's mouth returned to his sensual assault, and his fingers curled inside her, stroking, stroking, stroking. Sweat beaded on her neck, and her hand became a fist against the wall. Her hips rocked now, riding Pike's tongue and fingers—wanton and shameless—but she couldn't have stopped the movement if she tried. Sharp breaths caught in her throat.

"Goddamn," Darren said. "You're fucking his face, aren't you? I can hear it all. Shit, I'm gonna—"

Somewhere in the distance, Oakley heard Darren gasping through his orgasm. But she couldn't respond or focus on anything but the man here with her and the sensations rocketing through her. She made some desperate, choked sound, sure she was going to collapse to the floor with the impact of what she could feel spinning inside her. But Pike clamped a hand on her hip, steadying her, and everything exploded at once. She came with a shout, her body rocking and jerking against Pike's mouth.

A deep sound of satisfaction rumbled through Pike, and the vibration of it traveled up Oakley's belly. Her hand went to his shoulders to keep from falling as she called his name and rode the waves of pleasure.

Pike didn't back off until she was gulping breaths and wobbling on her feet. Arms wound around her and she sagged to her knees in front of him. He brushed his hands over her hair, murmuring soothing things and curled her into his hold.

"Jesus Christ that was hot."

The voice on the phone startled her in her buzzed state and she could only respond with *"Mmm."*

Pike took the headset from her and put it on his own head. She tried to protest but wasn't in the state to put up much of a fight.

"Sasha's off for the night now," Pike informed Darren.

Oakley couldn't hear Darren's response, but whatever he'd said made Pike smile down at her.

Pike pushed her hair away from her face. "She's sexier and more beautiful than I could ever describe on the phone. Words aren't enough. She's the kind of girl that makes you want to write music."

Oakley closed her eyes, letting Pike's words fall over her. For the first time in a week, she wasn't worrying about anything at all. The shifting soil beneath her feet had stilled . . . at least for a moment.

If only she could hold on to this feeling forever.

She knew that wasn't possible.

But a few hours of escape couldn't hurt. She leaned over to the mouthpiece. "Good night, Darren."

Then she clicked the Hang-up button and tossed the headset to the side. She wrapped her arms around Pike's neck. "I'm all yours now."

Pike's ravenous look stole her breath. He wasn't looking at her like she could be pregnant. Or like she was his lay for the night. He was looking at her like he wanted to own her. "On the bed, Oakley. On your belly."

Oakley's muscles were lethargic, responding slower than she wanted them to. But with Pike's help, she managed to get to her feet and walk over to the bed.

"Where's the box I sent you?"

She turned her head. "Back corner of the closet on the right."

She closed her eyes, listening to the rummaging, and not letting her mind drift to anywhere but here. She could worry about how this was a bad idea tomorrow.

The bed dipped as Pike crawled next to her. He told her to kneel up and he tugged off her shirt then he captured one of her arms. "Hands above your head."

She complied and didn't fight as he cuffed her arms to the headboard. The scent of new leather filled her nose as she settled back down on the bed, her knees tucked beneath her.

"You called me a dom on the phone," he said quietly.

"You are when you want to be."

"You want that side of me right now, Oakley?"

"Only if you want to give it."

He hissed out a breath. "You don't even realize how submissive you sound and what that's doing to me. You're fucking beautiful." His hand cupped the back of her neck. "Tell me your safe word."

"Oklahoma."

His grip on her neck eased her head all the way down to the bed until her ass was in the air and her cheek pressed to the cool sheets. "Tell me what you need tonight, baby."

"To not think."

"You sure Rae isn't going to come down here?"

"She's sound asleep. If she needs me, she'll ask for me on the monitor. And she can't hear anything from her room. I've checked because of the phone calls."

Pike glided a hand down her back and then he went to the box. She couldn't see what he grabbed, but she found out soon enough. He touched her back entrance and stroked. "I'm going to take you here tonight."

She groaned, unsure if it was from fear or anticipation.

"You lit up last time, baby. I can't ignore such a sexy reaction." Cool liquid moved over her opening. "But let's start with the plug."

Pike lubricated her thoroughly, dipping a finger in and then replaced it with the plug. Her eyes wanted to roll back in her head. The feeling was so goddamned decadent. Pleasurable in a way she never would've suspected before he'd touched her there the last time. He turned on the vibration and she pressed her forehead into the bed. "This thing's going to kill me."

He chuckled and then she heard the clink of metal. She peered over at him as he pulled his belt out of the loops of his jeans. He folded the black leather in his hand and tucked the buckle into his fist. "No, but this might."

A hard shudder moved through her. "You said you weren't a sadist."

He took the belt and drew the loop of leather over her backside in a slow, gentle stroke. "I'm not. But I'm addicted to hearing those noises you make when I get rough with you, so I'm beginning to see the appeal in meting out a little pain. Knowing you like it gets me hard."

He stalked around the bottom of the bed, and she turned her head to follow his progress. But before he appeared on the other side, she heard the slice of the leather through the air. The belt hit her with a burning-white sting. She arched against the sheets and clenched her teeth together, buffering the volume of the cry that escaped.

A few seconds passed as she panted through the pain.

"You good, mama?" Pike asked after she caught her breath, his voice deep and gritty as his fingertips traced over the mark he'd surely left on her skin.

It took her a moment to respond because she wasn't sure of the answer. The pain had been sharp and sudden, but now the burn was spreading over her skin, making everything pulse with heat, making the vibrator feel even more intense. "I'm good."

"You're perfect." He swung again, hitting high on her thigh and then followed up with a stinging blow across the middle of her ass—each stroke harder than the first. The pain was breath-stealing, and her mind blanked for a moment. She pressed her face into the mattress, restless, hungry. She wasn't sure for what.

He paused for a few seconds, not making a sound and not touching her.

Anticipation for the next strike filled her, like the feeling before the drop on a roller coaster. Tense thrill. "Pike, please."

"Please what?"

"More."

The word surprised her. She didn't understand it. But the rougher he got, the more she could feel the mantle of stress she carried dripping off her like melting snow, the tension breaking down and morphing into something entirely different, singular. Want. Need. *Pike.* Everything else became white noise.

He hit her again, three more times, no break, enough force to make a cracking sound in the air. Her brain buzzed, thoughts popping out of existence like soap bubbles. She shifted, writhing and rolling a little to her side. Pike's hand went to her hip. "Easy, baby. We can only do this if you stay on your knees. I don't want to risk . . ."

Her mind was fuzzy, his words not registering. "What?"

His hand slid to her belly, the weight of his palm heavy there. "We have to be careful. Just in case."

She lifted her head at that, some of the fog in her brain clearing, and looked at him. Gentle concern filled his face, and his hand stroked her stomach, something unreadable in his eyes.

For some ridiculous reason, she wanted to cry.

But as soon as the look was there on his face, it was gone, replaced by the hard-edged expression she'd started to recognize as his dominant face. "Get your knees back under you. You're still thinking too much."

Thankful that he was putting the focus back on the physical, she followed his instruction and braced herself for the next blow. He delivered in full, lightening the strength of the hits but increasing the pace until all the worries and thoughts began to empty again. She needed this, craved the oblivion of it all. Somehow Pike had known exactly what she needed most.

The seconds stretched into minutes and finally she lost all track of time and the number of strokes she'd taken. Pike dropped the belt, gripped her hair, and finished her off with a few open-handed slaps over her pussy and the base of the plug. Her skin was tingling and the burn was absolute, but it was a heady, dizzying rush. Every erogenous zone in her body ached and throbbed. She wanted to rub her thighs together, get some stimulation to her clit. She was dying.

Pike leaned down and drew her earlobe between his teeth, biting. "Still with me, gorgeous?"

Breath was wheezing out of her. "Yes. Need you."

"You fucking got me, babe. You've had me since the day I met you."

He kissed her neck, her spine, and his hands coasted over her burning skin, soothing it. The combination of the tenderness mixed in with the previous violence had her mind scrambling. The man was such a paradox sometimes.

He leaned over and unlatched her hands from the cuffs and

grabbed her bullet vibrator from her drawer. He tucked it into her hand. "Use this. It will make it easier for you."

Her fingers curled around it, and she shifted so she could tuck her hand underneath her body. The first buzz of it against her neglected clit almost sent her over the edge. She jolted.

Pike's laugh was low and dark. "Easy there. You're keyed up. Don't you dare come before I tell you."

"I won't," she promised, dialing the speed on the vibrator down. "I swear."

Pike positioned himself behind her, his hands still stroking her like he was sculpting her into something new and different. Maybe he was. Then his hands caressed over her hips and ass.

"Just relax for me." He tugged at the plug, easing it out of her. She moaned as the silicone slid past her sensitive tissues. "That's it. Gorgeous."

She heard the sound of the foil packet, the cap on the bottle of lube, and then something much more intimidating than the plug was pressing against her back entrance. Instinctively, she tensed. "Pike."

"Shh," he said, his voice like warm milk sliding over her. "You can take me. You should see how sexy and ready you are for me. You just have to breathe and let me in. I'm going to make you feel so good, baby. I promise I won't hurt you. I'd never hurt you."

She smiled into the sheets. "You just beat me with a belt."

He dragged the head of his cock over her opening in a maddening tease. "And you fucking loved it."

"God, I did," she said, rocking against him.

"You're going to love this, too."

"I'm ready."

With that, he shifted forward and nudged against her. The thick head of his cock felt like an impossible obstacle. She was going to be split in two.

"You're too big."

A choked laugh escaped him. "What every guy secretly wants to hear. But I promise, I'm not. Just trust me, baby. I've got you."

She sucked in a long breath, filling her lungs and working to ease the tight anticipation in her muscles, then she let it out. And as soon as all the air escaped her chest, her body gave way to him. He pushed past the resistance and eased inside, tentative at first and then seating deep when she made an involuntary moan.

Her fingers curled into the sheets, and she sucked in a long shuddering breath. She'd expected it to feel more like traditional sex once he was in, but this felt altogether different, the nerves more sensitive, the pressure more intense—the vibrator against her clit only making everything that much more Technicolor. "Oh, *God*."

"I second that," Pike said on a groan. "Fuck, you feel good. You okay?"

"I'm so okay."

"Thank God," he said, holding her hips and moving slow, seeming to stimulate every molecule in her body at once. "Now it's my turn to be tortured. Because damn, mama, the way you look right now . . . my cock deep inside you, your skin red with my marks, I'm fighting not to lose it and fuck you through this bed. You're like goddamned heaven."

"You don't have to be easy with me."

"Baby, don't tempt me." His voice seemed to be coming through clenched teeth.

She peeked back over her shoulder at him, finding him the picture of restrained violence. His jaw was tight and sweat glistened along his temples, but the sheer pleasure on his face was something to behold. A rush of pure, wicked need to let him off that leash filled her. She wanted him unhinged. His eyes met hers and she rocked her hips back against him. "Take what you need, Pike. I have a safe word."

He closed his eyes and his grip tightened on her hips. But then he inhaled a deep breath, a dragon preparing to breathe fire, and opened his eyes. He put a hand to her back. "Flat on your stomach, trap the vibrator between you and the bed."

She let him push her down to the bed, and she positioned the vibrator where she needed. Then his weight was on her, pinning her fully and completely, his cock deep in her ass.

He pressed his palm along the side of her head, pinning her to the mattress, and pumping into her in long, powerful strokes. "You're mine, Oakley."

"Yes," she rasped out, her release rushing toward her.

"Say it. I want to hear you say it."

"I'm yours, Pike." The words sounded like they came from someone else, her brain not keeping up with her body's overwhelming responses. Something about the position was sending her to a mental place she hadn't been before, one where her mind didn't fight anything. One where she just existed and enjoyed. Surrendered.

To him.

To Pike.

Pike braced his elbows at her side and dipped down to kiss her neck, his hips pumping furiously now. "Yes, baby. You're mine. All mine. Come for me."

He sank his teeth into the meat of her shoulder and fucked into her harder than she would've ever expected she could take. The motion jostled the vibrator hard against her clit and everything sparked inside her. She turned her face into the mattress, anticipating the size and scope of what was about to happen. And then everything went bright and brilliant behind her eyes.

She screamed. Real-deal screamed into the mattress, her body and reactions no longer in her control. Her fingers scrabbled at the covers as the orgasm took her over and yanked her under, drowning her with sensation and not letting her up for air. Pike grunted, dark and frantic behind her, fucking into her now with carnal abandon.

But she barely heard it over the noises she was making, her throat scraping raw with the primal, gut-deep sounds. The release seemed to go on and on without end, the power of it rattling her to the core and the vibrator not giving her a break in between.

And Pike, as if sensing she wasn't close to done, kept going, holding back his own release and driving her higher and higher.

Another wave of pleasure loomed within her and she worried, actually worried, that she couldn't take it. "James!"

"Let it have you, mama," he said, his words strained. "Give me one more."

And just like that, her body obeyed, making her go incoherent and nearly soundless as she gasped through the force of it.

Pike let loose a long sound of pleasure then, his body slick against hers as he flattened her fully onto the bed and shuddered through his own release.

She was boneless by then, boneless and sated and spinning.

Pike melted against her, careful to keep his full weight off of her, but burying his face in her neck and laying kisses there. "Good God."

"Mmph," she murmured in agreement.

"You all right?"

"Ask me tomorrow." Her voice was hoarse as the words moved past her raw throat.

He chuckled, the bounce of his body against hers making her shiver since he was still inside her. He reached between them, apparently grabbing the condom, and eased out of her. He planted another kiss between her shoulder blades. "I'll go run a bath for you."

"I can do that."

"Hush, woman. You can barely move. Let me take care of you, so I can feel manly and important."

"I think you fucked me into a stupor. Your manliness is affirmed." But she sighed into the blankets. "But maybe I will just lie here for a sec."

He brushed his fingers over her hair and looked down at her. "Rest. I'll take care of everything. I've got you."

She closed her eyes at the words and the tender tone of his voice. *I've got you.*

Yes you do, James Pike Ryland. Yes, you do.

TWENTY-SEVEN

Pike lay in bed, listening to Oakley sleep at his side, and stared at the slowly spinning ceiling fan. He should be exhausted. He and Oakley had fallen into bed after that phone call and had screwed like they were in combat—rough and hard and frantic. After her bath and his shower, they'd collapsed into the bed like they'd run a marathon. She'd told him not to say anything, that they should just enjoy the afterglow and go to sleep.

He'd agreed, not wanting to spook her with serious talk. But the fact that she was letting him sleep here at all wasn't lost on him. She'd told him he needed to be gone before Reagan woke up at seven, but the Oakley of a few weeks ago would've kicked him out right after sex. She'd wanted him next to her in bed as much as he wanted her there—even if she hadn't said as much out loud.

But what he couldn't get out of his head was that when she'd come tonight, it hadn't been the name Pike she'd called out, but James. At first, he'd figured it was because of the caller, that she was protecting Pike's identity by using James, the more common name. But it'd happened again when they'd made love. And hearing that name he'd so long ago left behind had made his chest tighten. Oakley saw him. The real guy beneath all the other crap. That's who she'd invited in her bed.

And Pike didn't want to leave it.

The broken condom had yanked him and Oakley apart before

they'd gotten a chance to give this a shot. Yes, this was only supposed to be a hookup, a fling, but he'd learned over the years that his gut didn't lie to him. And he'd felt the difference with Oakley from the beginning.

Pike got off on kink and daring sex. That's what got his motor going and held his interest when it came to women. And Oakley could play that game like a champ. But with her, it was an added bonus, not what drew him to her. Everything was different with her. The simple things lit him up—kissing her, conversations over dinner, watching her with her daughter . . . lying next to her while she slept.

A week away from her had been torture, especially knowing she was dealing with all that stress and worry on her own. Protective instincts he hadn't known existed had consumed him. And then tonight . . . when she'd said she was his, he'd wanted it to be true. The desire to claim her had been potent and absolute.

He had no idea what to do with that. Oakley could be pregnant. He was leaving for the tour in a few weeks. She already had a child. This had gotten complicated quickly. And the impulse that was pounding through him on how to handle the situation was a seriously idiotic one. He could hear all the words his mom and cops and social workers had thrown at him through the years—*reckless, impulsive, stupid.* He was so out of his depth with this.

He sat up in bed, careful not to disturb Oakley, and grabbed a pen and pad off the bedside table to scribble a note about having to go back to his place to feed Monty. His heart was beating too fast and his head was spinning, a panic attack waiting in the wings. But within a few seconds, he was up and dressed and headed for the door.

He needed fresh air.

And some perspective.

And he needed both right now.

Foster opened his door with no shirt on and his dark hair sticking up on end. He scratched his chest and yawned. "I swear to God this better be good."

Pike looked his best friend up and down. "What's with you? Usually you're up and halfway through your morning run by now. Your woman not giving you a chance to rest?"

Foster smirked and opened the door so that Pike could come in. "I wish that were the case. We babysat last night, and Lucy decided she wanted to pull an all-nighter with Uncle Foster and Aunt Cela. Apparently, she's not used to sleeping in strange places."

Pike chuckled. "The big bad dom taken down by an infant. Nice."

Foster flipped him off and led him into the living room, where a blanket was bunched up on the couch next to a harassed pillow. A few feet away, a playpen type thing sat near the unlit fireplace. Lucy's dark hair poked out between the netting of the makeshift baby bed.

Foster cocked his head toward the sleeping child. "Keep your voice down. Cela finally got her to settle down around three, but she didn't feel comfortable leaving her sleeping out here even with the monitor. I volunteered to stand watch in case she woke up again."

Pike peeked over the side of the playpen, a knot of nerves gathering. Jace, Evan, and Andre's little girl looked as sweet as an angel sleeping, but Pike couldn't help the rush of anxiety at the thought of being responsible for one himself.

He raked a hand through his hair and sat on the couch opposite Foster. "Sorry I woke you."

Foster's eyes narrowed, his ever-perceptive best friend evaluating him. "You look almost as bad as I do. What's going on, man?"

"You know that woman I was . . . am . . . seeing? The one you saw at Wicked?"

"Yeah."

Pike leaned forward, bracing his forearms on his thighs, unsure where to start. "Well, things have gotten . . . complicated."

Foster's eyebrow went up ever so slightly. "Meaning?"

"I may have gotten her pregnant."

Foster's eyes went wide. "*What?* Fuck, Pike. How did you do that?"

"Well, when a man and a woman get together and like each other, they can make a—"

Foster leaned over the coffee table and smacked the side of Pike's head like he used to do when they were kids. "Shut up. Don't joke. What the fuck happened?"

"Condom broke. She's not on the pill. We won't know for a few more days, though."

Foster sagged back against the couch cushions and rubbed a hand over his unshaven jaw. "Jesus, man. That's . . . I don't even know what to say. How is she taking it?"

"Oakley's tough—maybe too tough. She basically told me I could walk away and she wouldn't hold it against me. She thinks the responsibility is on her because she didn't want to take a morning-after pill."

Foster cringed. "Pike, you know you can't—"

"I'm not going to fucking leave her on the hook, man. What kind of asshole do you think I am?"

Foster blew out a breath. "Sorry, it's just—I mean, you've made it no secret how you feel about kids. And with your schedule and the band . . ."

"I wouldn't be the first musician with a kid."

Foster laced his hands together, letting them hang loosely between his knees as he took on a thoughtful expression—the businessman stepping in. "Well, obviously, you could help her financially. Maybe you could hire a nanny so that when you're not in town, she has an extra hand. And when you're in town, you could get visitation on the weekends and the nanny could help you. There are ways—"

"I think I might love her."

Foster looked up at that, a bewildered expression on his face. "What?"

Pike stood and shoved his hands in his pockets, hearing the words out loud sending him almost straight into hyperventilation. He paced around the couch, studiously avoiding looking toward the baby crib. "I know I sound crazy. That's why I'm here. You're good at talking sense into me. I'm having stupid urges. Talk me down, Fos."

Foster watched him as he paced. "Haven't you only known her for a few weeks?"

"Yes, but it's like I've always known her. I know that sounds weird, but there's this thing, this *stuff*, when I'm with her. I just . . . Everything's different. The vibe between us. The way we can talk to each other. The sex . . . God, it's like I'm a damn virgin again. I actually get it now—why you like the control. That need to dominate her came out of fucking nowhere. When I'm with her, I want to be everything to her, like this big, shining hero who she can trust to take her wherever she wants to go. All the bullshit that usually comes along with hookups just doesn't exist with her. Everything is better and real and new."

Foster listened to Pike's rambling speech without changing expression. He stretched his arm over the back of the couch. "Doesn't she already have a child?"

"Yes!" Pike said, keeping his voice down, but throwing his hands up. "That alone should make me want to run, right? But you should meet this kid. She's like . . . the coolest little girl ever. She likes Patti Smith, for God's sake. What eleven-year-old even knows who that is? And she's a musician, too, and has this voice that will knock you on your damn ass. Even Monty likes her."

Foster's mouth twitched.

Pike stopped pacing. "What?"

Foster shrugged. "Nothing. Just listening."

"You think I'm fucking nuts."

"Yep."

Pike braced his hands on the back of the couch and sighed. "I knew it."

"And," Foster added. "I think you're in love."

Pike lifted his head.

Foster's lips curled into a shit-eating grin. "Congratulations, man. Welcome to hell."

Pike simply stared, his friend's words sinking in, confirming Pike's worst fear. "I am so absolutely fucked."

"Why?"

"Because I leave for a big tour in a month. And she hates the musician life. All she wants is for me to go away. I'm only supposed to be the one-night stand. She doesn't even want her daughter to know that we're seeing each other."

Foster stood and walked over to Pike, putting a hand on his shoulder. "You can't control what she does or how she feels. But my advice is don't leave any cards on the table unturned. Don't fuck it up by trying to play cool about it. Lay it all out there. If she doesn't want more, you'll at least know you did all you could."

Pike's stomach twisted at that. The thought of putting his feelings out there, of offering that kind of vulnerability to anyone made him want to curl into the fetal position. The last time he'd made that kind of appeal had been with his mother. He'd put his heart on a platter for her and she'd served it as dinner to the man who'd beaten Pike. He didn't know if he could survive having someone reject him like that again.

And what did he have to offer Oakley? Money, sure. Love, yes. But if he was gone half the year or more, what were those things worth? And if there was a baby, he knew nothing of being a father. It's not like he could take notes from his own.

"I don't know what the fuck I'm doing," he said, pressing his temples with his thumb and middle finger.

"None of us do, bro." At that, Lucy began to whimper. Foster left Pike's side and went over to the crib. He lifted up Lucy with ease and kissed her head. "Good morning, diva. Didn't want to be left out of the conversation?"

Lucy wriggled against Foster then grabbed his hair in her tight little fist and began babbling happily.

Foster bounced her in his arms. "I think this one's going to be a domme. She's got a thing for pulling hair and demanding attention."

Pike tried to acknowledge the joke, but he couldn't muster up a grin. All he could do was watch how at ease his friend was with this child who wasn't even his. Foster would be a kick-ass father. All his life, Foster had been the responsible one, the one who knew how to take charge and make everyone else feel calm. Pike had been the fuck-up. He hadn't even been able to keep his siblings safe.

He was good at two things. Music and sex. Maybe he should stick to his strengths and let Oakley be. All he'd probably do is mess things up.

Foster tilted his head toward Lucy. "Want to hold her?"

Pike stuck his hands in his pockets. "No, I've gotta get going."

Foster frowned. "Come on, Pike. You're not going to hurt her. And she won't hurt you."

Pike swallowed hard as Foster walked over to him. Foster held Lucy out, and she gave Pike a curious look during the transfer. Pike awkwardly got his arm around her, his heartbeat ticking up a notch. She smelled of clean, sweet things—air-dried cotton and spring—and was heavier than she looked.

Lucy grabbed Pike's hair with surprising strength and declared with an air of triumph, "Da!"

Despite his anxiety, a laugh escaped him, her pure exuberance hard to be immune to. "All righty, then."

Foster smiled. "That's what she calls Jace. *Da* for him and *Pop* for Andre. I think she's telling you that you have blond hair like her daddy's."

Pike looked down at her. Her green eyes were big and curious, but there was a hint of mischief there. "She looks like Jace when she smiles."

"Like she's up to something?"

"Exactly." He took her little hand in his, testing out the feel of it. He hadn't held a baby since he'd helped his mom with his younger siblings, and the feel of her little fingers closing around his forefinger brought back a rush of memories—both good and bad.

Back then, he hadn't flinched around babies. They'd been part of his everyday existence. While his friends were riding bikes, he was learning how to mix formula and put a baby down for a nap. He was counting out the monthly WIC rations and hoping they would last. Helping his mom had felt like a prison sentence back then. He'd wanted to be like the other kids. He'd hated being stuck in that role. But holding Lucy helped him remember the good moments in between the stress of those days—the ways babies could look at you like you held the answers to the universe or how they could laugh from deep in their belly or how exciting it could be when they learned how to do something new. He remembered the goofy lengths he used to go to to get his brother or one of his sisters to smile—standing on his head, dancing like a fool, and making faces. They'd been the bright spots in his otherwise bleak existence in those early years.

He brushed a dark curl from Lucy's forehead and found himself wondering what his and Oakley's baby might look like. Would he or she have dark hair like Oakley and Reagan? Or maybe the white blond hair Pike had sported when he was little? Would their child love music like they did? Would she laugh with her whole body like his little sister had?

His lungs seemed to shrink in size as he tried to inhale a breath, his chest growing tighter and tighter.

Lucy moved her hand from his hair to give his cheek a light pat. "Da!"

He snorted, the sound coming out choked as he swallowed back the emotion that was trying to well up. "Goddammit."

Foster reached out and gave Pike's shoulder a squeeze. "Hey, it's going to be all right. You've got this. After all, who can resist the famous Pike Ryland?"

Pike snorted and shook his head. "Clearly, you haven't met Oakley Easton."

Foster grinned. "I look forward to meeting your woman then."

His woman.

That did have a nice ring to it.

TWENTY-EIGHT

Oakley sat in the control room with Pike, watching the kids rehearse through the viewing window, and trying to ignore how good Pike smelled. She hadn't seen him in a few days, but the night he'd come over while she was working hadn't been far from her mind since it had happened. Her heart had lurched when she'd woken the next morning and found him gone. But when he'd called her later that day to see if he could come by, she'd told him no. She had thought she could handle it, roll with the punches, deal with her feelings. But even a taste of that hurt had made her terrified of what it would be like if she got in any deeper. The fact that she was missing him so much when he wasn't around was stupid. And dangerous. And dumb.

He'd told her he'd landed the Wanderlust tour and would leave in a few weeks—on the road through the summer and into the fall. Baby or not, he'd be gone. And she needed to prepare for that.

Pike leaned over a microphone and hit a button. "That sounded great, you guys. Why don't you do a run-through of 'Blue Skies' now and we'll see if we're ready to record?"

The kids murmured to one another, their excitement evident to Oakley even though she couldn't decipher what they were saying through her headphones. She knew they'd all been waiting anxiously to do the real recording. Reagan hadn't talked about anything else for days.

Pike smiled her way, and she took off her headphones. He slid his set down to hang around his neck. "I think we're going to make it on time with this. They sound great. As soon as Reagan took over the lead, everything gelled. Even the kid on drums is finally getting his cues right. We may be able to get one track recorded before I have to head out tonight."

Pike had told her the rest of his band was meeting up here with the guy in charge of the Wanderlust tour to go over last-minute details with them—which he said meant going out, getting the guy drunk, and schmoozing him. So they were on borrowed time this evening.

She smiled at the scene in the window. "The kids sound fantastic. I can't believe how far they've come in just a few weeks. This might actually work."

He laughed and then put a hand over his heart, feigning a wounded look. "You doubted my immense ability to hone raw talent into greatness?"

She sniffed. "I will give it to you. You're pretty amazing at this producing thing. I know my experience is limited. I've only worked with two other producers in my life. But you definitely have that thing. You hear the opportunities in the song that I would've missed, the chances to elevate it. And you can pluck out the strengths in the performers. Like I never would've pegged Tenisha as a singer since her voice doesn't have a lot of range, but that girl can harmonize with the others like a champ."

Pike smiled, openly pleased. "Thanks, mama. That means a lot because most of the time I'm still feeling my way through this side of things. The guys thought I was crazy for buying this place. But I love it. That's always been my favorite part of being in a band— the creation side of it. I love performing, but figuring out how to create a song out of nothing, how to play to each person's talents— that gets my blood pumping."

The childlike enthusiasm in his voice warmed her. Pike was easy to look at anytime, but the passion he housed inside that outer shell was what drew her to him. The man loved what he did and it showed. She barely remembered what that felt like. "I get that. I used to feel that way when I'd write new songs. I didn't even care if anyone was going to hear them. It was the process that I loved."

"Yeah, that reminds me . . ." Pike leaned back in his chair, pulled a stack of papers from the counter behind him, the springs in the chair giving a creak, and slid a document in front of her. "I wanted to talk to you about something."

Her belly clenched, the legal document in front of her filled with lots of tiny print. What the hell? Her mind went straight in one direction. Was he already drafting up legal stuff in case there was a baby? She didn't know if she could handle that right now. "What's this?"

He rocked slightly in his chair, as casual as could be. "So I kind of did something behind your back. You can hurt me later if you feel the urge."

Her eyes scanned the top of the document but it was all legalese. "What are you talking about? What is this?"

"Remember that track you recorded here?"

Her gaze swung toward him, anxiety hopping like jackrabbits in her stomach. "Hard to forget, Pike."

He smiled. "Yeah, well, I edited out the uh . . . X-rated second half of the recording and layered in some more instrumentation to make a demo of the first song, 'Dandelion.'"

She blinked. "You did what?"

"I just wanted to see how it would sound when it was polished up. And damn, Oakley, it sounds great. You won't even believe how good it turned out."

"Why would you do that?" Her voice sounded thin in the small space.

"Look, I know if I would've asked, you would've shut me down. But I have a friend at a music publisher who was looking for some ballads. I had a feeling 'Dandelion' would be up her alley. So I *might* have sent it to her. And she *might* have loved it."

"*What?*"

He nodded at the document. "She wants to take on 'Dandelion.' They've been looking for a song for Harley Jay's new album and Harley loved it. The advance isn't crazy money or anything, but it's Harley Jay. Her last album went gold, and she's got lots of buzz around her, so this could mean real money down the line. And they want to see your other stuff."

Oakley stared at him, looked back at the document, then at him again. None of the words were making sense. This couldn't be happening. "Pike . . ."

He reached out and took her hand. "I know I should've asked you first. You're not committed to anything unless you sign the contract. But I wanted you to see that I wasn't bullshitting you about your songwriting. You're *good*, Oakley. You could do this for real. Make real money. Drop the late-night phone calls."

Pike's eyes were earnest, his hold on her hand tight, like he really was afraid she'd hit him or something. But all she could do was stare at him in disbelief.

Someone wanted her song. A popular singer wanted her song. *Her* song.

Tears came to her eyes, weird uncontrolled emotions surfacing. Excitement. Fear. Awe. She couldn't breathe.

"Hey," he said, squeezing her knee. "You okay?"

"I— Pike. Are you sure this is real? Like I sign that contract and it's real? Or can they change their mind? Or . . ."

His smile was quick and genuine. "It's real, mama. You're a gifted songwriter. This is your dream for the taking."

She put her hand on her forehead. "This is crazy. You sold my song. You *sold* my song. I'm not sure if I want to beat you for doing this behind my back or kiss you."

He gave her a roguish grin. "You could do both. Didn't I hear Reagan say that she was spending tomorrow night at your brother's?"

She snort-laughed. "Oh my God. You seriously just made my dream happen so you could get laid, didn't you?"

He nodded. "Totally. I have no scruples. Did it work?"

She shoved his shoulder. "No. I mean, I love you for this, but . . ."

Pike's smile froze halfway up. Shit. Had she just said I love you? She totally had.

"I mean, I told you we can't keep doing this," she said, trying to cover her slipup.

He grabbed the hand she'd pushed him with, his gaze going pensive, the humor leaving his voice. "Why?"

"You know why."

His thumb rubbed over her knuckles. "Tell me."

She looked down. "Come on, Pike. Don't make me say it."

"I want to hear it, Oakley."

She sighed. "Because it's starting to mean something, all right?"

He put a finger under her chin and lifted her face to him. "Newsflash, mama, I'm okay with that."

She closed her eyes. "Pike, if this is because I might be preg—"

"Stop. This isn't about whether you are or you aren't. I'm not asking you to spend tomorrow night with me out of obligation or some sense of duty. I like being around you. This is new territory for me, too. Believe me. This has gotten messy and complicated. Feelings are involved. But I'm of the school of living in the moment. And in this moment, I want to be with you. We'll deal with the rest another day."

"I take the test Saturday morning, Pike."

"I know, mama," he said quietly. "And we can be together for it. Spending the night together has got to be better than staying up all night worrying about things you have no control over, right?"

She raised her gaze to his and smirked. "But I'm so good at worrying about things I can't change. I'm like gold-medal good at it."

A slow grin moved across his lips. "And I'm gold-medal good at getting your mind off those things. Were you worrying about anything after I showed up at your house the other night?"

"Well, the donuts *were* a good distraction."

He reached out and pinched her thigh. "Never an inch with you."

"And always a good number of inches with you."

He laughed and rolled his chair a little closer until their knees were touching. "Is that a yes, Ms. Easton, to me and my inches?"

She indulged a bit and let her fingers trace a fray in the knee of his jeans, feeling the heat of his skin peeking through. "Why is it so hard to say no to you?"

"Because you're an incredibly smart woman. And an incredibly horny one. A fantastic combination, by the way."

She shook her head, smiling, and leaned closer, holding his gaze and feeling the instant spark that simple connection could create between them. "Guess it's a date, James."

"*Mom?*"

Chairs rolled back instantly, the little wheels on the wood floor obnoxiously loud as Pike and Oakley shoved away from each other. They might as well have had a blinking sign over their heads declaring their guilt.

Crap on a stick. How had she forgotten that they weren't alone? Oakley schooled her face into an all's-good expression, knowing that her cheeks were probably flaming, and turned to her daughter. "Hey, honey, what's up?"

Rae looked between Oakley and Pike, her dark eyebrows pinched together, and let the door shut behind her, blocking out the noise of the other kids. "I—well, we went through the whole song. We wanted to know if we can record now."

"Oh, right, the song," Oakley said, sending Pike a look.

Pike slapped his thighs. "Yep, I think we're good. Let's get set up for a run-through."

But Rae didn't move. She eyed the two of them like a judge evaluating guilty defendants. "Mom, were you about to *kiss* Mr. Pike?"

Pike waved a hand. "What? No. Don't be silly. I had something in my eye, and she was trying to help me get it out."

Reagan's head tilt said she wasn't buying it. "Y'all were looking at each other like people do in the movies right before . . . you know. And you didn't hear any of us when we asked if you liked the song."

Oakley let out a breath. Damn. She'd raised too smart of a daughter. Pike looked ready to come up with more of a story to protect Oakley's secret, but Oakley didn't want to lie straight-faced to Reagan. She got up and walked over to Rae. She put her hand on her head, giving that soft, short hair a stroke. "Yes. You're right. I wasn't going to kiss Mr. Pike, but we do like each other a lot, so that's probably why we were looking at each other funny."

"Like, *like* like?" Rae asked, poking a finger beneath her bright blue cast and scratching absently.

Oakley smiled. "Yes, that kind."

Reagan seemed to contemplate this for a moment, her forehead wrinkling, then she nodded. "Okay."

"Okay?" Oakley repeated.

Rae peered over at Pike. "If you marry my mom, would I get to live in your condo with Monty?"

Oakley choked on what she'd been about to say, and Pike froze in his chair, his stunned expression comical. "Uh . . ."

Oakley cleared her throat, trying to swallow past the constriction. "No, baby, it's not . . . We're just going to dinner and stuff. That's it."

Reagan's shoulders dipped. "Oh. Okay."

The disappointment in her voice was evident—surprising the hell out of Oakley. Rae, who didn't like any change in her routine, was bummed her mother wasn't getting married and moving her to a whole new place? Oakley couldn't wrap her mind around that.

"Reagan, why don't you go tell the group to get into their positions? I'll be in there in a second to make sure we're set up. We'll record vocals first, all right?" Pike said.

Rae tucked the hand without the cast in her jeans, a dejected expression hovering on her face, and turned toward the door. "Okay, I'll tell them."

She went back into the main room, and Oakley sagged against the wall. "Sorry about that. She doesn't understand—"

Pike raised a hand, halting her. "No worries. Monty will be very flattered. She actually handled that pretty well, I think."

"It helps that she thinks you're cool."

He stood and walked over to her, crowding her into a corner where the kids wouldn't be able to see them. He leaned in and brushed his lips over hers. "No, it helps that she's awesome. And her mom isn't so bad either."

Oakley gave herself the brief stolen moment, loving the feel of him pressed against her. She pushed up on her toes and kissed him long enough to make it count but not long enough that they could get caught again. "Guess this means you're all mine tomorrow."

He smiled and slid his hand onto her hip, giving it a squeeze. "For as long as you want me."

She smiled, a pang of sadness going through her.

If only that were the case.

Reluctantly, she stepped back and let him go into the recording room to set everything up. When he returned, he leaned over the mic. "Reagan, this is going to be all you, sweetheart. You'll hear the back tracks in your headphones. Let's just do the vocal alone first. Then we'll tape some of the background parts with the rest of y'all."

Rae gave a nervous nod through the glass, and Oakley sent her a thumbs-up. Pike flipped a few switches and the music filled the small space, saving them the trouble of headphones this time. He pointed at Rae and gave her the cue.

Reagan leaned close to the microphone, lips almost against it, and closed her eyes. Then the sweet strength of her voice filled the speakers around Oakley. She could barely stand to look at her baby and not cry. Her girl was so beautifully talented and brave. Eleven years old and singing with the conviction of a seasoned pro.

Pike looked over at Oakley. "You've done good, mama. She was born to sing."

"I'll say," said a voice behind them. "Damn."

Oakley startled at the interruption and turned, finding Braxton smiling their way. Geoff and another man were walking in behind him.

Pike rolled his chair back and stood. "Hey, you're early."

Braxton crooked a thumb. "Mr. Garrett came in on an earlier flight. Thought we'd check to see if y'all are wrapping up."

Oakley stiffened at the words. The name. She rose out of her chair like it'd caught fire.

"Yeah, grabbed a direct instead of that route that stops in

Albuquerque. Hope it's not a problem." The stranger stepped around Braxton and into the low light of the room. He held his hand out to Pike. "Liam Garrett. Nice to meet you."

Oakley couldn't move. *Liam.* Her daughter's voice rang through the room, and the man who'd fathered her stood steps away. Everything inside her went cold and still.

"Pike Ryland. Great to meet you." Pike shook Liam's hand firmly. Then he cocked his head toward Oakley. "And this is Oakley Easton. She's here working on a charity project with me. We were just finishing up."

Liam's gaze snapped her way, and she was almost surprised he remembered her real name. When they'd been together, he'd called her by her stage name, had told her it'd help her get used to answering to that name.

She felt frozen to the spot, all the anxiety from her teen self surging in her and making her throat want to close. Her muscles wouldn't move.

"Kris?" he said softly.

Pike frowned her way. "No, it's Oakley."

But Liam wasn't listening. He walked over to her. She'd always remembered him as this tall, imposing figure—intimidating. And though he still carried himself with that air, she now saw that he was shorter than Pike and not nearly as formidable. He was still attractive, his shoulder-length dark hair now shot with streaks of silver, but her stomach turned at the thought that she used to let this man touch her.

He stopped in front of her and shook his head. "It is you, isn't it?" His gaze raked over her, making her want to put some furniture between them. "I can't believe it. Still as beautiful as can be."

She swallowed past the constriction in her throat. "Liam."

"You two know each other?" Pike asked, frown deep.

Oakley's attention slid Pike's way. And as if he could read her mind, awareness dawned on his face. He wet his lips and looked toward Reagan, who was hitting the final verse of the song.

Panic was a living, breathing thing in her, but she needed Liam to not focus on the kids. She forced a smile. "Yes, we used to work together a very long time ago."

Liam's gaze held hers, and she could see it there—that old possessiveness. "Yes, very closely."

She wanted to vomit right on his expensive Italian leather shoes.

Braxton, completely unaware of the tension, grinned Oakley's way. "How's that?"

Liam tucked his hands in his slacks and rocked back on his heels, but his attention never left Oakley. "What? She didn't tell you. Kris was going to be a big star. Best singer we had in Pop Luck."

"Holy shit," Geoff said, coming up behind Braxton. "You were in that girl group?"

Pike put his hand up, halting any more questions. "Hey, guys, why don't we get going? We were just wrapping up, and Oakley's got this covered."

But right at that moment the music ended and Reagan's voice rang through the speakers. "Mr. Pike, how was that?"

Oakley forced her expression into neutrality, all the safety guards she'd put in place crashing around her.

Pike hit a button and leaned over a microphone. "Beautiful, sweetheart. I think we got it on the first take. Why don't y'all start getting your stuff together? We can finish this up tomorrow."

Liam spun around at that as if noticing there were children in the other room for the first time. He narrowed his eyes at the scene. "That was a kid singing?"

Pike stepped in front of the window, subtly blocking the view of Rae. His jaw twitched. "Yeah, just a little charity project thing."

Liam peered through the window with far too much scrutiny. "That girl's got a voice on her. She have an agent?"

Murder flashed across through Pike's eyes, and she got the feeling he was about to pounce on the guy.

Oakley surged forward at that. "Hey, Pike, I'm going to get them gathered up. I can lock up behind you."

Liam put a hand on her arm as she tried to pass. "Hey, you should come with us. We can catch up."

His grip was too firm, too familiar. She pasted on a smile. "Sorry, I've got a prior commitment."

"I'll be in town for a few days."

"All booked up, I'm afraid." She tugged her arm free and headed toward the door.

But Pike caught her hand on the way and guided her to him. He leaned down and kissed her, brief but not chaste. "I'll call you later, baby. Keys are in my office for you to lock up."

The move startled her at first, but then she realized what he was doing. He was trying to help. Trying to let Liam know in no uncertain terms that she was not available. When she caught sight of Liam's face, his eyes were calculating, sizing things up, but his pleasant smile was stiffly in place.

Oakley gave Pike's hand a quick thank-you squeeze. "Looking forward to it."

Then she hurried into the other room, her only mission to get her daughter as far away from the man in the other room as possible. But her hands didn't stop shaking until she saw the men leave and the door shut behind them.

Not until she was on the bus back to Bluebonnet did she let herself breathe a little.

A few minutes later her phone buzzed with a text from Pike.

Pike: U ok?

No. Not at all.

Oakley: Yes

Pike: I'm so sorry. I had no idea it was him.

Oakley: How could u?

Pike: I want to knock his fucking teeth in. The way he put his hands on you . . .

Oakley: Don't mess up your chance for the tour. He's an asshole but not worth giving up Darkfall's spot. Just do what you need to do and get him the hell out of town.

Pike: Let me come over tonight after I'm done with this.

She was so tempted to say yes. She knew her mind would be whirling all night, but they were going to see each other tomorrow night and Rae was home.

Oakley: School night. Let's just get together like planned tomorrow.

There was a long pause.

Pike: OK.

She could hear the hurt in the simple reply, but she couldn't deal with that right now. She just wanted to get home, get to bed, and forget today ever happened.

TWENTY-NINE

Pike sat across the table from Liam in the busy club, gripping his glass of Maker's Mark and trying to resist the urge to grab the fucker's head and bang it on the table. Pike was used to smarmy assholes. The industry was full of them. But Liam took it to a new level. And knowing this guy had taken advantage—no, had raped—a teenager who was in his care and sent her on her way when he got her pregnant made Pike want to do painful, maiming things to the man.

But Geoff and Braxton were yucking it up with Liam and playing the game. This tour was the biggest chance they'd gotten in a long time, and Pike was trying to keep his cool enough not to fuck it up for everyone. Once they got past this stage, they wouldn't have to deal with Liam. But it was digging under Pike's skin that he was going to do something to help put money in this asshole's pocket.

Liam kicked back the last of his Crown and water and ordered another, his voice getting louder and sloppier with each drink. A few more and the guy would be plastered. Pike hoped he'd fall right out of his chair and onto his face.

"So, Pike," Liam said, pointing with his empty glass, the ice cubes clanging. "You with Kris, huh?"

Pike's jaw clenched. "Excuse me?"

Liam waved a hand. "Sorry, sorry. I mean Oakley." He leaned

over to Geoff. "Can you believe anyone would name their kid that? Backwoods hillbilly motherfuckers. You met her parents yet?"

Pike gritted his teeth. "No."

Liam nodded and grinned. "Just fucking her then?"

Braxton straightened and looked to Pike, a what-the-hell look on his face.

Pike took a long sip off his drink, letting the burn of it keep him focused and calm. "You're drunk, Liam."

Liam shrugged and leaned back. "Just giving you fair warning, my friend. That girl's a clingy one. And emotional. Can go a little crazy when you're ready to drop her. Believe me. I know that pussy's sweet but—"

Pike's chair clattered behind him as he shoved it back and got to his feet, anger whipping through him like fire. "Maybe she was clingy because she was a fucking child, you sick bastard."

Liam's eyes flashed with something deadly, but Geoff jumped up and put a hand on Pike's arm before he could go after the fucker. "Hey, guys, I think maybe we've all had one too many. Why don't we—"

Liam just laughed and put his hand up. "Yeah, let's calm down. Sounds like she's fed you some lies. She was a consenting adult in my bed and more than a little willing."

Pike jerked forward, and Geoff's grip tightened on him.

Liam smiled, all charm and smarm. "I'm just trying to help you out, friend. No need to get all riled up about a girl who will be ancient history once the tour starts."

Pike was seething. In his head, he was already picturing what Liam's smug face would look like with two black eyes and a broken nose. But Geoff and Brax were sending him pleading looks. Pike raked a hand through his hair and sat back down. "Just keep her name out of your mouth, man."

Liam lifted his palms, sporting a good-natured smile but with victory in his eyes. "Didn't mean to offend."

Pike ordered another drink. This was going to be a long fucking night.

Oakley shuffled to the door in her pajamas, the incessant knocking making her head hurt. Pike had texted her late last night to tell her that he was going to stop by today, but she hadn't realized he'd meant this damn early. She pulled open the door. "Pike, isn't it kind of—"

But her words left her when she saw the man standing on the other side of the door. Liam gave her a sly smile and held out a single white lily. "These still your favorites?"

She tried to shut the door, but he put his foot forward, blocking her. She gripped the handle. "I don't want you here."

His expression turned cajoling. "Come on, Kris. It's not like I'm going to hurt you. I'm just here to talk. You up and disappeared on me all those years ago. You know how worried I was when you didn't come back? How heartbroken?"

"You got the letters that said I was resigning from the group. You knew I was fine."

"Letters with no return address. And what's with the Easton last name? Divorced?"

"It's my mother's maiden name. I wanted to disappear. Now let me."

She tried to shut the door again but he put a hand out and pushed his way inside, cooly aggressive. That was his way. "I will. After we talk."

"There's nothing to talk about."

He peered around her living room. "Sure there is. Looks like money's tight. Didn't have to be this way, you know. Leaving the group doesn't look like it worked out for you."

"I'm doing just fine."

"Still got that voice of yours?" He waved a dismissive hand. "Never mind, I know you do. I can tell by the way you talk. It's still there. I bet it's only gotten sexier with age." He gave her an up-and-down look. "Like other things."

"You need to leave."

"We could revive your career."

She wrapped her arms around herself, trying to keep her calm. She didn't think Liam would physically hurt her. That wasn't his style. But she needed to get him out of here before Reagan woke up. "I don't sing anymore. Lost interest."

The lines tightened around his mouth and actual remorse seemed to cross his face. "Because of me?"

"Contrary to popular belief, everything isn't about you, Liam."

He stepped closer and set the lily on the side table, his gaze softening. "Look, Kr—Oakley, I'm sorry about how things went down at the end. I should've realized how scared you were. You were always so mature for your age, so I just assumed you could handle it. I should've been there for you and gone to the clinic to be by your side. I never meant for that to be the end of us or your career."

The words were sweet, his tone gentle. He knew how to say all the right things. But he'd always been good at that part. "Apology accepted. But I have no interest in resurrecting my career. And why would you even want to? Seems like you've got a good gig managing a tour."

"Yeah, but it's a temporary role. I want to manage artists again. Things haven't gone so well the past few years. I need a star who can break out. You could slide right into the lane with the singer-songwriters that are popular right now. You've got the chops for it. And we used to be so good together."

She crossed her arms and frowned. "Liam, stop feeding me the line of bullshit. I'm no breakout star and you know it. You're here because even after all these years, you can't stand the fact that someone's in my bed and it's not you."

His lip curled. "Well, I was wondering why you're wasting your time with some punk-ass drummer. You know how many girls he's going to stick his dick in by night two of the tour? I saw him flirting with everything that moved at the club last night. He's an overgrown child with no impulse control and not fit for a woman like you."

Her teeth ground together. "How would you know what kind of woman I am?"

He leaned down, his cologne the same heavy musk from all those years ago. "Because I *made* that woman. Built her piece by piece just the way I wanted her. I bet you let him take control. You were always so eager to please." He dragged a knuckle over her cheek, making her shudder. "But I know how to please you back, how to take care of you, how to love you. You don't need a boy, you need a man."

She jerked away from his touch. "That boy is more man than you'll ever be."

Liam leaned back and smiled, his hands sliding into his pockets. "Give me one night, and I'll remind you how good we were together."

"Mom?"

The questioning voice came from the top of the stairs. Everything inside Oakley screamed a long silent cry.

Liam straightened like an arrow and turned his head, his eyes landing on Reagan.

"Hey, baby, I'll be up in a minute, okay?" she said, her voice high and tight.

"Who's that?" Rae asked, eyeing Liam shrewdly.

Liam broke into a genial smile. "I'm Liam Garrett, an old friend of your mom's. I heard you sing yesterday. You've got quite a voice, young lady."

Reagan crossed her arms. "Thanks."

"Reagan, go back to your room. I'll be there in a minute." Oakley's heart was bruising her ribs with the force of her frantic heartbeat. She silently prayed that Liam would be too distracted to put two and two together.

"Okay," Rae said begrudgingly.

"Wait," Liam said before Rae could turn her back. "How old are you?"

Oakley's heart dropped.

"Eleven and nine months." Reagan turned around then and headed back to her room. Oakley tried not to fall apart.

When Reagan's door clicked shut, Liam slowly turned back to her, wonder on his face. "You kept the baby?"

"She's not yours," she said flatly.

"The fuck she isn't. I was the only one in your bed back then." He carded a hand through his hair, his composure faltering. "You fucking disappeared and had *my* kid?"

That did it. Oakley lost all sense of self-preservation and stepped forward, poking her finger hard to his chest. "No, I had *my* kid. If you'd like your abortion money back, I'll write you a check. That's all I owe you. Now get the hell out of my house."

He didn't budge. "She's got your voice. And she's beautiful. And young. You know how perfect she could be for the market right now? I could help her. Help you."

She shoved him hard. "Oh my God, you find out you have a kid and the first thing you see is dollar signs? Fuck you, Liam. I want you out and away from me and my family."

He grabbed her wrist in a painful grip before she could shove him again. "You hid a pregnancy from me. Kept my child away from me. How do you think the courts would feel about that if I file for joint custody?"

Blind fear trampled over her. "They'd never give you that. You'd have to admit to statutory rape."

"We were recording in Vegas that summer. Age of consent is sixteen. I checked when you got pregnant. Didn't want you running to the police in some snit."

Her arm shook beneath his hold. "Please, Liam. Just let us be."

"I loved you, Kris," he said, his voice gentling. "You were all I wanted. I would've made you a star. Instead you chose this life? Single motherhood and letting some playboy musician warm his dick in you when he's got nothing to do in between tours? You're better than that. My kid deserves better than that."

"I deserved better than you," she said, her anger surging despite her fear. "And that playboy musician has taken better care of me in bed and out of it than you could've ever managed. You can't imagine the things he does to me, how good he makes me feel."

Rage filled his eyes, letting her know that old jealousy button could still be pushed. Even after all these years, he thought he owned her. And that told her all she needed to know. Vulnerability spotted, gun aimed. She stepped closer, her voice low and calm.

"You knew you couldn't get a real woman to touch you so you manipulated a child into your bed. That way you could look like you actually knew what you were doing. You're fucking pathetic."

Something ugly and hateful twisted his features and though she sensed it coming, she held her ground. His arm lifted and the back of his hand hit the side of her face with brutal force, knocking her sideways and stinging like a son of a bitch.

Dizziness took her for a second, her ears ringing, and she grabbed the side of the sofa to keep from falling. That would leave a mark.

Good.

She put her hand to her cheek and tasted blood on her lip. "Do it again, you fucking coward."

Liam surged forward like he was going to do just that. But before she could even brace herself for the blow, the door burst open. Pike was like a bullet coming through, giving Liam no time to process his presence. The right hook landed square, Pike's fist connecting with Liam's face, and Liam went sprawling to the floor in a crashing thud. Pike followed Liam's descent, shouting and hitting him a few more times, but it was clear Liam had been knocked out cold.

"Mom?" Rae's quavering question filled the air, her fear apparent, and Oakley rushed over to Pike, grabbing his shoulders before he could swing again.

"It's okay, it's okay, he's out. Not in front of Rae," she said urgently.

Pike turned, anger still hot in his eyes, but when he glanced up the stairs and saw Reagan, his fists unfurled and he released a harsh breath. He stepped back from Liam's prone form and dragged a hand through his hair, looking altogether undone.

"It's okay, baby, just give us a second," Oakley called up.

Pike reached for her, his expression pained, as he touched her cheek. "I couldn't get in fast enough. Are you okay?"

"I'm fine. It's nothing."

"I want to fucking kill this guy," he said, low enough for only her to hear.

She could feel the residual fury and adrenaline rolling off of him. If she left him here with Liam, it may only get uglier. "He's out. We're okay. We're all okay. Just take a breath."

He inhaled like an angry bull and let it out.

She licked her bloodied lip, thinking fast. Reagan would freak out if she saw her looking like this. "Can you go to Reagan? Try to calm her down?"

He frowned. "She's going to want you."

"I'm bleeding, and I can feel my face already starting to swell. I don't want her to see me like this. She feels comfortable with you. Just go up and tell her that Liam was drunk and not acting right and that everything's going to be fine. We're all safe now."

Pike peered up at Reagan, worry on his face. "I don't want to leave you down here with him. He could wake up."

"I'll go in the kitchen and call the cops. And I'll get my brother to come over and pick up Rae so we can file a report." She reached out and squeezed his arm. "But I need you to go to her. Can you do that for me?"

"Mom, what's wrong with that man?" Reagan called down, her voice small.

Pike held Oakley's gaze for a long second then nodded and turned toward the stairs. "He's going to be fine, sweetheart. Your mom's about to call someone to help him. Is it okay if I come up there with you?"

Oakley peered out the corner of her eye toward Reagan. Rae shifted on her feet then nodded. "Okay."

She released his arm. "If she doesn't calm down and needs me, just come get me."

"I'll take care of her," he said, his voice now resolute. He cupped her cheek then left her to go to Rae. She watched his trek up the stairs, not entirely convinced Reagan wasn't going to freak out anyway. But when he reached the top, he knelt down in front of Reagan and said something. Oakley stood frozen, waiting for Rae to ask for her, but instead she threw her arms around him and buried her face in his shoulder. She could tell by the way Pike's arms didn't move that he was taken aback by her reaction. But after a beat, he wrapped his arms around Rae and lifted her off her feet.

Oakley's lips parted as her daughter, who didn't hug anyone but her and her uncles, locked herself around Pike like a monkey and let him pick her up. When he turned around and met Oakley's eyes, she could see the surprise in his.

But she couldn't stand there staring for long. The man at her feet would rouse soon, and she wanted the cops here when he did. She glared at the slack body on the floor and gave it a little kick, getting entirely too much joy from the petty move. "Might be kind of hard to get custody with an assault on your record."

She went to the coffee table, grabbed her phone, and dialed.

Fuck Liam Garrett.

He may have seemed powerful back when she was a kid, but now she could see him for what he was—nothing.

THIRTY

Pike collapsed next to Oakley in bed after an exhausting day of talking to the cops and handling the fallout from punching out the tour manager he was supposed to be working with.

Oakley, who was sitting cross-legged on the bed, turned to him, her face less swollen, but the bruises starting to darken around her left eye. Every time he saw her injuries, he wanted to go find that bastard Garrett and beat on him some more.

"So did you lose the tour?" she asked, a wince already on her face.

He adjusted himself on the pillows and crossed his ankles. "I called Lex Logan, the lead singer of Wanderlust, and told him what I knew about Liam. Then I told him that he backhanded my girl."

Her gaze snapped up at that, and he could tell him calling her his girl had caught her off guard. She cleared her throat. "And what'd he say?"

Pike's lips quirked up. "He said, 'Fuck that guy. He's done.'"

"He believed you? Just like that?"

"Lex said he never really liked the guy anyway. The record company had hired him based on a recommendation. But yeah, regardless of the other stuff Liam's guilty of, Lex isn't the type of dude who'd put up with anybody hitting a woman. He said he would've beat the asshole down, too."

"He sounds like a good guy."

"He is. You'd like him. He's almost as handsome and talented as I am."

She sniffed.

But the smile she gave him held no humor. He could almost feel the weight of her thoughts pressing on her. "How's Rae doing?"

Oakley sighed and hugged her knees, sitting her chin on top of them like a little girl. "She's okay. She saw him hit me, though."

Pike pushed a stray hair away from her face, careful not to touch her bruises. "I know. She told me. Poor baby cried against my shoulder. She was so worried about you."

It had broken his damn heart to see it. To his amazement, Reagan hadn't let him go. She'd let him hold her and rock her while she cried it out. He'd almost cried with her because having her lean on him, trusting him to comfort her, had sent this surge of tenderness for Rae through him. He'd found himself wishing he could always be there for her to provide a shoulder or comforting words if she needed them.

Oakley blinked, her eyes a little misty. "I hate that she had to see any of that. I would've never tried to provoke him if I'd known she was there."

Pike stilled. "Wait, you provoked him on purpose?"

"He was threatening to file for custody. I needed proof on paper that he was a threat. He'd never hit me before, but I've seen him lose his temper with other people and get into fights. I knew what buttons to push and hoped he'd take the bait."

Pike shook his head. "Jesus, Oakley. What did you tell him?"

At that she smirked. "I basically told him how much better you were in bed than he was. Then I called him a pathetic pedophile who preyed on a kid because he couldn't get a real woman."

"Fuck," Pike breathed. "You've got some balls, Oakley Easton. He could've done a whole lot worse. Punched you or attacked you."

"I didn't need balls. I had my instincts. I was with Liam for too long. I know he's all hat and no cattle. He wouldn't have done anything that would've landed him in jail for real. He knows he'd never survive it."

Pike frowned. "I'm so sorry I wasn't here sooner."

She shrugged. "I think it was for the best that I took the hit. Gives us proof. I'd take that backhand ten times over if it means I can keep him away from Reagan. Hopefully the one hit was enough."

Pike ran the backs of his fingers over her cheek. "We'll get you a lawyer. Jace's friend Reid is an attorney at the Women's Center. He'll help us out. With all the back child support Liam would owe and the explaining he'd have to do about how he got a teenager pregnant, it'd be a tough one for him to win."

"Thanks. I doubt he'll really pursue anything. He was pulling that card to intimidate me. But I don't want to take any chances."

"I'd kill him before I'd let him near you or Rae. Jail would be worth it," he said, meaning it. When he'd stepped onto Oakley's porch and caught sight of the argument through the window, all he'd seen was red. Then Liam had hauled up and hit Oakley in a way he'd seen his mother hit too many times before, like he'd been hit as a kid—the backhand. The move that said the person on the receiving end wasn't worth a shit, that he or she was just some trash to smack around. Pike had never felt rage like that. It'd gone beyond when Red had broken his hand. It'd tapped into that protective part of him that blocked out all other logic. Knowing Oakley had been subjected to Liam, that her youth had been stolen from her, that her dreams had been taken. All because of this scumbag. It had opened up that ugly, dangerous side of him. If she hadn't been there to stop him, he probably would've beaten the guy bloody.

She rolled onto her back, peering up at him. "I'm so sorry you got dragged into all of this. Told you I suck at hookups."

He smiled down at her. "Yes. You totally do. Being all awesome and stuff. Making it impossible for me not to come back for more. I'm completely addicted."

Her gaze went to the ceiling, a distant look coming over her face. "Guess it's good the tour's about to start then. You can detox. We both can."

His smile sagged.

She looked over and reached out to cup his jaw. "Don't do that.

I didn't mean it as a dig, just stating the facts. We can't keep pretending that it's not happening."

"I'm not pretending." He put his hand over hers, the decision he'd made a few days ago slipping out. "If you're pregnant, I'm not going."

She sat up. "Wait, *what?*"

He shifted to be face to face with her. "I'm not going to leave for months while you're pregnant with my baby, Oakley. I'll find a drummer to fill my spot on the tour."

Her expression turned horrified. "Pike, that's . . . crazy. And completely unnecessary. I appreciate the gesture, but I can handle this on my own. You're not turning that opportunity down for this. I won't let you."

His jaw flexed. "It's not your call to make."

"Yes, it is," she said firmly. "I don't want that. You're going."

The way she said it stung. Cold. Final. "You don't want that or you don't want me?"

"Don't do that. Don't twist my words around." She sent him a warning look. "Last time I got pregnant, I walked away from my dream. If it happens this time, I'm not letting you compromise yours. I told you that if there's a baby, you can be part of his or her life, but I don't need you here holding my hand just because I'm pregnant."

"And what about being part of *your* life?"

She closed her eyes and rubbed the spot between her eyes. "I'm not going to pretend I don't have feelings for you. I think that's painfully obvious by now. But we knew going into this that our lives aren't compatible. You need to be on the road. I need to be here."

"You could come with me, you and Rae, as soon as she's out of school for the summer. Take a leave from work. I can cover whatever you need. Rae could see the country. That would give us three months together."

She lifted her head, giving him a look like he'd sprouted a unicorn horn. "You want to bring a girlfriend and a kid on a rock tour? Do you know how insane you sound? Do you even understand how confusing that would be to Rae? And what would happen after the three months?"

He could feel her slipping away, the walls going up. The night he'd originally planned had gotten screwed up by everything that had happened this morning. Now he was messing this all up, too. But he was taking Foster's advice and leaving nothing unsaid, no stone unturned.

He leaned back over the edge of the bed and dug in his overnight bag. When he straightened again, he plunked a little box on the bed between them.

"I don't want to take a girlfriend. I want to take my fiancée." He opened the box to reveal the sparkling ring he'd picked out a few days ago. "And I want to make it crystal clear to Reagan the role I want to take in her life, too."

Oakley stared down at the box with her lips parted and her face slack. "Pike, what the hell are you doing?"

Her voice was way too calm and still. Quiet in a dangerous way.

He took her hands in his, charging forward despite her lessthan-enthusiastic response. He'd expected that. "Look, I know it's fast. And yes, probably a little crazy. But you talked about your instincts earlier. Well, I have some, too. And the only time I've fucked things up in my life is when I haven't trusted them."

"Pike . . ."

"I know I'm probably not the type of guy you pictured having in your life. My job is bizarre and my family won't be inviting us over for Christmas dinner. Your parents will probably hate me. But I think we both know enough to realize that there's something different between us—something we shouldn't just walk away from."

Oakley looked down at their joined hands.

He gave hers a squeeze. "I've never felt about anyone the way I feel about you. Every time I think about leaving on tour without you, I get a knot in my stomach. And if you're pregnant . . . Jesus, Oakley, how could you think I wouldn't want to be a part of that process? So much happens during that time. Doctor visits and sonogram pictures and finding out the gender. I don't want to hear that shit via email. I don't care if we're here or there, all I want is for us to be together."

Tears filled her eyes, and she shook her head. "Pike . . . we—this is—we can't." She looked up at him, eyes shiny. "You are the best man for doing this. I can't even tell you what it means to me that you're offering this. But whether you can see it or not, this is about the baby."

He swallowed hard. "It's about us."

She pressed her lips together and shook her head again. "You would never be proposing right now if not for this potential pregnancy." She let her chilled hands slide out of his hold and met his eyes. "We would've ended our fling and gone on with our lives. You don't love me, Pike. You just don't want to walk away like your dad did."

He stiffened at that, her words like ice water rolling down his spine. "You think I'm trying to fucking *prove* something because I have some kind of daddy issues? Christ, Oakley, I'm telling you that I want to be with you, that I want to marry you. And you think I'm saying it because of my fucked-up childhood? Why the hell would you say that?"

She picked up the ring box, closed it, and placed it in his hands. Her eyes were sad when she looked up at him. "Because throughout all of that beautiful proposal, you never actually said that you love me."

"I did, I—" Hadn't he?

She swiped at the tears that had escaped and gave him a resigned smile. "You didn't. And that's okay, because you shouldn't. People don't fall in love that fast. The pregnancy scare has just messed with both of our heads, made all of this feel more intense."

The words didn't resonate with him. He didn't buy that logic. All he felt was the sting of her refusal, the pain of her rejection. Maybe she hadn't fallen in love with him. But he had with her. And perhaps the proposal was rushed because of the baby, but he wouldn't be doing it if his gut wasn't telling him that Oakley was meant to be his. That she was the one. That she was it for him.

But she clearly didn't feel the same way, and he wasn't going to be the pathetic guy who stuck around where he wasn't wanted.

He'd done what Foster said. He'd put everything on the table. Laid his goddamned heart out there and offered it to her.

She just didn't want it.

He clutched the ring box in his hand. "I've gotta go."

She frowned. "You don't have to—"

"No, Oakley. I really do." He climbed off the bed, every muscle in his body feeling tight. "I'll stop by in the morning for the test. Get some sleep."

"Please, don't leave like this . . ."

He grabbed his bag and headed to the door. "Good night, Oakley."

THIRTY-ONE

Oakley stumbled to the bathroom the next morning, unsure if she'd be able to perform for the pregnancy test. After crying all night, she doubted she had any hydration left in her.

She washed her face and tried not to look at her reflection in the mirror. The left side of her face was swollen from Liam's hit and had started to turn purple, and her eyes now looked like she'd been punched there, too. She peeked out the window. The sun was just starting to come up. Pike wouldn't be here for at least an hour.

She needed to get this done now. After last night, she couldn't handle doing this with him here. She'd hurt him last night. The way he'd looked at her, the wounded betrayal in his eyes when she'd turned him down was going to fucking haunt her. But she'd had to do it. It'd been the right thing to do.

Saying yes would've been selfish and destructive. She didn't doubt he had some kind of feelings for her, but the proposal had been a knee-jerk reaction. Pike being a stand-up guy. Maybe he'd convinced himself that he had strong feelings for her, but they couldn't get married after only knowing each other for such a short time. Even if there was a baby involved.

Pike was used to risk-taking, leaping on faith, a dreamer at heart. But no matter how hard she'd fallen for Pike, how badly she wanted to believe that she could have her own fairy-tale ending, she couldn't afford to marry a guy on a whim. She had Reagan to think about. Her daughter was already getting attached to Pike. What would happen if Oakley agreed to a marriage and then a year in, Pike realized he wasn't built for the family life? Or what if Oakley found she really couldn't bear to be with someone who was gone so much? If it ended, it'd tear them all apart.

It simply wasn't an option.

Oakley took a long, cleansing breath and reached into the cabinet beneath the sink, pulling out the two boxes she'd hidden in there a week ago. Her hands shook as she opened each of them and read over the instructions. She'd bought two different brands to be thorough, but the instructions were pretty much the same. Pee on a stick, wait three minutes to find out if your life was changed forever. One would give a plus or a minus, the other would give two lines for pregnant, one for not.

She carried the two tests into the small alcove that housed the toilet, trying to steel herself against the panic attack that wanted to overtake her. If she was pregnant, she could handle it. She'd be okay. Reagan would probably love having a sibling around. And Oakley was way more equipped this time around than she had been last time. Pike would help with the finances. Either way, this wouldn't be the end of the world.

With that in mind, she did what she needed to do and took the tests. When she was done, she set the two sticks on the counter, washed her hands, and then sat down on the edge of the tub. The clock on the wall seemed to tick slower and slower as she watched, and she had to put her face in her hands so she'd stop staring at the second hand. Tick. Tick. Tick.

She waited for longer than she thought she needed to and when she finally allowed herself to look, five minutes had passed. She stood, walked over to the counter, and braced herself for the result.

Pike leaned back on his couch, feeling more tired and gutted than he'd ever been. After getting back from Oakley's, he'd just felt numb. He'd come home, opened a bottle of whiskey, and had put his headphones on full blast—anything to get his mind off of what had just happened.

He'd screwed it up. He hadn't told her he loved her even though he knew it was the truth. He hadn't been able to take that extra step and leave himself completely stripped down. And without those words, she hadn't believed that he meant what he'd said. And hell, maybe he *was* fucking crazy. Maybe his instincts were shit. But he couldn't get past that feeling that they really would be great together. He just had to find a way to show her that he meant what he'd said, that this wasn't some obligatory proposal because he might've gotten her pregnant.

He didn't do obligatory anything.

If she needed more time, he could give it to her. If she wanted to slow down, date, and see how it went, he was open to it. He'd scared her and now he needed to make it right.

He would fix this. Somehow.

He set the whiskey bottle on the floor and rolled to the side. His music stopped, his hip accidentally depressing a button on his cell and his phone asked, "What the hell do you want?"

Normally, the question would've made him chuckle. Braxton had installed an app on Pike's phone that made the built-in assistant rude. But right now, he just wanted to throw the damn thing.

"I want Oakley Easton. Can you make that happen, genius?"

His phone dinged. "Found Oakley Easton, Perfect Match dating. Go to site?"

"What the fuck?"

He shifted up and pulled his phone from beneath his body, the screen bright in the dark room.

"Go to site?" the phone repeated.

"Yeah." He sat up, the room spinning a little.

The screen changed and the Perfect Match dating website opened up. He recognized the logo from the commercials they were constantly running. Oakley's picture was displayed front and center with the words *Profile: Active* beneath it. His heart lurched a little at seeing her bright smile, but dread was curling in his stomach. He touched the picture, opening up her full profile.

Status: Unmarried / Children: 1 / Seeking: men, age 26-40
Preferred career background of partner: Business, Engineering,
  Academia
Preferred education: Bachelor degree or higher
Ideal qualities: Smart, Stable, Romantic, Kind, Family-oriented,
  Funny
Turnoffs: Cockiness, tattoos, smoking

Pike sucked in a breath. His eyes skimmed the rest of her profile, but the message couldn't get any clearer. What Oakley labeled
as her ideal was everything he wasn't. She was looking for a suit.
Part of him hoped that maybe this was an old profile and that he'd
changed her mind on a few things, but when he scanned to the top
of the screen, he saw the date the page was created. The little numbers were like a punch to the sternum. She'd made this sometime
after their first night on the phone.

With a sick feeling washing over him, he closed out the window and tossed his phone aside.

This was why she'd tried to push him away when the condom
had broken in the first place. This was why she'd said no to his proposal. It wasn't because she was scared or didn't believe he had
feelings for her. It was because she knew the kind of man she
wanted in her life long-term and he wasn't it. He was the hot fuck,
the wild night—the disposable one, not the boyfriend.

How the hell had he thought it would've been any different?
Oakley wasn't a stupid or reckless person. Who would look at him
and think long-term or future father to my children or potential
love of my life? Not someone like her. No, she wanted a guy who
would be there every day, who'd work eight to five and be home
for dinner, a guy who'd take her to neighborhood barbecues and
coach the kid's baseball team. A guy like all these yahoos who'd
left comments on her page. Not one like him. Not one who came
from a fucked-up family and who had a drug history and who
thought a fun night was beating her with a belt.

The whole time he'd only been her distraction. Her fling. She'd been trying to tell him that all along. And he'd been too dumb to listen.

But now he heard. Loud and clear.

Oakley may have wanted him in her bed. But she'd never love him.

His phone buzzed against the couch cushion. Frowning, he reached over and grabbed it. Oakley's name blinked on the screen.

He looked at the clock. Why was she calling this early? He put the phone to his ear. "Hello?"

"I took the test," she said quietly.

He straightened, all the liquor threatening to come up. "*Without me?*"

"I—I figured it'd be easier, after everything," she said, her voice thick, like she'd been crying.

Oh, fuck, oh fuck, oh fuck. "Tell me, Oakley."

"It's negative. No pregnancy."

It was the news they'd both been wanting to hear, but this crashing feeling went through him anyway, like every hope and good thing inside him falling in a pile at his feet. "Are you sure?"

She sighed, like maybe her feelings on it weren't so clear-cut either. "I took two tests. They're supposed to be ninety-eight percent accurate."

He let out a long breath and rubbed a hand over his eyes. "Are you okay? It sounds like you've been crying."

"I'm all right. I think all the stress just got to me at once—seeing the test and finally knowing. I mean, this is a good thing. We're not—this wouldn't have been the right time for either of us to have a baby. I'm finally close to getting a promotion at work. You have this big opportunity for your band. Now you can go and enjoy the tour without worrying. There's nothing holding you here now."

He lay back on the couch and closed his eyes, his chest hurting. "No, I guess there's not."

She was quiet for a long moment. "I'm sorry I hurt you last night, Pike. That's the last thing I wanted to do. I don't want you to think your gesture didn't mean something to me. It meant . . .

well, it meant everything. Not many men would be willing to sac-rifice that much to be there for me . . . and for a baby. But you've got to know that it'd be insane for us to move that fast. I've got Rae and there's still so much we don't know about each other. I would never forgive myself for taking you off course for a career you've worked so hard for. You're brilliant, Pike, and talented, and the world deserves to see that. You're meant for bigger things than what I and the life I lead could ever give you."

Her words were meant to soothe, to soften the sting, and he had no doubt she meant them with only good intentions. But they cut through him like jagged-edged glass, hurting worse than anything else she'd ever said to him. He was meant for other things. Transla-tion: He was not meant for things like family and kids and loving, long-term relationships. He didn't fit in that world and never would.

"I'm sorry I can't be the kind of guy you want." The words slipped out before he could think to hold them back, and he cringed at how fucking pathetic he sounded.

"What are you talking about, Pike? Didn't you hear anything I just said?"

"I saw your dating profile, Oakley."

"You what?"

"It's fine. I get it. You want a Foster. Not a Pike."

"You're not making any sense. Are you drunk?"

"Never mind. It doesn't matter anyway." He pressed his fingers to the spot above his right eye where a wicked headache was start-ing. "Look, Oakley, I've got to go."

"Will I see you tomorrow for the last recording session?"

He grimaced. "I've got somewhere to be. I'll call Braxton, and he'll help you finish up the recording. He knows how to work everything, and I'll clean up the files afterward."

She was quiet for a long moment. "Are you going to be at their performance at the end of the month?"

"It's on my calendar."

"That's not an answer."

"As long as nothing comes up for the tour."

She let out a breath. "Don't do this, Pike. Don't punish them because we've fucked this up. They'll be crushed if you're not there. They need you there."

"No. They need their parents. They need the people who love them. They don't need me."

No one did. It's how he'd set up his life since he'd walked out of his house. If no one needs you, there's no chance you'll let them down.

"Pike."

"I've gotta go."

He hung up the phone before she could protest again. He couldn't stand to hear that disappointment in her voice, the resignation—like she'd hoped for better but wasn't surprised. *Yes, Oakley, I'm doing just what you thought I always would. I'm being the asshole.*

That's what he was good at.

He leaned over to grab his laptop off the coffee table and opened up a travel site. He'd been in this place before and he knew exactly how to handle it.

THIRTY-TWO

three weeks later . . .

Oakley stood near the wall in the auditorium, close enough to the stage to intervene if necessary but far enough back that the kids wouldn't think she was hovering. The room was full, parents and other family members chatting at a low-roar level before everything started, but she was way too tense to socialize.

Reagan had been a nervous wreck backstage, reverting to an old hand-flapping habit she hadn't had since she was six. She'd looked like a high-strung bird, flitting around the small hallway. Oakley had managed to calm her after a talk and some deep breathing exercises. But she was still afraid Rae would freak out before she made it to the stage. Or worse—freak out *on* stage.

Oakley chewed her thumbnail. Maybe it had been a mistake to let Rae take on this big of a role. It was too much pressure for her, too many people to be in front of. Maybe she should just go back-stage and get her. They had an understudy who could take over the leads if necessary for tonight.

Tessa waved at her from her spot in the second row, a big grin on her face. Oakley lifted a hand and forced a smile. Tessa had pulled her aside during rehearsals today and had told her how amazed she was at how everything had turned out. In its first week on iTunes, "Blue Skies" was already gaining momentum and making money for the kids' college funds, thanks to a spot Gibson had booked them on *Good Morning Texas* using his PR contacts. Now there was talk of the story getting picked up nationally.

Tessa had given Oakley the promotion right there on the spot. Full-time project coordinator—double the salary she'd been making as a receptionist, along with extra benefits. It was so much more than she could've ever hoped for. She wouldn't have to take another night call. No more faking it. No more getting called derogatory names. No more hiding. She could spend her free time on her songwriting.

But she'd barely been able to get excited about it. She hadn't seen Pike since the night he'd proposed. He hadn't shown up at any of the recording sessions, and Braxton had finally told her that Pike had flown to L.A. to take care of preliminary tour stuff. She'd known that night on the phone that she might never see him again. She'd heard the distance in his voice, felt the wall go up, the door slam shut. She'd known it would hurt. But she hadn't anticipated just how much. That absence had left a big fucking hole in her chest and had taken the shine off everything that would've normally made her happy.

She laced her hands behind her neck and closed her eyes, trying to release the tension she couldn't seem to shake. A hand touched her elbow and she jumped.

For one hopeful moment, she thought it was him. That he'd changed his mind, that he'd be here for the kids. That she'd open her eyes and he'd be here. But when she lifted her lids, there was no cocky smirk or chameleon eyes. A familiar face, but not the one she needed.

Gibson sent her an apologetic smile, as if he knew what she'd been thinking. "Sorry, didn't mean to startle you."

She blew out a breath. "Not your fault. A breeze could make me jump right now."

"They're going to be great. If they can do TV, they can do this."

"Thanks again for getting them on that show. The sales jumped immediately."

He shrugged. "It's the least I could do. And they're an easy sell. It's a great feel-good story. Plus, the songs are actually good."

She smiled. "The kids have worked really hard."

"You and Pike have worked really hard, too."

She looked away. "Yeah."

Gibson tucked his hands in his slacks, following her gaze toward the stage. "He told me what happened, that he proposed to you. Well—*told* is a strong word. I basically got him drunk and plied it out of him before he left for L.A., and I said I wouldn't watch Monty while he was gone unless he told me what had crawled up his ass."

She rubbed her lips together and nodded.

"He's freaking insane for doing it. Pike acts before he thinks."

Her instinct was to defend Pike. But hadn't she told Pike pretty much the same thing when he gave her a ring? "I think he was trying to be a stand-up guy."

"You're giving him too much credit."

She turned to him at that. "That's not a very nice thing to say about a friend."

Gibson smiled, dimples appearing. "Pike's spent his whole life giving a big *fuck you* to anything or anyone that put expectations on him. He makes his own rules. He lives his life on gut instinct. If he got a woman pregnant, he'd do right by the kid because he's not a dick. But he wouldn't marry the mother because he was supposed to."

She rubbed the chill from her arms.

"So I absolutely get it if you're not interested in that big of a commitment with him. God knows he can be a pain in the ass," Gibson said, affection lacing his tone. "But if you know Pike at all, you know that for better or worse, he's all heart. Maybe he didn't think through the logic of asking you to marry him after such a short time together. But that doesn't mean it wasn't genuine. He loves you. And he loves your kid. And I've been friends with him long enough to know that once Pike Ryland loves you, it's absolute. You'll never find a more loyal, giving, good-hearted man than him. He's the guy I'd call if I needed to bury a body, because he wouldn't ask questions. He'd trust that I had good reason and bring the shovel."

Her throat had gone tight, tears trying to fight past her defenses. "Why are you telling me this?"

"Because I'd help him bury a body, too, and I thought you should know the things about him that he'd never say." He rubbed a hand over the back of his head. "You should also know that he's not going to come back and try again or push. It's why he hasn't reached out to his sisters again even though I know it kills him that he doesn't have relationships with them. He doesn't hang around where he's not wanted."

"I didn't not want him," she said, meeting Gibson's eyes. "But look at what he's got in front of him. He shouldn't have to give up his dream to be with someone."

Gibson's smile went a little sad. "No, he shouldn't. No one should. But maybe his dream isn't quite what you think it is."

"What do you mean?"

"I need to be getting back to my seat." He pulled a small package out of the inner pocket of his jacket. "All I was supposed to be doing is giving you this."

She took the package from him. "What is it?"

Gibson shrugged. "Not my business. He sent me the package and told me to deliver it without commentary."

She lifted a brow. "Not one to follow rules either?"

A wry smirk touched his lips. "I never said that."

The words seemed innocuous, but something about the way he said it had her mind going back to Pike's vague comments about what Gibson did at The Ranch. "Oh."

He reached out and gave her elbow a quick squeeze. "Good luck with the show."

She thanked him and stepped around a column to get some privacy from the chatting audience. Her hands were shaking. She lifted the lid of a box and found a chain nestled inside. She pulled the silver length from the box to find a small black sparrow pendant hanging from it. She rubbed her thumb over it, surprised to find grooves. She looped the chain around her wrist and opened the card.

> *I wanted Rae to have this for her debut. The charm is made from my Patti Smith* Horses *album. I wore one like it my first night on stage (though my drug of choice was a Nirvana album), and it made me feel like I was part of something bigger, a new link in this big web of art and music and rebellion. Tell her nerves can't beat true punk spirit and that I know she's going to fucking kill it and be great.*

> *Best, Pike*

Oakley pressed the note to her chest and leaned back against the column, her lungs crushing under the weight of everything the simple gift stirred up. He hadn't sent something to Oakley. This wasn't an apology or a plea. This was for Rae and Rae alone and that got to her more than any grand romantic gesture he could've done.

Yes, they'd only known each other for a little while, but somehow he already intuitively knew what her daughter would need tonight, how to help her feel stronger, how to help her feel special and brave. It was a gesture a great dad would make.

Oakley closed her eyes, willing herself to pull it back together, and placed the necklace back into the box to bring it backstage to Reagan.

As expected, Reagan's eyes lit up when Oakley showed her what Pike had sent her. She grabbed the necklace, running her fingers over the grooved vinyl of the charm with awed reverence. "I wonder what song this piece was made from."

Oakley took the necklace from her and looped it around Reagan's neck. The little black sparrow nestled in the hollow of her throat like it was meant to be there.

Rae looked up at her, all big eyes and open emotion. "I wish he could've been here tonight."

Oakley felt a stab in her gut. "I know, baby. I'm sure he wishes he could've been here, too."

"I thought you *like* liked him. I thought you were going to fall in love—like in the movies—and that he could be my dad since I never got one."

Oakley took a long breath, the wistfulness in Rae's voice flaying her. Never before had Reagan expressed any desire to have a father in her life. Oakley had thought she'd surrounded her with enough to fill that gap—all the love she had to give plus her brother and Hunter heavily involved. But she should've known that it was still there—just like the empty spot Oakley had inside her where her parents used to be, just like Pike had for the family he was cut off from. "I do like him, but Mr. Pike has a very busy job and he has to be on the road. I'm sure we'll see him again soon, though."

She hated how the lie rolled off her tongue, but how could she tell her daughter that she'd sent Pike away? That they might never see him again.

A volunteer who was handling the backstage stuff clapped her hands and called for everyone to come take their places. Rae looked over her shoulder and then back to Oakley, worry flitting over her expression again. "I guess I better go."

Oakley took Rae's face in her hands and kissed her forehead. "You've got this, baby girl. Just go out there and have fun with your friends. The rest will work itself out."

Rae nodded and touched the sparrow pendant, rubbing it like a rabbit's foot. "I love you, Mom."

Warmth bled through Oakley. "I love you too, Rae. Now go rock it."

Reagan hurried off to get in her place, and Oakley went back out front to take her position against the wall again, still too anxious to sit. Before long, the lights went down and the curtains went up.

Reagan stepped onto the stage looking small and beautiful and overwhelmed. Oakley had one brief moment of panic that Rae was going to fall apart. But then Reagan touched her necklace, gave the audience a shy smile, and gave the drummer his cue to start. She closed her eyes and began to sway to the beat in a way Oakley had never seen her do before—and just like the way Oakley used to calm herself when she was on stage. By the time Rae opened her eyes and the first notes came out of her mouth, she was every bit the strong, brave girl Oakley knew her to be.

Oakley stood there, awed and proud and overwhelmed, tears filling her eyes.

The child who hadn't spoken until she was almost four, who had suffered panic attacks when she'd first had to be in a classroom with others, was now holding an audience in thrall with the power of not just her voice but her pure, shining presence.

Rae had stopped being afraid.

Maybe it was time Oakley did the same.

THIRTY-THREE

Pike jogged off stage, adrenaline pumping, the scream-ing roar of the crowd still ringing in the background. The audience had wanted an encore—from an opening band. That shit never hap-pened, but this was the third stop this week where Darkfall had gone back out to play a few more songs. It was happening. The new songs were taking off and grabbing people. Now instead of just seeing Wan-derlust T-shirts and signs out in the audience, he was seeing Darkfall merch. He could sense the shift, the swell of support growing.

And when he was out there on stage, he was flying. His drums around him, his head only filled with beats and song, the crowd whipping up into a frenzy—it was a high no one would've been immune to. But he knew what awaited him once he hit backstage—and what he'd faced every damn night of this first month on tour. The life. The girls. The partying. Another long ride on the bus.

As much as he loved that hour on stage each night, the rest of it was wearing him down. Braxton and Geoff had noticed and had tried to do their part, sending pretty groupies and high-end liquor his way. But neither held any appeal. He couldn't look at the groupies with any interest anymore. His goggles had been broken. Instead of seeing hot bodies and eager eyes, he'd notice all the other stuff—how much younger they were than him, how fake the conversation was, how empty the attraction. How fucking *boring* the whole game was.

And though he'd partaken of the liquor the first week or two, waking up with a booming headache and sick stomach had gotten old quickly, too. He wasn't built for this anymore.

So most of the time, he'd find his way back to his hotel room and tinker with the songs of the artists he was working with at the studio. Or he'd hang out with Lex and his woman since they weren't into the party scene either. But it was beginning to feel like a grind already.

He missed home and Monty and his friends.

He missed Oakley.

Pike weaved his way through the backstage chaos, people parting for him like he was a boat fighting upstream. He needed to get out as quickly as he could. This was Vegas and they were here for a three-day break, so the guys were dead set on dragging his ass out for a night on the town. Pike couldn't think of anything he wanted to do less.

A few people called his name, and he gave a nod or a wave of acknowledgment, keeping his feet moving forward. Fans, thankfully, weren't back here yet because the main act hadn't gone on stage, so he could at least avoid dealing with that. He made his way to the back door, the fresh air, and the limo that would drive him to the hotel.

Pike greeted the driver and climbed into the limo, inhaling the peace and quiet like it was the first oxygen he'd breathed all night.

"Where to, Mr. Ryland?" the man asked.

"Bellagio."

Something banged on the top of the car. Pike swung his gaze to the window. "What the fuck?"

The door yanked open and both Braxton and Geoff peered in. "Oh no you don't, asshole. You're not getting out of tonight. It's your birthday, and we're taking you out."

"Yeah, man," Brax said, sliding in and giving the driver an address. "Don't be a punk. We've been letting you act like an old man for the past couple weeks. No way we're letting you do that in Vegas."

"My birthday isn't until next week," Pike groused.

Geoff climbed in, shoving Pike all the way to the other side of the car. "But we won't be in Vegas then. Tonight's the night."

"I—"

"Shut the fuck up, Ryland," Braxton said with a smile. "We're taking you hostage. There is no choice here."

"Don't I even get a safe word?"

"Nope, we don't want to be safe, sane, or consensual with you tonight," Geoff answered.

Pike let his head fall back and rubbed a hand over his face as the limo took off. Normally he wouldn't let them strong-arm him into anything. But it would be a dick move to shut them down when they were trying to do something nice for him.

Pike blew out a breath. "As long as it's not that strip club we went to last time we were here. That was freaking bizarre."

Geoff snickered. "What? Not a fan of painted and bedazzled pussy?"

"Those sparkly things must hurt like hell when they pull them off," Braxton said, flipping the switch for the privacy window. "And your dick probably comes out tie-dyed when you fuck them."

Pike snorted. "I wouldn't go near that shit."

"Right. Like you'd go near anyone." Geoff fished a few beers out of the chiller. "You're like a fucking monk lately."

"That's changing tonight," Braxton assured him. "Don't want your dick shriveling from lack of use. We're getting you laid, son."

Pike accepted a beer from Geoff. "Worry about your own dick, Brax. Mine's not your concern."

Braxton sent him a shit-eating grin. "Oh, I make sure someone worries about mine every night, preferably multiple times."

Pike sniffed and sipped his beer. This was going to be a long night. He watched the scenery go by through the tinted windows, the colorful, dancing lights of Vegas a counterpoint to his dark mood. When they crawled past his hotel, he had to fight the urge to tell the driver to stop and let him out. But he forced himself to keep his mouth shut. He would do this for the guys. It wouldn't hurt him to sit in a club or bar and drink while the guys did their thing.

But soon the colors became muted outside the windows and the limo picked up speed, hitting open road after creeping its way down the strip. Pike frowned at the changing scenery. "Where the hell are we going? Finding a place to kill me and dump the body?"

Braxton stretched his arm over the back of the seat. "Need to go outside of city limits for what we're after."

Pike eyed him, annoyance setting in. "I swear to God if you fuckers are taking me to some brothel, I'm going to kick your goddamned asses."

The corner of Geoffrey's mouth lifted. "Come on, man. You know we've got more class than that."

"Says the man who picked out the painted-pussy palace."

"Just relax, Ryland." Brax gripped Pike's shoulder and gave him a little shake. "We've got something real nice set up for the birthday boy. Trust us."

The words were ominous in the dark of the limo. He trusted these guys with his life. He did not, however, trust them to have free reign over him in Vegas. "Ah, hell, I'm fucked."

Brax flashed teeth. "That's the spirit."

Finally, the limo pulled into a long driveway. Pike leaned forward to peer out the window. A sprawling house that seemed to grow right out of the desert mountain landscape glittered in the distance, the porch lights and windows glowing bright.

"What the hell is this?"

"Your birthday present."

He looked between the two of them, confused as shit. "You didn't buy me a damn house."

Braxton snorted. "No, we're not that good of friends. But we got you what you need. A few days away from the chaos, all the privacy you could want, and someone to keep you company."

He stiffened at that. "I don't need fucking company."

Braxton shrugged and opened the door. "Then send her home. But this is our last stop. We've got rooms booked at the kink club a few miles from here."

"There should be a rental car parked out back you can use."

Pike stared up at the looming house. The call of three days of privacy and quiet was a strong one. The hooker would be an issue, but he'd pay her whatever they'd promised her and call her a cab. Easy enough.

"You're just going to leave me here?"

Braxton clapped him on the back. "We know the last few weeks have been rough on you. Go. Recharge. Figure shit out. We've got a bag for you in the trunk."

Pike looked between the two of them, the simple gesture saying more than anything else could've. He'd thought all these weeks the guys had been pissed that Pike wasn't participating in the antics like he used to, but they'd been paying attention. They fucking knew he was struggling.

These were his brothers and they were trying to take care of him.

He reached out to grasp hands with each guy, thumping each on the back and thanking them. Braxton slid out of the way and Pike climbed out of the limo. He stuck his head back in. "Don't get yourself in too much trouble at the kink club, amateurs."

Geoff grinned. "Where's the fun in that?"

Pike laughed, wished them luck, and shut the door. After grabbing his bag out of the back, he headed up the driveway, ready to face the last obstacle before he could get a few days of peace.

The large iron-and-glass front door was unlocked, so he let himself inside and tossed his bag on the marble floor of the grand foyer.

"Hello?" he called out, his voice echoing.

"In here." The female voice was low and distant, but he could make out where it was coming from.

Pike sighed. The guys had gotten everything right except the hooker part. That was the last thing he fucking needed. But the good thing about working girls was that money talked. She'd go away happy for the weekend off probably. Way easier to send on her way than a determined groupie.

He headed to where he'd heard the voice come from and rounded the corner into a living room. An impressive wall of floor-to-ceiling windows looked out onto the pool and the dark desert mountains behind. That caught his eye first. But then he heard a shift of movement. He turned his head, expecting to find the hired help.

But a done-up woman with a practiced smile wasn't who greeted him. No, sitting in the middle of the couch was the girl he hadn't been able to get out of his mind since he'd left Dallas.

He froze half a step inside the room, all the air leaving his chest. "*Oakley?*"

Oakley smiled, tentative, beautiful. "Hi."

THIRTY-FOUR

The floor seemed to fall out from beneath Pike as he stared at the woman before him. He swiped a hand over his face, unsure if he was seeing things, but Oakley remained. His body moved forward, automatically heading over to embrace Oakley—but he pulled up short before he could make a fool of himself. He gripped the back of the chair opposite her. "What are you doing here?"

"The guys didn't tell you I was in here?"

"What? No they said—" They'd said they'd gotten him what he needed. Fuck, had the guys guilted Oakley into coming out here? His hope fell. He didn't need some pity party from her. "They brought you here?"

She considered him, those dark eyes scanning his. "They helped me work it out. But I'm the one who called them."

"You called them? Why would you— Why wouldn't you call me?" He stepped around the chair and sank into it, afraid his legs wouldn't hold him up. The rush of seeing her here was almost too much to process. He'd thought about her so many times since he'd left. Now she was here, just a few feet away from him, looking more beautiful than ever, like a mirage in the desert.

"I didn't want to have this conversation over the phone. I . . . I needed to do this face to face."

He leaned forward, bracing his arms on his thighs. "Do what face to face? Was the pregnancy test wrong?"

God, it was fucking ridiculous how his heart lifted at the thought.

She took a deep breath and then let it out, smoothing the skirt of her sundress. "No, it's not that. I'm not pregnant. But from the beginning we've promised that we would be honest with each other, right?"

He frowned. "Of course."

She pressed her lips together and nodded. "I wasn't honest with you before you left."

"What do you mean?"

"I said our heads were screwed up because of the pregnancy scare. I said I liked you, but didn't want a relationship. I lied." She lifted her gaze, finding his. "Yes, my head was screwed up with the pregnancy scare, but my heart wasn't. I fell in love with you before we ever got to the broken condom, Pike. I've been falling for you since the day I met you. And I pushed you away because I was fucking terrified of how powerful it all felt."

His breath stopped, the words seeming to hover and hum between them. She loved him? She *loved* him. He got up, planting a booted foot on the coffee table and climbing over it, not wanting to waste time walking around it.

"Baby . . ." He went to his knee in front of her, taking her hands, wanting to let her finish saying what she needed to.

She gave a wavering smile, her eyes going shiny, and she gave a self-conscious little headshake, like she was embarrassed she was being so emotional. "I know it may be too little too late. I've wanted to come find you since you walked out, but I needed to give us both time. Our relationship happened in this vacuum. Things were so intense and fast with us from the beginning that I wanted to make sure they weren't feelings that would fade just as fast. I wanted you to go on tour and remind yourself of that life, of who you were before we met. I needed to get back to my normal life and do the same."

He rubbed his thumbs over her cold hands, fighting hard not to just grab her and take her in his arms.

"But I realized I couldn't get back to my normal life because you've permanently altered it, altered *me*. All I felt was this giant hole in my life that hadn't been there before but now seemed to be all I could think about."

The air sagged out of Pike, and he put his forehead to her knee. He knew exactly how that felt. It'd been his story every night on the road so far. The world was the same. He was different. An alien on a formerly familiar planet.

Oakley's hands flexed in his. "But I know it's been almost six weeks since you left and just because I feel this way doesn't mean I expect the same from you. If how you feel about me has changed, I understand. I just didn't want to leave things how they were. You deserved to know the truth."

Pike raised his head. "If my feelings have changed?"

She rolled her lips inward and nodded.

He laughed, his body feeling lighter. "Are you kidding? I've been a fucking mess since the day I left. I'm surprised the band hasn't fired me yet for being so goddamned lame."

Her lips curved. "Really?"

He reached up, taking her face in his hands. "Yes. Christ, Oakley. I fucking love you. Like completely over-the-top love you. I wanted to say it the night I proposed and chickened out, but it was there the whole time. It's been there for a while. I can't even believe you're here right now. I've imagined you so many times that I'm not fully convinced I'm not going to wake up on the bus here in a second."

"You love me?"

He laughed. "Yes, goddammit. You have cotton in your ears, woman? I'm in love with you. Want me to tattoo it across my chest? Because I will."

Her smile went full throttle at that. "I'm in love with you, too. But I won't be tattooing it anywhere. Tattoos are dumb."

At that, he couldn't stop himself any longer. "I'm going to kiss you now."

"This is a good plan."

She barely had the words out before he leaned forward and claimed that lush mouth for himself. Oakley, his Oakley, was here. She loved him.

All his need and desperation surged in him at once, and she surrendered the instant they connected. Her hands gathered in his T-shirt like she was afraid that he was an illusion, too, like it'd all be ripped away. He groaned when her lips parted and finally, finally they were joined again—tongues stroking and breath mingling. His fingers slid into her hair and he angled her back against the couch, lifting himself and climbing onto the couch with her. If he wasn't careful, he was going to devour her in one swift gulp, all the weeks apart making him feel wild and possessive.

She moaned softly into his mouth and settled against the arm of the couch as he braced himself over her. Already, he could feel himself go hard behind his fly. Shit, he was acting like a horny, clumsy teenager. But then she grabbed his ass and dragged him forward until he was straddling her.

Hell, yeah. Maybe they could be clumsy and desperate together.

"Tell me to stop, mama," he said, trailing kisses along her throat. "Tell me to stop so we can finish talking."

She grabbed his hair and tipped her head back to give him better access to her throat. "We can talk later."

"Fuck yes, we can," he said, shoving the bottom of her dress to her waist and finding her heat. He pressed against the soft satin of her panties and rubbed. God, she was soaked already. "Talking later is an excellent idea."

He tugged off her panties and tossed them to the side and then lowered himself farther down the couch. He grabbed the backs of her thighs and draped her legs over his shoulders. For a moment, he let himself enjoy the view. Oakley breathless, face flushed, and body open to him like the sexiest, most tempting meal.

He ran a finger along her slick flesh, enjoying the way she quivered and gasped at his touch. He would never get tired of exploring every secret inch of her, of tasting her need. He lowered himself between her legs and replaced the touch of his finger with that of his mouth.

She groaned and her thighs tightened around him. She wouldn't last long. He could feel the tension in her, like a bowstring pulled tight. But he was going to take his time. He'd lost hours in the last month, torturing himself with scenes just like this, remembering her taste and the eager way she responded to his touch—so open and honestly sexual. Oakley was real in a way he'd never experienced with anyone else. Nothing was put on for his benefit. She was in this with him as much as he was with her.

He dipped his fingers inside her, his dick flexing at the feel of all that warm flesh tightening around his fingers, and he sucked her clit into his mouth, grazing it with his teeth. Oakley gasped and her hold on his head went painfully tight. He loved it, loved the feel of her losing her control.

He stroked slow and deep inside and nipped her skin again, knowing his woman liked a dose of pain with her pleasure.

"Oh, God." Oakley's voice was muffled above him, her thighs clamped over his head.

"Come for me, mama," he said, curving his fingers inside her.

She cried out, gritty and loud, and her muscles fluttered around his fingers. Her rise and fall were quick—an orgasm after a long break, sharp and spiked.

He slid her legs from his shoulders, kissing her thigh as he sat up. Normally, he'd give her a second to catch her breath, but he knew what he felt like after a long break. The first orgasm just made you hungrier for another. He reached for the button on his jeans and opened his fly. But as he was shoving his pants down, a sobering thought smacked him. "Fuck."

Oakley lifted her head, her eyes still a little glazed from the orgasm. "What's wrong?"

"I don't have any condoms with me."

"Got it." She arched her back, grabbing her purse off the side table and digging through it. She pulled out a chain of foil packets. "Brand-new, non-expired. I promise."

He grinned as he ripped one of the packets open and rolled on the condom. "Well, weren't you optimistic? What if I would've said I'd totally gotten over you?"

She shrugged. "This is Vegas. I've heard the male escorts here are the hottest in the country."

He laughed and pinched her hip. "Smart-ass."

"Hey, not all of us have groupies lining up for free services," she said, trying to pull off a teasing tone but not quite succeeding.

He frowned and leaned down, bracing his arms on each side of her. "There've been no groupies, mama."

Her eyes were serious as they met his. "It's okay if there were. We weren't together. I know how things can be . . ."

He sighed. "Honesty, right?"

She wet her lips. "Yeah."

He bent down and pressed his forehead to hers. "There have been no other girls. You've ruined me. Everything seems empty and ridiculous if it's not you there with me."

She closed her eyes and wrapped her arms around him. "I know what you mean."

He put his lips to hers, taking her mouth in a languorous kiss, and she reached between their bodies. When her hand wrapped around his cock, he groaned into her mouth.

He thought she was about to guide him inside her, but instead her fingers found the base of his condom. She rolled it up and off him.

He broke away from this kiss. "What are you doing?"

She slid her fingers over his bare cock. "I got on the pill after you left. If there's been no one else, I want you inside me, Pike. Skin to skin."

He closed his eyes, inhaling a harsh breath at how good her hand felt and at the trust she was putting in him. He'd told her he hadn't been with anyone, and she hadn't questioned it. That untwisted something inside him, opening doors he didn't even know had been locked. He traced his hand down her side and grabbed her thigh, opening her to him.

He'd never gone bare in a woman. And now he was happy he hadn't. His list of conquests and bad behavior was long, but he still had a few things he could offer just to Oakley. "You'll be my first. Bet you never thought those words would come out of my mouth."

She smiled, dazzling him with the emotion in her eyes. "I'd much rather be your last."

His lungs squeezed at that, but he didn't want to read too much into her statement. He was okay taking this one step at a time. He wouldn't rush her this time. "I love you, mama."

"I love you, too." She guided her hands up to his face, cupping his jaw. "Now fuck me, Pike."

He laughed. "Yes, ma'am."

He positioned himself against her entrance, hooked her leg around his hip, and pushed forward. Sound rumbled through him low and long as her wet heat enveloped him, taking him inside her body with a cashmere grip. "Fucking hell."

Her nails dug into his back. "Yes. That."

He eased his hips back then sunk deep again, taking it slow and reining in his reaction as much as he could. It'd been so long since he'd been with her and feeling her pussy clenching around him, flesh against flesh, no barrier to shield the intensity of the sensation, was enough to drive him mad with the need to fuck hard and fuck now.

He supported himself on the arm of the couch and rocked into her, his muscles tense with restraint, and as he lifted his head, he caught sight of their reflection in the wall of windows. The back of her head and him looming over her. Well, that wouldn't do.

He grabbed her leg and slid out of her. "Turn over, mama. Let's enjoy the show together."

Oakley didn't hesitate. She flipped over and he tugged her dress the rest of the way off and unhooked her bra. Now she was fully naked for him while he still had everything on, his jeans shoved down his thighs. The difference in their state of undress had a surge of power going through him—that burgeoning dominant side of his stirring now that his woman was back in his grasp.

He grabbed Oakley's ponytail and lifted her head so that she could see herself in the reflection. "Watch how fucking sexy you look taking my cock."

He slid between her spread thighs and watched as her lids went heavy in the reflection, a look of absolute greed coming over her face, like she wanted this more than anything. That hunger spurred him on. It wasn't a romantic look, it wasn't sweet. His girl wanted to be fucked hard.

"I want to hurt you, mama. Break you in two and put you back together." The words slipped out unbidden, some inner thought making it past his normal filter. And the truth of it resonated through him. He wanted to hurt her, hurt her in the best way possible. Make her beg. Make her scream.

"Then hurt me," she said, challenge and grit in her voice.

The words made every bit of his blood light on fire. "Keep looking in that window. And don't you dare come until I tell you."

"Yes, Pike," she said, the deferent words brazen coming off her lips.

He grabbed her hip with bruising force, pumping his cock into her, and with his other hand, he reached down and grabbed her breast. It was soft and warm in his hand, but when he found her nipple, he gave it a hard pinch.

She gasped and her cunt gripped him like a vise. *Fuck.*

He gave the same treatment to the other nipple, then tugged on it. "You'd be so fucking hot with clamps on these and a chain between them. Or maybe we should just pierce them and I can tug on them whenever I want."

Her entire body shuddered in his hold, and his teeth clenched as he tried to hold back his release.

Goddamn. It was one thing to play rough. He'd done it in his past on occasion. But feeling exactly what some extra bite did to Oakley made something inside him click into place. He'd always been the one to tease his friends about their sadistic streaks. But now he understood. Because when your woman is the one craving it, when you know you can be the one to give her that knife's edge of pleasure/pain, it's a freaking high.

He couldn't wait to get her to The Ranch and really explore that masochistic streak of hers. But right now, he just needed to fuck her and feel her fall apart beneath him.

He clamped his hands around her waist and dragged her back along his cock, shifting the direction of the motion and making his own hips go still. He could tell the instant it registered what he was doing. Physically, not much different, but mentally a big one. He was using her body how he wanted. Letting her feel like she was just the object to slake his need. And based on the way she moaned, it'd had the desired effect.

"That's right, mama," he said, his voice strained. "You're all mine right now. Just be a good girl and don't fight."

She pressed her face into the arm of the couch. "God, why does that make me hotter?"

He grinned and grasped her hair again. "Head up, gorgeous. You're going to watch every second of this."

She lifted her gaze to the reflection and met his—naked desire there. He let go of her hair and reached out for a throw pillow. It was canvas-covered, soft enough not to hurt but rough enough to make a difference. He shoved it between her thighs, positioning the corner of it where he wanted.

"Keep that there." He gripped her waist again and dragged her back over his shaft.

The pillow grazed over her clit and she jolted. "Oh, fuck."

He smiled to himself and draped himself over her, reaching around to palm her breasts. When her inner muscles tightened around him, he increased the strength and pace as he thrust into her. His fingers pinched and rolled her nipples as he rocked her roughly against the pillow.

He pressed his face into the crook of her shoulder, the smell of her shampoo mixing with the musky scent of sweat and sex. He'd never smelled a better combination. "You have permission to come, love."

"Don't. Wanna. Yet. So. Good."

He knew the feeling, but as her heat clasped around him, needy and tight, he knew neither of them would last much longer.

He put his lips next to her ear. "It's that good for me, too, baby. You're so hot and slippery around my cock. I'm slick with your juices and leaking for you. It's never been this good. Never. Your body was made for mine. You were made for me. You wreck me, Oakley Easton."

She cried out at that, the sound exploding out of her and echoing through the cavernous ceilings of the room as she tipped over into orgasm. Her body rocked and shook beneath him, the force of her release making his caveman gene flare full force. He'd done this to her. Made a put-together woman fall to pieces. And that's when he lost the last shred of his own control.

Fire rushed down his spine, drawing up his balls, and sending pleasure rocketing through him with shocking impact. His hips pistoned into her, the movement no longer in his conscious control, and soon the couch was sliding a little with each deep thrust, making a grinding sound that seemed to fit with theirs, mixing with Oakley's cries and his guttural grunts.

The release seemed to stretch on, making his vision blur and his mind buzz. Coming with her was a high like no other he'd ever felt—with drugs, on stage—none of it compared. He wanted to glut himself on her. Never let her go. He said her name like a prayer and kissed every place he could reach until they were both completely spent.

When they'd finally collapsed into a pile of sweat and unmoving limbs, he wrapped an arm around her waist and rolled them onto their sides, his cock still buried inside her.

He took a few moments to catch his breath and bask in the residual sensations, enjoying the feel of his erection softening inside her. It was a luxury he'd never had, always afraid of compromising a condom. Oakley didn't seem to mind a little quiet time either. He traced his fingers over her arm idly, enjoying the softness of her skin, her warmth, the feel of her against him.

"Mmm," she said on a long expelled breath. "I don't think we should move ever again."

He kissed her shoulder. "I'm okay with that. I can reach the phone from here. We can get people to bring us food and water."

She laughed and the movement made her clench around him again, sending a shiver through him.

"Though I think we may be ruining whoever's couch this is. And the pillow's a total loss."

She snorted. "I hope Kade's a good friend then."

"Kade?"

"When Gibson heard I was coming out here to see you, he asked his brother if I could use his vacation home. Kade said yes and also flew me out here on his company's private plane."

Pike propped himself up on his elbow. "You let Kade know about us? Doesn't that mean Tessa will find out?"

Oakley shifted then, separating their bodies and turning in his arms. "I needed to tell her why I was asking for a few days off. She seemed surprised at first and then muttered something about those Ranch boys."

Pike chuckled and grabbed a blanket off the back of the couch to drape over them. "She outed herself, then."

"Not in so many words. But yeah, I figured out that meant she and Kade probably weren't as sweet and vanilla as I thought."

"Definitely not. Hang around The Ranch long enough and you'll see just how not sweet Kade can be. He can give a caning that will make you hurt just from watching."

"Yeah, I saw one the other day. Not by Kade but by that guy Colby. His boyfriend seemed to enjoy it, but I don't think I'm quite that hardcore."

Pike's brows lowered. "Hold up. How the hell did you see Keats getting a caning?"

"Well, it's been a long time since I've seen you. A girl has needs. Gibson took me to The Ranch a few times to take the edge off."

He froze but when he caught sight of her smirking face, he gave her thigh a hard pop. "Not nice, mama. Not nice at all."

She laughed. "It's partly true. For the last two weeks, he's gotten me in so I can take a few training classes."

Pike blinked. "What?"

She bit her lip. "I didn't know how things would turn out when I came out here, but I wanted to learn more about . . . about that thing that happens between us. I knew about BDSM from my calls, but that wasn't real research. That was the silly porn version of it. I wanted to see the real-life stuff, see if what I was feeling fit into that. So Gibson set me up to work with Tessa's friend Sam."

"Gibson talked to Sam?"

"Yeah. It was kind of awkward. Is there something between them?"

"Yes. Unrequited lust and Gibson's hard head."

"Oh." She tucked her head into the crook of his shoulder. "Well, she's great. She kind of walked me through the basics of both sides. We did a few mock scenes."

He shifted higher so he could look down at her. "Hold up, you did girl-on-girl kink and didn't invite me to watch?" He groaned and lay back. "You are so dead to me, Oakley Easton. Dead."

She snorted. "It wasn't like that. She's gorgeous—and damn, is she intimidating as a domme—but I kind of have this obsession with this boy. It's super inconvenient."

He smiled up at the ceiling. "Yeah?"

"Love's a pain in the ass, isn't it?"

He closed his eyes and wrapped his arms fully around her, his world shifting into just the right place, maybe for the first time in his life. "The worst."

A few lazy minutes passed, and he was just about to suggest they find the bathtub before they fell asleep like this, when her quiet voice cut through the silence.

"Still want to marry me?" The question came out in a soft rush, like maybe she'd been working up the nerve to say it.

He sighed. "I'm not going to rush you this time, mama. I know I scared you. I'm just happy to have you here with me. I can act on impulse sometimes and forget that not everyone wants to take chances like that. You have Reagan, and there are lots of things we don't know about each other. I understand why you told me no."

"That's not what I asked."

He ran his fingers through her hair, staring up at the ceiling and forcing himself to be honest, even if he risked freaking her out again. "I know in my gut you're it for me. But I can wait as long as you need. We can do things the normal way, take our time."

Her fingers curled against his chest. "I'm kind of over normal."

"Hmm?"

"Ask me again, Pike."

He shifted to sit up, needing to see her face. "What?"

She sat up with him, wrapping the blanket around her shoulders, and met his gaze, her eyes as calm as he'd ever seen them. "Ask. Me. Again."

That's when what she was asking him finally clicked. He sucked in a breath. Ask her again. Hope bloomed in him, big and bright.

Without hesitation, he buttoned his jeans, hopped off the couch, and dropped to one knee. He took her hands in his and cleared his throat, the emotion trying to well up and block his words.

"Oakley Easton, I love you. I want you to be my first love and my last. My mission in life is to be the one putting that smile on your face every day. I promise you, I will give you and Reagan absolutely everything I have to give. Will you marry me?"

Tears filled her eyes and a wide smile broke across her face. She pushed the blanket from her shoulders and slid to her knees in front of him, naked and beautiful and more than he'd ever dreamed he could have. "James Pike Ryland, I love you back. So much that it takes my breath away if I think about it too hard. I love everything about you—including your reckless disregard for what's normal. Yes, I want to marry you. Not next month or next year. But this weekend. I don't need extra time to confirm what I already know for sure in my heart. You are going to be a wonderful husband . . . and an amazing father. Both to Rae and the children we may one day have. Our family will be filled with love and laughter because we're in it together—all the rest of the details will work themselves out."

He closed his eyes, the words pinging something deep within him. Family. Children. His.

He lifted his hands, cupping her cheeks, and pressing his forehead to hers, overcome with all the . . . feeling. Fuck. Was he crying?

"I'm totally ruining my badass image here," he said on a choked laugh.

She lifted his head away from hers and then kissed the escapee tears off his cheeks. "You have never been more irresistible to me than right now."

He smirked. "Sadist."

"No, that's you." She pressed her mouth to his. "And I love it."

He circled his arms around her and sat back, pulling her into his lap. "So this weekend, huh?"

She nodded. "Sunday."

He lifted a brow. "Already have ideas, I see."

"I'm getting better at leaps of faith. That doesn't mean I don't have a plan."

He kissed her mouth. "Just tell me where to show up and I'll be there."

"No fear, huh? Commitment? Forever? No other women for the rest of your life?"

A few months ago, those words would have sent him into a cold, blind panic. Now all he could do was grin. He brushed his thumb over Oakley's lips. "Haven't you figured it out? I'm already yours. Have been since the moment I laid eyes on you."

"When I was being rude and trying to kick you out?"

"You were so annoyed and so fucking cute. I wanted to climb right over that desk and undo you."

She adjusted her position until she was straddling him, her breasts pressed up against his chest. She bent down and kissed along his throat and then brushed her lips against his ear. "Mission accomplished, James. I'm completely and totally undone."

His blood stirred and he cupped her ass, lifting her up a bit to get his jeans open again and freeing his erection—his body as hungry as if he hadn't just been inside her a few minutes ago. "Not quite yet. But you're getting there."

He shoved his jeans down and off then seated her exactly where he wanted her, inhaling her soft sigh as he lowered her down onto his cock.

"God, it's like I can never get enough of you," she said, burying her face in his shoulder and shuddering with pleasure.

"You're insatiable. Didn't they tell you mothers aren't supposed to act like this?"

He could feel her grin against his neck. "Fuck *they*. No, better yet, fuck me."

"Your wish is my command, love."

THIRTY-FIVE

Oakley leaned against the wall of the dressing room. "I can't feel my feet. Is that normal?"

"I think the term is cold feet, not numb feet," Devon said dryly.

"I'm just wondering if maybe we should've done this on our own and without the pressure of an audience."

"And it would've been a short-lived marriage because Dev would've murdered you for not inviting him," Hunter said, tossing Devon his necktie.

"Damn straight." Devon caught the tie and efficiently knotted it around his neck.

"You both think I'm crazy, don't you?" Oakley slipped out of her heels and reached down to rub the feeling back into her feet. Her hands were shaking, though, and making it a difficult process.

"Yes," Hunter agreed. "But I like crazy. Plus, neither of us would judge you."

Devon's brow had a wrinkle in it, though. She remembered that look from when she was younger and he went into big-brother mode. She walked over to him in her bare feet. "Hey, you okay?"

Devon sighed and tucked his hands in the pockets of his black slacks. "You sure he's a good guy, Oak?"

"He's the best guy," she said without hesitation. "Like down-to-the-bone good."

"Don't talk about his bone, dollface," Hunter chimed in. "You'll have Dev picturing things."

Oakley smirked. "Well, that bone is certainly good, too."

Dev rolled his eyes. "I liked you better when you were too embarrassed to say anything about sex around me."

She smiled and grabbed his hands. "Dev, I know you're looking out for me. I love you for that. And I realize that from the outside looking in, I seem crazy. But you remember when you first met Hunter back in college?"

Dev slid his gaze over to his lover, the corner of his mouth twitching. "Not easy to forget."

"I remember, too. I watched it happen and was so worried about you. You had the hots for a straight guy. I tried to talk you out of it. I tried to tell you that you'd only get hurt. From the outside looking in—"

"It was crazy," Dev finished.

"And I was wrong because you knew your heart, and whatever was between you two, you felt in your gut." She put her hand to her belly, the soft fabric of her white summer dress warm beneath her fingers. "I feel that with Pike, right here, like I know. Like I've been waiting all my life to feel this."

Devon sighed and put his arms out to gather her against his chest. He sat his chin on top of her head like he'd done so many times when they were growing up. "Baby sis, you are the smartest and strongest woman I know. I just want you to be happy. You deserve that kind of forever love. And if you know this is it for you, I support you with everything I have."

She closed her eyes and breathed her brother in, that familiar scent of his cologne giving her peace. "Thank you."

He kissed the crown of her head. "And if you're just marrying him for his money and hot body, I can support that, too."

She snorted. "I've done just fine supporting myself, thank you very much."

He leaned back and looked down at her. "I know. You've always worked hard and landed on your feet. Your numb, cold feet."

She grinned and wiggled her toes. "I can feel them again. I think the shoes are a size too small. Think anyone will care if I'm barefoot?"

"Well, your flower girl is sporting a blue Mohawk, so I'm thinking no one's going to be looking at your feet."

Oakley laughed. "She wanted to be my something blue."

There was a knock at the door, and Tessa poked her head in. Oakley still couldn't believe that so many people had gotten here on such short notice. Apparently, Gibson had put all of Pike's friends on notice when he'd helped Oakley set up her trip. Tessa sent her a warm smile. "Ready to go? They're all set to start."

Oakley took a long, deep breath, finding no qualms or hesitation inside her. She nodded. "I am so ready."

Pike stood at the end of the aisle in the lush garden that he and Oakley had chosen for their ceremony. It was small and intimate, a little oasis in the Vegas desert. He'd figured that with neither of them having a connection to their families, outside of Oakley's brother, that they wouldn't need much room. But right now it was packed full of people, no seats left. A fact that stunned the hell out of him.

When he and Oakley had decided on Friday that they would get married, he'd had no idea that Gibson had put all his friends on standby. The minute the news had gotten out, plans had started flying. In a matter of hours, a wedding had been planned. Kade had offered company jets to fly everyone to Vegas and had one of his restaurants in the area handle the catering. Jace's wife, Evan, offered to do the photography. Foster had happily agreed to be best man. Colby and Keats would provide live music. And all of the rest of the friends he'd made through the years at The Ranch and his two bandmates had been there to help with whatever was needed. Foster had even managed to get Mama Flora and her boys on a plane.

Pike didn't know how to process all that support and kindness.

The kid whose family didn't want him now had a crowd of people who loved him. A family.

And now he'd start his own with Oakley.

The music started up, Colby and Keats on acoustic guitars, and Pike straightened his shoulders, beyond ready to see his woman walk down the aisle. But the first member of the wedding party made his way out first—and made Pike laugh out loud.

Coming down the walkway was a very annoyed Monty. Someone had dressed him in a doggie tux, and Monty was currently doing his best to get ahold of the bowtie so he could tear it to shreds. Monty only made it a few steps down the aisle before plopping on his belly, legs out behind him, as he apparently staged a protest.

Reagan was following behind, blue faux-hawk gleaming in the sunlight, and Converse on her feet despite the dress she was wearing. God, he loved that kid. She sent Pike a big grin and swept Monty up in her arms to get him out of the way. When she reached the end of the aisle, she pushed up on her toes to give Pike a kiss on the cheek. Monty joined in and gave him a sloppy lick.

Reagan giggled and pulled Monty back. She looked up at Pike. "Make sure to bend your knees so you don't faint. I saw that on TV."

He chuckled. "I'll be sure to do that."

Pike watched her, a strange pride swelling as Rae walked to her seat. He and Oakley had sat down with her yesterday to explain what was happening. Instead of her being upset or worried that Pike was a threat to her tight bond with her mom, Rae had taken it in stride, telling them, "I knew y'all were in love like the movies."

He knew it wouldn't necessarily be an easy transition for her. She'd had Oakley to herself all her life, and he didn't want to impede on their relationship. But he hoped that in time she'd come to see him as a part of her family, as a person she could come to, as a dad. The thought of being that to anyone still rocked him off balance, but now instead of wanting to run, he couldn't wait to take on the challenge.

The music changed and Pike turned his attention to the back of the garden. He hadn't seen Oakley since last night and already it felt like too long. So when she stepped into the sunlight, hair braided with flowers, barefoot, and looking as beautiful as he'd ever seen her, he had to stop himself from sprinting down the aisle and sweeping her into his arms.

Her gaze met his and for a moment, they were the only two people in the garden. A slow smile spread over her lips, and she let Devon guide her forward. The crowd had stood for her arrival and none of them could look away either. His girl was an angel—a fierce, kick-his-ass-when-he-needs-it, never-give-him-an-inch angel. And she wanted to be with him. She loved him.

When they reached the end of the aisle, he took Oakley's hand from Devon's hold. Her hand was warm in his, her eyes as calm and content as he'd ever seen them.

"You look beautiful," he said, low enough for only her to hear.

She touched the lapel of his jacket. "So do you."

He put his hand over hers, holding it against his chest. "Ready for forever, mama?"

The joy that lit her eyes made the colorful garden pale around them. "Only if it's with you."

He closed his eyes, breathing in her words, her love, the spaces inside him that had been empty and dark for so long filling with her light. He'd been to almost every corner of the world. But he'd never been here.

He was home.

Suddenly, forever didn't seem like long enough.

EPILOGUE

"What are you wearing?"

Oakley smiled into the phone. "My husband's vintage Guns N' Roses T-shirt and a pair of white cotton panties."

"Fuck, that's hot. Is he there with you now?"

Oakley rinsed out her toothbrush. "No, he's busy being some kick-ass drummer, the jerk."

"That must be hard, him being on the road so much. Has to get lonely."

"Mmm, it definitely does." She flipped off the light in the bedroom, plunging herself into darkness, her body already stirring in anticipation for what she knew was in store. This had been her and Pike's routine over the last few weeks while he traveled. They'd talk during the day about what was going on in their lives, and he'd have his daily chat with Rae when she got home from school. But at night, he and Oakley would find each other in the dark—touching through the distance.

This call was a bit of surprise, though. He'd told her he'd be in New York tonight and may not be done until after she was asleep. But she should've known he'd find a way. He rarely missed a night. Though after the summer they'd had, it never felt like enough.

After the wedding, he'd asked again if she and Rae would come with him for the summer leg of the tour. Reagan had been over the moon about it, and Oakley had fallen into that new-city-every-night routine again more quickly than she would've suspected. During the day, they'd all spend time together, see a little of whatever city they were in, and then at night, they'd watch Pike play. It'd been fun and exciting and a whirlwind. And to Oakley's surprise, Reagan had thrived despite the chaos of being on the road. The guys in the band had taught her some new things on her guitar, and Pike was trying to teach her drums. She seemed determined to learn every instrument out there. And while Reagan occupied herself with that, Oakley had gotten some quality time to work on her songwriting, strumming out new songs on the brand-new Martin guitar Pike had given her for a wedding present.

But schooltime had come up soon enough, and Rae had needed to be back home. Oakley had needed it, too. Both to get back to work so she could start her new position and to take care of the legal stuff she needed to put in place to protect Reagan from Liam.

It had gutted her to leave Pike after three months of nonstop togetherness. And she could tell it had torn him up, too, that they'd had to leave. But he also had a commitment to his band and to his fans.

"You want some company, then?" Pike asked, his voice low, tempting. "I bet I can make you feel good."

"You sound mighty confident. I'll warn you. The bar's set high. My guy is a pretty fantastic lay."

"I bet I can do better."

"Oh yeah? Try me."

The phone went quiet for a few long seconds, and Oakley toed off her socks, preparing to get in bed and curl up with the sound of Pike's voice.

"Still there?" she asked.

No answer.

Well, hell. Damn cell signals. She pulled her phone from her ear, but before she could check the status, a hand clamped over her mouth from behind. She screamed but the hand muffled the sound.

Lips brushed her ear. "Be a good girl and I won't have to hurt you."

She gasped—both out of relief that it wasn't some psycho and shock that Pike was actually here. She turned in his hold, feeling for him in the dark. "Oh my God, are you actually here or am I just having that hot dream again?"

He chuckled and his hand coasted over her hair as if reminding himself what she felt like. "I'm really here, mama. Fuck, you smell good."

She reached over and clicked on a lamp, needing to see his face. She blinked in the sudden light and then shifted back into his embrace. His hazel eyes were still smudged with liner and his hair mussed, but he looked as gorgeous as ever. She ran her fingers over his jawline. "You look like you just got off stage. How are you here? Did you get a break between shows or something?"

"I hopped on a plane right after the show. I couldn't wait." He brushed her hair away from her eyes. "I needed to see your face. I needed you."

She closed her eyes, inhaling his familiar scent, her entire body awakening to his presence. What a gift to have him here unexpectedly. She'd thought she wouldn't be seeing him until Halloween. "How long do I have you?"

His mouth kicked up at the corner. "Forever."

"I mean for this visit."

He lifted her hand and kissed her wedding band. "Same answer."

She frowned. "What?"

"Same answer. You have me here for good. I helped the band hire a touring drummer. I've been getting him up to speed over the last few weeks and tonight he did a few songs in my place. He's going to take over fully for the rest of the shows. I don't have to go back."

Her stomach dropped. "Oh, Pike. God, you didn't— We talked about that. I didn't want you to change things for me. This isn't—"

"Shh." He put his fingers over her lips, tenderness in his eyes. "I'm not doing it for you, mama. I'm doing it for me. From the start of this tour, my heart hasn't been in the process. I loved doing it over the summer while you and Rae were there with me, but I'm not built for being on the road like this anymore. I don't want that life.

I want this life. You. Reagan. Waking up in the morning and seeing each other every day. Farm breakfast on Sundays and movie nights on Friday. Going to bed every night and feeling you next to me."

"Pike . . ." The picture he was painting sounded so damn wonderful, but this had been her fear from the start when he'd proposed. She didn't want him giving up his dream to accommodate her. "Drumming is your life."

His hands slid down to her shoulders, his gaze holding hers. "I'm not giving up drumming or even my spot in the band. I'll still make music with them for the albums. But drumming is not my life. Not anymore. I want to be in my studio. I want to discover emerging artists and mold them into something better. And I want to be at home with my wife and family. That is, if you won't get too sick of me being here every day."

She shook her head, tears coming to her eyes. "I've missed you so damn much. I can't imagine getting to wake up with you every day."

He pulled her to him and hugged her to his chest. "I always thought nothing would beat the thrill of being on stage in front of thousands of people. But now I know without a doubt that something does. This does."

She leaned back and pushed up on her toes to kiss him slow and soft, savoring the feel of him here in the flesh. When she broke away, she gave him a saucy grin. "Guess I can get rid of that dildo now. I's got me a real man."

His lips curved, a dangerous spark coming into his eyes. "Well, I don't know if I'd go throwing stuff out. I can think of a few creative uses."

She lifted a brow. "Oh?"

He gripped her waist and drew her against him, his hardening erection brushing against her panties. "A month away is a long time. And seeing you look so luscious in one of my shirts is making me want to do very bad things to you."

She shivered in his grip, heat rushing downward where he pressed against her. "Guess it's a good thing it's Rae's night at Devon's then, huh?"

"Mmm," he said, tilting her head to the side and kissing her neck. "No one to hear you scream? Excellent."

He slipped his hand beneath her shirt and gripped her breast, his thumb grazing over one of the nipple rings she'd gotten while they were on tour. She groaned, the tight feel of the little tweak he gave the ring making her sex clench. She loved that secret they had between them. Looking at her, no one would suspect that nice mom down the street would have done such a thing. But with Pike she'd discovered just how effective a bit of pain was for her. Sometimes she felt like she could come just from him tugging and sucking on the rings. She could enjoy herself in bed with Pike no matter what the situation was—vanilla, kinky, or in between. But she'd found that her desire amped up to another level when Pike dominated her and exploited that newly discovered masochistic streak of hers.

One night on tour, Pike had taken her to a kink club while Reagan was hanging out with one of the crew members and her daughter. He'd given Oakley the reins that night, keeping his promise of taking the submissive role if she was interested in switching things up sometimes. Pike had looked like the most sinful gift ever. Arms chained above his head, chest exposed, his tattoos beautiful and harsh under the spotlight, and only the briefest of black briefs on. But the sexiest thing had been the look in his eyes—dark and full of challenge. *Try to tame me* those eyes had said. A cocky slave for her indulgence.

She'd tortured and teased him with her mouth, licking at his ink and biting his nipples, tracing her fingernails over his erection through the thin briefs. He hadn't been obedient at all. A terrible submissive in that respect. But she'd found his defiance hot as hell. When he'd told her to stop teasing, she'd backed away from him, sat on a chair and spread her knees. She'd been wearing nothing beneath her skirt and when she'd touched herself, Pike had lost his cool, yanking at the chains and telling her how much better he was than her fingers.

She'd wanted to let him take over, but instead she'd gotten herself off in front of him, enjoying the way his eyes had gone hooded and hungry. Then she'd strolled over to him and had gotten to her knees. She'd slid his briefs off, exposing him fully, and had warned him that he wasn't allowed to come. Then she'd put her mouth on him and tasted exactly how much he wanted her. She'd licked and laved and then when she'd worked up the nerve, she'd grabbed the lube and dragged her fingers back to his opening.

Pike had jerked in his bindings, but had groaned deep and low when she'd breached him. The sensation had been new and exciting for her. Never before had she penetrated a man in any way, and there'd been the surge of power with it—Pike clenching around her fingers, his cock leaking salty fluid onto her tongue, and dirty threats spilling out of his mouth. She'd fucked him with her fingers and sucked him until her thighs were slick with her own arousal.

But even though she'd found it to be one of the most erotic experiences of her life—Pike putting that kind of ultimate trust in her—she'd found herself wanting him to wrestle the control back from her. So she'd loosened his cuffs and then had teased him and goaded him until he'd broken free. When his hands had broken free, he'd charged across the room, eyes wild and body aroused. He'd grabbed her with rough hands and kissed her hard. Then he'd spun her around and pushed her down to the floor on her stomach. For a second, she'd caught sight of the faces peering at them through the window to the private room. They hadn't pulled the shade and knowing that others were watching had only ratcheted up her arousal.

Pike had pinned her arms above her head, nudged her legs wide and shoved up her skirt. The floor had been cold beneath her, but the hint of discomfort had only made it better, more untamed. He'd entered her without warning and had rutted into her like a man possessed—slick with sweat and grunting—and she'd found her mind slipping into a place she'd only flirted with, that sense of calm surrender. She would've happily lay there forever, taking what he wanted to give her. He'd come deep inside her, gripping her wrists tight, his weight heavy on her. And even without orgasm, she'd felt this humming sense of satisfaction. That's when she'd felt the truth. Submission nourished her. Pike's dominance nourished her.

But, of course, Pike hadn't been finished with her. He'd pulled out of her, lifted her onto a nearby bench, and then had put his mouth between her legs, heedless of the mess he'd just left inside her, and had brought her to a screaming orgasm right in front of the window.

The whole thing had been rough and sloppy and untethered. And it had showed them both what they needed to know. She could tell Pike had never felt completely legit taking the role of a dominant in the past—that he'd compared himself to the strict standards of his friends. But with her, he could own his brand of it. It wasn't neat. The lines were blurred. She'd never be the polite sub that called him sir and he'd never take on that cool, stoic persona—there was too much open passion in both of them. But their version was exactly right for them.

So when Pike tugged off her T-shirt and told her to go to the bed and brace her hands on the edge of it, she went without question.

"I brought some new toys home from my trip," Pike said, his footsteps heavy on the floorboards behind her as he went to his bag and unzipped it.

"Shopping at stores other than Wicked? Jace is going to be jealous."

Pike walked over to her, heat radiating off him even though he hadn't touched her yet. Something traced over her spine. "I had to order this one from one of his suppliers directly. Special order."

He shifted whatever he had in his hand, and soft, supple falls of leather coasted over her backside. Goose bumps broke along her skin. Pike had flogged her before, but this leather felt softer, more luxurious. "Ooh, what is that?"

Pike let the tails of the flogger tease between her spread legs. "Doeskin. It's a gentler sting than the elk hide we already have."

"Gentler? Going easy on me tonight?" She closed her eyes, the soft material tickling over her back entrance.

"Maybe," he said, wickedness in his voice. "Or maybe I'm just going to torture softer parts."

"Oh." Everything went molten inside her.

He laid the flogger to the side, putting it in her peripheral vision as a warning, then his hands reached beneath her and tugged both of her nipple rings, sending a shot of sensation straight downward. "I also got something for these."

The sound of metal on metal sounded and she looked down to

see his hands working a small chain through the rings. Two sparkly weights hung at the base of it. He fastened the clasp and the chain pulled downward and swayed, making her breasts feel heavy and sensitive. Pike gave the chain a tug and she groaned.

"You look so fucking hot right now, mama. I got half hard in the store when I picked that out and pictured you wearing it, but reality is so much better than I could've imagined." He coasted a hand over her backside then down her leg. He locked something around each ankle—a spreader bar. He kissed her inner thigh. "Now, all you need to do is to feel what I'm doing to you and enjoy. You can come as many times as you want. But I'm not letting you go until I'm done with you."

Arousal was already making her slick and needy. She shifted in the ankle cuffs, not sure how long she'd actually make it before orgasm. Having Pike here in the flesh instead of the phone had every part of her ready to burst.

She heard him tugging off his boots and chucking them to the side, and then the flogger disappeared from her view. She only had a second to prepare before the thing came down over her backside. She gasped. The impact was impressive. Yes, not as stingy as the other flogger, but that delicious thud still made her rock forward and shudder with pleasure—a hundred velvety tongues sliding over her skin.

But Pike was just warming up because after a few hits to the back of her thighs and ass, he landed one home, right between her spread legs. The shock of the sting on the tender flesh had her rearing up, but Pike pushed a hand to the center of her back and shoved her top half back down to the bed.

"Still think I'm here to be gentle on you?"

"No," she panted, her pussy tingling with the unfamiliar stinging sensation.

"You have the sexiest cunt, baby," he said, gravel in his voice as he slid his fingers into her. "All those long nights on the road, hearing your voice on the phone, this is what I pictured when I'd fuck my hand—you bound and spread for me, that pretty pink flesh sliding over my cock, that voice of yours calling my name."

She sighed and rocked back onto his hand, shameless. "Yes."

"I've neglected you." He twisted his fingers inside her, lighting her up. "I can see how ready you are for me. But the night is young."

The pressure from his fingers disappeared and she heard her bedside drawer open. Soon, Pike was back with a hand on her hip. Then something breached her opening—the dildo she'd bought at Wicked. The feel was familiar, the toy her go-to for her and Pike's phone calls, but having him insert it drove up the pleasure of it.

"Here, baby, this will help fill you up. You can use your hand to play with it."

She reached between her body and the bed and grasped the base of it and pumped it into her, getting a shred of relief.

Now it was Pike's turn to grunt, and the sound of his zipper cut through the air. "Fuck, baby, you should see the view from here."

She peered back over her shoulder to find him with his pants open and the heel of his hand rubbing his cock over his underwear as he looked at her. "Yeah, the view's mighty nice."

He smiled her way and lifted the flogger in his other hand. He swatted it across her pussy again, the tips brushing over the hand she had on the dildo. "I didn't tell you to lift your head."

She smirked and turned her head to face the bed again. "It was worth the punishment."

"Yeah? I must be going too easy on you."

That's when the real flogging began. Pike hit her across the backs of her thighs, her ass, and between her spread legs over and over again until all of her skin was burning and tingling. All the while, she used the toy to counterbalance the pain. All of it working in tandem. But she was breathless and sweating by the time he gave her a break.

She pressed her forehead to the bed, panting.

Pike put his hand over hers and pumped the dildo for her, a slow in-and-out drag that made her moan. His other hand traced over her back entrance. "Need to come, baby?"

"Please." The word was muffled by the sheets, but she couldn't lift her head.

Pike slid the hand on the dildo higher, leaving her to it, and found her clit. She nearly jumped out of her skin at the swift pleasure the simple touch ignited, but before she could fully process it, Pike's mouth was on her backside kissing and biting, getting precariously close to a zone they hadn't traveled yet. A choked sound caught in her throat.

Pike's teeth clamped into the flesh of one ass cheek, hard and unyielding, then he backed off and soothed it with his tongue. Oakley couldn't think, the pain/pleasure combo making her knees weak and arousal coat her fingers. But then his tongue moved to her most forbidden spot and she damn near jumped off the bed.

Pike's tongue traced over her back entrance, hot and wet and oh-my-God amazing. Her back arched. "Pike . . ."

His fingers stroked over her clit, his breath balmy against her sensitive opening. "Every part of you is mine, Oakley. I want it all. Everything that can give you pleasure, I'm going to find and use. Nothing is safe from me."

She squeezed her eyes shut—some weird combination of desperate need and ingrained shame coalescing. She wanted him to continue, but she couldn't help but wonder how he felt about it. "I've never. It's—"

"Sexy as fuck," he finished and gave her another slow lick. "You should see how your legs are trying to spread wider, how you're wanting to open to me. Come for me, baby, and I'll show you just how good this can feel."

He went back to rubbing her clit, and his tongue and lips lavished her most secret spot with sensations that made her whimper and gasp. She pumped the dildo hard inside her, riding his hand with the rock of her hips, and then Pike's tongue breached her and everything exploded behind her eyelids.

Her back arched and she cried out, every inch of her seeming to contract at once and then release in a flood of pleasure. She called out his name and came hard and loud.

Pike didn't back off until she was squirming and overwhelmed with all the sensations. But he only paused in order to unlatch her from the spreader bar and to take the dildo out. "Get all the way onto the bed. On your back."

"I'm not sure if I can." Her knees wobbled and her body felt ready to give way.

Pike grabbed her by the waist and hauled her up on the bed. When he flipped her onto her back, she lost her breath for a second. He was looming above her—naked and aroused and beautiful. His lips were puffy and slick from what he'd done to her, his gaze pleased. And that was all she needed. Any shame or awkwardness that kind of act might've caused in another situation faded away with the unabashed desire she could feel rolling off him. With Liam, she'd had to be the innocent, sweet girl—the girl who'd want the "correct" things. But with Pike, nothing was off limits. Everything was safe. They could explore things without fear of judgment or weirdness. Both in the bedroom and out of it.

Pike reached down and cupped her face. "You take my breath away, mama."

"You should come up for air when you're doing that to me then."

He smirked and gave the chain between her nipples a tug. "Never an inch."

"Never."

"Thank God." He lowered himself down to his forearms, the look of love on his face breaking her wide open. "Did you do what we talked about?"

She looped her arms around his neck, feeling the most at peace she'd ever felt in her life. "Haven't taken one in a month."

He touched his forehead to hers in that way that made her feel so cherished, and pushed inside her, filling her and making her sigh in pleasure.

"Then let's make a baby, Mrs. Ryland."

The smile on his face was one she'd never forget.

She felt it in her heart and filtering through her blood.

Fast and reckless and crazy. That's what the press had called their romance.

But she just called it perfect.

Dear Reader,

Thank you for reading Call on Me. *I hope you had fun with Pike! Before you go, I have a few more things for you. First, included in this edition is "House Call," a special bonus short story about Dr. Theo Montgomery.*

Theo first appeared in Fall Into You *as the physician who helps Charli when she's in a car accident, and then he nudged his way into* Nothing Between Us *when he examined Keats after a fight. We've gotten to see a little of the to-the-point, confident doctor who rules the ER but happens to be a submissive when he visits The Ranch. But "House Call" is finally going to give you his real story.*

I've also included two special previews for you after that. One is from Break Me Down, *the upcoming novella about Pike's friend Gibson, and the other is a peek at the first book in my brand-new Pleasure Principle series,* Off the Clock. *I'm really excited to share both with you!*

Also, if you haven't gotten the chance yet and want to read more about Devon (Oakley's brother) and Hunter to see how they first fell in love, check out their story in Yours All Along, *now available from InterMix!*

As you can see, I love writing about the minor characters who appear in my books. So if there's ever anyone you're wondering about and would like to see in a future story, feel free to let me know! I can be reached here: roniloren.com/contact.

Happy reading!
Roni

HOUSE CALL

ONE

He hated New Year's Eve. *Hated* it. Fucking drunk drivers and icy roads. Theo yanked his surgical gloves off and tossed them in the bin with a curse. The bloodied gloves disappeared beneath the slamming lid, and he ignored the twisting knot in his gut.

"Dr. Montgomery." The resident's voice was tentative as he poked his head into the small room, like he was expecting Theo to take a swing at him. "The family's asking—"

Theo held up a hand without looking his way. "I'll handle it. Just give me a minute to get cleaned up."

"Do you want me to call the chaplain?"

Theo went to the sink, scrubbing with scalding hot water. "Go ahead. But don't let him go out there until I deliver the news. They'll fall apart if they see him first."

"Yes, Doctor."

The resident slipped out of the room, and Theo turned off the water and braced himself on the sink. He could still hear the heart monitor going monotone in the trauma room—flatlining. *We've lost her, Doctor.* None of their resuscitation attempts had worked. It wasn't an uncommon occurrence in the ER. This was his job. But the woman had had hair the color of his former wife's. Gold tinged with auburn. No. Gold and auburn tinged with blood.

Sweat gathered on the back of his neck and that cold, sick feeling washed over him. He'd been calm and focused in surgery, had flipped that internal switch that let him shut everything out but the patient's needs and the tasks at hand. But now memories were trying to take over. He closed his eyes and took a deep breath, centering himself. There was no time for this. The husband and daughter of the woman were huddled in the waiting room, waiting for news of both her and the teenage son who'd been in the car when it'd been struck by a pickup truck. The boy would be okay. His mom would not. *Was* not.

Theo took a deep inhale, pulled his surgical cap off, and headed into the waiting room. Other doctors and staff quietly acknowledged him as he passed by. News had traveled quickly. Most days all these residents wished they were in his shoes—top trauma surgeon in the region, head of the department. But right now, the guy cleaning the bathrooms wouldn't want to trade spots with him. The only thing worse than losing a patient was delivering the news to the people who loved that person.

He pushed through the swinging doors that led to the waiting area. The place was packed—crying children, people coughing, family members lined up at the desk to ask how much longer they'd have to wait. Faces turned his way, everyone hoping they'd be called in next. But he wasn't going to be able to offer any of them relief right now. He took a turn down a separate hallway where they brought the waiting families of serious cases, offering them some privacy and quiet. There were a few separate families in the line of small alcoves, but he spotted the family he was looking for instantly. The daughter was curled up against her dad, looking younger than the preteen she was, her eyes red-rimmed. Her father had his hand on her hair, trying to soothe her, trying to be strong for her. God, this fucking sucked. Some idiot had decided to drink too much and not call a cab, and now Theo had to tell a little girl her mom wasn't coming back.

Days like this, he wished he'd gone for that engineering degree instead of to med school.

The husband's eyes locked with Theo's—hopeful at first and then . . . not. Families always knew. No matter how stoic Theo kept his face, you couldn't hide the aura of death on you. It stayed with you like a film that clung to your skin.

"Doc—" the man asked, standing up.

"Your son is in recovery and is going to be okay. His leg is broken, and we had to give him a transfusion, but you'll be able to see him when he wakes up."

The man's breath whooshed out in relief. "Thank God." Then he looked up. "And Brenda?"

Theo shook his head. "I'm very sorry, Mr. Allen. We did everything we could, but she'd lost too much blood by the time she got here. Her heart couldn't take it."

The man didn't shout, didn't scream. Instead he simply crumpled to the floor like a marionette whose strings had been cut and buried his face in his hands. "Oh, God."

The little girl hurried to her father's side, the word *no* falling off her lips over and over. She wrapped her arms around her dad and began to sob. Theo closed his eyes, wishing he could reach out and offer something, anything, to make it better, but what was there to do or say? When it'd happened to him, the doctor had put a hand on his shoulder and told him his wife was at peace now. Theo had wanted to attack the guy. The gesture had felt so useless, so trite. A pat on the shoulder was for when your team didn't win the game, not when you lose the woman you love. He wouldn't do that to someone else. Some of the residents and nurses thought he was cold, but this was his version of compassion.

He leaned out of the doorway and motioned for the chaplain, who'd been standing in the hallway. Father Bentley came out, his face full of his special brand of kindness. "Mr. Allen, I'm so sorry for your loss."

Mr. Allen stiffened and then got to his feet in an awkward rush. Theo saw the anger flare in his eyes before the words came out. He jabbed his finger to Theo's chest and stepped close. "You let her die! They told me you were the best. What did you do?! Why didn't you save her?"

The words reverberated off the walls and linoleum floors, echoing all around them and banging around in Theo's head. Theo didn't move. He could handle the collateral rage that sometimes got thrown his way in tragedies, knew it wasn't personal. But for some reason the man's words punched right through the doors Theo kept the bad shit behind. Flashes of that night so long ago flickered across his vision. Theo calling Lori's name, all of his medical training going to hell as his wife lay trapped and broken in the car. Lori begging him to help her, not to let her die.

Theo swallowed hard and then when that didn't work, cleared his throat. "Mr. Allen, this is Father Bentley. He'll be here if you need anything."

"I need my fucking wife!" the man shouted, his voice wrecked with grief.

The words sliced like daggers, and Theo simply nodded. "I know."

And he did.

Theo stepped away, leaving the family with the chaplain, and strode back toward the swinging doors, calling for one of his residents to go assist Father Bentley. Theo couldn't be that guy right now. The panic was trying to grab him, the memories rolling fresh even though seven years had passed. *Son of a bitch.* He didn't do this anymore. He'd mastered the panic attacks in the first year after the accident. But tonight, the past refused to stay quiet. He made a swift journey to his office to change his clothes and grab his things. He needed to get out of here before anyone saw him rattled. That would be completely unacceptable.

But even though he was exhausted after the twelve-hour shift, the thought of going home held no appeal. The demons were snapping at his feet, and he only knew one surefire way to shut them up. Oblivion. The sun would be up soon. A new year. But the same old monsters.

He got in his car and headed onto the open road.

TWO

"You heading out, chica?"

Maggie looked over her shoulder as she tugged down the zipper of her leather boots, weariness settling into her bones. She'd thought switching to a training gig instead of the paid domme role would be more fulfilling, but she was having trouble getting invested in the sessions. Lately, she felt like she was just going through the motions. The subs she was working with were great, but she hadn't felt that special thrill she used to get from a visit to The Ranch in a long damn time. "I think so. After two training sessions with newbies and that New Year's party, I'm wiped. I need hot chocolate and fuzzy slippers."

Janessa leaned in the doorway with a sly smile. "Might want to rethink that and find a second wind."

"Why is that? And don't tell me it's for girls' night in the employee bar. Last time I agreed to that, I had a hangover for like two days."

She laughed. "Lightweight. And no, it's not that. It's better. Guess which sexy doctor just walked in and is asking for you?"

Maggie paused, the zipper squeezing beneath her fingers and her stomach giving a little twist. "Seriously? He hasn't been here in months. I thought after last time . . ."

"The front desk told him that you weren't taking clients anymore and had moved into training, but you know how he is. He didn't exactly accept that answer, wants to talk to you first."

"Shit." She yanked her zipper back up. She'd already taken her hair down from the severe twist she wore here at The Ranch, but that couldn't be helped. There'd be no getting it back in place. She finger-combed her hair and checked her reflection in the mirror to make sure her makeup hadn't smeared.

"You are so adorable," Janessa teased. "The other dommes want a crack at the doc because he's so damn smug. They want to put him in his place. But you actually have a thing for him, don't you?"

Maggie ran her fingertips under her eyes to clean up her eyeliner. "I do not get *things* for my clients."

Okay, so maybe once upon a time she'd had a thing for Theo—or Theodore as she called him when he was in her dungeon. It was hard not to. The man was gorgeous, brilliant . . . and intense. Seeing such a stoic, powerful man submit to her flipped all of her switches. But she'd been stupid enough to think that what was developing between them over their sessions together was something real. Like some big-time doctor from the city would be interested in a small-town artsy chick. Please. She knew better than to get attached to anyone who was paying her money to dominate them. But it had happened. And when she'd crossed the line and gone beyond the physical and asked him a personal question—he'd said his safe word so fast she'd gotten whiplash. The man who could take a beating that would make even the toughest subs weep for mercy had safed out on a simple request of, "Tell me why you look so sad today."

"Well, the guy you do not have a thing for is in Room C," Janessa said.

"Thanks." Maggie adjusted her corset, made sure everything was still in place, and then crossed the dressing area to move past Janessa. But her friend put a hand on her arm. Maggie halted. "What's wrong?"

Janessa smoothed her lip-gloss. "Just a little advice, Mags. Don't forget that your decision to stop taking clients was yours. If that's really what you want, don't let the doctor sweet-talk you into breaking your rules."

Maggie laughed. "Sweet-talk? I think Dr. Theodore Montgomery is literally incapable of saying anything that would be deemed sweet. But I hear you. Thanks."

Janessa nodded. Maggie could tell her friend was in mentor mode now. Janessa had been her original trainer here, so though she was only a few years older than Maggie, Maggie had learned a lot from her about how to be a domme.

Once Maggie got into the cool air of the hallway, she took a deep breath and straightened her spine. Confidence always. That's how she walked around here—even if she didn't feel it all the time. And with Theo, she'd have to have all that armor in place because sometimes seeing him made her want to dissolve into the nerves of a swoony teenager. Even on his knees, the man was intimidating as hell.

She made her way down the hallway and opened up the door to Room C. Usually when Maggie saw him, he was already stripped down to his boxer briefs. He had a hard limit about nudity, so she'd never seen him completely bared, but today wasn't a session, so he was in dark jeans and a gray henley, black hair just a little past time for a haircut. He hadn't noticed the door crack open, so she took a moment to enjoy the view. That man always made her want to paint. Her fingers itched to map the hard lines of him with her brush, color in the dark shadows and the way the light fell on his face.

Tonight, he was sitting on one of the benches, forearms on thighs, hands loosely clasped between his knees. To most, he'd look relaxed, like he was simply waiting. But Maggie had studied him enough to recognize the tension in him. She'd call this painting *Storm Behind Glass*.

She stepped inside and he peered up at the sound of her heels clicking on the concrete. He didn't smile. He never did. But the flicker of relief in his eyes was its own reward. "Mistress."

"Theodore." She shut the door behind her with a click. "This is unexpected."

"I know." His focus flicked to her loose hair. "I apologize if I interrupted anything."

The feel of his gaze on her heated her more than it should. He always looked as if he was studying each little thing and analyzing it, filing it away in some data bank. She crossed her arms over her chest in an attempt to look annoyed even though all she really wanted to do was ask him what was wrong, why he was here, why a man who was so regimented would show up unannounced. "You interrupted me going home. I hope you have a good reason."

He sat up straighter, his eyes meeting hers with a businesslike air. "I would like a session. I know you're not taking clients anymore, but I'm willing to pay whatever you need to make it worth your time, mistress."

She frowned. She didn't deny that she'd taken money for her services. But when he said it that way, it made her sound like a hooker. Like she was just holding out for a better price. She didn't sleep with clients. She didn't kiss them. They didn't get to touch her. She administered pain, humiliation, whatever their kink was, but some things were still her own. And she didn't appreciate him making it sound like she could be bought out of a decision she'd made. "There are other dommes working tonight. Throw your money at one of them."

Frown lines appeared around his mouth. "I'm sorry. I wasn't trying to insult you, mistress. It's just, I'm not interested in other dommes. I came here for you."

She ignored the little flutter of he-likes-me-best! pleasure that gave her. *Focus, Maggie.* "I'm not taking clients anymore does not mean 'I'm not taking clients unless they pay me enough.'"

There was a flicker in his gaze—worry. It looked out of place on him. "Mistress, please make an exception."

"Why?"

He looked away, jaw tightening.

She took a few steps forward until she was right in front of him and snapped her fingers, the sound echoing in the cavernous room. "If you expect me to consider it, you will look at me and tell me why."

He turned his head toward her—the fight within him visible in the tense lines of his face. He was a proud man, one who was used to everyone deferring to him, but his submissive streak ran deep. He wanted to fight. He wanted to please. "I had a bad day at work and could use a distraction."

She kept her expression smooth even though a little surge of victory went through her that he'd actually given her an answer. "Tell me why it was so bad."

His jaw twitched. The request was razor close to the one that had made him use his safe word last time. She braced herself for him to bail. Instead he said, "Tell me why you stopped taking clients."

Her lips curved. "You're not the one who gets to make the commands in here, Theodore. But maybe if you comply with mine, I'll consider answering."

He sent her a steely look—one that she'd normally happily punish him for—but she hadn't agreed to play with him, so she couldn't go there. Their gazes held for a long moment, a silent war, but finally, he said, "A patient died on my operating table tonight. I had to tell her husband and daughter."

Maggie's lungs squeezed tight, all the breath whooshing out of her. "That's awful, Theo. I'm sorry."

He shifted, obviously uncomfortable with her sympathy. "Part of the job, mistress. We all have our own ways of dealing with it."

And his was getting the hell beat out of him by her. She didn't blame him. If she had to face that kind of thing every day, she may need those memories beaten out of her, too. But that didn't mean she could do this.

She grabbed a chair from the side of the room and pulled it over so she could sit in front of him instead of looming over him. What she was going to say wasn't coming from Maggie the domme but Maggie the woman. "Thank you for telling me. I stopped taking clients because a guy got angry one night when I wouldn't perform according to his wishes, and he backhanded me, split my lip."

Theo's attention snapped upward, fire in his eyes. "Someone *hurt* you? Who the fuck was he?"

The fierceness in the words took her breath for a second—the cool doctor looking like he could turn violent offender on her behalf if he got the guy's name. She wet her lips. "Who it was doesn't matter. The staff jumped in immediately. I wasn't hurt badly, just a little shaken. And a lot pissed. The guy was banned from the premises. But after that, I decided I didn't want to take money for this anymore. I never did this to be a performer in someone's play. And it was beginning to feel like that's what it had become. So now I know that when I scene, I'm doing it for me and the person I'm with. It's real." The last part slipped out and she winced inwardly. "Not that what we did together wasn't real—"

He lifted a hand. "I'm well aware I was paying you for a service, mistress. I didn't assume it was anything more than that."

No, apparently it was *her* job to weave fantasies that their business arrangement was more. She blew out a breath, unsure what to say.

Theo put his hands to his knees and nodded. "All right. I understand. I appreciate you telling me. Though, these are the times I wish I were one of the doms. I could order you to change your mind."

She laughed. "You realize that would so not work on me, right? I'd tell that dom to take his riding crop and shove it in his special place. You'd have a much better chance of persuading me than they would."

Theo lifted his head, and the little quirk of his lips could've been mistaken for a smile.

The sight nearly knocked her out of her chair. Goddamn. He was dangerously good-looking on any day. Broody and smug worked for him. But hell if that little hint of humor in his blue eyes didn't take the wind right out of her.

"Thanks for that, mistress." He stood. "I hope you have a good new year."

"I—" Seeing him head toward the door sent a sharp dart of panic through her. She'd been enjoying this—a taste of a real conversation with him. And she had a feeling if he walked out, he would never be back to see her. "Wait. I didn't say you could leave yet."

He turned, one eyebrow lifted. "I apologize. May I leave, mistress?"

She stood, trying to gather her courage. She'd put this man on her knees, had put her hands on him, but doing this was giving her heart palpitations. She cleared her throat. "We've both had long days. I'm really ready to get out of here. But what if . . . Well, there's a little diner up the road from here. They serve great pie. We could, you know, go have some pie together."

God. Her inner cringe was absolute. Badass domme, step aside, awkward teenager is here to humiliate you and undermine all street cred you've built with this man.

Theo looked stricken for a second then his expression closed down. He tucked his hands in his pockets. "That's generous, mistress. But I don't . . . have pie with people."

She frowned and put a hand to her hip, considering him. "You realize the pie wasn't a euphemism, right? There will be actual pie involved."

That half-smile appeared again but with a somber edge to it. "I don't date, mistress."

Her lips parted for a second at that bomb. "Like ever?"

"Ever. Good night, Margaret."

Her given name on his lips sent a warm curl of awareness up the back of her neck. He'd never called her anything but mistress. She hadn't even been sure he knew her name. But before she could respond, he turned on his heel and strode toward the door.

She stared at the empty doorway for a long minute. If she walked out to the main floor, would Theo be setting up an appointment with another domme? Would he let someone else exorcise his bad day? The thought sent a wash of hot jealousy through her.

She sighed and leaned against the wall. "Give it up, girl. You asked him out and he shut you down. You were just the hired whip. Let it go."

Great. Now she was talking to herself.

She massaged her brow with her fingertips, exhaustion settling in like a wet coat. She needed to get home and get to bed.

And she definitely needed to forget about the doctor with the ridiculously hot body and the haunted eyes.

Wrong tree. No barking allowed.

THREE

Theo sat in his car in the parking lot of The Ranch, watching the storm clouds on the horizon grow closer and closer. He needed to get moving or he'd be dealing with iced-over roads on the way back to Dallas. But somehow, he couldn't make himself put the car in gear.

He'd come to The Ranch hoping for swift and pain-laced oblivion. He hadn't been here in months, and the whole ride over he'd been planning to sign up for a session with one of the other dommes. The last time he'd scened with Margaret, it'd been the anniversary of his wife's death. He'd wanted to go out and get hammered that night, but he'd gone to The Ranch instead.

He'd been visiting Margaret pretty often back then. And though she always kept things focused on the reason they were there, he'd slowly gotten comfortable with her. Sessions with dommes used to be interchangeable. Selfish on his part. It didn't really matter who was on the other side of the whip as long as he got the physical release of the pain. But Margaret had changed that. She could be mean as hell, but she also had fun in the role and seemed to enjoy it. And her sense of humor was wickedly dry—something he couldn't help but be drawn to.

Once when she'd caught him trying to top from the bottom— something he'd gotten away with with other dommes—she put the heel of her boot against his crotch, the material of his boxers the only protection, and had made him recite the periodic table of elements because *if you're so determined to act like a know-it-all, show me what you've got.* He'd gotten all the way to Krypton before she'd relented. She'd leaned down, put her lips a breath away from his, her green eyes meeting his with a steady gaze. For that one moment, he'd thought she was going to break both their rules and kiss him. Right then, he would've let her, had wanted her with a ferocity he hadn't felt in so long, maybe ever. But instead she'd smiled, tapped his lips with the tip of her finger, and said, *Nothing makes me hotter than smart boys. But you missed Arsenic, gorgeous.*

He'd managed to smirk. "I left it out on purpose. Didn't want to give you any ideas, mistress."

A laugh had bubbled out of her at that—so genuine and unexpected that he'd found himself falling into that warm, welcoming sound, had wanted to come up with ways to make her do it again and again. She'd even let out this adorable little snort. That was the first time he'd gotten a glimpse of the real woman behind the role, and he'd yearned to find out more. He'd known then that he was in dangerous territory.

He'd found himself liking that he'd impressed her with his knowledge, that he could make her laugh so openly, that she thought he was attractive. It had started to feel like they were lovers playing this dangerous game together, like money wasn't being exchanged, like this was more than a business arrangement. But in doing that, he'd let his guard down.

Because that last night, he hadn't been able to hide from her. She'd sensed his struggles and had wanted to know what was going on with him. He'd been tied down, his back on fire from the cane she'd taken to him. All the ugly stuff had been obliterated from his mind in those blissful moments, leaving just sensation and the present moment. But her knowing eyes had drilled into him, seeking the truth, making him want to confess every damn thing he'd ever locked up. *Tell me why you're so sad today.* He'd never had to use his safe word, but he had that night. And he'd decided then to never put himself in that position again.

But tonight, when he'd walked through the doors, all he could think about was her. Mistress M. Margaret. She scared the hell out of him with her astuteness, her quick mind and spot-on instincts, but that's also what made the thought of seeking out any other domme unappealing. All of the others felt like playacting now in comparison. And seeing her tonight had confirmed it.

He'd gotten another glimpse of the real Margaret tonight. With her wavy hair down and the weariness of a long day hanging about her, she'd looked beautiful and undone and it'd made him want her. Not for a session but in his bed. He'd wanted to say yes to pie just to have her keep talking. And that alone was enough to send him bailing on the whole thing.

He'd originally picked Margaret because she was so opposite his type. A bold girl with dark hair, a Texas twang, and a stud in her nose. So unlike any woman he'd ever sought out. His wife had been blond, east coast, and refined. A brilliant lawyer. In the bedroom, he and Lori had been equal partners, vanilla.

Margaret didn't have one thing about her that reminded him of his wife. So it hadn't felt as much of a betrayal if he found a girl he'd never be interested in outside of The Ranch. He hadn't gone there for sex or to find another women, he'd gone for a service, to feed a need he'd always suspected he was wired for.

But now . . . his blood was pumping with a need for something way more basic. Conversation. Companionship. Pie.

He groaned and turned the key in the ignition. He needed to get the fuck out of here.

He knew he could go inside and get whatever he wanted. If he wanted to get laid, he'd have a lot of choices. He hadn't been a monk since his wife had died. But since he'd started coming to The Ranch three years ago, he'd stopped the occasional one-night stands and had become celibate. Vanilla sex wasn't worth the trouble. He didn't want to date the women or have them get attached or explain to them that he wasn't much of a partner. That he worked too much, that he could be bossy as shit, and that in the bedroom, he'd rather be humiliated than treated like a stud.

His wife had discovered how difficult it was to be married to him the hard way. The night of the accident they'd been in a screaming argument. She'd wanted to start trying for a baby, and he'd told her she was nuts. They'd just begun to get on their feet after med school and law school, and in his opinion, the last thing they'd needed was a baby. Looking back, he could remember how fucking terrified he was at the thought of being a father. But he'd been an asshole about it, and they never got to finish the argument. They'd been yelling in the car, and he hadn't been paying close enough attention to the road. When a drunk driver hazed over the line into their lane, Theo hadn't had enough time to get out of the way. Maybe if he'd agreed to a baby that night, he'd be tucked into his home tonight with his wife and child.

He blew out a breath, wishing the painful memories would blow away, too, and pulled onto the road as the sleet began to fall. The *tap tap tap* of the icy rain was almost a comfort as the black night closed around him. He could be back in the city in an hour. Maybe by then he'd be tired enough to sleep this bout of holiday ghosts off. Tomorrow things would get back to normal. He'd tuck the things he couldn't change away, take an extra shift at the hospital, and move forward like he always did.

He flipped on his windshield wipers as the sleet picked up and hit the button for the seat warmers. Just the open road and the quiet. Maybe that'd be enough. And by the time he turned onto the main interstate, it was starting to work, his mind settling and going over the patient cases he had to follow up on. But a few miles down the road, the inky night was split by the flashing of hazard lights. On instinct, he slowed. A small car had slid off the road and looked to be wedged against the highway sign announcing how far to Dallas. Someone was huddled in a jacket and knit hat in the rain, crouching next to the car. A woman by the looks of it.

"Shit." Theo eased the car to the side of the road and pulled his phone out of the cup holder. The other car had spun and hit on the passenger side. Bad news for the car, but if there was no passenger, then good news for the driver. Theo buttoned his coat and carefully made his way over to the car, the pavement beginning to ice beneath him. "Hey, are you all right? Is there anyone else inside?"

The figure turned, all shadows still. "I'm okay. And no one else. But my phone is somewhere inside, so I haven't been able to call anyone."

A breath of relief gusted out, resulting in a frosty cloud. But then the accent registered. He trudged closer. "Margaret?"

The woman straightened and turned. *"Dr. Montgomery?"*

The clouds rumbled above and pelted them with sharp pellets of ice. "Please don't call me that."

Everyone in his everyday life called him *doctor*. He expected it, liked it. But hearing her call him that felt altogether wrong.

"Sorry," she said, holding her hands above her eyes to shield them from the sleet. "That's what most people call you around The Ranch. I figured . . ."

"You're not most people, Margaret."

"It's Maggie," she said, stepping closer and into the shine of his headlights. Ice clung to her pink knit cap and eyelashes, making her look like she was dusted with tiny diamonds. "When I'm not there, it's just Maggie."

"Why do you change it there?"

She grinned, despite the storm and the shitty circumstances. "Because Maggie is the least intimidating name ever. No one is scared of a Maggie."

"Then they haven't seen you in session. You can be terrifying."

She laughed. "Oh, Theo, you say the sweetest things."

He glanced at her car. No way was that getting out of there without a tow truck. "Come on, let's get in my car where it's warm. You can call a wrecker."

"Okay, let me grab my stuff." She headed over to the backseat door and wedged it open far enough to get a bag and her purse.

He took the bag from her, recognizing the size and shape of it. Her toy bag. The thing had been in his line of sight enough times for him to know it by heart. He ignored the little ripple that sent through him. He held out his hand to her. "Be careful. This kind of ice puts people in the ER all the time. We don't need to add a broken arm to the list tonight."

Maggie eyed his hand for a second. Despite her knowing him in many intimate ways, there was rarely direct touching. She always wore thin leather gloves in session. Holding her bare hand seemed downright rebellious. But after a moment's hesitation, she wrapped her cold fingers into his. He ignored the pleasure that simple skin-to-skin contact gave him.

He guided her to the passenger seat, set her things in the backseat, and then hurried into the driver's side. He shut the door and she groaned. "Oh my God."

He glanced over at her as she wiggled in the seat and tilted her head back in what could only be described as pure bliss. The sight and the sound went straight to his dick.

"These seat warmers are the best thing ever. I think my blood may have frozen."

Theo adjusted in his seat. "Probably not."

She turned her head, a smile touching her lips. "Professional opinion, Doc?"

"You'd be pretty dead if your blood was frozen."

"Okay, my soul is frozen."

"Entirely possible." He handed her his cell phone. "You call for a wrecker. I'm going to get back on the road and find a gas station or something. Sitting on the shoulder with a patch of black ice out there is asking for trouble. Is there anything else inside your car that you're worried about?"

She frowned. "No, just my phone, but I have insurance on that. It's not worth sitting out here for it. But the nearest gas station is in BFE. I only live two exits up the road. Would you mind dropping me off there instead?"

"That's fine. Just type the address into the GPS and you can get on the phone."

She punched in the address and then started making calls. He concentrated on the road, the ice getting worse, making his BMW fishtail onto the shoulder a few times. When he finally turned onto her street, which really turned out to be more dirt road than anything, his fingers ached from his hard grip on the wheel. Maggie let out a sigh and set down his phone. "They said all the trucks are already on calls. They'll try to get to it by morning. Happy new year to me."

"New Year's sucks," he muttered.

She peered over at him, her expression softening, and reached out to give his arm a squeeze. "I'm sorry. I can only imagine what you see on nights like this. I shouldn't be bitching about car drama."

The sympathy made his chest feel tight. He didn't want that from her—or anyone. "Bitch away. Under that logic, we'd never be able to complain about anything. People are dying every day, starving, being abused. There's always something more tragic than what's going on in our own lives."

She gave him a grim smile. "That's a sunshiny outlook."

The words were delivered deadpan, but he could tell she was teasing him. He liked that she wasn't afraid to give him a hard time. He smirked and tapped his temple. "Oh, you have no idea. It's all butterflies and rainbows up here."

She laughed, the sound a frothy, honest thing. "Are there puppies, too? Please tell me there are puppies."

"Even better, baby penguins."

"Excellent!" She pointed to a small house off to the left, the porch light barely visible through the sleet. "That's me over there. You can pull in front of the garage."

His gaze scanned the area, seeing nothing but black night and trees surrounding the cottage. Not another house in sight. "Wow, are you all by yourself out here?"

She gave him a droll look. "Said the serial killer as he drives the unknowing victim up to her cabin in the woods to harvest her organs."

A laugh escaped, the act feeling rusty in his throat. "Don't worry. You're safe. I'm a surgeon. I've completely sublimated my antisocial desire to carve on people into my job."

She put her hand to her chest in dramatic southern-belle style. "Oh, thank the heavens."

He parked the car on the gravel drive. "But seriously, you don't get worried living out here alone?"

She shrugged. "I have an alarm system. And I know how to shoot a gun. Plus, there's a sunporch on the back of this house that's the perfect art studio. I couldn't pass it up."

"You paint?"

She narrowed her eyes. "Don't sound so shocked. There is more to me than bitch boots and riding crops, you know. My paintings pay the bills."

"Huh. That's impressive. Hardly anyone's art pays the bills."

"Don't I know it. Took me three years before I turned any kind of profit. But a few of the galleries in Dallas have been featuring my stuff, and they've sold really well over the last two years. Plus I get online sales."

"What kind of art?"

She glanced toward the house. "Why don't you come in, and I'll show you some? I'll make you a cup of coffee for the road."

Theo frowned, following her gaze. They were crossing too many lines for the neat arrangement in his head. Mistress Margaret existed in one place—a dungeon at The Ranch. He didn't have coffee with people who had seen him bound and begging. He didn't visit their homes. He wasn't ashamed of his submissive side, but he also kept his two worlds very separate.

"Come on, Theodore," she said, green eyes playful. "This is like the pie. Completely innocent."

"You, Maggie, are far from innocent. And maybe I should be the one worried. I'm a guy all alone in the woods with a woman who knows how to wield a whip and who tortures men's genitals for fun."

She leaned over and patted his cheek. "We all sublimate in our own ways, honey. Now are you coming in for a coffee or not? I promise ball torture is off the table tonight."

"Well in that case, never mind."

A laugh burst from her. "Doc, did you just make a joke? There's hope for you yet."

He didn't believe that, but he couldn't help but be charmed by her. Plus, it was cold as hell out there and coffee sounded like ten kinds of heaven. "I'd like to see your art."

She rubbed her lips together as if suddenly nervous, but nodded. "Okay, then. Let's go. And be careful on the front steps. They ice up like a son of a bitch."

He climbed out of the car, grabbed her stuff, and then went to her side. He offered her his arm. This time, she took it without hesitation.

When she swung open her front door, the blast of heat was a shock to his system but a welcome one. He shook the sleet off his jacket and followed her inside after swiping his feet on the mat as she punched in the code for her alarm.

"You can leave your shoes and coat by the door if you want them to start drying out." She bent and tugged off her muddy boots then tucked them under a bench by the door. When she slipped out of her coat, he was stunned for a moment to see her in ordinary jeans and a soft cable-knit sweater. He'd seen her in some of the tightest, sexiest clothes a woman could wear—things that revealed way more than these comfortable ones ever would—but somehow he felt like he was seeing her naked.

She glanced up and tilted her head. "What's that look for?"

"Nothing," he said as he slipped off his shoes.

Her lips hitched up at the corner as she tugged off her hat. "I'm ruining all my tough-girl cred with you, aren't I?"

"Not possible."

She nodded at his henley and jeans. "I bet your patients would be weirded out seeing you wearing that and no lab coat or scrubs, huh?"

"Yes. Doctors aren't real people who exist outside of the hospital. Didn't you know?"

"I remember running into my pediatrician in a grocery store when I was a kid. Totally freaked me out that he had a wife with him and Doritos in his cart." She waved a hand. "Come on, the kitchen's through here."

Theo followed, quickly taking in his surroundings. The house was old, based on the door casings and the original hardwood floors, but everything looked fresh and updated. White walls and art hanging everywhere. Sheer curtains and funky lamps. A bright blue couch with colored pillows. Daring choices. All of it should've looked out of place in the cottage, but somehow it worked. Just like Maggie—edgy and down home all at once.

Maggie bumped a light switch with her elbow, illuminating the kitchen. The space was cozy—small but bright with white cabinets and butcher-block countertops. It looked lived in and well loved—so unlike the stark utilitarian kitchen at his place. A ridiculous amount of vegetables were piled in a bowl in the middle of one counter and a stack of cookbooks sat beside it.

He strolled over as Maggie turned on the coffeepot, and he picked up a beet from the bowl. "Your doctor would approve. Looks like you're getting your five a day."

She peered over her shoulder and grinned. "I grow all that stuff out back. Can take the girl off the farm but not the farm out the girl, I guess."

"Farm girl, huh? How'd a girl from the farm end up an artist and dominatrix?"

She went to the fridge and pulled out a half gallon of milk. "A wicked-strong rebellious streak for the art. And a run-in with an asshole boyfriend in college for the dominance."

He lowered himself onto the stool by the counter. "Run-in?"

"Yeah. I went through a serious ugly-duckling phase in high school. Braces, bad skin, extra weight, the whole thing. By college, most of that had improved but not the self-esteem problem that came along with it. I found a guy who was happy to exploit those insecurities." She gave him a humorless smile. "It took a trip to the hospital and a firm talking-to by a doctor to get it through my skull that a man should respect me and that shoving your girlfriend to the sidewalk hard enough to break her wrist is not an appropriate response to being late for a date."

Theo frowned, his fingers curling into fists even though this transgression against her was clearly a long time ago.

"After that, I raised my standards. Eventually, I figured out I really, really liked being in control and that men who wanted me to have it were the kind who flipped my switches."

He considered her. "Because we're safe."

She smiled and poured the coffee, then set a full cup in front of him. "No, because you're the most dangerous. That's where the edge comes from. Nothing is more volatile than a proud man made vulnerable. It's why that guy hit me all those months ago. He couldn't handle it. Only the strong ones survive it. And it's a huge turn-on to know that a powerful man has put that kind of faith in me—that he'll let me see him the way the world never does.

"Plus, the kind of attitude it takes to be a submissive guy feeds my love of rebellion. That's a man who isn't afraid to give the world and its expectations for him a big, fat middle finger."

Her eyes never left his the whole time she spoke, and Theo's body took notice. He cleared his throat. "I've never heard anyone put it that way."

Her lips curved, and she slid a small sugar bowl toward him. "So same question back at ya. How's a big-time surgeon figure out that he likes to submit?"

Theo looked down at his cup, focusing on adding a spoonful of sugar to it instead of having to hold the eye contact. This woman saw too much too easily in him. "I've always liked strong women. And the masochistic streak has probably always been there. I mean, I did choose to go to med school."

She laughed. "Good point."

He could've left it there, deflected. But for some reason, he wanted to be just as honest with her as she had been with him even though he'd never talked about it aloud with anyone. "I figured out the masochism thing in college. When I used to get overwhelmed in school, I'd go to the gym and box. The best way for me to purge stress was through exertion and pain and pushing myself past what I thought I could take. It gave me this high—all the adrenaline, that victory in surviving it. Only when I got matched up with a mean-ass female trainer did I realize that the feeling could become sexual." He smirked. "I grew up in an affluent family. I was used to people treating me like I was some sort of royalty. But this woman talked to me like I was scum on her shoe if I didn't perform how she wanted. It pushed some button in me. My hand got quite a workout those few weeks I trained with her."

He looked up and Maggie was sipping her coffee, evaluating him with a hint of humor in her eyes. "That's hot. Young college Theodore in the gym showers dreaming about his drill sergeant trainer. I should've brought a whistle to one of our sessions. I could've done the whole Kelly LeBrock routine from *Weird Science*."

"Shit." Images of Maggie dressed up in snug workout gear, twirling a whistle and barking commands, filled his mind. "You might've just blown teenage Theo's mind into bits."

"Ha. Teenage Maggie agrees. I so had a thing for the one who played Wyatt in that movie. Guess that should've been a sign for me then that I wanted a smart boy who'd let me be in charge, but it took a lot more years for that to sink in. At least you figured it out early. Probably saved yourself some grief."

"I wouldn't say that. I saw the masochism as a separate thing—a thing only for my private fantasy life, not something to act on. I dated vanilla girls, married one."

The last part slipped out and his heart seemed to stop for a second. His hands tightened around his coffee cup.

Maggie's brows lifted. "You were married?"

He coughed, trying to get his throat muscles to work. "Yeah. Lori was killed in a drunk-driving accident about seven years ago."

"Oh my God, I'm so sorry. I didn't know."

"It's okay. No one around here does. We were living in Oregon at the time." He took a long sip of his coffee, uncomfortable with the turn the conversation had taken. Once again, he'd let his guard down and stepped into deeper waters than he'd intended. "Thanks for the coffee. I probably should get back on the roads before they get any worse."

"Sure." She hitched a thumb toward the back of the house. "Do you still want to see the studio before you go? It'll only take a minute."

He wanted to kiss her feet for changing the subject. "Of course."

"Okay, give me a sec. I'll be right back."

"Don't feel like you need to clean anything up for me."

"I'm just going to go flip on the space heater and hide that nude self-portrait I've been working on."

He choked a little bit on the coffee, coughing.

She grinned. "Kidding. It's really a photography series."

"Sadist."

"Yep!" she said happily and strode off.

He watched her go and even though they'd just talked about his embarrassing college jerking off, abusive boyfriends, and his dead wife, he found his lips curving into the unfamiliar shape of a smile.

Somehow this girl knew how to force sunshine through the clouds no matter how dark and threatening they were.

He should leave right now. This was getting more dangerous by the minute.

He poured himself another cup of coffee.

FOUR

Maggie hurried to slip one of the canvases she had laying out behind a leaning pile of farm animal portraits. She'd nearly had a panic attack in the car when he'd agreed to come in and she'd remembered what she had sitting out in the studio. She straightened a few more things, though getting the area neat was too lofty of a goal, and tried to settle herself.

After hearing about Theo's wife, her heart had broken for him. The guy had been through more than she could imagine, and it explained a lot about how he acted. How tightly reined in he kept his emotions, all the boundaries he set. He was the only client she'd ever had who didn't allow himself a release at the end of her sessions. Theo would get aroused, but it was almost as if he wanted to punish himself by not getting any relief. She'd thought it just a deep masochistic streak, but maybe it was more than that. Maybe there was some lingering loyalty to his wife. The sessions were about the pain, the catharsis, not the pleasure.

After seeing him at The Ranch, she'd often lie in bed at night, fantasizing about how he would look in release, what he'd be like when he really let go, what it'd be like to be the one giving him that moment. Maybe he wasn't capable of that. Maybe his heart and his desire would always belong to another.

"Am I allowed to come back there now?" a voice called from the hall.

"Yep. Come on in."

Theo stepped in, his looming height more obvious in the low-ceiling room, and gazed around. She had paintings-in-progress set up on two easels, other completed artwork hanging on the walls, and more canvases leaning in piles against the wall. The sleet was battering the wraparound windows and the tin roof, making it sound like they were in a rain barrel, but the space was warming up from the heater, and having Theo there with her made it feel almost unbearably intimate.

She'd long gotten over the anxiety of showing her work to others. But for some reason, knowing Theo was going to look at them had her heart picking up speed. He'd probably think her stuff was too bright, too whimsical. He probably had staid portraits of British nobles on his walls or something.

He strolled over to a series of three paintings of barnyard animals. She'd used bold colors and had tried to capture the quirky expressions of each animal—a goat giving a head tilt, a chicken eyeballing the observer with suspicion, and a cow looking pointedly bored (which she'd named *Udderly Bored* because she hadn't been able to resist). Those were the works she did when she wanted to simply have fun and play with her paints.

She stepped up behind Theo, who seemed to be taking in every detail. "That's Curly, Moe, and Larry."

He looked over his shoulder and smiled. "You named the paintings after The Three Stooges?"

"No, I named the animals that. They live on my friend's farm down the road. I use them as subjects often, so she let me name them. This series just sold online to a lady in Montana."

"They're great. You've captured a lot of personality in each of them. You're really talented, Maggie." He turned to her, the expression on his face impressed. "Do you exclusively focus on animals?"

"I like live subjects, so it's usually animals or people."

"People?" She could tell the second he caught sight of the wall behind her where she displayed her real income generator—the nudes. His entire face went slack with what she could only hope was awe and not horror. "Oh my God, Maggie, those are . . . Wow."

He walked past her to take a closer look, and she tried to ignore

the warm feeling that moved through her at his genuine appreciation of her work. She knew she was good. The fact that people paid
her big chunks of money to have her paintings told her that. But
hearing Theo say it affected her in a different way. He wasn't a guy
who would blow smoke up her ass. Had he not liked her work, he
would've been polite but wouldn't have offered false praise.

Theo leaned forward, examining one she'd done of two of her
female friends at The Ranch. The couple had happily agreed to pose
for her. She'd captured them in a naked embrace as they stood in a
row of grapevines at The Ranch. She'd painted more grapevines climbing across the ground and swirling up their legs to lock them together.

"This is stunning," Theo said, glancing back at her briefly
before turning back to the painting to continue examining it. "It
hits you right in the gut. I can feel their bond."

Maggie smiled. "Thanks. They'd just gotten married a few
weeks before and were in that honeymoon phase, so they were
great subjects. Gave me a lot to work with. I did a whole series
with them both together and separately."

"I imagine people pay enormous amounts of money for these."

"I'm not cheap."

He laughed. Actually laughed. And then he turned around,
eyes serious. "Good. I'm glad you know your value."

She wet her lips under that intense gaze, the words burrowing
right into her. She glanced away, pretending to focus on the paintings. "Took a while. I think creatives are inherently neurotic about
their work. But eventually I leaned how to take mistress mentality
and apply it to this as well."

"Speaking of which"—a little wrinkle appeared between his
brows—"I can't imagine why you'd need to work at The Ranch if
this is doing so well for you."

She sat on one of the stools in the room and he followed suit, taking a chair nearby instead of the other stool, putting her in a position
to look down on him. Her libido gave a little jump of recognition at
the subtle shift in the power dynamic. She also noticed that he didn't
seem to be as in a hurry to leave as he had been a few minutes ago.

She cleared her throat. *Down, girl.* None of this meant anything. He was a friend who wanted to see her art. That's it. "I don't need to work there. But when I first joined The Ranch, I didn't want any messy relationship stuff. I liked the idea of scening with paying clients. Boundaries were crystal clear. It made it easier. When it started to feel like work, I stopped." She gave a little shrug. "It was never about the money itself. I'm sure you understand that."

"What do you mean?"

"Well, you're a gorgeous, intelligent man and a fantastic submissive. You had to know that you could get whatever you wanted at The Ranch without dropping a dime. But you paid for sessions for your own reasons."

His eyes met hers. "No, I couldn't have gotten whatever I wanted. There was only one woman I wanted to see and she charged."

Maggie sucked in a breath, the admission hitting her right in the chest. "Theo . . ."

He ran a hand over the back of his head and looked away. "Sorry. I shouldn't have said that. I'm not trying to hit on you."

"You're not?" She let out a nervous laugh. "Well, why the hell not?"

His attention snapped her way. "What?"

She crossed her legs and eyed him from her perch, knowing she was treading into thorny territory but trying to trust her gut. "*Why* aren't you hitting on me?"

"I—"

"Are you attracted to me, Theo?" she asked, keeping her voice gentle.

He looked stricken for a second. "What? Of course. What man wouldn't be?"

She smirked. "Lots of them. I've heard I can be kind of a bitch in bed."

"Maggie . . ." he said, almost a protest.

She slid off the stool, her sock-covered feet landing without a sound. "I'm just asking for your honesty, Theodore. Do you want me?"

Her beautiful, sexy doctor closed his eyes and bowed his head, his shoulders hunching. "I can't . . ."

"That's not what I asked," she said, keeping her voice steady and calm even though her heart was splintering for him. She could see the turmoil, the loyalty to his wife, the guilt. He had to be breaking beneath the weight of carrying all of that all the time.

He shook his head, his eyes still closed, as if he couldn't bear another word.

She eased closer to him and laid her hand to the back of his neck, letting him feel her presence but also hoping to soothe. It was the place she always put her hand after he'd had a rough session in her dungeon. He tensed at the first touch but then the muscles loosened beneath her fingertips. "You can't say it, can you? Even if you want me, you won't allow yourself even a little piece of joy, even for one night, will you?"

"I don't know how," he said, his voice rasping out, grinding with the anguish that held him so tightly bound. "I don't know how to let it go. Even when I want to. Even when you've brought me to the brink in session, I seize up at the thought of taking enjoyment out of it. I feel sick inside with the guilt."

She believed him. Every damn word. This strong, proud man couldn't break free from those demons that chased us all—guilt, regret, grief. His loyalty to the woman he loved was admirable but it was also killing him. Maggie rubbed her lips together, an idea slipping into her mind like a serpent and whispering dangerous things to her.

Theo shifted beneath her hand. "I need to go, Maggie. I can't—"

She squeezed his neck hard and pushed him back down into the chair. "Tell me your safe word, Theodore."

He stilled. "Maggie . . ."

"Tell it to me," she said, trying to trust her instincts but her heart thumping hard against her ribs.

"Oregon."

"That will always work with me, you understand?"

He was quiet for a long moment, and she thought he'd call the word right then and walk out, but then she heard a tense "Yes, mistress."

She closed her eyes, gathering her nerve. Sometimes this role came naturally to her, like walking or breathing, but right now she felt like she was back on the ice outside with no tread on her shoes. She was about to enter slippery territory and had no idea if they'd be able to keep on their feet. But something inside her was telling her to take the risk, to let her gut guide her. She took one more breath and then bent down, putting her lips close to Theo's ear. "Listen, sub. You have spent almost a year teasing me—coming into my sessions, looking smug and sexy and so damn handsome I could barely stand it. You strip for me but not all the way. You let me beat you but not really touch you. You've submitted to me but with so much fine print that you managed to keep all the control."

"Mistress—"

"Do you know how many times you left me pent up and on my own to take care of my needs? A vibrator can only satisfy so much, Theo."

Theo let out a shuddering breath and gripped the underside of his chair. Maggie let her eyes travel downward where the outline of his burgeoning erection was visible. She smiled, the predator in her relishing the small victory.

"So I think it's only fair that you pay me back for all my trouble." She stepped around the front of his chair and tapped beneath his chin to make him look up. His dark blue eyes met hers—apprehension there, but also something else, something much more telling. *Need.* "Your hard limits and fine print are done, sub. We're in my house. My rules."

His gaze lit with panic, and he moved to stand. "Maggie, I can't—"

But Maggie had learned a few tricks in her time, and she pounced quick enough to catch him off guard. Her hand cupped his crotch and gripped. "You're not going anywhere, sub."

A choked sound escaped him when she squeezed his tender flesh in her palm. He was taller than her by at least six inches, and broader. He could toss her to her ass without blinking. But he didn't move. Just held her gaze with those fathomless eyes. "What are you doing, mistress?"

She pushed up on her toes, bringing her mouth within centimeters of his and whispered, "Taking you hostage."

Then she kissed him.

Breaking her rule and his.

FIVE

Maggie putting her mouth to his was like a thunderclap going off in his head—loud, shattering, and powerful enough to steal every ounce of sane thought in his head.

I'm taking you hostage.

She still cupped his testicles in a firm grip, the threat of real pain only driving up his arousal, but the soft, sweet touch of her lips was what almost killed him. He'd imagined kissing her before, had berated himself for the desire, but God, he hadn't come close to getting it right. This—this was the kind of kiss that erotic poems were written about. Her lips teased and coaxed, almost daring him to push her away, and then she eased his lips open with her tongue and took it deeper. In control. Commanding. But edged with such feminine sensuality that he wanted to moan into her mouth and beg for it to never stop.

Theo's brain was trying to kick in, trying to lay logic atop the situation, but his libido was too loud to hear any of it. Everything had gone hot and needy at the feel of her hands and mouth on him. *Maggie. Maggie. Maggie.* That's all he heard in his head. He wanted her more in this moment than he'd ever wanted any woman in his life. This sexy dominant woman. This beautiful, quirky artist. This strong girl who'd kicked an abusive boyfriend to the curb and made her own way. He wanted to feel her body beneath his hands, to be inside her, to bring her pleasure, to hear how she sounded when she came. That wanting alone was a guilty kick in the gut. But he couldn't bring himself to pull away. It was all too good, too in the moment.

She moved her hand up, sliding over his fly and finding the button of his pants. The feel of her fingers unhooking the button sent a frisson of panic in him. What was he doing? He couldn't do this.

Maggie had stopped taking clients because she wanted something more meaningful. He wasn't the guy who could offer that. He was fucked up. The fact that he was still struggling when a beautiful woman wanted to take him to bed proved that. He wasn't a guy who could take her on dates and be carefree and have a good time. She deserved better than what he could offer.

He put his hand on her wrist before she could unzip his fly and pulled away from the kiss. "Mistress, I can't do this. I can't be what you want me to be."

She lifted her face, meeting his gaze and holding it. Those laughing green eyes weren't laughing anymore. They were hard and serious. Unbearably sexy. "I don't want you to be anything but my fuck toy tonight, sub. Think you can manage not to screw that up?"

His lips parted. He'd seen Maggie in mistress mode many times, but this was a new level, and his desire stood up and took notice. She wasn't going to make this tender or sweet. She wasn't going to pretend this was a date. And she wasn't going to throw pity his way even knowing his past now.

But before he could respond, she reached out and yanked his zipper down then tugged his jeans and boxers down in one swift motion, leaving him exposed to the glare of the overhead lights and the darkness outside. His instinct was to grab for his clothes, but he forced his hands to his sides, his submissive training kicking in. His erection stood proud, belying all the protests he'd given.

Maggie's gaze traveled down his body, lingering on his cock. She eased her hand around it and gave it a stroke that nearly sent him to his knees. She nodded. "So this is what you've been hiding from me, huh? This will do just fine. Turn around."

He did, almost on autopilot.

The telltale sound of a belt being unbuckled sounded behind him, and he tensed.

"Bend over and brace your hands on the back of the chair, sub."

Theo closed his eyes. He could fight many things. He'd resisted a lot these last few years. But his submissive side was potent and starved and having Maggie behind him with a belt sounded like a gift from the gods delivered personally to him. He'd wanted so badly to get lost in the pain tonight. Maybe that's what she was going to give him after all. Maybe she would obliterate all the other stuff for a few minutes. He couldn't bring himself to walk away from that.

He put his hands on the chair.

But instead of feeling the welcome lash of leather against his skin, he felt Maggie's hands on his arms. She pulled his wrists behind his back and looped the belt around them, cinching it tight.

"Wh-what are you doing, mistress?"

"My bedroom is down the hall on the left. I want you in it." She yanked his pants and underwear back up to his hips, grabbed one of his arms and tugged him with her roughly, not looking at him.

He followed, taking in her profile as they went. Her hair was loose and wild, her lips wet from their kiss, and her jaw set. She looked fierce and beautiful and determined. In that moment, he wished he were the kind of guy who could be what she needed. One who could make that light come on in her eyes, who could make her laugh, give her pleasure, be her safe haven after a long day. A guy who wouldn't need to be beat to a pulp anytime old memories chased him. A guy who could be touched without thinking of someone else.

She led him into a large room in the back corner of the house. The hardwoods were warm and obviously original, the bed layered with colorful quilts, and the ceilings high. Books were stacked haphazardly on her night table and a small vibrator sat atop them.

A low kick of desire hit him at the sight. She'd said he'd left her frustrated all those times, had said she'd had to take care of things after their sessions. The thought of Maggie getting herself off and imagining him while she did it was almost too much to hold in his mind all at once. The man in him relished the fact that the sexual attraction hadn't been one-sided, that he'd stood out among her other clients. But the submissive part of him felt like a failure.

His goal was supposed to be his domme's pleasure and satisfaction. Thinking back over their times together, he'd been nothing but selfish. Yes, limits had been in place, so she hadn't expected him to reciprocate. But he'd assumed then that she was simply doing it as a job, looking at him as a client. He hadn't let himself consider that she was getting turned on as well, that beneath those sexy outfits had been a woman aching for more than he'd given her.

Fuck. She'd given him so much, and he'd left her with nothing. Even tonight, she'd somehow sensed that he needed to be forced into this, that giving him the choice was never going to work. She *got* him. Had understood him at some unspoken level from the very beginning.

Suddenly, he wasn't so worried about what she may do to him. She'd said she wanted to use him tonight. And goddamn, he wanted to let her. Fuck all that bullshit that kept him tied up in knots. Fuck the panic. Fuck the guilt. That was his crap to deal with. He wouldn't let it get in the way of giving Maggie every ounce of pleasure he was capable of tonight.

Tomorrow the ice would thaw. They'd go their separate ways. But tonight, he was going to worship. He would not be the stoic doctor he was out in the world, he would not be the guy afraid to let anyone too close, he would be Maggie's—whatever she wanted.

"Mistress?"

Maggie brought them to a halt at the foot of her bed and looked at him. "Yes?"

"You won't need the restraints tonight—unless it pleases you for me to wear them. I'm here willingly. I'm not going to leave unless you tell me to. I want . . ." The words got caught again.

Her eyebrows lifted slightly. "You want what, Theo?"

He inhaled a deep breath, forcing the truth out. "I want you. I want to please you. Serve you. Whatever that involves, I'm willing."

Her expression softened for a moment, and she reached out to stroke his face. "Thank you. I don't take that gift lightly."

He lowered his head, showing her his acquiescence, a sense of calm coming over him for the first time tonight. There was safety in this space. He was moving into uncharted waters, but the act of submission quieted a lot of the demons for him. If he could let himself fully go there, maybe they could both escape the outside world tonight.

Maggie undid the belt, releasing his arms, and then pulled his shirt over his head. She tossed it to the floor then stepped back and gave him a once-over. His jeans hung low and open on his hips, and his cock flexed at the attention of her gaze. "You are ridiculously beautiful, Theodore. I want to paint you just like this. Bare-chested and hard and waiting for my command. I'd never have to look at another dirty picture again. I could get off on this one view every time."

"I can stand here as long as you'd like, mistress."

She smiled. "I bet you would, wouldn't you? It'd be pretty challenging to keep that erection for as long as it'd take me to sketch. I guess I'd have to be creative with inspiration."

His lips hitched up. "It would be very meta for a nude to be sketched while the artist herself was nude."

She laughed. "Indeed. Next time."

He held back the frown that threatened. There would be no next time. He couldn't let there be. But he wasn't going to ruin that smile on her face with that reality.

She stepped closer again and curled her fingers around his erection. Her hand was like silk against him, and he let out a loud exhale, trying to keep his composure. She pressed a kiss beneath his ear. "How long has it been since you've come, sub?"

"About a week, mistress." Though with her stroking him like that, it felt like he hadn't come in oh—the last thirty-seven years of his life.

"How long since you've come with someone else?"

He swallowed hard. "About three years."

Her hand stilled for a moment, but then she seemed to catch her reaction and moved her fingers again. "That's a long time, Theo."

"It's easier that way."

She let her fingernails trace up along the line of hair at his navel all the way to the patch on his chest, sending shivers over his skin. "I'm not about the easy way."

She bent and tapped his leg, indicating that she wanted him to lift his feet. He did, one at a time, so she could take his jeans and underwear off, leaving him completely bare while she remained fully dressed.

She stalked around him, dragging her fingertips over his shoulder as she went. When she stopped behind him, she let the pad of her finger gently trace over the long scar that ran from his left shoulder to his rib cage. He shuddered and his hands curled into his palms.

"How did you get this?" she asked quietly.

He closed his eyes. That question had been one of his limits in his sessions. Don't ask about the scar. Maggie was proving the point that nothing was out of bounds for her tonight. He could safe word but all this would stop if he did that. He swallowed hard. "I got it in the car accident that killed my wife."

Maggie inhaled audibly behind them then pressed the flat of her hand along the scar. He braced for the sympathy, the empty words that any normal person would give him. But instead she moved her hand aside and put her lips to the scar, leaving a line of kisses along the length of it.

The injury didn't hurt anymore, but the feel of her gentle mouth soothing it knifed through him. He could handle her brutality, but he wasn't sure he could handle her tenderness. His hands trembled at his sides.

She slid her palms to his biceps, giving them a hard squeeze and digging her nails into him. The tiny points of pain dragged him back into the moment. He focused on the feel of it, the physical response, the grounded feeling of her holding him in place. He released a breath.

Her grip eased. "I'm so glad the accident didn't take you, too, Theo."

He sniffed. Fate had so gotten it wrong when it'd taken Lori instead of him. "Yeah, the world was so lucky on that one. Everyone needs another asshole to deal with."

Maggie pinched him hard on his side, sending fire to the spot. "I don't need the sarcasm, sub." She stepped in front of him, green eyes fierce, and put a finger to his chest. "The bastard routine doesn't work with me, so you can drop it. Insulting yourself insults me. You think I would welcome a jerk into my bed? You're a good man, Theodore Montgomery."

"Maggie, please, I don't—"

"You save lives."

"It's my job."

She stepped closer, her gaze holding his and her palm splaying against his chest. "And you saved *me*."

"What?" he looked down at her, confused.

"If you hadn't come along, I'd still be spending my nights taking clients, keeping everybody at a safe, professional distance. I thought I'd gotten past my shit with the old boyfriend, but I kept safe by not letting anyone really be with me. Until you came in and made me want things I thought I'd never want again—a real connection, a man's touch, a guy who would make me nervous and excited in the best way possible."

The words spilled over him, stunning him. "Maggie . . ."

She pressed her finger over his lips. "Shh. I'm not telling you this to put pressure on you. I'm not saying you have to be that guy. Tonight can just be tonight. But I'm not going to stand here and let you act like it doesn't matter that you are who you are and that you're in this world. You matter to the patients you help, and you matter to me."

Without bidding them to do so, his hands went to her head to clasp it and pull her against his chest. It was against the rules to touch her without permission, but she didn't stop him. Instead she settled easily against him, and he put his lips to the crown of her head, holding her tight, inhaling the wintery scent of her hair, and wishing once again that he could be a man worthy of her. "Thank you, mistress."

Her shoulders rose and fell with a deep breath, and then she grabbed his wrists and tugged his hands away from her. When she stepped back, the cool mistress expression was back in place. "Clasp your hands behind your neck and keep them there."

He did as he was told. His arousal had flagged when she'd touched his scar, but now the way she was looking at him was stirring interest anew.

"Three years is definitely too long. If I let you in my bed tonight, I want you to last."

He smirked. "I assure you my control is just fine, mistress."

Hell, he'd managed to keep it together for their long sessions all this time.

But she shook her head slowly and then she was moving closer. She stopped in front of him, lifted an eyebrow, and then lowered herself to her knees. "I think I need an insurance plan."

"Oh, fuck." He hadn't planned for the words to come out, but the shock of seeing Maggie kneeling in front of him, preparing to put her mouth on him sent fireworks going off in his head. So much of him wanted what she was offering. The thought of feeling her soft, lush mouth around him. *God.* But the last time he'd let a woman do this, he'd had a flashback to a night with Lori in the middle, and had lost his erection. It'd fucked with his head and ruined the night.

"Mistress, I—I promise I can last. And I want to please you. I don't need you to—"

She rose from her knees with swift grace and grabbed his chin. "What will please me is tasting my sub and not having him complain about it. Get on the bed."

When he didn't back up immediately, she gave him a shove and the bed hit the backs of his knees. He sank down onto the mattress.

She pointed to the headboard. "Lie down."

His heart was beating wildly now, but he listened anyway. Maggie strode over to her bedside table and pulled out a few things. Before he could form an additional protest, she'd locked his hands to the headboard with cuffs and had wrapped a blindfold around his eyes. His throat felt like it was closing, but his erection had gone solid as steel.

She gave his thigh a vicious pinch. "Knees up and legs spread, sub. Make room for me."

"Mistress . . ."

"Shut up, Theodore. Unless it's your safe word, you don't get to speak. Remember, you're the one who is making this harder on yourself."

His mouth clamped shut. He could call his safe word, but his libido was overruling all veto options right now. This may turn into a disaster but there was no turning back now.

The first touch of Maggie's lips on the head of his cock nearly made him leap off the bed. But she held him down with firm hands and took him deeper—the hot, wet glide of her tongue enveloping his flesh and every bit of sense he had left. *Holy mother of God.*

His hands curled in the cuffs and he let his head fall back onto the mattress. Maggie, Mistress M, was giving him head. He could barely process it. Maybe he'd fallen asleep in his car and was dreaming. Behind the blindfold, he let himself imagine how she must look. That sweet pink sweater and that wild hair, those full lips slippery and hot on his skin, that unyielding confidence in her eyes.

So much of him wanted to just let go in that moment, give himself over to the sensation of it all, to Maggie. But he'd trained himself for so long to hold back that he was worried he wouldn't be able to give up that control. His body wasn't going to cooperate.

He was almost at the point of telling Maggie that when he felt cool liquid against his anus. He flinched then froze. "Mistress."

She released him with a pop, and he instantly missed the heat of her mouth around him. "I need you to relax, Theo. Your body is mine tonight. You have to trust me to make it feel good."

"I—"

Her slick finger pressed against his hole and rubbed. The intense sensation of it sent him groaning. Medically, he was aware there were nerves back there, but goddamn, he hadn't expected that level of sensitivity. His head tilted back again.

"There you go, gorgeous," she said, her breath hot against the head of his cock. "I don't let boys inside me who won't let me inside them."

He sucked in a deep breath, trying to relax for her, taking a leap of faith, and was rewarded when she worked her finger past the tight ring of muscle and slipped inside right as her mouth closed over him again.

His back arched and he let out a string of curses. Every nerve in his body seemed to awaken at once, all heading straight to his cock. "God, Maggie."

She made a satisfied hum, which vibrated over his skin, and then took him deeper, enveloping him fully and gently pumping her finger inside him. Stars blinked in and out in the darkness behind his eyelids. He couldn't remember ever feeling so damn alive.

He sunk into the feel of it all, forgetting to think about all the stuff that usually plagued him, forgetting to worry, and forgetting that he wasn't supposed to enjoy himself.

And when she curved her finger, finding his prostate, every worry about not being able to let go was obliterated in one sweet press. Orgasm slammed into him with the force of a tidal wave, dragging him under and sending him flying all at the same time. He cried out, calling Maggie's name and pumping his hips, losing himself as his release went on and on.

Maggie didn't back off, swallowing him down and continuing the roller-coaster ride for as long as possible. When he couldn't take any more, his little sadist gave one more nearly painful suck and then pulled back, leaving him panting and blown to bits on the bed.

"Maggie, mistress . . ." He didn't know what he wanted to say but he wanted to say something. His ability for English was impaired at the moment, though.

"Shh," she said. He could feel her climb off the bed and then the rustle of fabric.

His belly flipped. Was she getting undressed? Fuck this fucking blindfold. "Mistress, please let me see you."

"Would you rather use of your hands or eyes? You've only earned one privilege back."

He groaned. Look and not touch? Or touch but not see? "You're evil, mistress."

"And you love it."

He chuckled, feeling looser and more relaxed than he had in years. "I do. And if I only get one, I choose hands. I can't make you feel good with my eyes."

"The way you look at me makes me feel quite nice, actually." Her fingers brushed along his wrist. "But good choice."

She unhooked his hands from the cuffs and told him not to move.

He lay still, his arms above his head. But then she circled his wrist and lifted his arm to her. She pressed his open palm against her soft flesh.

A shudder went through him at the feel of her full breast in his hand, and she let out a soft sigh. Her skin was silky soft and so warm. He wanted to bury his face against her, to touch and taste and feel her. He brushed a thumb over her nipple, which promptly rose to the occasion. He wet his lips. "What do you like, mistress? Soft? Rough?"

He realized now he had no idea what she liked in bed. She was a sadist, but did she like a dose of pain herself? Or maybe she liked the sweet-and-gentle approach.

She pressed her hand over his and squeezed, making him tighten his hold on her breast. "I want you to trust your instincts, Theo. I bet you know how to make a woman feel good. You have permission to explore."

The pronouncement sent a surge of desire and confidence in him. He'd never had sex with a domme, so hadn't known how far the roles would go. But having a green flag to make Maggie feel good was like winning the lottery. It'd been a long time, but once upon a time, he'd known just how to drive a woman wild in bed.

He let his hand trail down Maggie's arm and then tugged, pulling her into bed with him. She laughed when she landed with an *oof* and knocked the air out of him for a moment. He slid his hands up her thigh. "Are you laughing at me, mistress?"

"Of course I am. I enjoy seeing you wince like that." She straddled his waist, the damp heat of her sex pressing against his abdomen. He bit back the groan of need. She was soaked for him. Even having just come, his cock was already perking up for the party again. But he wouldn't rush this. He moved his hands over the tops of her thighs and up her waist. When he reached her breasts, he brought the tips to points again, and then guided her down.

At the first sweet taste of her against his tongue, she moaned and shivered in his grip. It was the best damn sound he'd ever heard. He sucked and caressed, mapping her curves and relishing the taste of her—warm and lush and all woman. "You're so beautiful."

She gripped his shoulders, trying to keep her balance as he worshipped her breasts. "Says the man with the blindfold."

He smiled against her skin. "I've memorized every part I've ever gotten the privilege to see, Maggie. That little freckle on your collarbone, the way your bottom lip juts out when you're planning something particularly tortuous, how your hair color changes in the light. I know what I'm talking about. You're an artist, but you're also art."

"Theo . . ."

He heard the ache in her voice and knew he'd probably let too much slip out, but the combination of his orgasm and this beautiful woman beneath his lips made him forget to be careful. He was drunk on her. He put his hand on her waist. "I need to taste more of you, mistress."

"God, yes."

In his previous life, he would've shifted her beneath him, spread her out, but Maggie pushed back and then scooted herself up his body. His belly went tight with need when the scent of her arousal curled around him. She was above him, knees on each side of his head, and her pussy presented like the best prize he could imagine.

He'd never pleasured a woman this way, but the position and the blindfold only edged his arousal higher, and when she grabbed his hair and adjusted him just how she wanted, he decided he was having some kind of pornographic dream. Maggie riding his mouth and using him for her own pleasure? Yes, let's order that. A double serving, please.

"Show me what you can do, sub. Do a good job and maybe I'll take that blindfold off."

"Yes, ma'am," he said, his voice rough with aching desire. He placed his hands on her waist and lowered her to him. When he got his first taste of her and heard her uninhibited moan of pleasure and his name on her lips, all became quiet in his world. The earth stopped spinning. The past and future ceased to exist. It was just him and Maggie and this moment. For the first time in as long as he could remember, the demons loosened their hold with no pain involved.

This woman was all that mattered right now. And he was going to make her fly.

SIX

Maggie had lost all sense of composure by the time Theo slipped his hand between them and pushed two fingers into her while he licked her. She had one hand braced on the headboard and the other gripped in his hair as she tried not to go over too quickly. The stoic doctor was a fucking master with his mouth. Often she had trouble getting off without the help of a vibrator, but goddamn, this man seemed to know exactly what spots to hit and how to bring her to the edge and then back.

And seeing him so into it only ratcheted up her arousal higher. She'd been worried that she'd push too hard and scare him off tonight. His wounds ran deep, and she didn't want to compete with his wife's memory. But she'd also seen glimmers of that part of him that wanted to break free of it all. Even when she'd gone down on him, she could sense how locked up he was—like even allowing himself the briefest of pleasure was too much.

She could've changed tactics then. She'd known if she had flipped the night to focus on pain, he would've gotten lost in that, it would've made it easier on both of them. But then they would've been back to where they'd started. She didn't want to ignore his need for pain. She'd loved those sessions with him. But she also wasn't going to let him use it as a crutch anymore. So she'd done the most sadistic thing of all; she'd forced him to focus on pleasure.

And when she'd felt him go over into release, she'd almost cried out with him. Feeling his body clenching around her fingers, his taste spilling on her tongue, hearing the gritty sounds he was making—all of it had given her the sweetest high. Her body had throbbed for him. The man was sex personified when he let go. But she'd also gotten this warm contentment bleeding through her, this sense of being right where she needed to be.

She wasn't stupid. She knew this was probably a temporary reprieve while he was still riding the high of his own orgasm, that when cold reality crept in again, he'd probably run. But right now, she was going to enjoy every moment. And maybe, just maybe, this one night could put a chink in that brick wall he kept around him. One tiny shaft of light sneaking through could be a start.

She wished she could be the one to break down the wall completely. She wanted the man with a ferocity that scared her. She didn't understand it. In a lot of ways, she hardly knew him, but something inside her had latched onto him from day one—this feeling of fate, of destiny. Her flighty, artistic heart had fallen for the guy. Luckily, her brain was much more rational and kept her in check.

She wasn't going to fool herself into thinking this was any more that a hot night for him. A breakthrough in some ways, sure, but still just sex.

Theo twisted his fingers inside her, putting pressure in just the right spot, and sucked her clit between his teeth. The move sent pleasure rippling outward, and all thoughts in her head shimmered into the sweet nothing of sensation. She rocked her hips against him. "Theo, Theo, *God*."

He seemed lost in his own version of pleasure, and murmured a response against her. Suddenly she couldn't bear to not see his eyes for another second. She reached down and tugged the blindfold off. Theo blinked in the lamplight, his head falling back to the pillow, then his gaze focused on her. She knew she had to be a sight from that angle, but his eyes didn't move away from her face. Lines appeared around the edges of his eyes, like looking at her hurt him in a good way, and then he pushed his fingers deeper into her, pumping them slowly, and pressed the flat of his thumb against her clit. His lips were swollen and slick from her arousal, which was sexy enough, but the look in his eyes, that I'm-going-to-make-you-come confidence did her in.

She reached down, lacing her hands in his thick hair and cried out as orgasm took over. Theo put his mouth against her again and everything went white in her vision. She held on tight and ground against him, taking every bit of pleasure he was offering and not caring how wanton or desperate she looked.

When she couldn't bear any more, she rolled off of him and collapsed onto her back. Her chest was heaving, trying to grab air, as aftershocks reverberated through her. Theo rolled onto his side and looked down at her, a satisfied smile playing around the edges of his lips. He traced a finger around her navel. "I guess that was okay."

She laughed and reached for him, brushing her fingers over his stubble. "There's my smug doctor."

He pushed her hair away from her forehead, his gaze tracing the details of her face. "I've thought about what you would be like when you came so many times. My imagination wasn't even close to how sexy that was. You're so vocal. And loud."

Heat crawled up her neck. "Oops. Guess it's good I live in the woods."

"It was ridiculously hot." He wrapped a lock of hair around his finger, his attention traveling down her body, making every inch of her skin hyperaware. "I want to hear you do it again, mistress."

She knew what he was requesting. And the fact that Theo was asking to fuck her was a victory in and of itself. She'd planned for that to happen tonight when they'd started. But now she could sense her own attachment to him growing. Letting him inside her body would only make that worse. She'd only slept with three guys in her life. She played with strangers, but she'd only slept with guys she cared about. When he left afterward, this would hurt.

She swallowed hard. "Am I going to see you again after tonight, Theo?"

A muscle ticked in his jaw. "Would you want to?"

"I would."

He leaned down to press a soft kiss to her lips. "Then you will."

She didn't know if she believed it. But she believed that he believed it in this moment and that had to be enough. She reached out to her bedside drawer and pulled out a condom. "Kneel next to me."

He got into position and she rolled the condom on. And though she was almost always on top with a guy, she wanted him to guide the pace this time, wanted to see this beautiful man above her. She grabbed his hand and dragged him on top of her. Heat flared in his eyes when their bodies aligned, her outer lips sliding along his length.

He didn't rush it, though. Before entering her, he kissed her eyebrows, her nose, and finally her lips. "Thank you, Maggie."

She forced a casual smile, despite her heart flipping over in her chest. "For what, gorgeous?"

He pressed his forehead to hers. "For being exactly what I never knew I needed."

Her lips parted, his words knocking the air from her. But he closed the space for words by kissing her again, cutting off any response as he entered her.

Her entire body surged with need as he stretched her. He inched in slowly, making sure not to hurt her until he seated himself fully. She couldn't tell if the shudder that moved over her originated with her or him. All she knew was that feeling them joined was possibly the most perfect moment she'd ever experienced—this sacred, still space where the physical met all the things that had built quietly between them over the last year. He seemed to recognize it as something special, too, because he paused for a long moment, just looking down at her with this heartbreakingly sincere look on his face.

And she knew in that moment that he wasn't thinking of his wife or his past or the tragedy at the hospital tonight. That look was singular and just for her. She thought she may dissolve under the weight of that look, but then he closed his eyes and began to move. He made love to her in long, unhurried strokes, a man who was going to savor. And just when she thought it couldn't get any better, he grabbed her behind her knee to open her up and get as deep as possible. She got lost in the feel of it. His strong body against hers, his skilled hands, and his tongue stroking over hers when he bent down to kiss her. She wanted to fall into it and never come up for air. She wanted to cry. She wanted to keep him.

And when he brought her to orgasm a long time later, he whispered her name against her ear, his tone full of ache and heat, and came along with her. Joined for one perfect night. The doctor no one could touch and the mistress who never let anyone in.

And in those few moments, Maggie allowed herself to hope that this wasn't the end but just the beginning. She fell asleep next to him, holding on to that impossible hope.

And when Theo climbed out of the bed later that night, she never heard a sound.

SEVEN

Theo looked out at the still-falling sleet, the pattering sound one he probably would always associate with this night, and let the tears track silently down his face. His chest hurt, his eyes burned, but the pain felt good. Cleansing.

Sometimes in medicine, you couldn't remove a tumor because doing so would damage something else vital for life. All these years, he'd felt that way about the accident. The guilt, the anguish, the grief had been his tumor, but he'd felt like if he let that go, if he cut it away, there would be nothing left that would survive. It was what held his pieces together.

But tonight Maggie had taken a scalpel to him, carefully carving away the mass and giving him a glimpse of life in the aftermath. A life where despite the sadness in his past, he could still laugh and feel pleasure without it always having to be paired with pain, and where he could make someone else smile. He'd always love Lori and would always miss her. But maybe that didn't have to mean a life sentence of being alone.

Maggie had showed him that he was capable of more. She was a masterful domme—one who had sensed what he needed and somehow had known just how to get around his walls—but she was also just an amazing woman with a big heart. She'd seen his need and had helped him. He didn't know what he could be to her or what she wanted from him. Maybe just to be play partners without so many boundaries. Maybe to be friends. He wasn't going to assume more than that. But for the first time, he was willing to open his mind to having someone else in his life.

He swiped his face with the sleeve of his shirt as the rising sun started to lighten the rain clouds, and he strolled around her studio, taking in her artwork. He could spend all day in there, noticing all the little details she included in her paintings. She was a gifted painter who captured emotion on the canvas with a masterful hand. He'd already decided he needed at least three of them for his own place.

He went over to a stack that was leaning against the wall and flipped through another few animal portraits, looking for the rest in that series of nudes she'd talked about last night. But when he got to the last one, he stilled. It was a nude but definitely not female. And, holy shit . . .

He pulled out the canvas, setting it down in front of the others, his heart picking up speed as he looked at it again. It was of a man in submission on his knees, his back to the observer. His head was bowed, his face hidden, but his muscles were tensed and strong, his hands fisted at his sides. Chains were locked around his forearms and wrapped all the way to the biceps, but the metal was straining. It was a painting of powerful submission—a man about to break free of his bonds. But that's not what caught his attention. No, what drew his eye and had his breath catching in his throat was the long jagged scar on the man's back—right from the left shoulder to the ribs.

Theo sank to his knees and touched the corner of the painting where Maggie had signed it with her flourishing signature. Above the signature was a simple title for the work: *Mine*.

Theo braced his hands on his thighs, this sense of peace coming over him. Maggie had said she wanted to paint him, but she already had. And she'd captured his image in a way that said she had spent a long time memorizing every angle of his body, every intricate nuance of his posture, but also in a way that said she knew *him*. His heart. His struggles. And despite all that, she wanted him anyway. *Mine*. The word echoed through his mind, settled in the center of his chest.

Hers.

That thought didn't scare him like he thought it would.

"You are in so much trouble for digging through my paintings," said a firm voice from the doorway.

He looked over to find Maggie standing at the entrance to the room—silky robe wrapped around her body, hair piled on top of her head in a messy knot, and a threatening look in her eye. He'd never seen anything more beautiful.

"You painted me."

She rubbed her lips together, her eyes going to the painting, then she shrugged. "So, news flash: I may have had a wee crush on you once upon a time."

He rocked to his feet and tucked his hands in his pockets. "Yeah? You're all done with that now?"

She wrapped her arms around herself, looking bored. "Totally."

"So that's how it is, huh? Use me for my impressive skills in bed and then move on?" His lips lifted at the corners.

"Well, they *were* quite impressive. I may need you to do another audition if I'm going to reinstate this aforementioned crush, though."

He walked over to her and grabbed the belt of her robe, pulling her close. "I may consider this audition. May take me a few times to get it right, though."

She blew out a breath and put her hands to his chest. "I woke up and I thought you'd left."

He frowned. "I thought about it. I woke up and freaked out for a few minutes. But then I saw you lying there, and you were snoring so loud I figured you might have sleep apnea and needed a doctor to stay nearby."

She gasped and then shoved his chest. "I *do not* snore."

He chuckled. "And how would you know that?"

Her nose scrunched up into this adorable scowl and she shoved him again. "Because I know."

He dragged her close again and kissed her wrinkled nose. "You're right. You don't. What I really thought when I saw you lying there was that the world wasn't fair. That a bastard like me should've never been given a shot with one amazing woman much less a chance with a second one."

Sympathy crossed her face. "Theo . . ."

He brushed a hand over her hair. "Shh. No sadness, okay? It's a new day and a new year. I want to start this off right."

A saucy smile touched her lips. "I can think of a few ways."

"So can I. And I know just where to start."

"Oh yeah, how's that?"

He took a step back then lowered himself down to one knee, grabbed her hand, and met her eyes. "Mistress Margaret, would you do me the great honor of having pie with me? And by pie, I mean pie."

Her eyebrows arched.

He kissed the top of her hand and then squeezed it between his. "I can't promise that I'm not going to be difficult sometimes. I can't promise that my past won't still bite me on the butt on occasion. I work a lot and I'm a know-it-all. Feel free to kick my ass about those things."

She laughed at that.

"But what I can promise you is that when I'm with you, I'm one hundred percent with you. You are not competing with a memory. And I will never be so stupid as to turn down a date with you again. I want to know you, Maggie. And I . . . want you to know me."

Her gaze went soft, shiny.

He stood and took her face in his hands. "So Mistress Maggie, artist extraordinaire, will you have pie with me?"

She put her forehead against his and wrapped her arms around him. "Nothing would make me happier, Dr. Theodore Montgomery."

"Don't call me doctor."

She gave his hip a hard pinch. "I'll call you whatever I want, mister."

He laughed. "Yes, mistress."

"And if you're good, after pie, maybe I can find that *Weird Science* outfit for you."

He groaned. "Are you trying to get me to propose? Because now I'm thinking about it."

She grinned. "One thing at a time, Doc."

Yeah. One thing at a time. One sweet, beautiful thing at a time.

He kissed her then as the rain pounded the windows and all the farm animal paintings looked on, and knew without a doubt that the sun would come out for him today and was going to stick around.

It'd been a very long time since he'd seen it.

Continue reading for a sneak peek at

Break Me Down

A Loving on the Edge novella
Coming October 2015 from InterMix

"Are you *trying* to torture me? I thought your husband was the sadist." Sam dropped the tray of clean glasses onto the rack behind the bar and gave her best friend the stink eye.

Tessa frowned. "Kade didn't tell me Gibson was coming along. I would've suggested another bar if I'd known, but I wanted to see you before we left for Bermuda in the morning."

Sam sighed and snuck a glance over at the table where Tessa's husband, Kade, was chatting with his brother. Gibson didn't look her way, but she got the distinct impression he knew she was watching him and was purposely not looking her way. Good, she didn't need to see those gorgeous blue eyes, didn't need to remember how he'd looked at her when she put him on his knees. "Does he have to look so goddamned good in a suit? It's ridiculous. Who gets to look that good after a whole day of work? By the time I'm out of here, I look like I've been rolled around in a pile of sweaty bodies and beer. He looks like he's ready to pose for an Armani ad."

Tessa smirked. "You know, pining isn't good for your health."

Sam rolled her eyes. "Please. I'm not pining. I just went on a date two weeks ago, and last weekend I scened with Julian at The Ranch. This girl"—she swept her hand over her black T-shirt and jeans—"is moving on."

Tessa lifted a brow, clearly not buying it. "If the date was two weeks ago, that means it wasn't worth a second date. And you and Julian are friends. I bet you didn't even bed him."

Okay, so she hadn't. Julian was a fun submissive to scene with and more than a little hot, but Sam had never taken it very far with him. In fact, none of the submissives she played with at The Ranch ever inspired her to take it to that level. She rarely let them touch her. She enjoyed the dynamic, the power, but she always took care of her own needs afterward. The only one she'd ever allowed to truly touch her was sitting at the table a few yards away. And the minute she'd crossed that boundary with him, things had gotten complicated, and he'd bailed like she had some plague.

Shit, maybe she was pining.

"All right, the date was a bust. But I really am moving on. If Gibson wants to pretend that what happened between us was a fluke, that's his business. I deserve a guy who's not ashamed or afraid to be with me. I don't have time for games."

Tessa leaned against the bar. "If it makes you feel better, I think he's pretty miserable over it, too. You should've seen his face when he found out we were coming here."

"Good." She gave a terse nod. "In fact, since he's here anyway, I may as well enjoy his suffering. What are y'all ordering?"

"A Blue Moon, a Crown and water, and a dirty martini."

Sam grabbed a glass and started pouring the drinks. "Give me a minute and I'll bring them over. How's my hair?"

Tessa laughed. "Uh-oh, it looks great, but what are you up to?"

Sam adjusted her shirt, letting the V-neck show off a little more cleavage than she usually revealed at work. "Torture."

"Sadist."

"Yep."

Tessa smiled and headed back to the table, and Sam finished up with the drinks. She carried them over on a tray, making sure to put a touch more sway in her walk. She'd learned how to do it early on to get tips before she'd become the manager of the place, but she hadn't lost the skill. And she wasn't afraid to use it to torment the man who'd walked away from her.

When she stopped at the table, Kade looked up and grinned, all blond hair and broad smiles. "Hey, Sam, long time no see."

She smirked. She'd just seen the couple a few days ago when they'd all gone to a music festival together. She and Tessa rarely went long between visits, but Kade didn't seem to mind. "Hey, stalker boy, I presume the dirty martini is yours."

He took the drink from her, not blinking at the nickname she'd given him last year when he'd been doggedly pursuing her best friend like a knight on a quest. She set the beer in front of Tessa and then finally turned to Gibson. She kept her smile poised, but it took everything she had to keep her composure when Gib looked up. He'd let his jaw go a little scruffy and the dark shadow of a beard only made him look more edible. But the look in his eyes sucked the air right out of her. Hunger flared in that deep blue gaze, open and naked, but he shuttered it quickly. "Hey, Sam."

She swallowed past the tightness in her throat, completely forgetting her plan to look seductive and so over him. "Crown and water."

She plunked the glass on the table without grace, causing some of the drink to slosh over the top.

"Thanks," he said gruffly.

Silence ensued and Tessa cleared her throat. "Do y'all still have those potato skin things? I'm starving."

Sam snapped out of her daze and turned to Tessa. "You bet. I'll tell Angie to put in an order. She'll be handling your table. I just wanted to come over and say hi."

Gibson took a long gulp from his glass and then brushed a hand over his dark wavy hair, trying to smooth the unsmoothable. A move she'd learned was his sign of discomfort. God, this was so ridiculous.

And she was done with it. So things had gotten a little out of hand during that last training session. He'd been helping her out, bottoming for her so she could learn how to use a whip. They'd been through a few weeks of lessons and everything had gone well. All had been done under the assumption that he was a fellow dominant who would be guiding her from the bottom—a friendly exchange. He wasn't supposed to get hard when she whipped him. And she wasn't supposed to get so turned on at the sight. And they weren't supposed to kiss. And she definitely wasn't supposed to let him push her against a wall and put his hand beneath her skirt to get her off.

But all that had happened, and when she'd tried to take control back and take him to bed as her submissive, everything had exploded in her face. He'd snapped out of whatever spell he'd been in from the flogging and had told her that nothing could happen between them because they were both dominants. The training had ended right there—even when both of them knew that he'd gotten hard as a rock in the submissive role, that the more pain she'd given him, the more turned on he'd gotten. For whatever reason, he wasn't going to take that role. Period. End of sentence.

She wasn't worth the risk to him.

Fine.

"Is there anything else I can get y'all for now?" she asked, her voice coming out a little too bright.

"No, I think we're good," Kade said, cutting an annoyed look his brother's way.

Sam headed back to the safety of the bar. The crowd was picking up, and she didn't have time to waste trying to figure out an indecipherable man. She had a job to do. So for the next hour, she managed her bartenders, poured drinks to help them keep up, and made rounds of the floor to greet customers. By the time she made her second walk around the place, every table was taken and the noise of all those different conversations reverberated off the walls.

This was her favorite part of her shift. Managing the bar wasn't always the most glamorous of jobs, but when the crowd was buzzing and the energy pulsing around her, she couldn't help but feed off it. She cruised by the back corner, and a sharp whistle caught her attention.

She fought the instinct to ignore it. Nothing ticked her off more than being summoned like she was a dog that needed to come to heel, but a customer was a customer. She turned around and forced a tolerant smile at the two guys swigging cheap whiskey at a back table. "Can I help y'all with something?"

"Hey, sweetheart," one said, tipping his ball cap up and revealing narrow green eyes. "I dropped my keys. Mind getting them for me?"

She looked down at the floor and the keys at her feet. She bent over, swiped them from the ground, and tossed them on their table. "Here ya go."

His friend grinned her way and pushed the keys onto the floor again. "Maybe bend down a little slower this time, baby. I didn't get a good view the first go-round."

She straightened, irritation surging. "I'm not here to give you a show. Do you need a drink or what?"

Idiot Number One smirked and leered at her chest. "Yeah, how about two buttery nipples? Are they pierced like your eyebrow? I bet they are. You look like that kind of girl."

She wanted to reach over and bang their two skulls together. It'd probably make a hollow sound. Usually guys got over the buttery nipple joke by the time they were out of high school, but clearly these two hadn't moved beyond that maturity-wise. Next they'd be ordering a Sex on the Beach. "Two drinks coming right up."

She strode off and told one of her male bartenders to bring the drinks over to the guys. She'd be damned if she let any of her staff get harassed. Flirting from customers was part of the deal. People got tipsy, and their tongues got loose. But Sam didn't put up with idiots who took it too far.

Sam slipped back behind the bar and started clearing empty glasses. But only a few minutes passed before Idiot Number One made a reappearance. He leaned against the bar, snapping his fingers at her. "Hey. I need to talk to you."

She clenched her jaw and turned. "Is there something wrong with your drink?"

He slid the drink across the bar. "Yeah, you didn't serve it to me. What? You're too good to talk to your customers?"

"I'm managing the place. My staff serves the drinks."

"You're a stuck-up bitch is what you are."

"Hey," a booming voice came from behind him. "You watch your goddamned mouth."

Sam's attention snapped to the spot behind the guy. Gibson's face appeared out of the crowd as he shoved his way closer to the bar.

The guy turned toward Gibson, his features twisting into a scowl. "And who the hell do you think you're talking to?"

Gibson was the picture of cool rage, completely unruffled and terrifying in his calmness. "You. Disrespect the lady again, and we're going to have a major problem."

"Fuck you, man," the guy said, words slurring. "This cunt's job is to serve me my goddamn drinks and she's not doing it."

With lightning-fast movement, Gibson grabbed the guy by the shirt collar and jammed him against the bar. "Wrong answer, asshole."

"Shit." Sam hurried around the counter and yelled for Angie to get their bouncer, Herb. "Gib, stop. Let us handle this guy."

But it was too late, the drunk idiot was already taking a swing at Gibson, and his equally idiotic friend was heading their way. The punch missed wide when Gibson ducked out of the way. A glass broke. Gib looked smug at the guy's failed attempt and knocked him hard against the bar again. But before it could turn into a full brawl, Herb got in between to break it up. He dragged the guy away and told him and his friend to get out.

The two men continued cursing and throwing insults her and Gib's way, but they weren't dumb enough to try to fight Herb. If they did, she'd have the cops on the phone before they could blink, and they'd be sleeping it off in the drunk tank down at county lockup.

The customers in the bar had stopped to watch the ruckus, but as soon as the two jerks were out the door, all the conversation kicked back in like hitting Play after pausing a movie. Sam released a breath and turned to Gib, who was straightening the cuffs of his shirt.

She shook her head. "I could've handled that, you know."

He looked up, frown lines between his brows. "No one gets to talk to you like that. I saw them giving you a hard time earlier and could tell he was headed up here to cause trouble. What did they say to you earlier? You looked pissed."

She shrugged. "They kept trying to get me to bend over and pick up things off the floor. Then they ordered buttery nipples while ogling me. Juvenile stuff. Idiotic but probably harmless."

His jaw flexed. "Customers or not, they don't get to disrespect you like that."

She smirked and stepped around him to get back behind the bar. "Getting respect around here is hard to come by. I have to go other places to get that."

"Too bad you can't bring a single tail to work."

She laughed. "No kidding. That'd get people's attention. Talk back to me, and I'll paint a stripe across your ass."

His gaze flared at that. "That could make it worse. Some people might misbehave for that privilege."

She cocked a brow. "People like you?"

He frowned.

She sighed and grabbed a rag to start wiping up the drink they'd spilled during the altercation. "Sorry. Guess we haven't reached the point where we can joke about everything with each other yet."

He rubbed the back of his neck. "Sorry. It's fine. I just hate that things are weird between us now. I miss hanging out with you. And my brother's married to your best friend. We're going to run into each other."

She focused on cleaning the bar top, using a little too much vigor to wipe up things. *Out, damn spot.* "Doesn't have to be weird. We can be friends."

"Hard to be friends with someone you want in your bed."

She looked up, and something tightened low in her gut when she saw the invitation in his eyes.

God, it would be so easy to just give in and let him have the control. Sex with him in whatever form would probably be amazing.

But she knew what she wanted, had finally figured out what flipped her switches, and she was tired of doing things halfway. "You know the price of admission for my bed, Gib. You're not willing to pay it."

Gibson leaned forward, bracing his arms on the bar and getting way too close for her to concentrate on anything but his dark eyelashes and full bottom lip. He kept his voice low enough for only her to hear. "We don't have to be in any roles at all. We could just do things the old-fashioned way."

She closed her eyes, a hint of his cologne hitting her and bringing her back to those sessions in the training room at The Ranch. Never before had she felt such an utter need to make a man hers like she had when she and Gibson would get into a scene. Something about him stirred those dark desires she'd only toyed with in fantasies before then. But the sessions had been her own kind of torture because they'd kept it so business-like. He'd never taken off anything more than his shirt. There'd been no sex. He'd guided her from the bottom as her trainer and never gave over real control. Not until that last session when she'd somehow broken through that outside layer had she gotten a glimpse of what things could be like if they ever did those things for real, without restrictions.

And she knew without a doubt that if she agreed to an old-fashioned hookup with Gibson, physically she'd probably be over the moon, but deep down she'd be left unsatisfied afterward because she'd gotten a glimpse of what she'd be missing. She was done compromising. In her endless search to find Mr. Right, she'd spent too many years of her life dating guys who she'd jumped through hoops to please. No more. Even if Gibson was stupid beautiful and looking at her like he'd light her world on fire.

She poured a Crown and water and slid it his way. "Gib, let's not pretend that either of us would be satisfied with old-fashioned. You don't pay that exorbitant fee at The Ranch for nothing."

His frown deepened and he straightened, taking the drink in his hand. "I can't be what you want me to be, Sam."

"Why?" The word slipped out before she could stop it. But she'd seen how he'd reacted after that flogging. He'd been on the verge of subspace. Submission did something for him. She hadn't imagined that.

His gaze slid away. "Because it's not who I want to be."

She pressed her lips together, considering him for a long moment. She knew some submissive guys struggled with their desires. Many thought big, strong alpha men weren't supposed to be anything but dominant. But Gibson was so confident in his everyday life, she couldn't imagine he gave a shit what societal norms or traditional gender roles called for. But for some reason, this was a no-go for him.

She needed to accept that. She reached out and put her hand on his arm and squeezed. "Hey, that doesn't mean we can't be friends. Friends who are not weird with each other."

His lips tilted up at the corner, but his eyes didn't hold the same humor. "Yeah, guess we'll have to get some practice at that."

She nodded. "Definitely. We'll go have lunch or something soon, okay?"

"Sure." He grabbed for his wallet. "What do I owe you for the drink?"

"It's on the house for trying to protect me from drunk assholes. Thanks for that, by the way. I would've handled it, but seeing his teeth rattle when you shoved him against the bar was pretty entertaining."

He smirked. "Anytime."

After one last look, he headed back to his table, and she didn't talk to him again until he and her friends said good-bye for the night. When he walked out of the bar, all the starch drained out of her. She tried to stay busy, keep her energy up, but as the crowd thinned and the night stretched on, the finality of her and Gibson's situation weighed on her. When the last customer headed out the door, she sagged back against the counter and closed her eyes, rubbing her brow.

"Everything okay?" Angie asked.

Sam opened her eyes to find her current manager-in-training cleaning a glass and giving her a concerned look. Sam shook her head. "I'm fine. Long night."

Angie nodded toward the back. "You should get out of here, then. Billy and I can lock up. I've got the hang of the closing procedures by now."

Sam stretched her neck and glanced at the empty bar. Usually she stayed and helped put things back in order, but she'd worked every night this week and the thought of staying any longer suddenly felt like too much. "You sure?"

"Of course. Your vacation can start now. Go. Get some rest."

Sam smiled. "Why haven't I made you assistant manager yet?"

Angie grinned. "Because you're too much of a control freak. But I'll be more than happy to accept that promotion when you get back."

Sam pushed off the bar and patted Angie's shoulder as she passed. "Consider it done. And if anything happens this week, you can call me—"

"I'll call Marvin," she said, cutting her off. "You're on vacation, not on call. Forget about us for a while."

"You're a bossy thing."

" 'Hello, Kettle, you're black,' says Pot."

Sam rolled her eyes. "Fine. Point taken. I'm out of here. Don't forget to lock up the safe and check—"

"The side door. I know. Go." She shooed her with her hand.

Sam didn't protest this time, and went into the back room to grab her purse and keys. The spring night was cool and dry as she exited the side door and headed through the alleyway toward the parking lot. Her worn Vans were silent on the pavement and after the constant roar of the bar, she welcomed the quiet night around her. But despite the peacefulness, she held her little bottle of mace in her right hand.

This area of downtown was pretty safe, but she knew not to take that kind of thing for granted. You were never really safe. She'd learned that the hard way bouncing around foster homes and group homes, running into people who thought her petite size and vulnerable circumstances made her an easy target. Danger pounced when you let your guard down.

It's why her first semester in college, she'd taken a Krav Maga course and learned how to protect herself. It's why she knew how to shoot a gun. And it's why when she turned the corner around the building and saw a familiar face heading her way, she didn't hesitate to raise her hand and aim.

Idiot Number One from the bar fight was glaring back at her, but he lifted his hands. "Easy now, sugar. I'm not here to cause trouble."

"Bullshit," she said, finger on the trigger of her mace, her heart trying to pound out of her chest. "You need to back off and go home."

He smiled. "I was just coming back because I realized I left my wallet at the table. I need to get back inside."

"You can come back tomorrow. I'll let the staff know to put it aside for you."

"I can't wait that long." He took a step closer.

She stepped back.

And ran into something solid . . . and warm.

Her body jolted at the impact, but it was too late to react beyond that. A hand came around and clamped over her mouth. Another arm banded around her chest, knocking the mace out of her grip and dragging her back into the alleyway

"Well, hi, there," a voice said against her ear, stale whiskey breath burning her nostrils.

Panic kicked through Sam, and she wrenched her body, trying to break the grip and screaming behind the hand. She'd been through self-defense. She knew there was a way to break this hold, but none of the moves would come to her. All she could think of was to stomp on his feet. But when she tried, her tennis shoes did little damage.

The first guy followed them between the buildings and came closer, his smile satisfied. "You know, we never did get those buttery nipples. But how about I taste them without the butter for now."

He reached out and grabbed the collar of her T-shirt and yanked it down, ripping it and exposing her bra.

Tears jumped to her eyes, and she kicked and writhed like a wild thing. This was not going to happen. These disgusting men were not going to touch her. Her foot connected with the guy's crotch and he doubled over, crying out in pain. She felt the small surge of victory, but then he hauled up and slapped her hard in the face, making her see stars and sending her ears ringing.

"You stupid, fucking bitch," he seethed, still hunched over, one hand cradling himself. "You think you're so high and mighty, but you're not going to be anything when we take you to the van and fuck that attitude right out of you."

The man who was holding her tightened his grip, and her throat began to close up with abject fear. Not again. She would not go through this again. She shook her head with a violent, sudden motion, breaking free of the hand over her mouth and let out a piercing scream.

Idiot's eyes went wide, and she hoped to God they would run, but he just looked out toward the street. "Come on, get her to the van. Hurry."

But before they could drag her a few steps, the door to the bar opened and Angie ran out. When she saw what was happening, Angie lifted her arms and pointed a gun their way. "Let her go or I swear to God I will blow your fucking balls off."

The guy holding Sam tensed behind her and then let her go like a sack of grain. Her knees hit the ground hard and the two men ran off, shouting at each other to hurry.

Angie ran down the back stairs and toward the parking lot, and Billy came running behind her, cell phone to his ear. Billy stopped at Sam's side. "Jesus, are you okay? I called the cops."

Sam braced her hands on the pavement, panting and trying not to hyperventilate, and held her torn shirt to her chest with her other hand. "I'm all right. Check on Angie."

But Angie stepped back into the alley a second later, face red with exertion. "I couldn't get a license plate, but I saw what kind of van they were driving." She hurried to join Sam. "God, honey, you're bleeding. Billy, get some ice and a new T-shirt."

Billy jogged back into the building, and Sam sat back on her calves, tentatively touching her lip where it'd been split. "I'm fine. They didn't get a chance to do more than hit me, thanks to you."

And no thanks to Sam's own instincts. Every goddamned lick of training she'd gotten had gone down the tube in an instant. She'd always felt so strong and confident after arming herself with all those self-defense tools. And then when she'd needed them most, she'd been useless. She was just as vulnerable as she'd always been. A victim waiting to happen. The thought shook her down to the core.

You're never safe.

Angie put her arm around Sam. "Come on. Let's get you inside. You're trembling."

Sam let Angie lead her back into the bar, and Billy brought her ice and a new staff T-shirt. They were babying her, but Sam didn't have it in her to protest at this point. She just wanted to give her statement to the police and get the hell out of here so she could put herself back together.

The cops arrived a short time after that and took all of their statements. Sam doubted they would be able to find the guys by description alone, but she hoped the van may give them a good lead. Either way, she didn't think the men would come back to the bar. The staff would recognize them. Everyone had seen at least one of them during the altercation with Gib. But she'd ask Marvin, the bar owner, to pay for extra security for the next couple of weeks anyway.

By the time she got in her car to go home, she felt numb. But as she drove toward her place, that numbness gave way to anger. Anger at the men who'd attacked her. And anger at herself for panicking so completely. She was not that person. She was the girl in her Krav Maga class who had taken down an instructor twice her size. She was the domme at The Ranch who had men willing to kneel at her feet. She was not going to be the girl to go home to her empty apartment and cower behind the locked doors and jump at every sound. That wasn't who she was anymore.

So when she got to her place, she grabbed the suitcase she'd packed for her vacation and added another black bag that was meant for only one place.

Tonight she didn't need to be alone. Tonight she needed to be in charge.

She tossed the bags in her trunk and got on the road. The Ranch was only an hour away. She couldn't get there fast enough.

Continue reading for a sneak peek
at the first Pleasure Principle novel

OFF THE CLOCK

Coming January 2016 from Berkley Books!

Then

"I'm going to wrap my fingers in your hair and slide my other hand up your thigh. You have to be quiet for me. We can't let anyone know."

Marin Rush paused in the dark hallway of Harker Hall, her tennis shoes going silent on the shiny linoleum and the green Exit signs humming softly in the background. She didn't dare move. She'd been on the way to grab a soda and a snack out of the vending machine. Her caffeine supply was running low, and watching participants sleep in the sleep lab wasn't exactly stimulating stuff. But that silk smooth male voice had hit her like a punch to the stomach, waking up every sense that had gone dull with exhaustion.

She'd assumed she was the only one left in the psychology building at this hour besides the two study subjects in the sleep lab. It was spring break and the classrooms and labs were supposed to be locked up—all except the one she was working in. But there was no mistaking the male voice as it drifted into the hallway.

"I bet you'd like being fucked up against the wall."

Holy. Shit. Marin pressed her lips together. Obviously someone else thought they were alone, too. Had students snuck into the building to get it on? Or maybe it was one of the professors. Oh God, please don't let it be a professor. She should turn around right now and go back to Professor Roberts's office. Last thing she needed was to see one of her teachers in some compromising position. She might die of mortification.

But instead of backing up, she found herself tilting her head to isolate where the voice was coming from, and her feet moved forward a few steps.

"Yeah, you like that. I know. I bet you're wet for me right now just thinking about it. Maybe I should check. Keep your hands against the wall."

A hot shiver went right through Marin and she swallowed hard.

"I'm so hard for you. Can you feel how much I want you?" That voice was like velvet against Marin's skin. She closed her eyes, imagining the picture the stranger was painting—some hot guy behind her, pinning her to the wall, his erection hard against her. She'd never been in that situation, but her body sure knew how to react to the idea. Her hand went to her neck and pressed against her throat, her pulse beating hard there.

She waited with held breath to hear the woman's response, but no voice answered the man's question. *Can you feel how much I want you?* he'd asked. And hell if Marin wasn't dying to know. She strained to hear.

"I tug your panties off and trail my hand up your thighs until I can feel your hot . . ."

Marin had a hand braced against the wall and was leaning so far forward that one more inch would've sent her toppling over. Your hot . . .

"Goddammit. Motherfucker."

The curse snapped Marin out of the spell she'd fallen into, and she straightened instantly, her face hot and her heartbeat pounding in places it shouldn't be. There was a groaning squeak of an office chair and a slew of cursing.

Whoever had been saying the dirty things had changed his tone of voice and now sounded ten kinds of annoyed. A wadded-up ball of paper came flying out of an open doorway a few yards down. She followed the arc and watched the paper land on the floor. Only then did she notice there were three others like it already littering the hallway.

Lamplight shifted on the pale linoleum as if the person inside the office was moving around, and Marin flattened herself against the wall, trying to make herself one with it. *Please don't come out.* The silent prayer whispered through her as she counted the doors between her and the mystery voice, mentally labeling each one. When she realized it was one of the offices they let the PhD students use and not a professor's, she let out a breath.

Either way, she had no intention of alerting her hallmate that he wasn't alone. But at least she could stop worrying she'd gotten all hot and bothered over one of her professors. Now she just had to figure out how to get past the damn door without letting him see her. She'd gotten used to skipping meals since she'd started college a few months ago. Her scholarship only paid for her tuition. But she wasn't going to make it through the next two hours of data entry and sleep monitoring if she didn't get some caffeine. No wonder none of the upperclassmen had wanted this job.

Marin's gaze slid over to the stairwell. If she stayed on the other side of the hall in the shadows, she could probably sneak by unnoticed. She moved to the right side wall and walked forward on quiet feet. But as soon as she got within a few steps of the shaft of light coming from the occupied room, a large shadow blotted it into darkness.

She'd been so focused on that beam of light that it took her a moment to register what had happened. She froze and her gaze hopped upward. A guy had filled the doorway. A very familiar guy. Everything inside her went on alert. *Oh, God, not him.*

He had his hand braced on the doorjamb, and his expression was as surprised as hers probably was. "What the hell?"

"I—" She could already feel her face heating and her throat closing—some bizarre, instant response she seemed to have to this man. She'd spent way too many hours in the back of her Intro to Human Sexuality class memorizing each little detail of Donovan West. Well, his profile, really. As a teaching assistant, he usually only stopped in at the beginning of class to bring Professor Paxton papers or something. But each time he walked in, it was like some Bat-Signal for her body to go haywire. It'd started with the day he'd had to take over the lecture when Professor Paxton was sick. He'd talked about arousal and the physical mechanics of it. It was technical. It shouldn't have been sexy. But Lord, it'd been one of the hottest experiences of her life. He'd talked with his hands a lot and had obviously been nervous to be in front of the class, but at the same time, he'd been so confident in the information, had answered questions with all this enthusiasm. Marin hadn't heard a word in the rest of her classes that day for all the fantasizing she'd been doing.

But now she realized she was staring. And blushing. And generally looking like an idiot. Yay.

She turned fully toward him and cleared her throat, trying to form some kind of non-weird response. But when her gaze quickly traveled over him again, all semblance of language left her. *Oh, shit.* She tried to drag her focus back to his face and cement it there. His very handsome face—dark scruff, bright blue eyes, hair that fell a little too long around the ears. Lips that she'd thought way too much about. All good. All great.

But despite the nice view, she couldn't ignore the thing in the bottom edge of her vision, the thing that had caught her attention on that quick once-over. The hard outline in his jeans screamed at her to stare—to analyze, to burn the picture into her brain. The need to look warred with embarrassment. The latter finally won and her cheeks flared even hotter. She adjusted her glasses. "Uh, yeah, hi. Sorry. I thought I was alone in the building. Didn't mean to interrupt . . . whatever."

He stared at her for a second, his brows knitting. "Interrupt?"

Goddammit, her gaze flicked there again. The view was like a siren song she couldn't ignore. *Massive erection dead ahead.* She glanced away. But not quick enough for him not to notice.

"Ah, hell." He stepped behind the doorway and hid his bottom half. "Sorry. It's uh . . . not what it looks like."

She snorted, an involuntary, nervous, half-choking noise that seemed to echo in the cavernous hallway. Really smooth. She tried to force some kind of wit past the awkwardness that was trying to overtake her. "Ohh-kay. If you say so."

He laughed, this deep chuckle that seemed to come straight out of his chest. Lord, even his laugh was sexy. So not fair.

"Well, okay, it *is* that. But why it's there is just an occupational hazard."

His laugh and easy tone settled her some. Or maybe it was just the fact that he was obviously feeling awkward, too. "Occupational hazard? Must be more interesting than the sleep lab."

He jabbed a thumb toward the office. "It is. Sexuality department. I'm working on my dissertation under Professor Paxton."

She could tell he didn't recognize her from class. Not surprising since she sat in the back of the large stadium-style room and tried to be as invisible as possible. Plus, she was wearing her glasses tonight. "I'm with Professor Roberts. I'm monitoring the sleep study tonight."

"Oh, right on. I didn't realize he'd taken on another grad student. I'm Donovan, by the way."

I know.

"Mari." The nickname rolled off her lips. No one called her that anymore. But she knew he probably graded her papers, and the name Marin wasn't all that common. She forced a small smile, not correcting him that she was about as far from a grad student as she could get. She wanted to be one. Would be one day if she could figure out how to afford it. She'd managed to test out of a semester-and-a-half worth of classes, but high IQ or not, that dream was still a long way off—a point of light at the end of a very long, twisting tunnel.

Marin shifted on her feet. "I was just heading to get a Coke so that I don't fall asleep from doing data entry and watching people snore. You need anything?"

"A Coke?" He glanced down the hall. "Don't waste a buck fifty on the vending machine. I've got a mini-fridge in here. You can come in and grab whatever you want."

Are you an option? I'd like to grab you. The errant thought made her bite her lips together so none of those words would accidentally slip out. She had no idea where this side of herself was coming from.

Not that she'd really know what to do after she grabbed Donovan anyway. This was a twentysomething-year-old man, not one of the few boys she'd awkwardly made out with in high school.

"No, that's okay, I mean . . ." She shifted her gaze away, willing her face not to go red again.

He caught her meaning and laughed. "Oh, right. Sorry. Yes, you should probably avoid strange men with erections who invite you inside for a drink. Good safety plan, Mari." He lifted his hands and stepped back fully into the doorway, the pronounced outline in his pants gone. "But I promise, you're all good now. You just caught me at an . . . unfortunate moment. And now I'm going to bribe you with free soda so that you don't tell the other grads in the department about what you saw. I keep these late hours and work through holidays to avoid that kind of torture."

He gave her a half-smile that made something flutter in her chest. She should probably head straight back to the office she was supposed to be working in. He was older. Kind of her teacher. If he found out she was one of Pax's students, he'd probably freak out that she'd seen him like this. But the chance to spend a few minutes with him was too tempting to pass up. Plus, the way he was looking at her settled something inside her. Usually she shut down around guys. Being jerked around from school to school on her mom's whims hadn't left her with much time to develop savvy when it came to these things. But something about Donovan made her want to step forward instead of run away. "Yeah, okay. Free is good."

"Cool." His face seemed to brighten. Maybe he'd been as lonely and bored tonight as she had been. He bent over and picked up the papers he'd thrown into the hallway then swept a hand in front of him. "Welcome to my personal hell. The fridge is in the back corner."

Marin stepped in first. His desk was stacked with photocopied articles and books. A Red Bull sat atop one of the piles, and a microphone was set up in the middle with a line going to the laptop. Controlled chaos. Along the back wall was a worn couch with a pillow and a blanket. She made her way to the fridge and grabbed a Dr. Pepper.

"Did you want me to get you something?" She peered back over her shoulder.

Donovan was busy gathering a pile of papers off the one other chair in the small office. "No, I'm good. Just opened my third. I think my blood has officially been converted to rocket fuel."

She smiled and stepped back toward the door. "I hear ya. Well, thanks for the drink. I'll let you get back to—uh, whatever it was you were doing."

He pointed to the spot he'd cleared. "Or you could stay for a sec and take a break. God knows I need one."

She hesitated for a moment, knowing she was taking the I'm-a-fellow-grad-student charade too far, but then she moved her way around the desk and sat. What could a few more minutes hurt? "Yeah, you sounded kind of pissed off when I walked by."

He stilled, and she cringed inwardly when she realized what she'd revealed.

He lowered himself to the chair behind his desk. "You can hear me in the hallway?"

"I— Sound travels. The hall echoes."

"Good to know. So you heard . . ."

"Enough."

He laughed. "Well, then. Guess I should probably explain what I'm doing then so I don't look like a total perv."

"It's fine. I mean, whatever." She wasn't sure if she sounded nonchalant or like her throat was closing. She guessed the latter.

He lifted a paper off his desk. "This is what you heard."

She leaned forward, trying to read the scratchy handwriting.

"Scripts," he explained. "I'm doing my dissertation on female sexual arousal in response to auditory stimuli. I'm recording potential scripts of fantasies that we may use in the study."

"Your study is about dirty talk?" she asked, surprised that the university was down with that. And if he was the one doing the dirty talking, where did she sign up to volunteer?

He smirked and there was a hint of mischief in that otherwise affable expression. "Yes, I guess that's one way to put it. If you want to be crass about it, Ms. Sleep Disorders."

"Just calling it like I see it."

"Fair enough. But yeah, I'm focusing on the effect of scripted erotic talk on women who have arousal disorder. A lot of times, therapists suggest that these patients watch erotic movies to try to increase their libido. But in general, porn is produced for men. So even though that method can be somewhat effective, the films don't really tap into women's fantasies. They tap into men's. Erotic books have worked pretty well. But I want to test out another method to add to the arsenal—audio. It'd be cost effective to make, wouldn't send money to the porn industry, and could be customized to a patient's needs. Plus, it's easy to test in a lab."

Marin liked that he was talking to her like a peer, and his frankness about the topic saved her the weirdness that would normally surface when talking about sex. Plus, his passion was catching. That's what she loved about this environment. In high school, everyone acted like they were being forced to learn. She'd always been the odd one for actually enjoying school. Books and all that information had been her escape. Schools changed, the people around her changed, but the stuff in the books stayed constant. But here at the university there were people like Donovan, people who seemed to be mainlining their education and getting high off what they learned. "So what were you so frustrated about?"

He grabbed his can of Red Bull and took a sip, keeping his eyes on her the whole time. "I'm discovering that women are complicated and that I'm having trouble thinking like one."

She sniffed. "This is shocking news?"

"Well, no. I knew it was going to be tough, but the fantasies are turning out to be harder than I thought. We did a round of romantic ones in a small trial run, and they were a major fail. My friend, Alexis, one of the other grads working under Pax, told me that I needed to go more taboo, tap into the forbidden type of fantasies, that sweet romance makes a girl warm and fuzzy but not necessarily hot."

Marin's neck prickled with heat, but she tried to keep her expression smooth. "Makes sense."

"Does it?"

"I—uh, I mean . . ."

"Never mind. I retract the question." He leaned back in his chair and ran a hand through his messy hair. "I met you like five minutes ago and I'm already asking you if forbidden fantasies do it for you. Sorry. Hang out in this department too long, and you lose your filter for what is acceptable in normal conversation. I spent lunch yesterday discussing nocturnal penile tumescence with a sixty-five-year-old female professor, and it wasn't weird. This is my life."

Marin smiled and played with the tab on the top of her soda. "I'm clearly hanging out in the wrong department. My professor just talks about sleep apnea. Though I monitor the sleep lab and can confirm that nocturnal penile tumescence is alive and well."

"Ha. I bet."

She wet her lips and, feeling brave, leaned forward and grabbed the script he'd left on his desk. He didn't make a move to stop her, and she squinted at the page, trying to decipher his handwriting. The fantasy looked to be one between a boss and subordinate. She saw the parts she'd heard him read aloud. *I'm hard for you. I tug down your panties.*

She crossed her legs. The part he'd gotten hung up on had various crude names for the female anatomy listed and scratched out—like he couldn't decide which one would be appropriate. But just seeing the fantasy on the page had her skin tingling, her blood stirring. She shifted in her chair. Kept reading.

"Okay, well that's a good sign," he said, his voice breaking through the quiet room.

Marin looked up. "What?"

He leaned his forearms against the desk, his blue eyes meeting hers. "You just made a sound."

"I did not."

"Yeah, you did. Like this breathy sound. And your neck is all flushed. That one's working for you."

She tossed the paper on his desk. "Oh my God, you really don't have a filter."

He smiled, something different flaring in his eyes, something that made her feel more flustered than those words on the page. "Sorry. It's all right, though. Seriously. You already saw me with a hard-on. Now we're even. But this is good information. I thought this one may be too geared toward the male side—a fantasy that'd appeal to me but not necessarily to a woman. You're telling me I'm wrong."

"I didn't say anything."

"You didn't have to. You're like . . ."

She could feel her nipples pushing against her bra, their presence obvious against her T-shirt, and fought the urge to clamp her hands over them, to hide her traitor body. She stood. "Okay, so I'm leaving now."

"No, no, come on, wait," he said, standing up. He grabbed her hand before she could make a clean escape, and the touch radiated up her arm, making her breath catch in the back of her throat. "You can help. I've got a stack of these. I need to know which ones to test next week and which ones to trash. Or maybe you can offer suggestions? I promise to keep my eyes to myself. And I swear, if you help me, I'm yours for whatever you want. I can take a shift in the sleep lab for you or something."

"You want me to read through fantasies and tell you which ones turn me on?" His hand was so warm against her cold one. She might just die. "Can't you ask your friend who's in this department to do that?"

"She's a lesbian so her fantasies don't line up with these. I need a straight girl's opinion. Wait—are you straight?"

She pressed her lips together. "I—yes. But this is beyond embarrassing."

"Why? Because you get turned on by fantasy stuff? It's not embarrassing. It's human. You'd be shocked by how many people struggle to tap into that part of themselves. That kind of responsiveness is a good thing."

"Donovan, I don't know . . ."

He let go of her hand and opened a drawer. "Here. I have an idea. I'll give you some headphones and a thumb drive with the ones I've already recorded. You can take them back to your office and listen to them while you do data entry. Then you can just tell me which ones you recommend when you're done. You won't have to feel self-conscious sitting with me. Plus, I need to record some more tonight, and I can't do that if someone's in here with me."

He held out the earbuds and a blue thumb drive. She stared at them like they would bite her, but on those files would be Donovan's voice in her ear, saying those explicit things, things she'd never had a guy whisper to her. The temptation was a hot, pulsing thing low in her belly. She took them. "Okay. I'm not making any promises, but I'll let you know if I've listened to any before I leave tonight."

His grin was like a physical touch to her skin. "That would be amazing. I'll owe you big-time, Mari."

She got caught up in that smile like a fly in a spiderweb and she wanted to linger, wanted to stay there all night and listen to him talk about his research, what made him passionate, what else made him smile like that. But she knew she'd only risk embarrassing herself further, or worse—get herself in trouble. Because the thing blooming inside her with him this close was intoxicating and potent. She wanted to cling to it, to wrap herself up in that feeling and jump into the unknown without thinking about the consequences. Something she couldn't do.

She lived her life carefully, always making sure to stay between the lines on the road. No alcohol. No drugs. No risky behavior with boys. She'd learned from her mother that one foot on the path, one chased whim, could lead to chaos. She knew enough about her mom's disorder to know that those genes probably lingered in her, too, and this pulsing desire to flirt with Donovan, to push this charade further, could be a dangerous one.

She probably shouldn't listen to the tapes, shouldn't open that door. Things were safe right now, calm. She needed them to stay that way.

Marin headed down the hall with the thumb drive tucked in her pocket and the soda in her hand. She needed to focus on her job. Get those little numbers entered into the computer, get lost in the monotony.

But it wasn't more than ten minutes after she stepped back into Professor Roberts's lab that she had the recordings cued up. Donovan's voice filtered into her head.

"I spot you first across the bar. You look beautiful and I know you've come here with someone else. I can see him getting you a drink. But I can feel your eyes on me, and I know that tonight, it's going to be my hands on you . . ."

Marin didn't get another lick of work done that night.

Roni Loren wrote her first romance novel at age fifteen when she discovered writing about boys was way easier than actually talking to them. Since then, her flirting skills haven't improved, but she likes to think her storytelling ability has. Though she'll forever be a New Orleans girl at heart, she now lives in Dallas with her husband and son. If she's not working on her latest sexy story, you can find her reading, watching reality television, or indulging in her unhealthy addiction to rock stars, er, rock concerts. Yeah, that's it. Visit her website: roniloren.com.